SOCIETY RULES

Society Rules

Katherine Whitley

Library of Congress Control Number:		2009912544
ISBN:	Hardcover	978-1-4500-0169-4
	Softcover	978-1-4500-0168-7
	EBook	978-1-4500-0224-0

To order additional copies of this book, contact:
Xlibris Corporation
1-888-795-4274
www.Xlibris.com
Orders@Xlibris.com
71845

ACKNOWLEDGEMENTS

People to thank. Well. Where to begin?
Kathy Couture, for donating her precious personal time, acting as my private editor? Without her kind words, wonderful feedback and encouragement, I don't know where I would be.

Or maybe Raz Blackstone, for agreeing to be one of my first victims, reading, and offering excellent advice.

Suzanne Adsit and Ashley Mears, for valiantly taking home the rough draft, and TRYING to read that mess!

My mother, Kathi Fielder, for suffering my e-mail attacks, hurling chapter after chapter to her, until she finished the whole thing, and my husband, Jon, who bravely tackled the same project, and acting as my consultant on all things military and Warrior-like.

My children, for providing me with material and tolerating long periods of neglect, while I typed away into the night.

And we must not forget, my personal photographer, Erin Partlow, for her mad skills with the digital camera!

Last, but certainly not least, all of my co-workers who allowed my constant chatter, incessantly boring and repetitive talk, about
"this book I'm working on."

Thank you and I love you all!

The game's in full swing
Its players, intent
On besting the other
They sit with heads bent.
The Beast and his Master
Lift their cards from the table
The corners singed black
From the claws of Death's grasp
'You believe you can beat me?'
God hid his kind smile
'You know not my plan'.
He lay down his cards
Never showing his hand
As the Horsemen appeared
Death smiled, then he spoke
'Four of a kind'
Beat that if you can
His smile now a gloat
His Master, He answered
'There's nothing to best,
My cards I hold tightly
And close to my chest'
Your Horsemen, all four
They answer to me
Now pick up your cards
Stand well back
And you'll see

Katherine Whitley
From "Strategy of the Apocalypse"

CHAPTER 1

As the sun burned brightly through the glass panes of the French doors, it painted a path of brilliant light that stretched lazily across the bedroom floor. The day promised to be unseasonably warm for early March in Vermont, and Indiana Taylor was feeling sulky.

Unreasonably so.

What she didn't feel, was ready to face the world yet. Her bed was soft and comforting and her body was still achy with fatigue. But the official start of her day was ticking its way toward her.

"Not yet," her mental groan echoed through her head as she breathed in and out in a slow and steady rhythm, despite knowing there was no need for the performance.

It was easy to continue a habit that had become part of her ritual for life management. Out of necessity, she'd become well practiced at feigning sleep.

The thought of leaving her four-hundred—thread—count sanctuary shoved her into a mental cringe, but Indie knew that allowing the obnoxious blast of the alarm to actually sound off was the more unpleasant option. She detested loud noises. The only exception to this rule was music, whose decibel levels never seemed to assault her in the same manner as other sounds. Music was her sanctuary, and soothed her in an almost hypnotic way.

Her ears were painfully sensitive, and her children often accused her of having "superhuman" hearing. Superhuman vision as well, but this was either a sign of her ocular acuity, or the mark of mental issues that Indie simply refused to address, because she sometimes saw things that were not only disturbing to her, but obviously unseen by others.

Still, thinking of her children's suspicions made her smile into her pillow. Those suspicions were true and she admittedly used it to her advantage. After all, wouldn't it be a shame not to acknowledge and use a God-given talent?

A faint click announced the impending buzz, just seconds away. Indie launched a preemptive strike against the unfortunate piece of timekeeping equipment, silencing the alarm before it sounded. Just the thought of the intrusive noise made her shudder.

Alarm clocks.

It was Indie's personal opinion that the inventor of this instrument of torture should be forced to submit himself to the endless ringing, clanging or buzzing of a few of his creations for several hours a day. She clenched her entire body in horror at the very thought.

In spite of the knowledge that she never needed the nasty brain-smacking things, she always set one at any rate.

Just in case.

Because she never know when normal behavior would covertly steal into her life, and maybe sleep would happen.

Right. Sure it would.

As early as she could recall into her past . . . even in her childhood, Indie had never needed an alarm. This was because of the admittedly bizarre fact that she never actually slept.

It was something that Indie didn't let get around. No, she knew the reactions news like that would prompt; one of many lessons learned the hard way at a very young age. Not sleeping seemed to be regarded by the world as a little freakish, she'd found.

When Indie was fourteen years old, a cousin with whom she had lived for a short time made Indie painfully aware of the insanity of such claims.

Kristen had indulged her with a rare moment of attention, and Indie, overwhelmed by a rush of release from her loneliness, had blurted out her secret.

"Never sleep?" Kristen had asked, skeptically. "Everyone sleeps, Indie. What you're having is called insomnia." Her cousin had then run down the tired list of "remedies" for curing this simple problem, from warm milk, to sleeping pills as a last resort.

When Indie tried to explain that her condition went way beyond insomnia and into the absolute absence of sleep, Kristen had become impatient.

"All human beings sleep! People cannot survive without it. You would be wild, crazy and hallucinating right now if you never slept. It is a mandatory human function!"

"But . . . but *I* don't," Indie had persisted in a whisper, tears stinging her eyes, mostly because she had wasted the rare moment on what had turned into an argument.

"Then maybe you're not really human," her cousin had stated coolly. "And by the way . . ." she tossed the words over her shoulder as she escaped into the hallway, "I wouldn't go around telling people stories like that if I were you. You might earn yourself some special time in a padded room!"

Indie was horrified by her cousin's sarcastic retort about not being human. Her extreme reaction to words she knew were obviously spoken with only the intention of causing pain had confused her as well.

She knew very well that her cousin didn't believe that she was anything but a normal, if possibly crazy, human being; but something in that comment crystallized her years of unrest and feelings of not quite belonging.

A strange sweeping sensation swirled through her head that as absurd as Kristen's statement was, she had somehow hit the nail on the head.

It had been a small but defining moment in her life. Not only did Indie feel that she now had proof that she was different, but the look on her cousin's face inspired her to toughen up her outer shell. She had no wish to be vulnerable to anyone's suspicious scrutiny.

And who cared if Kristen believed her anyway? Her claim of being incapable of sleep was simply the truth.

Climbing into bed at the appropriate hour was now part of her nightly show. Indie would turn off the light, and close her eyes. She could experience fatigue, exhaustion even, and feel the need to curl up in her bed, becoming comfortable . . . drowsy and warm, and her body would rest. However, Indie had long ago stopped waiting for unconscious slumber to take her to the places where people dream. That realm, she'd never visited.

She could keep her eyes closed for six to eight hours at a time, but her mind remained alert . . . aware. It was the perfect time to think . . . make plans, or simply map out her "to do" list for the following day. Perhaps ponder important issues, such as Hannaford versus Shaw's, and whether Pricechopper really does, in fact, chop prices.

A time to listen to the small and unimportant noises that happen in a house late at night, when the occupants are supposed to be peacefully oblivious.

Indie was almost positive that she was able to hear the creaks and groans of the house as it shifted with the imperceptible rotation of the Earth. She rolled onto her back and squinted at the textured ceiling.

It wasn't entirely impossible, she mused, that maybe she truly *was* insane. Years ago, Indie had reconciled herself to this frightening possibility, and congratulated herself with a silent round of applause for each day that she successfully completed the astounding feat of normalcy.

Indie's husband, Will, was gloriously self-centered and unaware of any action or reaction that did not hold him accountable in some way. He never noticed anything, at least not anything concerning Indie; the two of them floating around one another in a dance that never quite included a partner.

The twins were another story. Jake and Cassidy had what Indie could only define as the extrasensory force that surrounds most twin siblings. Nothing escaped their attention and nothing remained hidden. They seemed to share the ability to reach into your head and pull out the truth within.

The sensitivity toward others was no doubt there . . . most definitely between themselves, and from the way she caught them scrutinizing her, then meeting each other's gaze knowingly, she knew they could see through her too. In those moments, she felt outed—exposed as the imposter she feared she was.

Nevertheless, she also knew that they loved her and she them in the perfectly proper way for mothers and their children to feel about each other.

"Their love is what saves me," Indie speculated, "and stops them from revealing what they see."

It was funny. She had an uncanny knack for reading people; knowing what they were feeling, but the twins' minds were a mystery to Indie. There certainly never appeared to be any sign that they were suffering any fear or self-doubt, thank God. They were cheerful and happy children, albeit somewhat on the serious and studious side. Her twins had no disability when it came to sensing her own thoughts, Indie was positive.

Jake and Cassidy would be described by anyone as perfect children. They'd always gone along with anything needed of them without question. As often as the family uprooted due to Will's job, it might be expected that the children be overly clingy or overly anxious, or suffer some such issues common to the insecurity caused by instability.

But they were not.

They were never overly anything, and accepted all things with a serenity that defied their young age.

They had each other to supply most of their companionship needs, but spoke to others easily and when they did, people listened. Indie knew she was very lucky, and was relieved that they didn't suffer the same shut out feelings that she had dealt with for most of her life.

Moving constantly, though stressful and a pain had helped Indie learn to become an accomplished actress, observing others and learning how to better blend in with the masses.

Who would have to do that, though, she often wondered. *I'm pretty sure other people don't walk around trying to figure out how to be normal!*

The thought frustrated and distressed her, but also made her all the more determined to blend. If moving helped, then she was grateful for the opportunity. The most recent move, however, had nothing to do with Will.

At the family's last address in Portland, Oregon, Indie had been restlessly flipping through the pages of an historic romance novel, which, like her IPod, were her always present addictions. She'd been turning the pages much too quickly to fool anyone into thinking that she was actually reading, when suddenly she tossed it aside. Looking up, she caught Cassidy eyeing her shrewdly.

Will noticed nothing, absorbed in a book detailing the most recent findings on the worlds beyond the "black holes". A ridiculous thought had seized her out of nowhere. Ridiculous, and yet it demanded to be spoken aloud.

Indie drew a deep breath and tossed out her opening statement abruptly. "I think we should move to the northeast . . . Vermont, maybe."

Will looked up from his book.

"What?" he asked, his attention surfacing slowly.

"I want to move . . . to Vermont . . ." Indie repeated, feeling a little confused herself at this revelation.

"What for?" Will had laughed. "I mean, you're telling me that you are actually *suggesting* a move . . . one that isn't necessary?"

"I guess I am," Indie had replied thoughtfully. She had no idea why this had occurred to her.

Indie had absolutely no ties whatsoever to the state of Vermont. Not that she had them anywhere else either, but still, how weird was this impulse? And how crazy was it that she was going to make the move happen? She knew with a sudden unexplainable urgency that it simply had to be.

Indie made few requests and even fewer demands, but whenever she did, she got what she wanted. Indie had learned one thing over the years, and that was that whenever she made herself seen and noticed, she was a force to be reckoned with . . . she just had to demand it.

This was not her natural M.O., because these days she spent most of her time trying *not* to be noticed, but at times things just had to be made to happen. Always, her demands had been on behalf of another . . . a patient, a cause . . . something other than herself.

This was different.

It was something she knew had to be done, and it didn't set particularly well with her that in the fact that it was all for a need of her own. To further complicate her feelings, Indie had no idea what that need was.

She pressed her case anyway, and in only a few months, the move took place. Will was able to obtain a transfer to an office complex near Burlington. After Will completed his third round of service in the Army, he was offered what was supposed to be a prestigious job working for the government, but Indie imagined him toiling away at what she assumed was a bland and grey desk position.

He had to travel often for work anyway, so the move seemed easily arranged and the family soon found themselves firmly planted in the center of the Green Mountain state.

No magical thing happened when they arrived; no amazing clarity on the issues of her life manifested themselves after the move . . . things were as they always were . . . only now they were happening here.

Indie had given up trying to understand why she'd had a sudden urge to become part of the New England landscape. She decided to attribute it to some sort of violent boredom seizure perhaps. Or maybe since she'd lived nearly everywhere else, she just naturally felt the need to be the perfect storm and hit every region.

Regardless of the reason, here she sat, and more than two years had passed with nothing more than the usual feeling of unease, and the occasional glimpse of something fleeting and momentarily terrifying in what would appear to be average citizens walking the streets.

That, along with the sometimes nail munching fear that she'd caught sight of something that didn't belong on this astral plane . . . her teeth clacking together as she thought of the sharp-toothed *thing* that sometimes appeared in the shadowed corners of her vision.

This thing she'd seen sporadically throughout her life, and had named him the "Gator Man" when she was younger, just to humor herself; because these were ridiculous thoughts, of course.

Combine those eerie ideas, with the feeling that kept her looking over her shoulder in recent months . . . the feeling that someone or some*thing* was watching her with an unnatural interest, and it was easy to see why she had one kettle of nerves on her stove.

Still, she felt that the decision to move was a good one. They'd discovered that Vermont was a great place to raise kids, and this was important to Indie. During this time, Indie had given up waiting for the reason motivating the move to appear before her. But she knew she wasn't moving again, not for a while. She'd told Will that if the house they'd bought was put up for sale anytime in the near future, that it would come complete with a wife and children.

A soft explosion of music popped through the air as the sound of her children's alarms shooting off simultaneously created a stereo-phonic effect throughout the house. They set their alarms to awaken to the local radio station, and their clocks were apparently well synchronized.

With a snort and a forceful effort, Indie lurched out of the bed, squinting at the unusual amount of sunlight beaming in through the glass doors. She deftly maneuvered around the dog, Max, who scrambled out of the way and darted into Cassidy's room as Indie made her way to the bathroom.

An avalanche of romance novels thumped to the floor, sliding off the bed one by one.

Her collection was huge and ever growing, as Indie gathered the books that held her most hidden desires and fed her secretly romantic heart. This was her only real concession to "girliness". Chick flicks made her impatient and irritable and fluffy songs had much the same effect. She was more action/adventure oriented, and her musical tastes were eclectic, but usually had to fill her with energy and motivation.

But the books . . . the books understood her yearnings, and she devoured them the way oxygen and wood fed flame. She kept them close at all times, and the small mountain stacked precariously at the foot of her bed had collapsed when her sudden movement had tipped the scales.

With the soft breath of a sigh escaping her lips, she stooped to retrieve them. Her fingers lightly traced the outline of the beautiful woman on one cover. A handsome man stood protectively behind her, lips against her neck.

She stared at the couple, feeling her yearnings wash over her like cold spring water. What was missing . . . what she needed . . . was the passion.

Bring it on back, Indie, she laughed to herself, snapping back to reality. She replaced the stack of books carefully and continued on her way to the sink.

The woman in the mirror loomed in front of her, and Indie leaned forward, nose against the glass, confused as always by the lost and hollow look in her eyes.

"I have no reason to look like this." She scolded herself impatiently. "I have everything. I should be grateful!" And she was, in a sense.

But sometimes she would become just plain irritated by the fact that she looked as if she were hiding some great personal tragedy; one that she could not name, or even imagine. It bothered her, because it sometimes caused people to notice her. This was rare, and so not the kind of attention Indie was comfortable attracting.

That kind of attention was totally unwelcome. It caused a whole lot of *"thanks for your concern, but go away and stop looking at me!"* to bang unevenly around in her gut. Besides, she never had an answer for them. Everything was fine . . . was it not?

Indie splashed cold water on her face, then hastily pulled a brush through her thick, dark hair, smoothing back the waves and closely examined her deep blue eyes.

Aside from the inexplicable look of longing, her face was perfection. She had not a single wrinkle or any other sign that would reveal her age. Her porcelain strawberries and cream complexion was identical to her pictures from twenty years ago.

She had perfect bow-shaped lips, which she now slicked over quickly with a sheer gloss, then smoothed on her mandatory SPF 20 moisturizer.

Indie had no need of any other make-up. Her skin was unblemished, her lashes long, black and lush. Her body was also still in peak form, which she credited to her daily running habit. This was normally part of her morning routine, but today she would have to do it after work. She had put off leaving the sanctuary of her soft bed for too long.

In her youth, Indie had been fragile and dainty, her tender heart easily damaged by even the slightest act of brutality, such as her father smacking a spider with yesterday's newspaper.
Not the case anymore.

After suffering the heartbreak of loss, and the knowledge that she was somehow different, Indie had Darwin'd up a nice hard shell, which she polished daily. She still would kill not even an insect herself, but she held stoic whenever she witnessed others do such things.

But Indie also needed strength around her for support as well, which was evident in her choice of husband, movies and music. Only her reading material gave her true inner-self away.

With her youthful beauty and slim athletic body, one would think she would spend most of her time busily shoving her way through throngs of eagerly gathered men.

This was not the case. Conversely, Indie had no better luck finding friends of her own gender.

Despite the outer shell, she was good-natured, had a quick and sometimes wicked sense of humor wrapped around a kind and generous heart.

Yet Indie had no true friends.

She didn't "hang out" with anyone, simply because she was never invited. Her breaks were spent alone, devouring her escapist love stories.

Co-workers, if asked, would have nothing but positive things to say about Indie, and yet she would watch as groups of them would make plans to meet up after work for parties or bowling, knowing that no one would turn to her and invite her to join them.

This caused an ache in the people-loving part of her heart, although she was resigned to the probability that things were not going to change.

It was a sad fact that neither men nor woman gave Indie any indication that they knew she was anything more than part of the surrounding furniture. Only when she spoke did people snap to attention, studying her as if some sort of new entity had just appeared out of nowhere, after which they would slide back into the routine of overlooking her as soon as the conversation ended. It was all very strange, but Indie'd had the luxury of many years to become used to this odd reaction from everyone around her.

Indie was feeling a heightened amount of nervous energy today, as if some kind of premonition was trying to tap her on the shoulder, warning her of impending elements that would change her life.

So the drama, she laughed at herself. *I suppose I should be expecting a major break from my soccer-mom world any second now!* Her laughter slowly faded.

Yeah, right.

What composed her world was an incredibly odd combination of unrelenting boredom and predictability, combined with freakishly strange happenings and feelings. It wasn't going to just magically change overnight, of that she was certain.

Shoving off these thoughts, she wiped down the sink and then headed for Cassidy's room. Indie stopped as her eyes fell upon a suit jacket that Will had apparently planned to wear today, but then cast aside for some reason. Why, she couldn't imagine.

His suits were all pretty much the same; black, black and more black, always Brooks Brothers, and always with the white shirts, rounded out with his mirrored sunglasses.

You would *think* it would make getting dressed everyday a little less challenging, wouldn't you, she thought dryly. As she hung it back in the closet, her mind wandered again.

Earlier, she had kept her eyes closed while suffering and clenching her teeth at his jolting alarm, set every day as was his habit, for a half an hour before he actually needed to get up.

Will enjoyed the satisfaction of smashing the snooze button at least four times before finally dragging himself out of bed.

This forced Indie to distract herself every morning from this outrage to her senses by playing out mild fantasies of planting her feet into her husband's back and launching him through the bedroom wall.

Although aghast at having such thoughts, Indie wondered if she could really do it. She had always been freakishly strong, and the thought of really letting loose with her full strength both excited and repelled her.

On a daily basis, she kept her strength folded closely around her like the wings of a small bird . . . but a part of her longed to stretch those wings and test the limits, but only in a benign way. The thought of ever hurting anyone in any fashion made Indie nearly physically ill. She spent her life on the opposite end of that spectrum, offering help and comfort to those around her.

Indie always continued the charade of sleep while Will poked around the room getting himself pulled together and off to work. It knocked off an extra few minutes of her daily hurt feelings from his refusal to acknowledge her presence. But every day, through her eyelashes, she would watch him.

The purely female part of whatever type of creature Indie feared she might be enjoyed spying on him.

Will undressed, was a sight to behold, and once dressed, handsome and professional, yet still hardcore in his dark suits and ties.

She felt guilty, because she never really asked him about his work, and he certainly never seemed compelled to talk to her about it . . . or anything else for that matter. Conversation between herself and Will consisted of comments instigated by Indie, regarding household issues, or updates about the kids.

These things prompted courteous and brief replies from her husband, which never progressed to what you could call an actual conversation.
Indie told herself she was over being wounded by this fact.

But still, she felt ashamed of her lack of interest in his daily grind. The essentials she knew; *where* he worked and the name of the office complex, but nothing about what he actually *did*. Indie and Will had never shared any kind of true passion of either mind or body.

Oh, Will could be made to be interested in the physical part if Indie so chose, but that didn't seem like the way it should work.

On their honeymoon, Will had been startled and quite thrilled to learn that Indie, at age thirty, was still a virgin and had no idea what to expect. He had been patient, gentle and skillful, Indie supposed.

She had no point of comparison, but it definitely appeared as if Will knew what he was doing.
"Tell me what you need, Indie . . ." Will had whispered in his deep husky voice. His breath was warm in her ear, his hands and body working what she instinctively knew *should* be magic.
But she couldn't tell him what to do for her, because she didn't have a clue. Indie was still a virgin as far as the orgasm factor was concerned, not even understanding what she was missing.

Well, that wasn't exactly true, was it? The romantic stories that Indie clung to for companionship held numerous descriptions of physical and emotional feelings that were supposed to happen during lovemaking, didn't they?
Fire. Heat.
She ached for it.

Passion and lust . . . the very words made her blush, but at the same time, drew her even further into her conclusion that her marriage was seriously lacking in that regard. However, in classic Indie style, she was sure that it was due to some defect within her that was causing the problem.

Indie was observant enough to know that Will was not emotionless; he just kept his feelings and reactions tightly under his command.

In the beginning of their marriage, she had tried to make whatever was missing magically appear by playing out the female lead in her stories, attempting to grab Will's attention.
This never failed to work . . . for moments all too brief.

The fact that he almost never approached her on his own after the honeymoon, and yet was a very eager participant any time Indie set up a scenario in which to fire up some passion, left her frustrated and bewildered.

She had decided that she wanted children right away, feeling that they might fill the void in her life and clinically knew just what had to happen in order for her to become a mother. During that time, Indie sought Will very frequently, ambushing him in the bedroom wearing temptingly small amounts of lingerie.

It played out the same way every time.

Will would enter the room, find her there and become aroused instantly; his expression similar to one that a sixteen year old boy would sport after finding a naked supermodel lounging in his bed. He would then approach her with his notoriously deliberate pace, reaching out to touch her and looking for all the world as if he expected her to pop like a soap bubble and disappear.

Will would then attack her with an enthusiasm that never failed to take her breath away, at least in appreciation for the effort.

They would make love, Will giving his all and then some, using his hands, mouth and other appendages in a quest to give her satisfaction. Indie was savvy enough to know that Will was well equipped to give any woman serious quantities of pleasure, but the grand finale' never made its appearance for her, and she took this on as just another failure of her own doing.

The only true pleasure she could honestly say she gained from these encounters was the closeness they shared afterwards, however brief.

Will was heavily into "after play", and the attention he gave her after the act itself was golden to her.

He would hold her close to his warm, tight body, offering soft kisses and words of love. It was the only time, as far as Indie could tell, that William Taylor opened himself up . . . offering his emotions to her freely. She could feel in him a desperate need; the loneliness caused by burdens to great to bear.

Although it did nothing for her sexually, the attention made her feel needed . . . *there*. She responded instinctively to him when he let down that virtual force field he'd created around himself. It made her feel—well—almost . . . *loved*.

As if she actually existed and mattered.

Sometimes, forgetting her own emptiness, she thought her heart might break for him. He seemed so in need of *something* from her . . . something she obviously could not give him.

But she wanted to feel the fire. Hell, she wanted *eye contact*. It seemed as if Will never really even *saw* her except in sporadically rare and increasingly far flung moments. Why couldn't she feel the way the girls in her books felt?

And why did she always have a vague sense of unease whenever she *did* use the art of seduction on her husband . . . an odd feeling that she was doing something that she shouldn't.

It was creepy and annoying.

No wonder Will never sought her out on his own. For all of his enthusiasm during the act, and emotional outpouring afterward, as soon as he left the room, their relationship went generic and static once more.

Will would return to his role as the man so very well in control that Indie would be forced to wonder if she had imagined the whole thing.

The only thing that seemed to really break through his emotional barrier were his children.

He loved them. Anyone could see that. And he was fiercely protective of them. Cassidy, the more "in your face" of the twins, would roust him from his computer and demand his attention. He almost never said no, although he always tore himself away a bit too soon for the kids' liking, stating that he had to "get back to work."

Will wouldn't even have them, if it hadn't been for Indie's pride imploding efforts. She had wanted children badly enough to open herself up to the embarrassment of basically "begging" for it, for as long as it took.

Once Indie finally conceived, she made it a point of pride never to be the one to approach Will again for sex. She couldn't bear the thought that perhaps he didn't truly find her enticing, or worse, performed only as an obligation. Oh, what a revelation that would be. She had heard others gossiping in the break room at work about someone being a "pity-lay."

Indie knew what this was, and had no intention of having that handle tattooed across her forehead! If she ever found out that was the case, she was more than a little sure that she might strangle the man she'd married. The very idea made her cringe. Besides, if he wanted it, he knew where to find her, didn't he?

As a result, Indie and Will had made love exactly twelve times during the last nine years, and each time there had been some kind of event that had forced Will to look over and acknowledge Indie and apparently light his fire for that moment.

In other words, there had been a heck of a lot of dry spell in Indie's world.

At times, her need to feel loved was so overwhelming, she was ready to take it any way she could get it, pride be damned . . . but then her sensibilities would return, and she would refocus her energy on other things.

Mundane things.

The running helped burn off a little frustration, but it was a hollow relief.

She'd briefly considered the idea that Will might have a girlfriend on the side. This possibility hurt Indie, but oddly didn't devastate her. That idea was quickly dismissed though, because Will was unfailingly where he was supposed to be at all times, and a work-a-holic to the extreme.

A computer genius, his HP seemed to be the recipient of all of Will's passion these days.

At any rate, he was gone for the day, and Indie needed to get moving. Cassidy was already awake as usual, stroking and cooing to the dog.

"Get dressed honey, and come to the kitchen for breakfast," Indie chirped cheerfully to her daughter. Cassidy nodded, and looked up at her mother, her eyes twinkling mischievously.

"Max needs a bath, Mommy. He smells like Poo-Bear!"

Indie coughed back a laugh.

"Maybe that could be a project for you and Jake after school today then, huh? No one appreciates a dog that smells like Fritos and tail feathers! Now hit the breakfast table, okay?"

Cassidy snickered and bounced off to do her bidding.

Amused, Indie watched her go.

Is it even necessary for me to get up with them? She wondered with a touch of exasperated pride, just as she did every day.

She wandered into the hallway and peeked in at Jake. His eyes were closed, but opened as soon as she looked at him. Indie came in and sat down on the edge of his bed.

"Hi, Mommy," he whispered in his sweet little boy voice.

She loved that he still called her "Mommy", even though at nine years old he was pushing the "Mommy" envelope. Indie hoped he didn't get grief at school from all of the other little kids for still being her baby. She doubted it.

The kid was simply dripping with confidence and serenity.

"Hi, little pup." She gazed at his soft, sweet face . . . looking so much younger than his years. He had the face and build of a six year old, as did his sister.

Indie looked much younger than her age as well. No one could ever believe that she was forty years old. Not that this fact displeased her. She rather enjoyed hearing the gasps of disbelief whenever the subject of her age came up. It never failed to boost her spirits a bit, making her feel special, but not in a weird way, although lately it *was* getting to be a little ridiculous. It seemed that the years were simply not catching up to her.

Will was five years younger than Indie, but no one would ever dream this was the case. People generally guessed her to be in her early twenties, but she had once been told that she could pass for a "mature teenager," whatever that meant.

"Time to get up, little son," she smiled as she pulled the covers off of his warm body. Of course, he was fully dressed.

Like always. Just another game they played. The kids were always awake and ready on time.

After a short struggle so that she could pin her son down and kiss his whole face, Indie sent Jake scurrying into the kitchen and followed, tripping over her husband's boots that he had left in the hallway.

Flash of irritation, then remorse. Negative feelings unnerved her and it struck her as all wrong whenever her thoughts went dark.

She loved her husband in a warm, comfortable way and her feelings of discontent made her feel guilty and vile. She knew he was a good person at heart.

Lack of sexual interest aside, William Taylor was just your typical distracted, self-absorbed, let your wife take care of everything *guy*!

She shook off her vague feeling of annoyance, and proceeded to get the kids' breakfast. Today they wanted Greek yogurt and honey. Luckily, they always had matching cravings, which made mornings much easier, and their health-food obsession was one installed in them by Indie from the very beginning. Indie herself, devoured a piece of toast and then got dressed for work while they ate.

She'd been able to negotiate the perfect schedule at Central Mountain Manor, the local nursing home. Her personality was perfectly suited to the nursing profession, and she loved her job. Previously, Indie had worked at the hospital, but as had happened many times before, her gift for unnerving people in her profession drove her out the door to a less conspicuous location.

It was nothing that she could ever explain in a way that didn't freak people out, but Indie was always able to tell what was basically wrong with her patients as soon as she put her hands on them. She could tell if a person was dehydrated, or if the injury or illness was minor, or something more ominous right away.

Her habit of speaking while touching them, and making these pronouncements aloud without thinking, had caused many of the doctors and other nurses some distress.

Indie supposed that they thought her a freak.

Whispers of "psychic" hit her from behind, and once, while leaning over a patient that she felt had internal bleeding, a doctor had made a ridiculous comment about Indie being some kind of witch, heard clearly by her sensitive ears.

She'd finally requested a transfer to a nursing home that belonged to the same corporation, and this was granted with unusual speed and efficiency.

Indie fit in much better with long-term patients. Whenever they did notice her, the staff here thought she was great, so in tune was she to every resident's slightest change in condition.

She always knew when it was someone's time to die. If Indie put her hands on a person and felt the burn in her belly that meant death was inevitable, they had better start scrawling out a last will and testament on a napkin, because it was about to be all over.

Indie spent many a night at the nursing home, staying over after her shift ended, simply holding the hand of a patient she knew was on the slide toward home plate . . . the return to their maker. If someone had no family, Indie flatly refused to leave them.

No one should die alone, in her opinion, although during these times when she would stay and give the gift of her compassion to the dying, Indie always had the distinct feeling that they were in fact not alone. She could sense a presence in the room with them, and felt sure that some sort of entity had come for her patient, waiting to escort them to the next realm.

Sometimes she saw things; images in her peripheral vision that gave the impression of comforting presence . . . human shapes. Other times the things she saw were nothing more than disturbances in the air . . . a rippling in the fabric of this dimension.

These little things were some of the reasons that Indie, at times, questioned herself. Not that she *really* believed that she was crazy, or a freak, but then, she knew how others saw her. She knew their reactions to her actions, and heard their whispers. It was one of the curses of having "superhuman" hearing.

This was nothing new. Indie had faced these kinds of public relations issues her entire life. She had always felt like she was outside of the glass of humanity, trying to find a way in, like a winged creature flailing away at a window.

It wasn't so much that she *wanted* to "fit in", as much as having a strong sense that she needed to.

There was also the odd feeling that there was some sort of duty she was fulfilling by trying to blend in seamlessly with the rest of the human race, although she usually felt that she failed spectacularly.

She was also fairly certain that other people . . . *normal* people, did not have to work at getting through the day without freaking others out.

Since she married Will though, she had discovered that she could plod her way through life by taking up the most mind paralyzing—no, that was much too exciting—mind *numbing* pattern of repetition.

For the last ten years, no matter where the family had moved, Indie immediately set out to pound in the stakes of a normal routine. Get the kids settled, get a job, and begin to play the role that was beginning to show a little wear and tear around the edges.

She had always had a faint sense of unease and discontent since her life began. Or at least after the sudden death of her mother when she was only three. She could remember her mother clearly, in spite of her young age at the time of her death.

Beautiful. Bohemian and hippy-chick-ish. She'd named her daughter Indiana, after the state in which she had been born.

After the accident, Indie's distraught father pawned her off to various relatives, to be raised by them in short increments; passed around like a Christmas fruitcake until she was old enough to flee.

This allowed her father to slowly drink himself to death without interference. The only stability she had ever had was within herself, and she had become self reliant, as well as a nurturer and caretaker of others at a very early age.

Though she tucked them back into hiding every day, the feelings of nameless despair were beginning to feel a little more insistent. They began to press on her throat in a sudden escalation on the very day she had married Will. For ten long years, she had denied the angst its place on her forehead, forcing it to live in her belly and burn like a forgotten coal in the barbeque . . . quiet mostly, but flaming up suddenly, and taking her by surprise.

In more unnerving moments, she had the skin prickling feeling that someone was calling to her, but just out of range, always elusive. It was like a dream, she supposed, although she could not actually relate to that experience.

Today, the vague shadow grew until Indie felt sure that she could taste it's slightly metallic flavor on her tongue.

She swallowed convulsively, and pulled on her plain light blue scrubs, throwing her shoulder length dark waves into a ponytail and sighed at her reflection in the mirror.

"Now I really do look like a high school kid," she thought with a laugh.

The world would just have to suffer through it she supposed, and shut her eyes, picturing the family members of her patients, and how it seemed that their days were incomplete until they could tell her once again, how ridiculously young she looked.

Oh yes, it was a good thing she liked that kind of attention, wasn't it?

She flicked on the news to catch the weather report for the day, and heard the tail end of a news story about a local girl, brutally raped and murdered by her uncle. Indie leaped to snap off the television, too late, and felt the tears spring into her eyes, her hand pressed to her belly. The story made her sick . . . and made her question humanity . . . the direction the world was taking.

It filled her with a sadness that would probably seem extreme to some. Indie knew that she would carry this story in her heart, quietly mourning this young life, taken so senselessly. She often felt as if she couldn't bear the suffering of the world. The tough front Indie presented to the world was her only way of protecting the soft underbelly of her emotions.

Shaking her head to clear away the tears, she drew a deep breath. With an effort, Indie pasted on a happy face for the kids, though she still felt faintly ill, and entered the hallway calling out to the twins. They were standing outside the front door on the deck, their backpacks slung over their shoulders.

Indie watched as Cassidy raised her small hands into a frame, and peeked up through them at the bright morning sun.

"What are you doing, Cassidy?" Indie called out to her daughter. "Nothing, Mommy . . . just checking. It looks different today!"

"Well, you know not to look directly at the sun, right?" Indie knew that the warning was unnecessary, but some mommy phrases can't be fought. They just roll off the tongue at moments like this.

Cassidy looked back at her mother and rolled her eyes, grinning. "*Everyone* knows that, Mommy!"

"Okay then guys, are you ready to face another day?" she fought a sudden tremble in her voice that came from nowhere, and tried to smile through it. The twins eyed their mother slyly and sang out "Yes, Mommy" in unison and in a deliberately goofy tone that she could tell was designed to make her laugh.

And so Indie laughed, a little too loudly, as they stumbled their way out the door.

CHAPTER 2

When Fate comes to claim you
In the stark light of day
His hand, so persistent
Grasps firmly His prey
Don't bother to struggle
To cry or to fight
For Fate has no pity
For your mere mortal plight
Just follow His lead
You have no recourse
Just go without doubt
No fear, no remorse

"Go In Peace"
Katherine Whitley

Every day after Indie dropped the kids off at school, she played out her ritual of stalking the Cumberland Farms convenience store, where they have good coffee, cheap.

Health wise, it was her only vice.

Okay, make that coffee and chocolate. Dark chocolate could always give her a nearly drug-like high, but she indulged infrequently. She tried her best to behave herself, and scarfing down a family sized bag of Dove dark chocolate treasures, didn't particularly strike Indie as constructive.

The coffee, however, was a must. And it had to be large enough to have its own undertow for it to suffice.

Technically, coffee could be made at home, she supposed, but making amazing coffee that came in unlimited quantities on demand, just happened to be one of the very few skills she had never mastered. Indie figured as long as she worked, she had no reason to deny herself this (very) small indulgence.

She parked her car in the farthest parking space from the front door, as she always did.

All part of her life of boring predictability; an attempt to keep her natural tendency to accidentally unnerve others at bay. She couldn't bear the frightened looks on people's faces when they noticed the occasional slip up, and some form of her oddness broke free from their self imposed restraints.

It wasn't so much the fact that it made her feel like an oddity, but she truly hated to upset others, or cause distress that she knew was fully her doing.

She swung out of the car and hopped up onto the walkway, sidestepping lightly to avoid a small pack of high school students that had congregated around the front of the store on their routine pilgrimage to buy the unhealthy but necessary items that would carry them through their brutal day of learning. Their bantering and keyed up speech made her head hurt, as though she could hear all of their thoughts at once.

A thin sheen of perspiration gathered on Indie's forehead instantly, and she brushed it away, glancing upward. Winter had come to an end with a creak and a groan, and an early spring had attacked central Vermont with the enthusiasm of a Jenny Craig dropout confronted with a Dunkin' Donuts buffet.

It was crazy hot today, she thought as she gently but firmly squeezed her way through the swarm of backpacks and book bags.

The sound hit her with a nearly physical force. It made her feel as though her knees had been removed and replaced with overcooked pasta, or something equally supportive. Indie grabbed the cement post in front of her hastily, in an effort to remain upright.

It was ... what? A gasp, maybe? Someone's sharp intake of breath that she instinctively knew was directed toward her. At the same moment, she felt an odd warming sensation on the back of her neck.

Alarmed, but determined not to attract attention to herself, she shot an uneasy glance over her shoulder.

Nothing but the oppressive crush of teenagers.

Indie felt an instant, desperate need to get away, and quickly.

She darted into the store with the same feeling she used to get when she had to take her Aunt's dogs out at night when she was a kid. The feeling she recalled that began once she was walking back toward the safety of the house.

When she just *knew* something large and fang-y was walking right on her heels, drooling with anticipation, until finally, it would force her to lose all composure that last few feet and run in panic through the door, slamming it shut behind her.

Yes, it was like that.

Indie raced to the coffee bar, poured with ferocious speed and sprinted to the counter, only to meet with toe tapping frustration as the cashier slowly counted the contents of the drawer, looking up only when Indie waved her money in the air.

"Excuse me . . ."

The girl jumped, her pierced eyebrow shooting upward in surprise. "Oh my gosh, I'm sorry. I didn't even see you there!"

Well that was the running theme of Indie's life, was it not? Utterly forgettable.

Of course you didn't, she thought irritably. The unrest continued to build as the girl gave her back change, until Indie finally made her escape to the safe confines of her car. Flipping the locks shut, she laid her head back on the headrest, panting.

"What is *wrong* with me?" she wondered in disbelief. A crush of unease was seeping into her belly, and she couldn't shake the feeling that something was terribly wrong with today.

"Stop it. Everything is fine. Look around. No one is paying the slightest attention to you." This was her baseline, wasn't it?

"See", she spoke to herself, trying to soothe her clenched intestines. "Perfectly normal, right?"

She took a deep breath, and tried to look around casually. Her head began to pound with the pain that began while she was in the throng of kids.

No doubt, her brain was trying to claw its way out of her skull, and was very close to making its escape. Indie had to laugh shakily at the visual.

She needed a Tylenol, which was positively unheard of for her. Luckily, where she was going, they had plenty of benign, over-the-counter, painkilling pharmaceuticals. Backing carefully out of the parking lot while trying to keep the coffee steady, Indie drove determinedly toward her workplace.

As Indie pulled in to her usual parking spot, she sat for a moment and considered the sound that had forced her to take flight. The feelings created by the sound were four steps beyond disturbing to her, yet . . . why? It was a sound of shock.

Surprise . . . or maybe fear. What could someone have possibly seen in *her* to generate that kind of reaction? No answer spontaneously popped into her head.

With small sigh, Indie decided that she couldn't play chicken with the time clock any longer. She had to get her butt in there and do her thing. She flew into the building through the back entrance to use the stairs to the second floor where she worked.

The front entrance had only the elevator to get you upstairs, and although no one spoke to her, it always made her uncomfortable to ride in what she felt was awkward silence.

Indie was painfully inept at the art of creating conversation just to fill an empty silence, although she had little trouble speaking to people when there was something meaningful to say. She was rarely armed with anything interesting when she met people in the hallway or in small confined spaces, but it just seemed plain rude not to try.

And, if forced to admit it, she would have to say that there was a part of her whose feelings were constantly hurt by the surprised looks on people's faces when she spoke to them, reinforcing the paranoid feeling she sometimes grappled with, that she had been invisible to them before she had opened her mouth.

Every time it happened, her self-esteem took another swan dive off the edge of a great canyon. She had to be very careful now, because there wasn't much left.

Swallowing down that depressing idea, Indie loped up the stairs. She switched from being afraid, to becoming thoroughly disgruntled as she thought back to the stop for coffee.

What really happened, she asked herself, more calm now as the trauma was left behind. Did I overreact? Did I imagine something strange in a perfectly normal setting? She wondered.

She wasn't able to think about it anymore. The instant she greeted her co-workers in the nurses' station, she was assailed immediately by a worried voice.

"Maggie Conner isn't looking so well." Ashley, one of Indie's best nursing assistants was speaking and looking stressed as Indie set down her purse and coffee. She tried not to panic.

"Really? How can that be? She was just fine yesterday."

Ashley jumped at the sound of Indie's voice, and then repeated her concerns about the wiry little woman whom Indie had come to love.

"She's refusing to get out of bed, refusing breakfast . . . she wouldn't even open her eyes and look at me. And her breathing sounds bad. I told her I was going to get her nurse, and she told me, "don't bother!"

Ashley looked around the nurses' station and shrugged. "I'm 'bothering' anyway. She's acting really weird."

The news made Indie's heart go pat.

Miss Maggie was one of the residents with whom Indie truly connected. She felt a strange kinship with her, and enjoyed being in her room talking about anything and everything with her, while her radio played a constant accompaniment in the background.

It was never shut off, even in the night; the small notice taped to the front of it stated in no uncertain terms, "do not touch!" was placed there by Indie's own hands, after well-meaning nursing staff would sneak in to the room, thinking Maggie asleep, and turn it off.

The interruption of Miss Maggie's music was perhaps the only thing that could take the smile from the face of the gentle and patient woman. This Indie could totally understand, having an extreme love for music herself.

Their conversations were fascinating; the older woman was well-traveled and able to talk happily about any subject that happened to pop up, even though she could be a little loopy, Indie had to admit. She had once casually announced that she was very nearly three hundred years old. Indie had laughed.

"Well, we seem to have your age down as closer to ninety five!" "Oh, I know all that," she'd replied, waving her small hands delicately in the air.

"What would people think, after all, if you went around trying to convince them that you were nearly three centuries old?" She had laughed her sweet, clear laugh.

She didn't seem to have any kind of dementia, other than claiming to have lived an unusually long life. One thing had always struck Indie as odd, though. She had often appeared as though she wanted to confide something more. Something further, and, most likely along the same line as that unbelievable revelation, but something always seemed to keep her in check. Maybe it was the way that Indie would immediately steer the conversation back to reality, whenever it seemed that a detour was coming.

"I'm going down to check on her," Indie said to no one in particular. Who was listening anyway, right?

She quickly trotted down the hall to Maggie's room, and entered cautiously; stepping carefully to avoid knocking over the multiple stacks of books that were the room's only decor, save for one silver frame on her bedside table. The shiny five-by-seven outlined the handsome face of a white haired gentleman, of whom Maggie had always refused to speak.

Sure enough, she found her in bed, which was already a bad sign and no, she did not look good.

"Miss Maggie?" Indie whispered anxiously. Maggie kept her eyes firmly shut. She quickly took in the rise and fall of the thin, pink cotton gown covering the frail ribcage of her only . . . *friend*. The movements were irregular and the respirations fast.

Yeah, this was bad.

Indie inched closer to her bed, afraid of what she would feel in her belly . . . of what she would *know*, if she put her hands on her.

"Go ahead, Indie, come closer," Maggie said softly. "You know, don't you?" she whispered.

"I don't know anything, Miss Maggie," Indie returned the whisper.

Maggie laughed weakly. "Oh, you do so! And, you know, it's really ok. I've been alone for five long years . . . and after all, I *am* nearly three hundred years old . . . I think I'm ready!"

"So that's it then, ready to pack it in after only three centuries?" Indie nervously tried to joke, just so she wouldn't start bawling. Maggie laughed again before she was overtaken by a spasm of wet coughs that seemed to strangle her.

Without thinking, Indie rushed to turn her to her side so that the thick secretions could drain from her airway, and stifled a cry. The burning was fierce in her gut. She tried to shake it off, but it was undeniable.

Her favorite person had been sentenced to die, and there would be no stay granted by any doctor. Maggie was her own guardian, and had an advance directive, Indie knew, and so no one was to try to save her anyway. She fought the tightening of her throat that warned of the unprofessional tears trying to force their way out.

"I told you so," Maggie rasped in an eerily casual manner, finally opening her green opalescent eyes to look up at her. Indie tried to set her in a comfortable position, pointlessly fussing with the woman's soft sea-foam green comforter, the tiny floral pattern blurring as the tears insisted on making themselves known.

"Okay, so what would you like me to do for you," she asked, stroking the silver white curls framing Maggie's face, determined to remain calm for the sake of her patient.

"Oh, there is nothing you can do for *me*, but I am going to try to do something for *you*. Actually, I'd hoped to put off dying until I saw you again. I know something about you that even you don't know, and I wanted to be the one to finally tell you that you are NOT crazy!" Maggie shifted in the bed to better see Indie, and spoke to her in a somewhat sly voice.

"You are a music lover, are you not? Not simply a lover . . . you become almost entranced by it. You *need* it, don't you?" She smiled at the look on Indie's face, and then closed her eyes for a moment with a satisfied sigh.

Indie stared at Maggie's face, trying to quell the instant unease caused by her words.

"What do you mean by that, Miss Maggie?" Maggie snapped open her translucent sage-colored eyes, and fixed them upon her.

"Indie, I know you try to act like one of them, but you're just simply not, and today is the day you will hear the truth."

Indie was becoming even more alarmed now. Was her patient finally succumbing to senile dementia, on her way out the door? She was frightened that the answer was a resounding "no". She felt a rising anxiety, because the words she spoke brought to life the sense of foreboding she had felt earlier. Now, it began to spread throughout her body.

Maggie knows that I am not normal. Well, okay, so much for my charade, thought Indie.

A movement in the doorway caught her eye, and she turned to face the intruder. Instinctively Indie knew that she was onto something here, and some other nurse or aide, was going perform a terrible information-denying feat by cutting in on the conversation; one that she knew was going to be interesting, but sadly, also very short.

The feeling burst through her in a flash . . . the burning intensity in her head catching her off guard. The interloper was a tall and obviously very fit young man, dressed simply in dark jeans and a white button down shirt, worn untucked under a dark leather bomber-style jacket. He had obnoxiously unkempt hair, although Indie found it strangely appealing.

The color was perhaps two shades shy of jet black, like molasses, with glints of warmth snapping through the thick mixture of straight and wavy locks and he looked at Miss Maggie with compassionate eyes.

Eyes that were an exquisite blend of cobalt and turquoise in color. Those eyes then flicked toward Indie's, and a jolt of electricity slammed through her body. The oddly colored blue eyes widened, and she heard his quick intake of breath.

This caused an instant dizzy and disorienting feeling to rush through Indie's head, because it was the same sound that had triggered her senses this morning. The sound that had come from an unknown source, and now, she had identified it.

This stranger looked like he could have easily blended in with the hoard of high school kids there at the time.

Indie shook her head briefly, trying to clear it when the obvious hit her. It was here! The source of her early morning angst . . . in her workplace . . . her safe zone . . . *her patient's room!*

In full protective mode, she threw off the fuzzy feeling and stood between the door and Miss Maggie's bed, arms outstretched in warning.

"Don't come near her, do you hear me?" Indie's foremost thought was to protect her patient, and in an unprecedented reaction, she was ready for a throw down with this person, if that's what it took.

"What do you want?" she demanded in a choking voice that sounded nothing like her own. The stranger took a step back as though pushed by an unseen force, with a sickened look clouding his perfect features.

"Indie let him be," Miss Maggie wheezed in what still managed to be a commanding voice.

"Do . . . do you know this person," Indie asked, suddenly appalled at the idea that she may have just threatened a legitimate visitor.

"Oh I don't know him, but I see his markers, and I know he is one . . ."

He is *one*? A chill raced through her body.

"He is one . . . of *what*?"

"Please," the stranger broke in softly, "if I may be allowed to speak . . ." His voice was intoxicating in tone and cadence, a hint of a British accent apparent.

"I heard Miss Conner was here, and I came to see her. We . . . know some of the same people".

He cautiously approached the bed, eyes never leaving Indie's, moving with a lithe grace that suddenly made Indie feel a strange sensation in her lower belly, and some very inappropriate thoughts swung through her mind. What was happening to her?

Indie burned with ten shades of shame, and cleared her throat. Confused and embarrassed, she stepped out of his path as he came around to the chair next to the bed and sat down slowly, taking the hand of the dying woman.

Miss Maggie allowed this, looking up at him through half closed eyes.

"Ah, so warm, these hands. I can feel the bloodlines of the warriors flowing through them." She smiled and gestured with her chin toward Indie before continuing. "But hers are even more powerful, you know . . . in the way only warm, healing hands can be. However," she sighed, "we are beyond healing now, and the next life awaits us."

We?

Before Indie could ask what she meant, Maggie closed her eyes and dragged another ragged breath through her failing lungs.

"Let me get you some morphine, Miss Maggie," Indie begged, "it will help your breathing." She was desperate, if not to keep her alive, then at least to keep her comfortable.

"Keep still, child. I have only a short time left." Maggie spoke firmly. She opened her eyes and looked at the disconcertingly handsome man sitting inches away from her, his arms poked through the side rails of the bed, still holding her hand.

He pulled his gaze away from Maggie and lifted his eyes back to Indie's. She had to fight to stay on her feet. He was, well, stunning; she had to admit this in spite the discombobulating things that were happening, as well as the words accosting her in the cool dimness of Ms. Maggie's private room.

The look in his eyes was familiar to her in some odd way. She had seen those lost and tired eyes somewhere, very recently. The answer slammed into her. With a shudder of recognition, she realized that it was in the mirror. *She* had those same eyes; that same look of desperate yearning.

Indie tried to focus, and study him stealthily. He looked so very young, but there was something about him . . . a weariness that comes from years spent . . . unfulfilled? His were not the eyes of someone young. And there was no way to pinpoint it, exactly, but there was something about this person that was creating a nearly irresistible pull toward him, as if she should simply walk over and sit in his lap! If that wasn't ridiculous enough, she also felt as though he would welcome her doing this . . . as if she would actually do such a thing.

She could picture it now;

"Hello, stranger, mind if I plop down on top of you?"

"Why no, not at all. In fact, please do!"

Aside from the obvious reasons, such as the situation as a whole, there was another reason Indie was becoming more than a little uncomfortable with her reaction to this man. He physically did not look a day over nineteen . . . twenty maybe.

Moreover, he was a complete stranger. This whole thing was strange. In a rush of emotion, her throat tightened and in an instant, the overwhelming urge to flee took over her thoughts.

"Do you tell her or shall I, young Jackson, because she is about to bolt!" Miss Maggie seemed to sense her sudden inexplicable fright, but her words locked Indie into place and stopped her breathing. She stayed where she was, staring stupidly at the two of them.

"I suppose it may be easier, coming from you," sighed the young man in a resigned and weary voice, but it was achingly smooth and lulling. It had the disturbing effect of both putting Indie both at ease and on edge simultaneously.

"She knows you . . . and loves you," he added quietly.

Wow. That was quite the intimate statement, uttered by a person upon whom she had never set eyes before. Indie fought a defiant urge to demand that he explain just how he could possibly know anything about whom or what she loved.

Instead, she focused on the young man's eyes, reading his unease and wariness . . . and some other unfathomable emotion in them that inexplicably made her heart ache.

He needed comforting. She had no idea why she knew this, but the young man in front of her was on the edge of heartbreak and despair.

The knowledge made Indie's own heart shrivel with pain. His pain was hers also. The thought slid through her mind like strong hands through her hair, and made her unsteady on her feet once more. As she thought further about the statement that he had just made, suddenly, it wasn't so hard to keep her mouth shut. She was becoming nervously intrigued.

"Then we haven't much time," Miss Maggie croaked. "Sit down Indie, and I am going to tell you a story." Indie snapped back to reality with a gasp.

"I am on the clock," she remembered, speaking in a small voice, "they will be looking for me, wondering where I am in just a few minutes. I'll have to count first . . . get report . . . ." her voice trailed away.

"No one is thinking about you right now, trust me," Miss Maggie said airily, as she shifted uncomfortably in her bed. "Nor me either."

Indie silently tried to process this statement, and decided that even though it made no sense, she was just going to have to go with it. She knew Maggie was going to die very soon, and she was suddenly desperate to hear what she had to say.

"I will warn you right now, Indie, my story goes back further than your mind can probably accept; your carefully cultivated normal mind. I'm talking about billions of years . . . one hundred and twenty, to be more precise."

Indie listened with outward calm, but was already wondering where Maggie could possibly be going with this introduction. And why was this strange and beautiful man at her side not shrinking away, or at the very least, looking appropriately mystified by these words?

Indie shifted nervously, noticing at that same moment, that all of the unending sounds of the nursing home . . . call lights buzzing, aides talking, etcetera, had gone frighteningly silent.

She dared not look into the hallway, for suddenly, she suffered a gut twisting terror that she would see everyone frozen in place, as if in an episode of the Twilight Zone, and she had no wish to begin screaming uncontrollably.

"Pay attention Indie Allen!" barked Maggie, hoarsely, "Stand still and listen, because my time is unfortunately, quite limited now!"

Indie gaped at her. She knew her mouth was hanging open, but she couldn't seem to fix it, for Maggie had called her by her maiden name. Indie knew without a doubt, that this name had never crossed her lips in this town . . . not in this state.

She carefully pulled her mouth up to its correct position, and dropped her head, clinging to the wooden footboard of Maggie's bed for dear life. She was so very grateful for its ability to hold her up, because as her eyes made contact once more with the one called Jackson, Indie felt the current snap through her again, and his intensity made her legs feel shifty.

She steeled herself.

"Ok, you know what? I . . . I am positive now that I absolutely need to hear this, and I'm . . ." she gulped down the slight feeling of nausea that was scratching at the inside of her belly. "I am ready to handle whatever you want to tell me, Miss Maggie."

Indie hoped that she sounded more convincing from the outside of her body, than she sounded to herself.

Maggie replaced her head on her stack of pillows and smiled.

Jackson's face creased with a look of momentary distress, and she squeezed his hand in a comforting way before speaking.

"Good. Now we can begin"

CHAPTER 3

Miss Maggie's Tale

"When you have eliminated the impossible, whatever remains, *however improbable*, must be the truth."

The Sign of the Four, chapter 6 (1890)
Sherlock Holmes in *The Sign of the Four*

"First you must clear your head of all your preconceived ideas of the possible, please, or you will never be able to hear me," she began. Indie winced but kept silent as a burst of coughing shook Maggie's tiny frame. She recovered, and pressed on.

"As I said, this story begins approximately one hundred and twenty billion years ago, long after the Ancestors had watched this planet boil, flare and finally cool. This, they observed with clinical detachment, interested in the shaping of the materials, and what they were becoming."

At this point, Indie opened her mouth, ready to interrupt this dialog right away, but she caught Jackson's eye, and somehow read a gentle warning from him, and a slight negative movement of his head. Indie closed her mouth with a snap as Maggie continued.

"And then there was life! As the first microscopic being drew breath, the fascination grew, as did the complexity of those beings. And the Ancestors grew excited, amazed at the life evolving before their eyes.

It has been said that Baghdad is the cradle of civilization; however, this is a myth. One of a thousand civilizations was born there, but this was not the beginning. The birthplace of human kind truly began in the Nurnanov Region approximating Russia, near the city of Ufa.

The wild lands were cleared, the waters drained away in preparation for a great Society.

A city where people would be born to learn, to understand and put to full use the gifts that they had been given by the Creator. They were granted the great knowledge by the architects of this Society, to create a highly advanced community.

Two hundred maps were created, carved from dolomite and diopside. They were inscribed with intricate three-dimensional maps of the world, including every mountain range, forest, the Rivers Bely, Ufimka and Sutolka, as well as the Great Ufa Canyon. These were distributed by Society Elders to various parts of this planet, given as gifts to all life forms there.

The plan was to bring to this world the greatness that is shared beyond it. All over this beautiful but still new and wild land, grand structures and chambers were built using a system that the ancients referred to as 'Sacred Geometry,' based on mathematical measurements in relation to simple shapes.

Society Ancestors taught the people to construct the sacred places using specific geometrical ratios. This allowed them to better connect with their Creator, and to feel the vibrations, the language of the Earth."

Maggie sighed and shook her head

"I will not waste time speaking the names of those races yet to be discovered from so very long ago. The remnants of those Societies have gone back to the Earth, and may never be known by the general masses. Instead, I will focus on the recent history . . . the known cultures, and how our Ancestors have touched them.

At first, in the earliest years, it was simple. The Ancestors would present themselves to the strongest and most intelligent of colonized life forms, moving to tribal leaders as time wore on. The life here believed, and listened eagerly to what the strange visitors had to say, and absorbed their knowledge with boundless thirst. It wasn't like it is today, with modern sensibilities so cynical they refuse to acknowledge the new and unknown."

It was this last statement that caused Indie to briefly interrupt the story with her own fit of coughing, as she struggled to keep herself silent at this revelation.

Both Jackson and Maggie watched this with contrasting emotions stamped on their faces . . . one wary, one faintly exasperated.

"Compose yourself, Indie!" Maggie demanded with a surge of strength, "and listen!" She hit Indie with a frown of disapproval.

"With the Inca's, the visitors focused on teaching engineering and agriculture, showing them how to build their steep mountainsides into terraced farms.

"The Huari-Tiahuanaco learned quickly, and became skilled engineering marvels. They could fit giant stones together so seamlessly, they needed no mortar. Why, most of their forts are still standing today, in perfect condition. Look at Manchu Picchu! This knowledge did not simply materialize in their heads. *Our* Ancestors gave this to them."

Our Ancestors?
Indie noted the word, used several times now and although confused, remained quiet, not wanting to interrupt Maggie's momentum, although her still lingering strength was evident in her voice.

"The Nazca showed thanks to the original Society Members with their enormous Earth drawings, still viewed by tourists to this day. Society Elders came to give advice on the governing of their tribes, and their cultures thrived. However, when left on their own, instability was allowed to destroy them as they became too focused on the "ruling class", and they were laid open to defeat.

The Maya culture was also birthed by the Society, and was considered the greatest hope for humankind, so well did they learn. They were given the secrets of technology, mathematics and in an unprecedented show of confidence, the true origin of the world.

The early visitors taught them the concept of time and the written word. So successful were they that theirs is the most accurate calendar to date, accurate to the point of losing only one day every six thousand years.

The Mayas called the first Society visitor "*Ah Kin Mai*", meaning "highest one of the Sun." Those that followed, were simply "*Ah Kin*", or "from the sun." Every culture from the Maya's forward have stories about the so called "Children of the Sun", for that is what they saw . . . visitors who for all appearances, came to them from a bright light in the sky."

This made Indie shift uncomfortably where she stood.

Light from the sky? She didn't like where this story seemed to be drifting, but struggled to remain silent as Miss Maggie continued.

"The Egyptians gained much architectural knowledge as well, such as the ability to build the most universal of sacred shapes, the pyramid, and were possibly the most demonstrative of their thanks, with their worship of Ra, the sun god. But they also fell for the trickery of the Fallen, who presented himself as a god as well, gathering a huge following among the Egyptians, and later the Greeks also."

"*Sobek*!" Jackson's growl broke through the room at this point, fury quite apparent in his simple utterance of the word. In an instant, he seemed chastened. His eyes met Indie's again, and he looked away. He was clearly embarrassed by his outburst, and turned to Maggie once more.

Maggie had taken this moment to recover her breath, and she placed her hand to Jackson's face in a comforting and indulgent gesture.

"I know the mention of this incarnation of the Fallen disturbs you, young Jackson, but it must be told, don't you agree?"

"Of course, Miss Conner," he responded instantly.

Respectfully.

"This worship of the one called *Sobek* did not bode well for either culture, unfortunately." Maggie added, shaking her head sadly while drawing shallow breaths that made Indie uneasy.

"The greed of man was fatal to the cultures; instigated and encouraged by the anger and jealousy of the Fallen. The power hungry moved in when the teaching was over, after our members left. Mere mortal men took on these titles, these positions of Gods, and began to rule by fear and violence. They called it just, in the name of religion.

"The Maya began human sacrifice. The Society broke with their usual protocol of allowing destiny to unfold as it will, and put an end to this, when it could be tolerated no longer. In nine hundred AD, the Mayas were quietly removed by order of the highest ranking of the Ancestors.

Society members visited the Mayan lord Pacal, as well as Viracocha of Peru, and the great Emperor Ch'in Shi Huangdi of China. These three were known to be Keepers of the Sacred Science, and given the understanding of the heavens and the immortality of the human soul."

At this point, Maggie released a sharp gasp that cause both Indie and Jackson to jump toward her in a panic, but she waved them back as her face contorted momentarily with what looked like unspeakable pain. Maggie gripped the side rails of the bed tightly, and closed her eyes briefly.

With a wince that made Indie's heart ache, she pushed herself to continue.

"It was only a little over two thousand years ago, that this Chinese Emperor, knowing his death was imminent, constructed an army of over eight thousand terra cotta soldiers. These, with over five hundred sculpted horses drawing his chariots, were covered with symbols and codes which he used to write out the secrets of creation and the sun, from the beginning of time.

This was crafted and kept in a very secret location, but has been unearthed in this century, for all to see, yet no one believes the words he took such care to record and then conceal. In 210 B.C., China gained the knowledge to construct a Great Wall. If anyone cared to dig deeper into the secret language written on the terra cotta chariots, they would find the instructions for this massive undertaking.

The Aztecs simply moved into the remains of one of these Societies, learning a fundamental understanding of the positions and alignments with the heavens that were important to our being. The sacred structures allowed their spirits to become one with all matter, and to allow the fluids and chemistry of their bodies to resonate at the perfect ratio to commune with the heavens.

In the Aztec language, Maya means "Old Ones", named so because the Aztecs believed *them* to be the creators of society. They *were* an old civilization, but by no means the oldest.

Mayas carved stones; giant heads the size of a compact car . . . the Olmecs. The Aztecs thought them to be Gods. There have been many found in the jungles of southern Mexico. The features of these "Gods" are quite African, and the symbols covering them are nearly identical to that of Nubian, Kush, and the Vai of West Africa. These things are no coincidence.

The knowledge was brought to all of these different regions and different cultures by the same ancient visitors . . . our Society Members. They began and lost civilization after civilization . . . watching them destroy themselves and others. They tried again in Mexico, then Egypt, and so on. Each time, attempting to teach humankind the wonders of learning and of the endless possibilities provided by technology, only to have the Fallen gain victory over the weak of mind, and begin wars over land, power and possessions repeatedly, destroying what was good and right.

The inhabitants of Mexico City, (actually the longest inhabited city in the world, predating Rome, Athens and even Baghdad) . . . the ancient Incas, and the Mayas knew that the Earth was round. They knew where they were located on the planet, and about the existence of other cities around the world. Their discovered writings show this knowledge. Because of *our* teaching, *our* maps, they knew even how far these were and how to get there."

Maggie now began a spastic round of coughs that were wet and choking, but before Indie could move, the young man beside her carefully slid his left arm under Maggie's shoulders and lifted her up and to the side with all the skill and care of a devoted son; one with a little medical training.

He held her firmly as she worked to clear her airway, and once she had somewhat done so, Jackson offered her a sip of water from the insulated jug that was within reach on the side table. This, Maggie accepted gratefully, but when Jackson asked if he should perhaps take over the story, which Indie decided had taken on the feeling of a college lecture, Maggie shook her head and struggled to sit up once more.

"No, young one, I must do this. I promised myself that *I* would tell her the tale when the time was right. Although the situation is now forced, as my beloved is leaving this world. I claim for myself this right, because it is *I* who have waited and watched her struggle within. It is *I* who have been silent, while looking into her eyes and seeing her pain!"

Jackson abruptly sat back in his chair. The look of sickness was back, twisting his features into a mask of misery, and he nodded his head, gesturing for Maggie to continue, as if he didn't quite trust his voice.

Indie watched this exchange feeling strangely detached . . . as if this was taking place on a movie screen, where she was not a participant of any kind. It was probably the only way she could remain in place, listening to this bizaar tale.

She also noted the overly formal way of speaking that the other two had slipped into; the words sounding as though there was some sort of textbook being read. And the feeling that a chain of command had been established; the older woman a General, to Jackson's Sergeant. Maggie definitely held the higher office, Indie was somehow sure.

Her attention was jerked back by Miss Maggie's hoarse voice, wearily continuing her long and for some reason, frightening story, the dying woman picking up once more, exactly where she'd left off.

"As Cortez destroyed the Aztecs," she wheezed, "all libraries were burned, gold melted, records lost forever, people forgot. Think of it, Indie. Archeologists have unearthed many great cities, their citizens seemingly vanished. Most of what they find are things made of very hard stone, metal and other impermeable materials. Things most likely to survive wars using advanced technology to destroy and kill. Things that can withstand even cosmic catastrophes, such as when the comet Marduk slammed into Mars sixty-five million years ago, causing large chunks of the planet to break off, and hit the Earth, instigating mass extinction."

Indie drew in her breath as she considered this. Could this really have happened? There was a feeling of suddenly becoming privy to a deeply guarded secret about the history of the world, and it fed her anxiety as she continued to listen, while at the same time, thinking frantically.

"And so, the Society began its efforts once again," Maggie spoke more sharply, as if to regain Indie's focus. "At the direction of the Creator, they will never give up on making this grand experiment a success until mankind truly destroys the Earth or the end of time descends."

Indie's eyes shifted back to Jackson, who had been utterly silent, and seemed, impossible as it was, familiar with the history lesson. His eyes blazed back at her. She looked away and the lesson continued.

"The early Society Members, who were visitors to this place, began leaving behind some of their own, by direct order, instructing them to assimilate into humankind in every way. They were to embark on missions with several goals in mind. Most are here only to teach, to learn, and to monitor the energy flowing from this planet, and the sun's response; this being key to the survival of the planet. There are those, however, who are employed in a more active role; a hands-on kind of guardianship, defending against elements either unnatural, or harmful to the destiny of the plan.

They were also to try to protect people from themselves, yet without true interference, to try to rebuild the great Society that was planned for them all along, but has been destroyed repeatedly by greed, apathy, the quest by the few for power, all marks of the Fallen. What the Population does not understand, is that this world has been restarted and reset hundreds of times over. Where negativity brings destruction, the Society brings resurrection.

Ms Maggie stopped suddenly, and looked up at Indie. "Is this difficult for you to comprehend? I realize that I am all over the map in time, and geographical locations, but I am trying to fit a very long history into my very limited time frame. I want you to see how many things Society Members have affected throughout the history of the world."

"Not really", Indie spoke slowly. "I don't understand the reason behind this episode of Mysteries of the Ancient Worlds, and I have never heard of . . . *society members*, but I have heard similar stories before . . . myths, legends."

Maggie eyed her determinedly. "Yes . . . I think you *do* know . . . you *do understand*. Think, Indie!"

"What *are* you trying to tell me, Miss Maggie?" Indie felt a sudden rush of apprehension, as if she knew that what was taking place, right here, right now, in this room, was about to throw her tightly wound universe off its orbital track forever. She could sense that Maggie was leading up to something so incredible, so unbelievable . . . but trying to do it in such a way that Indie didn't run screaming from the room before she had finished.

Indie took a deep shaky breath, and decided to meet her head on. "So, you want to tell me about . . . about a group of . . . others, (She flatly refused to use the first word that popped into her mind, which was *aliens*), that came down to Earth, eons before there were supposed to be even *people* here yet, and that they were trying to create some sort of advanced Society?"

"Yes, I am," Maggie stated with an eerie calm, staring Indie straight in the eye. "Life as we know it did not begin here; it was brought here, and then perfected through a conscious purpose."

Indie swallowed hard. "Um, okay, I guess that's not totally inconceivable."

Indie believed in UFOs and aliens the way others do; she may believe in the possibility of their existence, but if anyone told her that they'd seen one, she would think that they were probably a kook.
Just like with ghosts. These concepts seemed especially hard to hear about in the benign setting of her everyday work environment.

She noticed that Jackson was frowning at her now, and he once again shook his head slightly, nearly imperceptibly.

Maggie smiled at him, but weakly, nearly spent from the exertion of telling a tale of such length and detail. Indie could see that she was struggling to hang on, and she wanted to do something medical for her. Indie started to speak, but Maggie shook her head, as if she knew her thoughts.

"I know, you would like to think I'm crazy or senile. That's the much more acceptable reality, right? It would be easier that way, but I'm sorry. I'm not." She shook her head again. "And it's about to get more difficult for you. Much more." "Remember, I told you about the original members leaving some of their own behind, to assimilate into humankind . . ."

"Okay," Indie whispered, now terrified to hear what was coming next.

"Well, they assimilated quite nicely; breeding with the native life forms and effectively upgrading, if you will, carrying forth the best possible genetics of both races. There are different ranks among our kind, hierarchies.

Two hundred of our Ancestors, all from the various ranks, came to mingle with the genetic make-up of the human beings. However, only one of our very highest order came, directed to spread the genes that he possessed. His rank is the only genetic sharing achieved through a sexless union. The highest of our kind are a pure and perfect species, and have no carnal needs or desires."

"How sad for them," Indie couldn't resist, trying desperately to convince herself that this was total nonsense. Maggie ignored this and continued; however, Indie was sure that she caught the man called Jackson's mouth twitching in an attempt to hold back a laugh. Yes, there was a definite sparkle of humor behind those blue eyes.

Indie looked away as the soliloquy continued.

"Hybrids were created by this blending of the species, but the genes themselves remain separate . . . intact. They combined well with other genes to make new products, but at times it happens that people with the right combination of these hybrid genes mate, and a complete set of genetic markers come together, making a full-blooded descendent of the original Society.

"One Society Member can always see the markers of another, if they are taught, and know what they are looking for. Forgive the cliché' but it's as plain as the nose on your face!" Maggie waited while this sunk slowly into Indie's thought process.

It hit its mark.

"What are you saying? You can't mean . . ." Indie gasped, yet the sound went nowhere. "What do you mean, as plain as the nose on *my* face?" The room began to tilt precariously and her hands clawed the footboard ferociously now. Was her suspicion that she was truly some sort of unnatural creature about to be confirmed, her status irrefutable?

"Mathematically speaking, my dear, the measurements of the spaces between your eyes, nose and mouth have a perfect symmetry that belongs only to Society Members. It is a mark of the Sacred Geometry, usually too subtle for human cousins to notice."

Indie's thoughts raced in a desperate attempt at denial. She had heard psychotic ranting like this before, but only from the truly deranged and sick. It was impossible to think of Maggie in this way, but it was a whole lot easier than accepting her shocking words as truth.

"Indie," she sighed, "I'm neither deranged nor sick, and neither are you!" Indie once again experienced the unsettling feeling that Maggie had plucked the thought right out of her brain.

"I DID, Indie!" Maggie gasped, "There is no time for pretending anymore. My *Equal* is dying, and I have only minutes left." She closed her eyes and rasped out a deep breath. "Jackson is yours. Listen to him, *please!*"

"Jackson is my *what?*" Indie felt an urge to scream at her, to tell her to stop whatever it was that she was trying to do to her. She didn't want to hear anymore of this . . . insanity.

"He is your *Equal*, Indie . . . your rightful partner. Hear what he tells you. It will be the truth, and you will know it, as soon as you let your mind accept it, as soon as you feel his touch. *Equals* can never deceive one another." She raised slightly upward, her frail shoulders leaving her pillow.

"Listen to me! I knew your real name, did I not? I know your thoughts. You can't just dismiss me as some crazy old lady and go on about your life as if today never happened, because I've said too much to you that *makes* you believe, even as I tell you things that you cannot! You have the markers. You have not been found until now, because you are an *orphaned member* . . . you have the gift of *invisibility*, but now you have been identified and your *Equal* has come for you! Jackson, you *must* make her hear you. You will teach her . . . protect her. And there is more . . . she is in possession of something so *precious* . . . !"

Maggie's voice was disappearing. " . . . Must be protected *at all cost* . . ." It trailed away to a gasp. Indie watched, both hands covering her mouth, horrified by not only Maggie's words, but also what she was seeing. Miss Maggie drew one last agonized breath and was still. She then seemed to deflate as her life force flowed out of the empty shell of her body.

Indie, rooted to the spot, moved the only things that she could—her eyes—to the young man at Maggie's side. He gently stroked Maggie's snowy curls and whispered, "Go into your true form . . . be reunited!" in his soft lilting voice. He stared for a long moment at the lifeless form that had been Maggie, and then rose to stand in front of Indie. She backed away until the wall became a solid barrier behind her, noticing that at exactly this moment, the hallway had come back to life.

The buzzing, the chatter.

Inescapable.

"Indie . . ." he spoke her name with a familiarity that made her throat ache with the need to cry, and he started to reach out his hand to her. Indie flattened herself against the wall, whimpering in terror.

With a stricken look, he dropped his hand quickly.

"Of course," his voice sounded distraught. "You are afraid. I am so sorry, but . . . ." he hesitated, as if making a decision.

"No," he finally spoke sadly, shaking his head, "it won't begin this way!"

He swiftly breezed past her, his hands shoved deeply into his pockets, and was gone. As he passed by her, Indie caught his warm masculine scent, which unleashed a surge of vertigo. She remained against the wall for balance, and felt a peculiar sensation in her lungs. They were beginning to ache, and she realized that aside from the whiff of deliciousness that she'd caught as the stranger had rushed past, she had been neglecting to breathe for God knows how long.

She dragged down deep gasps of welcome oxygen, and turned to race down the hall. Of course, he was nowhere in sight. She hadn't really expected to see him . . . after all, he was only a dream . . . wasn't he?

Indie staggered into the nurses' station.

"Miss Maggie is dead," Indie intoned, in a weak, flat voice.

"What? She is not! I was in there with her like, five minutes ago!" exclaimed the aide who had met Indie with the news that Maggie was unwell. Ashley turned and sprinted down the hall.

Indie stared after her, and looked at the clock in the nurses' station. It read 7:05 AM. Not five minutes had passed since she had walked in to work this morning. "Impossible," she mumbled, completely numbed out by the events of the morning. She found herself suddenly jarred back to life by a braying voice.

"Are you ready to count or what?" The unwelcome voice barked in her ear, referring to the job requirement of having to count all of the narcotics locked up on the med cart.

"Uh, yeah, sure . . ." Indie cringed. Her ears hurt. "Who is working Maggie's hall today?" Indie asked.

"Erin is on it!" shrieked Brenda, the cause of the pain in her hypersensitive ears. Indie looked pointedly at Erin, and spoke with authority.

"You need to get down there!"

Erin nodded once, her expression shocked, and hurried down to Maggie's room.

Indie noted that for the first time, every eye in the nursing station was on her. Okay, so she had accidentally brought her personality to work with her today. Well, well, wasn't this rapidly becoming a day of novel events.

She counted mechanically, listened to report, and clawed her way through the rest of her day in a haze of grief, mixed with disbelief and a growing sense of panic.

Even after the funeral home came and picked up Miss Maggie's body, Indie purposefully avoided the hallway that had been the scene of this insane exchange of information this morning.

She had to have dreamed the whole scenario, right? Miss Maggie had spoken for half an hour, and yet, no time had passed? Into what realm had she slipped? It simply was not possible, and yet . . . and yet . . . she knew it had happened.

Pulling Maggie's chart, Indie noted that there was some sort of legal document forbidding any kind of autopsy or post death exam . . . something about religious reasons. She was to be cremated within twenty-four hours.

As she scanned the documents, she also noted for the first time that Maggie routinely refused all labs, and Indie already knew that she took no meds. Not even a vitamin.

This did not necessarily stand out, as many residents lived at the nursing home as a matter of convenience, having no family, and an inability to care for the maintenance of a home any longer, but Miss Maggie had been incredibly healthy.

Inhumanly healthy.

Until today. Indie slammed the chart shut and thrust it back into the rack with trembling hands. She had never been as eager as she was that day, to clock out and race at top speed out the door.

CHAPTER 4

Jackson

Jackson leaned against the wall at the bottom of the stairwell, having fled like a coward from the miserable scene upstairs. The cry of terror that had erupted from Indie's lips when he approached her had ripped out his heart.

Ripped it out and stomped on it with steel-toed boots.

Then set it on fire.

To put it mildly, Jackson was devastated.

He slid down the wall and sat on the floor, resting his forearms on his knees and agonized over his next move. A most unfamiliar sensation was taking place somewhere near the back of his throat. A tightness that made him think that it may be possible for a throat to slit itself.

He pressed his hand uneasily to his neck and swallowed repeatedly, feeling his eyes begin to burn.

His hands moved to his eyes and they felt damp.

Tears? What was happening?

He ground his fists painfully into his eyes to rid them of this embarrassment and slid his fingers through his hair.

Jackson stared at the peeling paint on the wall adjacent to his slumped form. How had his plan gone so horribly wrong? Although he was not so naive as to believe that Indie would come skipping down the hallway with him, without a second thought, he *had* come here today on a mission, determination that *he* was going to tell her the truth. He would reach out to her, she would take his hand, and he would at least have the opportunity to explain everything to her.

She would have let me speak to her, had I touched her! He thought, exasperated. He had not counted on finding Miss Conner on her deathbed.

Not only was it sad, but inconvenient! She had blurted out nearly the entire story to Indie, and he had allowed this in silence. It had been his only choice, given the circumstances.

But now, she is truly freaked out, he thought with a groan. And very afraid . . . of me, he added, rubbing his sternum to try to quell the ache that had just lodged there.

He was also at a loss as to what Miss Conner, or Maggie, as he now knew her to be called, had meant about Indie having something that had to be protected "at all cost."

He pondered this for a moment. He was somewhat gifted at knowing other's thoughts, although far from perfect . . . for now; but Maggie was the strongest of his kind that he had come across in a very long time. Not since his trainer in London had he met someone so able to cloak his or her thoughts.

Well, he decided, it does not matter, because I am already committed to protecting Indie and whatever is important to her. I am sure the answer will show itself soon enough.

Just exactly how he was going to accomplish this, well . . . he had no specific plan thus far.

Perhaps I'll just throw myself down a flight of stairs in front of her! he thought humorlessly. If I fracture every bone in my body, maybe she'll feel sorry for me, and allow me speak.

That was stupid.

He closed his eyes and rolled his head back and forth against the wall in frustration and despair, fighting a violent impulse to race back up the stairs and spirit her away. It was agonizing to sit here trying to pull his mind back into an acceptable state, after having her so near, just moments ago. And he . . . ah well, he had bathed in the light of her presence. After all of these years.

The searching, and then the waiting. It was over and yet not.

Because here he was, sitting just literally yards away from her, and there she was, so close, but as far away as ever. He knew he must not frighten her further. He didn't *want* to frighten her. He wanted to hold her . . . kiss her.

Comfort her. However, this was obviously not possible.

Not yet.

Jackson sighed, and rubbed his eyes again with both hands. He ached all over. Having been this long without her, how could the longing have reached this unbearable fever pitch? He felt like doing something as pointless and lame as curling up into a ball, here at the base of the stairs.

Jackson knew that he was about to throw Indie's carefully constructed life into chaos, and a large part of him shrank away, horrified at the very idea; but a larger part knew that he had to do what he had to do.

It was simple, really.

He had to at least give her the option to have the life for which she was born. If she chose to reject it . . . well . . . he would figure out how to endure that possibility if it arose. He desperately hoped he wasn't going to find out.

Looking around uneasily, Jackson slowly clambered to his feet. His usual strength and ease of motion seemed to have evaporated, leaving him feeling heavy and clumsy. It was an odd sensation for him, as was the faintly nauseous feeling rolling through his belly.

I feel like a reject . . . like I've been dumped! He thought with bitter amusement.

I can't hurt her, he sobered, whatever this costs me; I don't want to do that . . . oh, but by all that is holy . . . he countered himself, I also know that I won't be able to leave her alone, not until she makes the choice.

He slid his fingers in to the pockets of his jeans and stared at the bits of grass and debris lying on the indoor-outdoor carpeting on the landing.

"Are you okay, sir?" The voice made him jump. Allowing someone to sneak up on him like that was further evidence that he was not in his usual form. No one was ever able to take Jackson by surprise, as a rule. He looked around, a bit wildly, to find the source of the question.

A pretty blond girl in brightly colored scrubs, with pictures of Tinkerbelle decorating the top, stood on the stairs above him, eyeing him with concern. She also wore an obvious appreciation for the disoriented, but incredibly handsome man in front of her. As Jackson looked up, piercing her with his brilliant blue eyes, she moistened her lips, her own eyes heavy with invitation.

"Oh . . . uh, yeah . . . I am fine. Yes, very well, thanks . . ." he stammered. Okay, where *did* he leave his head, he wondered. He was always so calm and controlled. Now he was babbling like a complete fool.

This would not do. He had to regain a little of his manhood before he had to swing by Wal-Mart and buy himself a tutu and a Glamour mag. He took a deep breath and tried again.

"Thank you for your concern." He smiled at the girl. "I just needed a moment to collect myself, and this seemed as good a place as any. Just sulking in the stairwell!"

The girl flushed, and returned his smile, her eyes bright.

"Anything I can help with?" she asked hopefully, subtly thrusting her breasts forward and assuming what Jackson understood was supposed to be a provocative pose against the wall.

He tried to hide the laugh that wanted to ripple its way out of his throat at her thoughts.

A genuine laugh.

He never quite got used to the effect he had on people; women especially, although he'd never had but one woman on his mind, who he wished to find him irresistible.

"You're very kind, but I am okay, really. I'll be on my way." With a quick wave of his hand, he turned to push his way through the door. He heard her call out as he left, trying to stop him, and it wasn't just so they could have pleasant conversation, he thought wryly. He didn't like to seem rude, but he knew he wasn't interested in wasting time with this female.

He had no thoughts for any woman other than Indie, and never had. Even when he hadn't known exactly who she was, he knew she was out there, his soul mate, and he had no time for anything less.

Although he was always unfailingly polite, and the perfect gentleman, he had left scores of bemused and frustrated women in his wake, for as long as he could remember.

He tried his best never to lead anyone on, but women always appeared to be up for the challenge of the seemingly "unobtainable". They became ensnared in his eyes, and bound by his voice. It was comical at times, actually.

Batting away these unwanted images, he jogged lightly toward the parking lot, hoping the girl did not try to follow. People were always drawn to him, and he normally didn't mind playing the game . . . acting the part of the good-natured loner. Today, it was just too much of a project. His mind was elsewhere, daydreaming about the beautiful face that he could truly *see*, not just his mind's image, but her actual face, seen for the first time at close range.

His fists clenched as a shameful burst of a powerful emotion shook through him.

She is *my Equal* . . . my rightful mate. She must be made to see! She must . . . . Jackson unclenched his fists in remorse.

"She must . . ." he whispered out loud," . . . be free to choose her path."

The Society trained part of Jackson . . . the contained and controlled part, knew that her choice was his law. If, after he made contact with her, she chose to stay in her current life, he would have to honor her wishes.

But in his blood ran a genetic predisposition toward winning. A predisposition further fueled by six years of training with the SAS while in the UK. He was simply taking what belonged to him.

And although he didn't think of her as a material possession, he did think of her as his, and therefore it was all quite righteous.

The idea that she was returning to her house tonight, behind closed doors with her false mate brought about a cold feeling of sickness and, much to his chagrin, fury.

"If he touches her . . ." Jackson's fists were back, his body tense. But then, he *had* touched her, hadn't he? They had children, so the answer was pretty self-evident.

If there had been no children, he could have enjoyed a nice hot cup of self-delusion, and pretended to believe that they had played house for ten years, but only as platonic friends.

But no.

They had laid together, made love together . . . made children together. Jackson felt the blood drain from his face, leaving him deflated and cold.

Well, get over it, old boy, he told himself despondently. She didn't even know you existed. Why should *she* have remained celibate?

He considered the idea that this was his own fault. His warrior mode kicked up a little, as he chastised himself.

If you had been more competent and found her earlier, you wouldn't have this problem, would you? His brain pointed out helpfully.

With a fierce exhale, Jackson delivered a burst of speed, sprinting just to burn off a little frustration.

Regardless, he had found her now, and he was going to proceed from here. Nothing he could do to change the past. She was still perfection in his eyes, and one hundred percent pure as well. He loved her, and by extension, her children who were part of her.

Flesh of her flesh.

All of them were now entered into the Jackson Allen protection program. Unfortunately, nobody knew about the program's benefits yet.

Jackson finally reached his car and dove into it, slamming the door behind him quickly. He sat low in the seat, prepared to wait.

I hope she doesn't try to have me thrown in jail for stalking, or worse, sic that husband of hers on me, he thought, with a nervous laugh. He would *hate* to have to hurt him, wouldn't he?

He knew he was going to follow her . . . show up wherever she happened to be, for as long as it took to convince her to talk to him. She simply had to let him.

He stretched his legs out in front of the seat, and shook his head at the irony. Here he practically had to beat away every other female, run from them even, to avoid their unwanted advances. But the one *he* wanted . . . the one he *needed*, like air to breathe, was terrified of him!

Oh, she found him attractive; that much he could read from her. She felt the inevitable draw toward him, but was so overwhelmed by the revelation of the morning, that all she could conceivably react with was suspicion and fear. What, was this someone's idea of a joke? His eyes lifted to the ceiling of his car, as if awaiting some kind of response to that thought.

"Ah, well," he sighed, "we shall see what the day brings . . . or eternity, whichever. I am prepared to wait for her, either way!"

He rested his head back on the seat, and visualized again the sky blue of her eyes . . . the silky rich sheen of her flowing hair and her perfectly kissable lips.

Desire leaped on top of Jackson like a hungry bear, its claws digging deeply into his flesh. This forced him to shift uncomfortably in his seat, as certain physical reactions began to manifest themselves; the direct result of his mental caresses upon her body.

Well, this was so not appropriate!

With admirable force of will, Jackson cast off his aching need to touch Indie, and get as close to her as humanly possible.

Maybe even closer still.

The IPod he'd connected to the auxiliary outlet in his car suffered the usual abuse as he restlessly flipped through song after song, in a hopeless attempt to distract himself.

Irritated with his self-acknowledged musical ADHD, Jackson ripped the cord free of the outlet, wondering how it was possible to load your IPod with the songs you love most, but then feel the need to skip over five to ten songs at a time once they were captured for your anytime pleasure.

The FM station blasted on, and a song that under most circumstances he would have changed immediately, assaulted him at high volume.

A much too slow and sappy song by Finger Eleven.

Jackson was familiar with the band from their much more energetic material, but as he reached forward to press the tiny scan button, rhythm of the acoustic guitar ensnared him, and the verse caught his attention . . .

. . . *it's nothing I planned, and not that I can . . . but you should be mine, across that line . . .*

He froze with his finger still poised in the air.

. . . *If I traded it all, if I gave it all away for one thing . . . just for one thing . . .*

For perhaps the first time in his life, a song hit Jackson in an emotional way, instead of just to escape his thoughts, or to amp him up for action. He listened to the words, and he could feel them. It was like the song understood his torment and it made him feel better. He dropped his hand, and placed it awkwardly on the gear shift, deep in thought.

The music encouraged Jackson to return his head, both physically and mentally to the headrest; only raising it again hours later, when he spied Indie running out the back door of the facility, and jumping into her car in a fashion that was eerily similar to his own earlier dive for cover.

He glanced quickly into the rearview mirror and made a face at his reflection. His hair was impossible. The wild and windblown appearance probably wasn't helping him make his case to Indie that he wasn't some raging lunatic. He raked his hands hastily through the tangled mess, and sighed. It wasn't going to get any better. Jackson started his car.

CHAPTER 5

———

Indie sat in her car for a moment and contemplated the events of the day. It hurt, knowing that there was absolutely no one in the entire world with whom she could confide about what had happened today. Not if she wanted to remain out of the psych ward. Not even in a state as ready to accept the strange and improbable as Vermont, would she find someone okay with this topic.

She sighed, and started her car.

Miss Maggie had told her that she couldn't just act like today never happened. Well, she would see about that.

Get back to normal, she told herself, shakily. Stay in your routine, and everything will be okay.

Sure it will, her uncooperative inner voice spoke sarcastically.

Indie drove briskly to the grocery store, determined to stay focused and grounded. She parked and jumped out of the car, walking fast, keeping her head down, afraid to make eye contact with anyone, lest they see the frantic gleam in her eyes.

Produce and cans, she tossed them carelessly into her cart with no real plan or thought, just going through the motions of your average shopper. She finally decided that she had enough supplies to make it look as if she were there for an actual reason, and got in line.

Almost immediately, she felt a warming sensation on the back of her neck.

Not unpleasant. Rather soothing, actually.

She exhaled deeply . . . a heaving shuddering breath, like after a good hard cry. In a flash, her body suddenly tensed, and Indie turned slowly. She knew exactly what, or rather who, she was going to see.

Sure enough . . . it was the man. He was standing much too closely behind her, his eyes brilliantly blue and focused sharply upon her.

———

This was too much. Indie started to walk away from her shopping cart and leave the store.

"Wait!" He had spoken softly, but it startled her like a shout, and brought her to an instant halt.

"Please . . . just tell me why you are stalking me. What do you want?" Indie stammered helplessly.

"Just a moment of your time, please . . . nothing sinister, I assure you." The sound made her sway.

That soothing voice. The rhythm of his accent was like a soft song to her hypersensitive ears.

Indie shook the thought away and whispered, "Why though? Why would you want a moment of *my* time?"

"Don't you want to talk about it, Indie?" She could see the concern in his eyes. Concern and a hungry yearning that made Indie feel restless and fidgety.

The way he spoke her name was like a physical touch . . . a caress. His soft voice made her shiver, just a little. Indie could not help but notice that his hair looked as if he had attempted to sort it out a bit, and failed.

It was still endearingly mussed.

God, stop it! She commanded herself, wanting to scream. She clutched at her head with both hands as she backed away.

"There is nothing to talk about!" Indie spoke decisively, dropping her arms so that she could fold them defensively across her chest.

"Oh, okay . . . whatever you say," he said with a slight shrug. "But I think you may change your mind."

"Do you, now?" She tried to sound sarcastic, but it was pathetic, even to her own ears.

"Yes, I really do!" *My beautiful, defiant one*, he added silently. For the second time, she detected the sparkle of humor in his teal-blue eyes. He then turned serious.

"You'll have to agree that today was a lot to take in, and I'm sure it won't make it to your dinner table tonight as a topic of casual conversation, will it?" He held her gaze, now projecting an elusive emotion in those eyes, and then exhaled sharply.

"Look, just know that I am here for you, when you *are* ready to talk about it."

"*You* are here for me, huh? You, who I have no idea who you are . . . waiting for me to turn to you?" Indie placed her items on the counter to pay for them, and turned back toward him. "Well, I wouldn't hold my breath if I were . . ."

He was gone.

A pair of teenage girls in the next line snickered at her and she felt her face ignite. She paid the bill, collected whatever it was she had purchased, and fled.

Her thoughts crawled frantically through her brain, their tiny sharp claws prickling as she guided her little green Volvo through town. How could a day that started out so ordinary, so like every other day, take such a turn for the surreal? Indie dreaded walking in the door to her house. She tried to picture the scenario:

"Hi honey, how was your day?" Will would ask . . . and she could reply with something like, "Well, you won't believe this, but I was told by one of my patients today, that I am some sort of alien! Ha. Oh, you're not surprised, are you? You've always suspected as much, right?"

Indie silenced her internal monologue. The reality was this; she did not need to worry about hiding it from her husband at all. He was not going to ask how her day went.

He never did. Indie's thoughts continued to race.

He comes home, eats his supper and hops on to the internet until his bedtime, she reasoned. This would be no problem. Then she sobered.

The twins. They would not let her off so easily. It felt like her skull was made up of crystal clear glass whenever they looked at her. They read her brain like a manuscript.

Well, she breathed deeply, *I have to face them all . . . I have no choice. I have to go home, don't I?*

She pulled in to the driveway and cut the engine. Everyone was inside. She could see the lights and hear the patter of nine-year-old feet, and giant stomping size 11 boots. Indie saw Will peek out through the window at her. She drew in another deep breath and let it out slowly.

And here we go!

She readied herself for the worst, which would be the interrogation from the children. With an inaudible groan, she pulled herself out of the car and popped the trunk. She gathered the bags of groceries, picking up all five with her free hand.

Indie knew better than to expect a spontaneous offer of help from her husband. He would never think, all by himself, to help her carry anything. Oh, he would if she went upstairs and asked him to please bring up the groceries . . . but something about the fact that she would have to ask always exasperated her, so she just carried them in herself.

She was not into being a martyr; she did this knowing that he wouldn't notice that she had, nor would he have any redeeming thoughts, like "Oh, I'm so sorry. I should have gotten that for you!" No, it would not enter his mind.

Indie trekked up the stairs, the front door opening before she had to fumble her fully loaded arms to try to open it herself.

"Mommy!" It was Jake. "Can I carry something for you?"

"Yes, thank you, pup!" At least her boy was a gentleman. Cassidy appeared, and little helper that she was, began putting away groceries. Indie noticed at once the twins' sneaky, corner of the eye glances, and sighed. And so it begins.

"Mommy, what happened to you today?" It was Cassidy, always the first to start. She spoke with a deliberate casualness.

"Nothing out of the ordinary, why?" Indie lied calmly and ineffectively.

"Oh?" Cassidy stood with a loaf of bread in her little hands, seemingly lost in thought.

"What is it?" Indie asked wearily, although she did not want to encourage this line of discussion. Her daughter squinted up at her, in a way that made Indie's head feel as if it were being pried open by some invisible tool.

"Cassidy, come help me with my homework!" Jake spoke suddenly, looking meaningfully at his sister. She broke off her mental attack, and looked at Indie reproachfully. Then she sighed.

"Fine, I'm coming," and they left the kitchen together. Indie watched them leave, somewhat relieved.

She quickly made her way to her bedroom and shed her now crinkled scrubs, not noticing how the light blue color matched her eyes just so. Kicking them off, Indie didn't bother removing her Reeboks. She jerked on her black running pants, and pulled one of Will's undershirts roughly over her head.

Without a word to anyone, Indie sprinted out the door, pausing to grab her IPod on the way, looping the earphones around her head with one hand.

Ten circles around the block later, ears nearly on fire from the thought destroying volume of her music, Indie bounded back in the front door. Her tactic had worked; the loud and pounding music had made it nearly impossible to focus on anything else. But now, here she was, right back where she started.

Her body almost collapsed under the realization. There was no way she was going to be able to summon the will to cook supper, although this made her feel guilty. Indie sagged visibly, her energy sapped.

Dominos Pizza was simply howling her name tonight, she decided, and dialed the number.

One extra large pepperoni pizza, light on the sauce and a side of wings; Will's favorite. She chose the pay by phone option, including a tip, so that whoever answered the door need only take the food and place it on the table.

The kids were not big pizza fans, oddly enough, but they would deal with it. They almost never complained about anything. Indie remembered a bag of pre-washed salad greens in the fridge, and dumped it unceremoniously into a large bowl. She hesitated, then grabbed a lemon from a basket on the counter and sliced it into wedges, and brought down the olive oil. This was her children's only acceptable "dressing", but Indie approved. It was healthy.

Feeling slightly less guilty about supper now, she took a moment to poke her head in to Will's office.

"I ordered pizza for you guys, and it should be here in a few. It's already paid for, tip as well."

"Didn't you just go to the store?" Will asked absently.

"Yes, but I've . . . had a long day. I just don't have the energy to cook." He shrugged, never lifting his eyes from the computer screen.

"Well, then," she cleared her throat. "I think I'm just going to take a shower and climb in to bed. I don't think my stomach can take any food tonight." He glanced up and gave her a quick smile, eyes distracted.

"Okay, I'll take care of the kids for you." Ugh, Indie made a face. He actually said it.

Will is going to take care of the kids *"for me."* How nice of him. And, as if, anyway!

Indie knew that when the pizza came, Cassidy would answer the door. Jake would get the plates, and tell Daddy the pizza was here. The kids would be done before Will was able to tear himself away from the computer. They will have already put their plates in the dishwasher, started their own bath, and would be brushing their teeth before he came out. His involvement would most likely be the unnecessary words, "time for bed," as they were already climbing in.

Yes, Honey, thanks so much.

Indie was both annoyed and relieved. She knew she was not going to have any trouble hiding what had happened to her today, not from him, but at the same time, she wanted somebody to care. Not nine year olds, who she didn't want worrying about Mommy's mental health, but someone . . . grown up.

Indie suddenly felt a craving for strong arms around her, telling her that everything was going to be okay, offering her the feeling of the utmost comfort and protection . . . her own hero in her very own romantic love story.

She wanted a partner who was involved in her life . . . her thoughts . . . someone who knew how she felt about things. Someone who understood how hard every day was for her, she thought, stifling a small sob.

Jesus, just someone who thought she was worth talking to, even.

She felt the tears welling up in her eyes, and bit her lip to still the trembling. Indie allowed herself a very rare moment of intense self-pity as she leaned against the wall in the hallway. Was it so much to ask that her partner be someone who was on her emotional level. Someone who was her . . . equal.

No. Her *Equal.*

Yes, it definitely felt like a proper noun. Indie clutched at her head, aghast at what had just shot through it.

Am I crazy, she asked herself, swallowing the lump in her throat. *What could I possibly be thinking,* she wondered, freaking herself out at the thought.

Turning to stumble down the hallway, Indie stopped short as she passed the window on the way to the bath. Her hand shaking, she pulled the curtain back and stared out into the utterly opaque darkness, seeing nothing but her own reflection . . . but yet . . . Her senses were screaming.

He was out there. Somehow, she knew it.

And he was watching her.

With a gulp of panic, she drew back from the window, realizing that she was backlit, and very visible to any handsome and mysterious voyeurs who might be lurking in the shadows. Crazily, she wanted to peek out again.

Confused at her unexplainable compulsion, Indie hesitated, then re-focused on the project at hand. Oh, yes. She was late for a date with the showerhead, wasn't she.

Disentangling the scrunchi from her hair, and shaking out the now knotted waves, Indie hastened to lose herself in a scalding hot shower. Closing up her mind into a tight little box, she dried off methodically and put herself to bed. She closed her eyes, and the face of Jackson appeared, as if conjured purposely by her traitorous brain.

She allowed herself to study his features behind her eyelids. Indie had perfect recall. His face was, she had to admit . . . perfect. His eyes were the most unusual shade of dark, almost teal blue, under a frame of black lashes and brows. The curve of his jaw line was gentle, not too angular.
This contributed to his youthful appearance, in spite of the shadow of a beard that was making itself visible by day's end, although he didn't seem overly endowed with an abundance body hair, thank God.

Thank God?

Whatever. As if it mattered to her.

She mentally kicked herself as the assessment continued, unable to stop her virtual voyeurism.

His somewhat full lips looked as if they could do some real damage . . . the kind any woman could appreciate, and they remained frozen in that patient smile that he had last given her, before he had dematerialized like a ghost.

She wondered again, how old he really was, feeling a little uneasy; he might be young enough to be her child! Technically, Indie could easily be the mother of a twenty-two year old, at least. Indie shuddered. This was such a terrible thought, that she snapped her eyes open with a nearly audible pop.

What kind of perv would that make her?

She wondered though. Something inside of him seemed older . . . wiser. He didn't have the lanky build of a teenager, either. He was tall, and muscular, but not in a bulgy He-Man kind of way. She'd never found that look attractive. There was definitely nothing gangly about him.

No, his was more of a focused and graceful power; lean and potentially dangerous, a tiger, ready to pounce. She could see the pent up energy in him, like a tightly compressed spring that could release at any moment, but well controlled. Indie liked this in a man.

It was probably the reason Will had first appealed to her . . . that promise of lethal ability, kept under lock and key.

Her speculation continued as she pictured him again. His eyes were not the eyes of a young man. They had the look of someone who had suffered for a long time, she recalled. An almost unendurable sadness yet, at the same time, he was calming to her.

When he had reached out to her in Miss Maggie's room, she had shrank away, terrified, but not of him exactly. She was terrified because a very central part of her core was convinced that what she had just heard was truth, and it was too much.

It was true sensory overload, and his close proximity, she feared, would toss her over the threshold of madness. In addition, she'd noted that her rejection had nearly destroyed him. She had felt it, without a doubt, yet that made no sense.

He didn't even know her.

She thought of his voice. Indie shivered as she remembered the way her name had flowed sensuously from his lips. His voice sounded as if it was created just for her. The perfect pitch to calm the havoc in her brain, the soft breath of his accent was just an added bonus.

Her thoughts shifted to absorb the possibility of a partner who was *there for her* . . . in every possible way. Someone who wanted to take care of *her*.

A lover who was also actually interested in her thoughts and struggles.

She gasped and pulled the covers over her head. This was so wrong.

Completely unacceptable.

What, was she going to *fantasize* about the person who was part of the psychosis-inducing scene that had taken place, Christ, was it just this morning? She didn't want to do it . . . but then . . . she *did* want to.

Maggie had said he was her *Equal*.

Indie shamefully acknowledged to herself that she liked the sound of this. She shivered again.

However, what exactly did it mean, her *Equal*? It sounded good, in theory, except that she was a married woman, and he could not conceivably be her anything, could he? She had no answer.

After glancing longingly at her latest fantasy romance novel and deciding that reading it would only further her torment, Indie flipped on the television and lost her thoughts to the Discovery Channel. They were running a special on ancient civilizations.

Perfect.

CHAPTER 6

If just yesterday, someone had asked Jackson Allen to describe himself, he was quite sure that the words sick-o, obsessive, disgusting, and Peeping-Tom would not have immediately leaped to mind.

How things change, he thought dryly.

Repulsed by his actions, he leaned his back against a large birch tree situated across from the split-level home that concealed the cause of this all-new tendency to lurk in the shadows like a monster from a horror story.

He cursed silently. What in the hell *was* he doing?

I mean, really, he thought to himself, like this would be considered Society approved activity, right?

Groaning softly, overcome with the need to see her face once more, Jackson turned, pressing his chest and belly to the smooth tree trunk, and faced the house; the windows glowing with a cozy light. He stared at the window; feeling for the connection that he knew was inside.

There was no doubt about it . . . he could sense her presence now that he had been so close to her, even though they had not made physical contact.

William Taylor. Jackson had gleaned the name from Indie's mind when they'd faced off in Ms. Maggie's room, though he'd picked up on nothing else. She'd thought of her husband because of her guilty conscience. She felt attraction to Jackson, and it made her feel all wrong.

It's not wrong, he thought violently. In fact, it was *so* much more than right.

And this William character . . . Will, she called him, didn't appreciate her or give her the love that she needed. Jackson could see it in the pain reflected in her eyes. She was lost, and needed to be found.

And so she had. And Jackson stood more than ready and able to give her what she needed. He was literally drowning in his feelings for her.

Maybe she was feeling him right now too, he mused. Surely this enhanced sensory kick wasn't all one-sided, was it?

He stopped breathing as a shadow passed in front of the window that had drawn his stare. The shadow went by, paused, and then returned to stand directly in front of the glass.

Jackson's strong hands were now strangling the poor birch, his fingers digging deeply. He watched as the curtains were slowly moved aside, and the lonely looking figure of Indie stepped forward, her face cupped right against the glass.

Was she looking for him, he wondered breathlessly, or did she simply sense an unwelcome presence in the night? Earlier in the evening, he had perched in the tree that held him up now, and watched as Indie attempted to break the three minute mile record; racing around the block for what seemed like hours. She was clearly running *from* something.

Oh, let's see, maybe it could be the book of weirdness laid open and shoved at her feet by some crazy old lady and a creepy strange guy?

Nah, couldn't be *that*.

And he had felt like an intrusive predator, hanging out in the trees and spying on her desperate attempts to get away from the events of the day. Maybe he would sprout fur and fangs next.

Brilliant. Then he could really creep her out.

It almost looked as if Indie's eyes were reaching across the distance and making direct contact with him. He lifted his hand on impulse, and then quickly dropped it again, feeling foolish. There was no way she could see him, concealed in the darkness as he was.

But she knew.

Oh yeah, she knew he was there. Jackson closed his eyes and wished fiercely that he'd touched her today. He so needed to read her thoughts clearly. Was she looking out with longing . . . or fear?

Maybe a little of both. Or was it just curiosity?

Was she just interested in hearing his little story, and then planning to send him on his way with a *"thanks for stopping by, now get lost before my husband kills you,"* kind of vibe?

The figure in the window stepped back and let the curtains fall shut, and he watched her shadow move away. The light in the smallest window at the center of the house flipped on, and Jackson got the distinct impression of water running.

"Ok," he sighed to himself. "I've broken enough laws for tonight." With one more quick glance up to the lighted window, Jackson shoved himself away from the tree and took a slow stroll up to the small park where he had left his car.

His head was throbbing with the pounding ache of unmet needs, along with a chaser of uncertainty and worry. What if she didn't want him? Just what would he do with himself if he made contact with her, and she wanted nothing to do with him? Could he even survive such horror?

Technically, he should just be able to carry on with his life, right? He'd lived without her for forty years. He could live another forty without her. Or eighty.

Or two hundred.

He cringed inside and out at the idea, and felt it punch through his guts in a bowel twisting earthquake. It seemed that continuing on the journey through this life without her was almost impossible to think about, even in the abstract. The "what if's" were nearly destroying him, impaling his head with the pain of this possibility.

No, Jackson's brain spoke for him. *I cannot allow her to slip from my grasp. Not now.*

Unlocking the door to the Mercedes, he then pulled himself heavily inside. He wasn't sure how to approach the situation without coming off like a really scary bastard.

This was something to be done with caution.

He fired up the engine, and pulled out into the deserted street and moved at a crawl, lost in thought. But in the blink of an eye, or so it seemed, Jackson found himself surrounded by a dark blanket of tree boughs and in the clearing that was the entrance to his home.

Parking the car on the carpet of pine needles and dirt, he dragged himself from the car with an exhaustion that was becoming annoyingly familiar. A bone-deep weariness that comes only from completing several triathlons in one day . . . or needing something you don't have so desperately that it literally slaps the energy from your body, rendering one all but useless.

It was all Jackson could do to make it down the steps and into his house, where he sat on the floor and rested his back against the door. His joints hurt, and the dull aching pressure behind his eyes was disconcerting.

Using the moment to recover the last of his flagging strength, Jackson bounced upright and moved his miserable party of one to the master bedroom. Pulling open the bottom drawer of the apothecary chest that he used as a nightstand, he withdrew a small box made of highly polished wood that was exquisitely hand carved, and he flung himself down on the bed.

He lifted the perfectly fitted lid from the tiny work of art, and removed a pair of wide, highly polished platinum bands, each inscribed with the words, "*Ego dilecto meo et dilectus meus.*"

Jackson could read Latin like nobody's business, having really gotten into the teachings of the old languages. This had been an unbelievable help through law school, and allowed him to move through his classes with relative ease.

Reading the inscriptions aloud, though he'd memorized it years ago, Jackson's voice was rough with weariness.

The words were so fitting.

Plus, he knew the story, from The Song of Solomon, chapter six, to be precise. The translation; "*I am my beloved's and my beloved is mine.*"

As he stared down at the heavy shimmering weights in his hand, he could not help but add the next line; "*He feeds among the lilies.*"

Ah yes. He was feeding all right. Absolutely gorging himself on a feast of want, need and dread.

All well done, naturally.

Jackson had received the little box on his sixteenth birthday . . . the age when Society Members are committed to their *Equals,* the bands normally exchanged at the Ceremony of Recognition and worn as a symbol of their everlasting bond.

At first, he had thought it a particularly nasty little joke; after all, his *Equal* was MIA, wasn't she? His nanny, who left him on this same day, to re-join with her *Equal,* had pulled him into her arms and asked him to look at it from another perspective.

"*Someone,*" she'd said so kindly that it made him want to weep, "*has faith that you will connect with your mate, and they wish you to be prepared. I believe the Elders had these sent to you so that you do not lose hope.*" She had pushed him back gently and looked in his eyes as she spoke the next words; "*You have always been extraordinary, Jackson . . . there is something I see in you . . . your strength and faithful tenacity, that makes me believe that you have a destiny to fulfill, and that your Equal must be part of it. You are extraordinary, and so must she follow in that mold. You will see.*"

Ms. Rihanna had smoothed his hair away from his expression of brave resignation.

"*You live, so you know that she lives. As long as there is breath in you, you may find her. You will feel the draw, and find your way to her. Pray that you do before she succumbs to the madness that takes our orphaned members.*"

With love and tears, she'd kissed his forehead, and left him at the boarding school. He'd been prepared for this day, and although losing Ms. Rihanna was like losing his mother all over again, he knew that he was a man now, and as such, had to conduct himself with maturity and reason.

Which meant that he went to his room, locked the door and bawled like an infant.

After that one-time shameful indulgence, however, Jackson threw himself into his schooling and physical training with a focus that was frightening in its ferocity. After all, he had no female distractions, and he definitely needed an outlet for all of the frustrations that he didn't even understand . . . his body demanding a physical release that was never satisfied.

Hitting things for righteous causes helped a lot.

Jackson enjoyed the combat training way more than he thought to be appropriate, but what could he do? After all, he reasoned, a person can't help how they feel, right? And sometimes, it just felt *so* right to smite the enemy, even if in training it was all play-acting.

The energy release was real enough.

More difficult was the Society training that demanded that he have complete control over his body and his emotions at all times, as it was imperative that all Society Members reflect only positive or neutral energy, in order not to contribute to the negativity that could potentially destroy the world. It had been insanely challenging, but he'd finally mastered it.

For the most part.

And he'd grown into one of the most prolific of his kind, performing his duty with fearless strength. So fearless, that his name had become well known even before accomplishing a feat of bravery, skill and daring that had resulted in a setback of phenomenal proportions for the Common enemy of Society and humankind. He'd accomplished this at age nineteen, and afterwards Jackson was almost legend among the Society, respected and revered. But he also knew the pity they felt for him because he was alone.

Pity didn't anger him, for it was truly only compassion openly expressed. But it made him uneasy and unhappy, for it was a constant reminder of what was missing in his life.

Not that he could possibly forget.

With a long hard sigh, Jackson stroked the smooth polished surface of the rings with his forefinger, and then pressed his lips to the smaller one, wishing that he were a drinking man. He could use a little chemical restraint right now . . . something to stop him from terrifying Indie with the actions that he knew he would continue tomorrow.

Stalker. There was no other word he could think of that fit the activities on his to do list for the following day. In spite of the fact that it made him feel, well . . . *dirty* and foul, it didn't matter.

He was going to come after Indie until he put his hands on her, and she was going to let him do it, too.

Of her own free will. It had to be that way, he knew. And he wasn't going to stop until then, and only if afterwards, she sent him away. If that was her choice, he would honor it . . . at least he was pretty sure he would.

There were other complications related to his joining with her; things that would bring her pain, but he chose to ignore those issues for now. He wanted to focus only on his goals right at this moment. The other stuff . . . well . . . if she wanted nothing to do with him, then it would all be a moot point, wouldn't it?

Why stress over it now, right?

Frowning now at the rings in his hand, he felt the tug of guilt in the back of his mind. If things went well for him, then other parties would be hurt. Jackson didn't like this idea, as selfishness was not generally part of his protocol.

I don't care, he lied fiercely to himself as he covered his eyes with a tensely muscled forearm. *This is not my fault . . . it's just what I have to do!*

He brought down the curtain on these thoughts with a mental thud, and with a motion that was smooth and quick as a camera flash, the rings were shoved back into the box, and thrust into the drawer once more.

Using more strength than he'd known he possessed, Jackson got to his feet and slinked into the kitchen, knowing with the instinct of the warrior that he was, that his body had to be nourished, even though his belly was threatening him with violence if he tried to put anything down there.

With a dully hollow joy, he found a can of a high protein energy shake, and popped the top after giving it a viciously satisfying shake to mix it up properly. He swallowed the contents in six deep pulls, and tossed the can into the recycling box.

Sighing with relief that the deed was done, Jackson returned to the bedroom and shed his clothes. As he entered the bathroom to shower, he caught sight of his body in the large mirror above the sink, and stopped short.

Leaning toward the mirror, hands white-knuckling it on the counter, Jackson took careful inventory of what he saw; a toned, tight body, without an ounce of fat or excess in any form, his muscles very much in evidence under his skin, all coiled and ready to get down to business.

Physical business of the ass kicking variety, or maybe some other kind of purpose where his stamina and control would come in handy.

Jackson considered this for a moment. Could he bring pleasure to a woman? He hadn't the slightest idea what exactly it involved, but he knew there would be kissing . . . touching and other things, aside from what he knew to be nothing more than the invasive penetration of the female.

It had to be more than simply that.

As he pictured Indie and her face . . . her body, he watched in amazement as his own body reacted to the memory. He was beginning to think that maybe, just maybe, he was getting the idea, as his mind wandered to things that he knew instinctively that he would enjoy doing to do to her, at any rate.

Maybe she would like those same things too.

As he brought down his hand to feel the part of him that was now throbbing with unaccustomed sensations, Jackson's body did a jackknife backwards, hitting the wall behind him with violent force. The shiver of pleasure he felt at the touch shocked him. Oh, what would it be like if it were her hands on him?

Her body pressed to his?

He spun around abruptly and moved into the shower. He had no business thinking of her in those intimate ways; not now. Not yet.

It was much too early in the game for that, for it was her heart he was after first, wasn't it?

Wasn't it?

As he roughly yanked the lever, the tap exploded into his belly, all cold water and stinging pressure. Yes, he'd pegged it right before. *Dirty.*

His thoughts for Indie weren't all pure, he knew. But then, wasn't that part of love? Was he not constructed to respond to the one with whom he belonged in the physical sense? He'd never had these carnal knifings through his belly at the thought or sight of any other female, had he?

No, it was all for her.

As he mechanically lathered his body, Jackson closed his eyes, carefully avoiding the now swollen and sensitive area between his legs. Yes. It was *all* for her, and he would give her *his* all, if she would allow it. He rinsed quickly and found himself rebounding with a surge of energy that was begging to be released.

Shutting off the stream of Arctic water and reaching for a towel simultaneously, he headed out of the bathroom at a near sprint, snatching up a pair of drawstring workout pants as he jogged through the room.

Pausing only to throw on the pants, Jackson kept moving until he found himself in the fully equipped gym at the far end of the house, and flipped on his CD player. It was already loaded with Muse.

Jackson looked around for another CD. Given his current emotional climate, he was feeling more inclined to get "Down With the Sickness," but it was nowhere around.

Jackson didn't use music to soothe. He thrived on it as an outlet to vent. It allowed him to feel and enjoy his power, while he maintained his outward show of passive calm, and he needed it like food or air.

Moving around the pile of available music on the table did not reveal the CD he was looking for.

Fine.

He listened as the intro to "Assassin" rolled into his airspace and began to pump him up. Actually, this was the perfect complement to the muscle shredding workout he was about to brutally put his body through.

Just to warm up, he dropped and knocked out a quick set of fifty push-ups, and then sprang to his feet and snatched up two heavily weighted mini barbells. Curling the hand weights of around one hundred and twenty five pounds each, Jackson suddenly found that he couldn't wait for the sun to rise. His thoughts pounded in rhythm to both the music and the pull of the weights that were popping his biceps like they were inflatable.

No. He could . . . Not . . . Wait.

CHAPTER 7

The Irresistible Stalker

Indie somehow made it through the night, resolutely keeping her eyes clamped firmly shut. Will came to bed at some point . . . she never opened her eyes to look at the clock. She listened to him fumbling around the room, getting ready for bed. For some reason, Will never seemed to feel any particular need to try to be quiet as he went through his bedtime rituals.

Maybe he's on to me, Indie thought absently. *Maybe he knows I am never sleeping anyway*. He never tried to talk to her, though. She felt his weight as he sat down on the bed, trying to sort out the covers.

A sharp pang of guilt wound its self tightly around her throat as she remembered the thoughts that had played out in her mind.

Inappropriate thoughts for a married woman. As Will began snoring almost immediately, the pangs grew sharper. He was just so oblivious. *Oblivious to my moods, my needs, my struggles . . . just plain oblivious to me*, Indie thought with a stab of pain.

Usually, she pretended that this fact was just fine by her. It meant her charade was working. However, a deeper part of her felt constantly hurt by the idea that the only way her husband actually saw her was if she spoke first . . . or when she approached him.

She thought that she had become used to this pattern over the years, but she found that it still stung.

Does he just not care? She wondered, wounded. *If he really loved me, he would have noticed that I was not okay. He would be in tune to my needs, right? We'd be each other's yin and yang, each knowing instinctively what the other needed.*

Indie crinkled her nose, suddenly impatient with herself. She wasn't being fair. In her heart, she knew that he cared—that he loved her. He just was not . . . demonstrative. He never had been, really, and now she had the nerve to feel hurt? And she had married him for an escape, she knew, as a pathway to a normal life.

Though Indie did *love* him, it wasn't as if she was ever truly carrying a flaming passion torch for him either, she supposed, although God knows she'd tried to work it up for him.

Why she couldn't was a real mystery to her.

He was certainly handsome enough, with his sandy blond hair, cut just shy of military style, and his body was one that could make any man years his junior, suffer serious insecurity issues.

Will was rock solid and in peak form, yet moved with the smooth and cautious stalk of a man used to walking in dangerous places.

Indie had no problem appreciating the masculine appeal that radiated from the man, especially when he came home after work and shed his suit jacket, his shoulder holster strapped across his crisp, white button-down shirt. It gave her a little jolt to realize that he could be very dangerous in the right circumstances, yet he gave Indie not even the slightest feeling of fear toward him.

She knew from the depths of her gut that Will could never harm her.

His sienna brown eyes were warm and lit up when he smiled, allowing the crinkles around them to show, and his teeth were perfect . . . straight and white; the result of six months of his mother's salary back when Will was a teenager, and worth every penny.

She rarely saw the investment anymore, though. He was serious minded and dedicated to his work, and the brief flashes Will gave her now were usually tight-lipped and offered in what seemed an obligatory fashion.

He had seemed a decent man when they met and had acted as though he had loved her at one point, once he took notice of her. Hitting someone with a car will force a person to take notice, Indie supposed.

Ten and a half years ago, Will had backed directly into her while she was running, knocking her flat.

Luckily, she wasn't hurt, but when Will jumped out of his car, horrified and all apologies, it was as if he was seeing her for the first time, although he and Indie had traveled in the same circles. Indie had known who *he* was, at any rate.

Will was attending training at Ft. Benning, and Indie worked as a civilian at the on-base clinic part time. She had noticed him, because all the girls did. Indie listened to the other females in the clinic going all a-twitter whenever he made an appearance, swooning and fanning themselves and finally, she decided to see for herself what all the fuss was about.

Indie got her chance when Will came in for a follow up on a minor injury he had sustained during a combatives course he was taking. She learned from him that the combatives level four class was, as he put it, "a real ass-kicker", and then enjoyed his blushing apology for the self-proclaimed crude comment made in her presence.

Indie knew from eavesdropping that Will was quite gifted in the use of creative and colorful language, and Indie found it . . . *sweet* that he censured himself around her.

Actually, around women in general. Most men these days were not worried about such details.

As Will had stripped to the waist and Indie took his vitals, she could see with one hundred percent clarity what got the office nurses in a lather. He seemed to appreciate Indie as well, although he remained appropriate and polite, calling her ma'am, much to her dismay.

Then he was gone. She had halfway expected him to seek her out, as she remembered his endearingly shy looks at her when he thought she wasn't aware, but he never came around again.

He apparently never gave her another thought until he nearly killed her, and incredibly, showed no signs of recognition. However, he seemed determined to "win her forgiveness" afterward, though Indie had assured him that it was all very unnecessary.

Will had persisted, taking her out nearly every night and proposing to her after only a few short months, when a transfer out of state was imminent.

His being a handsome and decent man seemed a good enough reason to marry him at the time. And, after all, Indie had been nearly thirty years old. People were supposed to be married by then, and on their way to family life, and she was all but obsessed with doing the "right" thing . . . the "normal" thing. And so in the span of only a few months, Indie found herself with a husband.

Will's mother had been horrified . . . trying right up until the organ music began to signal Indie's cue to start walking, to convince Will not to "rush into marriage to a total stranger".

Marie Taylor was outwardly friendly toward Indie, but she could feel the woman's slight resentment of her clearly. Will had been adamant, and told his mother that Indie was "the one", and the wedding had gone off without a hitch.

Once they were married, however, it seemed that Will lost focus again. After the honeymoon, he seemed only vaguely aware of her presence . . . as if, whenever she spoke, it startled him . . . reminded him that she was still there. This hurt Indie terribly, even though she was used to it from others.

She thought Will would see her differently than did the rest of the world. This was not the case, however. Her presence was no more appreciated or noticed by him than it was by others. As far as Indie could tell, Will thought that the clean underwear fairy kept his drawers stocked, and kitchen elves did the cooking and cleaning.

Indie rolled over, burrowing deep into the comforter, careful to keep her eyes closed. She counted the minutes ticking by, listened to the sound of Will's snoring and wondered what was in store for tomorrow.

Somehow, she was positive that things were going to escalate, and come to some sort of explosive conclusion. And there seemed to be no way to head this off.

Did she even really want to, was the real question that had Indie tossing and twisting the sheets around her body as if in combat with an anaconda, or some other long and tangle-y creature. She absolutely refused to cave to the pleading of her brain for more visuals of this man, Jackson.

Nope, she told her inner self, *we will not be going there again!* Scrunching her eyes shut in an unnatural clench, Indie forced herself to lie motionless and rigid, making it through the rest of the night in painful silence.

When morning arrived, Indie bounded out of bed as soon as Will left. She called out of work, which was a first, but she strongly felt that she needed a mental health day, and felt that it was quite honestly the truth when she told them that she didn't feel well. She thought that they would be shocked, but the disembodied voice of the unit secretary was distinctly bored, as she wished Indie to "feel better soon."

"Oh God, yes . . . I hope so too," she breathed into the phone after the other person had dropped the phone back into its cradle. She sent the kids off to school on the bus today.

Cassidy looked at her mother questioningly, but said nothing.

"I love you Mama," Jake sang out, as he crossed the yard. So it was "mama" today, huh? Indie wondered idly if it meant anything. After the bus collected the twins, she walked around the house, aimlessly picking up clutter and washing some larger dishes. She looked down at Max, and he sneezed expectantly.

"I guess you want food?" He answered with a short, sharp bark. She filled his bowl, and stroked his soft black and white fur, combing out several clumps of the stuff with her fingers, and then stood looking out the window until the mail truck startled her out of her torpor.

"That's crazy," she mused. She had been standing, frozen in place for quite a long time, gripping the clouds of dog hair in her palm.

Ugh. Max's phenomenal shedding skills always caused Indie to stay tight with the lint roller. She tossed the fur, and scrubbed her hands clean.

Indie threw on some jeans and Will's Red Sox sweatshirt, and dashed out to the mailbox. She retrieved the mail, and sifted through the advertisements and required daily quota of junk as she walked slowly back toward the house. She stopped dead in her tracks as if blocked by a wall.

Indie felt the now familiar warmth spread across the small of her back. Swinging herself around, she saw him, leaning casually against her car, arms folded across his broad, muscular chest. Today, he was dressed in jeans, a dark blue button-down, though fully unbuttoned, with a white tee shirt underneath. Over this, he wore the same dark brown leather jacket, in spite of the heat.

The sunlight caught in his unruly hair, exposing the promised hints of red throughout the deep brown color. He had on a pair of ray-bans as well, which was a shame, Indie caught herself accidentally thinking. Those eyes of his should never be covered. The picture he presented was . . . arresting.

Gah! No! He is NOT getting to me just because he is pretty! Indie spoke sharply to her brain, which was busy clapping its little hands and squealing with happiness at the sight of him.

"What are you doing *here?*" Indie hissed, looking around desperately. "And why are you so persistent?" What would the neighbors think?

"What can I say? I'm a go-getter!" He pushed his sunglasses to the top of his head, and his blue eyes stunned her, but only for a second. "Yeah, you know, I sense that!" Indie parried back. "What do you want?"

"I thought I would come to see if you'd changed your mind," he offered with a smile that was heart stopping in its sincerity. "I mean, about that moment of your time," he added hastily, as if to head off a misunderstanding of some kind.

"Nope," Indie threw back in what she hoped was a disinterested tone. She began walking back toward the house while pretending to be fantastically interested in an ad for some pest control service. "But thanks for stopping in. Goodbye!" Indie spoke without looking at him, trying not to trip over her own feet as she fled.

Jackson stared after her, bemused for a moment, then looked around quickly and released a sigh.

"May I come in?" He fixed his suddenly weary, but intense eyes on her hopefully, while removing his sunglasses, and hanging them from the collar of his tee shirt.

Indie stopped in her tracks and looked back at the man in disbelief. "Bring you into my house? Are you out of your mind?" Indie whispered in the most ferocious voice she could make, which was somehow lamely unthreatening.

"First of all, I don't even know you, and second of all, what I DO know about you is weird and scary, so why on earth would I bring you into my house?" she demanded.

He pushed away from the car, and began moving towards her with appealing grace, hands in his pockets. Indie became immediately distracted by the way he moved. The man seemed amused by some private joke when she met his eyes.

At once it became clear . . . he *knew!* The idea filled her with horror, but somehow, she realized that he was clearly aware of what she was thinking; how the motion of his body moving in her direction mesmerized her.
She felt a full on face burn as she clapped her hands over her eyes.

"Get out of here!" she ordered, but it sounded more like begging. He stopped instantly, the amusement in his eyes dying just as quickly. "I'm sorry. I truly don't mean to upset you." he spoke very seriously.

"But you DO! You ARE, and I really don't know why, exactly!" Indie almost wailed.

"Don't you? Can you truly think of no reason why my presence disturbs you in . . . various ways?" he asked in his devastating voice, his eyes appraising Indie in a way that felt almost possessive.

He then stopped speaking, as if uncertain what to do next, no longer smiling. He was beginning to take on a look of despair. Turning his back to her, Jackson dragged his hand through his dark and wild hair. He looked for all the world like a soul in pain.

Indie had never been able to bear pain in others, and this stranger's pain seemed particularly difficult to witness, as if it affected her physically as well.

It was a natural part of who Indie was; to give comfort to those who suffered, and this threw her for a moment. She looked around, and sighed. Oh, well. Let the neighbors make of this what they will. Like anyone was watching anyway.

"Listen," she drew a deep breath, "you can come in for a minute, but . . ." she hesitated. He turned around cautiously, stress playing across his features. Then abruptly he smiled at her.

"Really?" he asked with all of the disbelief at his good fortune hanging out for the world to see.

"Yes," Indie sighed, "I—I guess I really would like to . . . talk to you. About yesterday, I mean," she admitted reluctantly. Indie did not know why the need for that clarification sailed out of her mouth, but oh well. She was resigned to some serious weirdness at this point.

"I must offer you heaps of admiration for being such a risk-taker," he said with disarming humor. "After all, what would life be without the occasional surrender to impulse?"

Indie frowned, and wondered if she had been played. Somehow, she didn't think so. It seemed like she could truly feel his emotions, and she also knew that her distress had been the cause of his pain. She did not know what to make of this idea, but felt a sudden need to find out, and to find out now.

"Listen, if I bring you in, and you cause me trouble, I will have no trouble kicking your butt, understand? And if you don't give me some answers, I just might end up killing you!"

Jackson looked surprised at her words, and then spoke with tightly suppressed laughter. "You might want to re-think the killing part, just in the interest of your own self-preservation!" He couldn't hold back the soft laugh that managed to break free at the confused look on Indie's face at his comment.

After taking a short moment to scowl at the intruder for his continuous use of odd statements, she led him up the stairs into the living room, wishing she had done more cleaning and less staring out the window this morning. Really though, did she honestly care what this stranger thought of her housekeeping skills? Well . . . she kind of did, didn't she?

He looked around politely.

"Um, have a seat," Indie waved nervously to the couch, snatching off the pile of newspaper that Will had left behind, along with his coffee cup on the end table. Indie wasn't sure, but she almost felt that the man suffered a flare of . . . anguish maybe, at the sight of the errant cup.

But that was ridiculous, wasn't it?

He sat, and looked at her with a scorching gaze that would bring any woman to her knees. This unfortunately happened to include Indie, so she sat down with a sigh. In the same instant, Max immediately came and curled up at the feet of this stranger, no sign of tension in his shaggy body.

How strange, thought Indie. Max was usually timid around new people. She caught herself staring at the stranger's build, admiring, against her will, the way his arms were taut, firm and well muscled. He smiled that enigmatic, uncertain smile again, and dropped his eyes, looking somewhat embarrassed. Indie flushed and sighed again, letting her own embarrassment wash over her.

Oh, whatever, she thought, a little irritably. Obviously, she couldn't hide her rotten little thoughts, so why try.

"Can I ask you something?" she ventured.

"Anything!" was his prompt response, and she was a little taken aback by the heat in his voice.

"Er . . . can I ask how old you are?"

He smiled fully now. "I am forty years old." Impossible, Indie thought, looking at his youthful face.

"Surprised?" he asked innocently.

"Well . . . yes." She admitted. "You look much . . . *much* younger. In fact, if you told me you were a day over twenty-five it would be hard to swallow."

"One could say the same about you, could they not?" he challenged with a frown.

"I guess so . . ." she couldn't deny *that*, wondering if he somehow already knew her age.

"You know so," he said seriously. "You hear it all the time, from everyone."

"How could *you* know that?" she asked, a little defiantly.

This caused a short burst of a laugh to escape the man, although Indie could see nothing funny about the question. The laughter was short-lived, as the humor faded.

He closed his eyes briefly and sighed. *Just lay it out there and reel her in, Jackson*, he urged himself . . . *spark her intrigue.*

"This was not supposed to be a battle. Don't you want to know who I am . . . who YOU really are, and why I am here?" Indie's insides quaked. He had a point, and was apparently getting right to it.

"Right . . . okay, yes," she agreed. "Tell me then, who you are, and what do you want?"

"Alright," he breathed out slowly. She waited, watching his eyes play out some sort of argument within himself, the emotions flipping across his features; seeming to run the gambit from determination, to complete and utter desolation.

He looked up and met her stare, then suffered an obviously torturous bout of full-fledged despair and uncertainty. It was impossible not to feel his torment. His hands clutched at the air and his voice was unsteady. He laughed nervously, mirthlessly.

Help me through this . . . please someone . . . I cannot blow it!

"I . . . don't know how to start, now that I have obtained an audience with you, which is exactly what I was seeking!" He shook his head. His face . . . the pain in it became simply unbearable to look at.

"What is it?" Indie asked, alarmed now. "What can you have to tell me that is so awful, that makes you so sad?"

He stood up suddenly, and she thought he might streak out of the house. What would she do if he tried, she wondered, because he looked as if he wanted to do just that?

Could she take him down, she wondered wryly.

"Ah. I'm so afraid this is all wrong," he whispered, jamming his hands deep into his pockets. He looked up, and seemed to be speaking to someone other than Indie.

"I don't know how to do this. To bring on the pain this will initially cause you. There's never been a case like yours, like *ours* before!" He pulled his hands through his hair once more.

"The *children!*" He shook his head again and fixed her with a breathtaking stare. "No, there is no way that this can be right," he decided, and began to walk toward the back door.

Indie leaped to her feet. "Wait! Where are you going?"

"I—I am going back to where I came from, and I am going to find a way to be without you, for a little while longer, at least!"

She stared, open mouthed, at his answer.

"Be without me?" Indie asked, weakly. "Explain yourself, please, before I go mad!" Yeah. If he tried to bail on her now, he was definitely getting tackled. He was still backing away from her, and the look on his face caused a strange urge to cry to manifest in her throat. He stood looking exactly like a man sentenced to hang for a crime he did not commit. The suffering was intolerable to look at. He was shaking his head, eyes now closed.

"No," his voice shook. "I can't do it now. I *won't!*" It sounded like an argument was taking place in a realm apart from where they stood now, and Indie was instantly filled with an irrational fear that if he walked out the door, that she would never see him again. Inexplicably, this idea filled her with terror.

She tried to tell herself that the terror was sparked by the idea of never understanding the words of Miss Maggie, and having the events of yesterday remain a mystery forever. However, deep down, she had to admit to herself that mostly she knew that she just plain did not want him to disappear from her life.

She did not know how this could be, exactly, as she didn't even know him, but there it was, a simple fact. Indie was not letting him get away.

Not yet, anyway, she'd already decided.

"Stop!" she shrieked, and he froze. "How *dare* you follow me around, show up at my work, my *home*, convince me to let you in here so you can explain things to me, and then try to take off, without any explanation? And after the things you've said!" Her voice was tight with anger and some other choked back emotion.

"I wasn't kidding when I told you I might just kick your butt if you don't tell me what's going on!"

He held her stare for a long moment before giving her a bleak smile. "Actually, you said you'd kill me."

"You told me I wouldn't want to do that, remember? 'In the interest of self-preservation,' right? You need to tell me what that means, before you go anywhere." Indie spoke with determination, mingled with a touch of desperation.

Jackson then moved very slowly back toward the couch, and he sank down, almost in some sort of trance.

"I've done it anyway, haven't I?" he said, softly. "No matter what I do now, you will be hurt. I can't bear it, I honestly can't."

The agony in his voice had to stop. She couldn't bear *his* hurt, either, somehow. But how can this be? She wondered, bewildered by her strong reaction.

"Jackson," Indie began, more gently now, and he visibly leaned toward the sound of her voice saying his name as if pulled by some unseen force. She liked the sound of it coming from her lips as well. Insane.

"Whatever it is that you came here to tell me, I need you to do it, because I will lose my mind if you don't, do you understand? Don't worry about causing me pain, because nothing in this world could cause me more pain than if you

---

walk out of here, and leave me forever in the dark. Whatever you have to say, I want you to spit it out, brutally, if it helps you, but I *must* know, and right now!"

There was a noticeable change in Jackson's demeanor now . . . his visible reaction to the unquestionable command that Indie was so capable of delivering when the situation warranted.

She sat down across from him and crossed her arms, waiting expectantly. Jackson frowned, and narrowed his beautiful eyes.

"I'm afraid . . . I am a slave to your wishes." He smiled painfully, as he dropped his head in a strangely submissive posture. He drew a deep breath once more, and began.

"My name is Jackson Riley Allen," he spoke slowly, raising only his eyes to her face, taking in her reaction. "My birthday is June 26th, 1968"—Indie drew in a sharp breath—"I am forty years old, and I am . . . your *Equal!*"

These words made no sense to Indie, even though she'd heard them from Miss Maggie before. And yet . . . and yet, she felt instinctively that they could also mean everything.

"But I don't understand what this means!" She bit out between her teeth. "That's *my* birthday. Same day, same year!"

And my maiden name, she added silently, though somehow she felt that he knew this.

"Yes." He spoke cautiously, eyes never leaving hers as he slid off the couch and moved forward, ending up on his knees directly in front of her. His knuckles were white as he kept his hands tightly pressed to his body, as if to avoid doing something he knew he shouldn't do.

"What are you, my long lost twin brother or something?" Indie demanded, darkly. *That* thought was sickening to her.

"Hardly," he laughed a little, still looking down. "I was born . . . *for* you."

Indie was silent. She could feel his heat, wrapping around and pulling her toward him. He didn't move.

"What can that possibly mean?" she finally pleaded with him, her voice thin and desperate.

"It means that I have come to claim what is mine. Because you . . . you were born for *me*," he whispered shakily.

After a long silence, something snapped in Indie's head. She stood up abruptly.

"This—This is insane!" Indie stuttered, backing away. "You have to get out of here!" He stared at her, motionless, his eyes haunted, and he dropped his head, a ruined look upon his perfect features.

"NOW" she shouted, and he winced, as if she had slapped him. Max whimpered in protest.

"I didn't want to do this," he reminded her in a wounded tone. "Don't be upset, please. I'll go." He leaped to his feet lightly, but leaned toward her once more, his eyes impaling hers with their brilliance. "But I know you feel the draw. I can *feel* it in you," he spoke heatedly.

"Do you not realize that it doesn't matter what I feel?" she looked back at him, wild eyed. "I am *married*, plain and simple. This isn't right!"

Jackson shook his head.

"There is nothing *simple* about this situation." He moved to stand directly in front of her.

"Don't you think I *knew* all of this?" he demanded. "Don't you see that this fact, as well as the fact that you have children, was the very reason I wanted to leave? I would *not* have you upset like this!"

The very blatant possessive look had reappeared in his eyes. He looked as if he was going to reach out to take her hand, but he hesitated, and drew back.

"If I touch you, you'll know," he said in a weary voice, "but I won't . . . not without your invitation." he looked at Indie, the implication very clear.

"Somehow I don't think my husband would be on board with my inviting strange men to put their hands on me," she sighed lamely.

Jackson flinched at the word *husband.*

"I am *not* just some 'strange man,' and William Taylor is *not* your *Equal!*" he growled through clenched teeth.

This sent a short laugh snorting out of Indie. "Like *that's* supposed to be news to me!" she stopped, and clamped her hand over her mouth in horror.

She had never stated such an insulting thing about Will out loud before, and it felt so vicious and wrong. She was ashamed and sickened by her outburst.

Jackson noted the horror reflected in Indie's face at her words, and recoiled. "Indie, I'm sorry. I . . . I'm just going to go," he spoke, his voice defeated. At that moment, they both jerked their heads toward the door, a fraction of a second before the knock sounded. Indie looked at Jackson, confused.

"Your senses are not complete until you've joined with whom you belong." he spoke, a little ruefully. "But you were getting so close!" he added in a hoarse whisper, his eyes now on her carpet.

She had no time to ponder the meaning of these words as the knock sounded again, insistent. The dog went ballistic, barking furiously. Indie looked out the window and groaned. "Oh perfect, it's my Mother-in-law," she whispered in disbelief.

Wherever the family moved, Marie always found a way to join them after a few short months. She always claimed that she liked moving often—that she got bored staying in one place too long, but they all knew that the reality was that she could never let go of her son. Most of the time, Indie thought it was a little humorous.

Today, not so much.

"Of course it's *Marie* . . . wouldn't you know? What am I going to *do*?" she panicked, looking at Jackson.

He was calm.

"You will let her in, of course" his voice was comforting. "There will be nothing here to arouse her suspicion." He turned to look at her one more time, smiled wistfully, and was out of sight.

Indie leaped up and stumbled to the door.

Jackson deftly leaped over the railing of the deck, and ducked out of sight. With a deep sigh, he lowered himself to the cool soft grass underneath.

And so, it has come to this, racing out of the back door and hiding like the clichéd two timing lover! Oh, would the setbacks never end? He ranted silently.

And the look on Indie's face. Was this sheer madness? What was he about to set in motion?

Yet he felt that this could very well be the decisive moment. As soon as the older woman left, he could sense that Indie's quest to know was possibly going to override her fear, and she was going to let him make contact.

Jackson's stomach muscles contracted with anticipation and excitement.

You belong with me, Indie Allen. He deliberately snubbed her married name, and sent his focused thoughts into the house, into her brain, although he knew that they didn't connect that way yet. But she might feel the emotions.

You are mine, as I am yours . . . . He leaned forward, clasping his hands together and resting them on his forehead, rocking back and forth, as he chanted the words in his head;

My angel. My blessing. My love.

Indie was burning with curiosity . . . and need. He could feel that, too. Jackson tried to slow his racing heart with deep, steady breaths, but he could hear her voice from inside, and her very essence was competing with his efforts.

How impossible it had seemed, to sit there before her and maintain his act of composure.

She was everything. There was simply nothing else that mattered. He did not feel forty years old at this moment. He felt like a hormonally driven sixteen year old.

Come on, Jackson, pull yourself together! He tried to put himself back into his usual state of cool, calm assurance.

Yeah. *Not* happening.

He flipped over onto his belly, plucking absently at the dandelion weeds while he listened closely to the conversation from inside the house. He was prepared to slip further out of sight if necessary, but he wasn't going far.

Because this was it.

Jackson knew it in his soul, and he could barely contain himself. He closed his eyes and waited anxiously for Indie to be alone again. Then he was going to make his move.

There was nothing in the world that could change his mind.

CHAPTER 8

As far as work days went, Will had seen worse. Much, much worse. However, as he clamped his right hand tightly to the top of his head, covered just as firmly by the left hand as well, he had to concede that things just weren't flowing for him this morning.

He started out the day feeling a little like crap. Nothing he could pinpoint exactly.

Just a vague gut discomfort. Like maybe he could hurl if he really wanted to. As always, whenever he woke up feeling sub-par, he tossed around the idea that he would call out sick.

And as always, he didn't.

As much as Will had grown to hate his job, it was his personal belief that unless you are face-down in an oily pool of death, you should drag your ill carcass to work because people were counting on you. Will was reliable to a fault, and expected no less from others. So here he was, and already the morning had made him wish he *was* the loser no-show type.

He'd come in to find six new files on his desk; people whom he was expected to root out every detail of their lives by five o'clock this afternoon, right down to their favorite color, and even the answer to the familiar "boxers or briefs" category of private info. This was about three more than on any average given day, so the stress began immediately. In between data searches, Will had also been unsuccessfully trying to locate his partner, who was somewhere in the building, but making himself very scarce.

The reason behind his partner, Baker's MIA status was totally understandable, but still . . . Will needed his ass back here to help work on some of this shit, even if it meant that Baker would have to man up and face the persistent female agent who worked upstairs in . . . well, hell, he wasn't really sure *what* department she worked in; mostly because he didn't care.

The woman, Agent Lockhart, was as repellent a creature as Will had ever met, and the conversations that she tried to engage he and Baker in were filled with sexual innuendo and other grossly inappropriate content. Besides, she was just nasty in general. And if that wasn't enough, the rumors about her would scare off anybody in their right mind.

In spite of the fact that the office was just as bad as any junior high school lunch table when it came to gossip, Will knew that with most gossip came a kernel of truth, and if just *some* of what was said about this lady was true, well . . . it was probably safer to keep your distance.

But it was really Baker upon whom she was focused. Her blatantly fake and transparent excuses to show up around them were tiresome and embarrassing, but God damn it, it was time for Baker to either give in and have sex with her, (he shuddered) or tell her that her interest was not reciprocated . . . or file a formal complaint with HR, because Baker was now into taking extended breaks and leaving Will here to face both the Beast *and* all the research.

Now, topping off his irritation was this; since he and Baker were lucky enough to have a coveted spot up against a real wall among the acres of cubicles with moveable boundaries, maintenance had installed two huge cabinets above Will's desk to provide extra storage.

This was fine and dandy, but the sons of bitches jutted out of the wall pretty far, and twice today, Will, having arisen from his desk in a hurry, had impaled the top of his skull on the corner of one of the things.

The first time it happened, Will sent the "F" word ricocheting around the office at high volume, causing titters of laughter to erupt throughout the space.

The second time made him see stars, and was the reason that he was now clamping down on the top of his skull, feeling a strong need to try to keep his brains from oozing out.

He was proud of himself though; the "*fuck*" that shot from between his teeth this time was barely audible, and he didn't have to suffer the humiliation of being caught making the same mistake twice.
That would so blow his rep.

Will was known for his calm, authoritative efficiency, and he'd worked hard to earn that kind of confidence from his peers. He wasn't exactly down with looking like the class clown, walking into sharp pointed objects and yelping like a kicked dog.

Gingerly, he lifted his hands from the top of his throbbing head, and checked for blood. Nope, didn't break skin, thank God, but the lump was impressively high. He probably needed ice, but to hell with that. He would just suck back the pain before he walked around with an ice pack strapped to his head.

Because of those same head-stabbing m.f.'ers, Will also had to waste time tracking down a florescent light to secure to the underside of the things, because they cast a nice dark shadow onto his workspace.

Rather than wait for the maintenance team that was still busy installing deathtraps throughout the office, Will sought out a light source independently. He was only able to find a corded plug-in style light, so after he'd installed it, his sense of neatness and order demanded that he spend another thirty minutes trying to MacGyver the cord so that it wasn't hanging down in his face.

Baker's head appeared over the cubicle wall, and his eyes darted nervously around the office.

"Is she around?"

"No, and she shouldn't be back. I told her you left early for a doctor's appointment; told her you had a nasty little infection you couldn't seem to shake, and that the burning and discharge was getting in the way of your ability to concentrate."

"Nice, Taylor. She'd better not spread that shit around as fact." Baker looked a little worried. "That could do real damage to my afterhours recreation."

Will leaned back in his chair and gathered up three of the folders, handing them to his partner.

"Yeah, well that would be a shame, but I'm sure you could still sweet talk the girls into coming home with you, even if you had an active case of skank. You're good like that."

Baker grinned back at Will. "Okay, 'A', I never bring them back to *my* place, and 'B', what can I say, dude; I'm simply irresistible!"

"Great. Now sit your irresistible ass down and start gathering some Intel on these subjects of interest. And I'll thank you not to quote lame, eighties Robert Palmer songs in my office."

Baker took the files with a sigh, and sat down at his desk.

"Well, you knew the song, pal, so don't . . ." he cut himself off as he looked through the thick stack of requirements. "What the hell? We're supposed to get all of this done *today?*"

"That's right, and you'd be pretty much done with at least one of them if you weren't busy playing 'hide-n-seek' with the blond."

Will locked a stare onto Baker.

"This shit's gone on long enough. You need to grow a pair and tell her to back off, or I will file the complaint with HR myself, on your behalf. Unless, of course, you're actually into her."

Baker looked horrified.

"Jesus man, are you kidding? She turns me on like a fly-covered tuna melt!" He turned toward his computer while Will tried to control his gag reflex at the analogy, deciding that he, himself, would probably go for the insect-ridden sandwich before making contact with *that* woman. His partner made himself busy by logging on to the network and glanced quickly over at Will.

"You're right, though. I'll handle it."

Baker entered the first name on the list and after a few seconds of frustrated clicks and curses, threw the file down on the desk.

"Okay, so this dude, like, doesn't exist, right? I can't find his name anywhere in the cyber world!"

The first step in even the most complicated and detailed invasion into a person's life, always started with the simple square one of a Google search. Baker excelled at square one. However, if the results weren't thrust in front of his face instantaneously, Baker's youthful impatience took over. Obviously, he had hit a wall.

Will, expelling a sigh, rolled his chair backwards until he was next to Baker's computer, and after thinking for a moment, pulled up a list of cell phone providers. There were only three that were popular in the state of Vermont because of coverage difficulties, and with only a few strokes of the keyboard, will pulled up the customer data base for all three, minimizing them into separate windows.

"There you go," Will slapped Baker's back nice and hard. "Try sifting through those customer lists first. I'll bet he has an account with one of them. If not, then his girlfriend . . ." Will rechecked the folder, "Sarah Rydell will be in there, I'm almost positive. When you find it, let me know. We'll break into their cell phone records and get all his contacts."

Forcing aside the look of awe that had accidentally found its way on his face, Baker turned back to the keyboard as Will skated his chair back across the linoleum floor to his desk.

"Show off," he muttered under his breath. It was bullshit. Will should just handle all this info-digging crap on his own, shouldn't he? Since he was such a God damned know it all.

Oh, and let's not even get started with the profiling master he was reported to be. Christ, he was so good, some people thought he must be some kind of closet psychic medium.

Will Taylor could look at almost any action performed by a human being, and tell you all kinds of character traits of the person who did the deed, and several outstanding theories on the motives behind the action; one of which was always found to be correct.

Always.

Irritatingly enough, he never appeared to be watching or listening to anyone or anything with any particular interest, yet he missed nothing, even regarding his co-workers.

And field work . . . well, forget about it. He could catch anyone in the slightest lie, and by the end of the interview, trip a person up so badly that they usually ended up confessing and offering up even more info than was originally hoped for.

Baker wanted a little of that glory, and even though he thought well of Will, and even admired him, the somewhat immature side of Baker resented the hell out of the fact that people thought Will was *better* than him. The guy was middle-aged for God's sake. Probably should be maxing out his IRA's by now, thinking about which golf course he was going to haunt.

It didn't occur to him that with age comes experience, most of the time. It also didn't occur to him that maybe he could learn from his partner. No. It was easier just to be pissed, and taunt the guy about his age. It never seemed to bother Will, but then again, what did?

Just once, Baker thought with annoyance, he would like to see Will get shaken up. See him freaking out about something. Yeah. That would be kind of enjoyable, actually.

Will worked diligently on his task, ignoring the resentful vibes coming from the direction of his partner. They were so strong he almost felt them as physical blows.

What a crybaby. Baker should really work on sharpening his own skills, rather than being pissed about *my* abilities, he thought an impatient jab at the keyboard.

The guy was great when they had to go out and do a confrontation, but abilities using just your brain power are just as necessary, and very teachable, if the fool would just listen. But Baker was restless and young and thought his way was the only way.

What-the hell-ever. Someday he would figure it out.

Will's secretary, Kaitlyn, stuck her head over the wall. "Um, Mr. Taylor, Mr. Levinson said for me to tell you we have a guy who made visual contact with an unknown, and is planning to go to the media. He said you're available, and to go do a chat with this guy . . . like, um . . . now." Kaitlyn winced as she spoke; trying to soften the message she was sent to deliver.

Will leveled his copper stare at the young girl. "What the *fu* . . . I mean, what in the world is Mark thinking? *I'm* available? I am? *Really?* He needs to get . . ." He stopped suddenly.

Ah, hell. He shouldn't go off on the secretary, he decided.

No need to shoot the messenger.

Everyone, including himself, was still on edge after the urgent meeting called yesterday. Every agent in his department at least, had been put on a priority assignment that was going to be stressful and difficult, on top of being distasteful as hell to Will, as a matter of morality.

In spite of this fact, he had added that assignment to his *"do it right now"* list to juggle with the other stuff that piled up daily. And now this interruption.

Expelling a lungful of frustrated breath, Will rose to his feet, strategically avoiding the "cabinet-slash-dagger" beautifully this time.

"Fine. Thank you, Kaitlyn. I'll go see Mr. Levinson, 'k?"

Kaitlyn smiled, relieved. "Thanks, Mr. Taylor. I'll be at a staff meeting until eleven in case anyone's looking." Will forced a smile back, and the secretary left, after allowing a dreamy look back over her shoulder at Will.

She walked off with a slightly exaggerated sway that Will could not help but notice.

As did Baker.

Will cleared his throat as his partner smirked.

"Yeah. Well. I'm just going to see what's what with Mark, okay? I'll be back." He nodded toward Baker's computer. "You might as well bookmark that shit, because I have a feeling we're going on a field trip."

"Sure thing, stud muffin. I never noticed your natural flair with the ladies before. Interesting."

"There's nothing interesting, and I don't have a flair . . . I have a *wife*, you dig?"

"Oh I can dig it, dude. I sure can," replied Baker with infuriating smugness.

He was elated. Nothing pleased him more than busting free of the confines of office space, for a little "hands on" work.

Will grunted with irritation. No doubt, the expectation of the six files getting researched would remain intact, in spite of this unexpected detour in the plan. This just meant that he would have to work on Intel at home tonight.

Just like he had the past three hundred and sixty-five days this past year.

Just like every year.

He just hoped he could get the guy with an itch for media glory to see reason quickly. He *would* see reason, without a doubt. There would be no compromise. It was just a matter of escalation, and how high up the scale they would have to go to make the man see things the Federal Government's way.

Grabbing his laptop, he stuffed it into its case with careful hands. He was going to have to do a stat background of this individual on the way to the scene. He wouldn't have time to learn the guy's entire life story, but if he was married or had kids, just the mention of their names and schools, or places of employment was usually enough to show people that the strange visitors meant business.

The threats were vague but implicit, and most recipients of a visit from Will or any other member of his team tended to capitulate very quickly.

Single citizens were tougher, but not much. They had family too, and there was generally at least one person whose potential safety could be used as leverage. When he had enough time though, Will could really terrify a person by reciting to them every intimate detail of their lives, starting from their date of conception, and ending with what they bought at the supermarket the night before.

His quiet demeanor only served to further freak people out, which was very helpful in his line of work.

If it came down to it . . . if someone played at being unusually stupid and defiant, then things could get very ugly very fast. A removal of an individual was rare, but not unheard of.

Whatever was necessary for the protection of the people.

It was this aspect of the job that Will hated. Intimidating civilians really sickened him, especially using the thinly veiled implication of harm to someone's children.

That was down and dirty, and damn near unforgiveable.

He knew that he would never actually touch someone's child, for any reason. It was all for effect, and worked incredibly well.

Although Will, straightforward as a bullet from a gun, was not one for superstition or self-delusion, one game he played within his own mind, just so he could continue to live with himself, was a simple game of words.

He worked with excruciating care to make sure he never directly spoke the actual *words* that he would take action against someone's family. The threat was there, but he refused to say it.

It was a bullshit game, he knew, and made no difference, but it allowed him to keep breathing.

Speaking the name of a subject's significant other or child in the right tone was as far as he would go. And true statements, like *"We would hate for anything to happen to your beautiful family"*, were part of the game.

He told himself that it *was* true . . . he really *would* hate for any harm to come to anyone's family. But that's not how the subjects would take it.

Oh no.

His emotional control was such, that it left no doubt in the minds of his targets that he would follow up a visit with them by swinging by the school or daycare or workplace of their offspring or spouse if they did not agree to forget all about any alien or otherworldly encounter that they had actual proof of, and to surrender any footage or artifacts supporting their claims.

It took Will days to recover from the internal torment of a really tough assignment. He could visualize the faces of all of his targets as it slowly dawned on them that they were helpless, and that their own government was capable of such strong-armed tactics. That's when the terror set in.

And it was always made one hundred percent clear that should the target attempt to call or try to meet with someone to tattle-tale about the evil government's threats, that it would be known immediately, and that the penalty for that kind of stupidity would be unthinkable.

"Even if you whisper about us to your wife while you are making love to her . . . we will know it . . ." Will had spoken those words in his deep menacing voice to his last terrified target, who was shaking with fear. *"And the ramifications would be quite severe."*

No one ever guessed at the silent burden that Will carried with him on a daily basis because of these confrontations at which he famously excelled.

"Ah, yeah . . ." Will sighed to himself. *"The good old Federal government, in league with the Air Force Special Activities Center; breaking down overly loudmouthed citizens since 1946."*

Obviously, they did not confront everyone with a claim to the odd or supernatural. Only the credible ones with irrefutable evidence. The crappy, grainy, and shaky video footage of Bigfoot or flying saucers, people were welcome to share with the public.

Most personal encounters were unprovable, and therefore no threat either.

The people who earned a visit had to be in possession of very special evidence or stories, and they had to be made silent.

One way or another.

It was a dirty job, and he did it better than anyone . . . and it was slowly killing him. Every confrontation caused Will to draw just a little deeper inside the emotional cocoon he'd spun around himself.

He could only imagine what it would do to him to think that his kids were in danger from anyone. It made him crazy and overly protective of them, probably out of the guilt he carried.

He hoped the theory of Karma was a load of crap, but he wasn't so sure.

Will was trying to get moved into more of an investigative role on the team, but so far, all of *those* positions would require a transfer, and Indie had made it clear that she wasn't leaving this area anytime soon.

So for now, the idea remained shelved; nothing more than a wistful twinge in his gut.

Oh well. He was going to see his boss, wasn't he?

At least Baker would be pumped.

Will returned from Levinson's office twice as irritated as when he left. Shit, this day was going from bad to worse. What else could go wrong, he wondered as he punched his arms through the sleeves of his jacket, and slipped his sunglasses into place.

He shifted his shoulders a little uncomfortably at the snug fit.

It was seriously time to plan a quick shopping trip to Boston, and soon. His lunch hour workouts had become increasingly aggressive, and the results were beginning to show.

This was perhaps Will's single vanity, except for maybe his pride, and the Brooks Brothers shop at seventy-five State Street in downtown Boston was his personal clothing oasis. Well, he would have to think about when he could make that happen later.

He looked over at Baker, who was draped over the cubicle wall in meaningless verbal play mode with a woman from the public relations department.

"Baker!" Will barked, and he watched as Baker slowly turned his head, a sexed up look in his eyes.

"Let's go. You can request some *private* relations when we get back." "I'm ready, Grandpa, just waitin' on you!"

Will ignored the jibe, as always.

"Right. Let's put this mother on the road, shall we?"

"Put it to it, Taylor!" The two men walked purposefully out of the office, stopping to collect their weapons from small lockers before exiting the building. The keys to those lockers were guarded closely by a well-armed young man. Shawn took a look up when they reached the outside entrance.

"It's God damned *hot* today, man!" Baker exclaimed, as he shoved back his aviators. Will looked neither left nor right as he moved steadily down the granite steps. It *was* hot. Bullshit hot.

"Yep. Kind of warm for March." He handed Baker the file and opened his computer case as he activated his earpiece. "Blake, we're ready for the car, please."

All business, aren't you, Taylor, thought Baker, feeling somewhat sulfurous.

A sleek, black limo pulled up in front of the building almost immediately, and as he got inside, Will took a stealthy look up at the glimmering sun above him, and pushed aside a sudden foreboding that planted itself in the center of his belly.

He gathered up his strength and used it all to keep his non-committal expression in place, and after an imperceptible hesitation, slammed the door firmly shut.

CHAPTER 9

"What took you so long to answer the door? Are you okay?" Indie's mother-in-law eyed her suspiciously. Marie Taylor kicked at Max with a pointed shoe as she spoke. She detested dogs, being decidedly more of a cat person.

"I'm fine, Marie, really," Indie fibbed.

"But I called your work, and they said you were sick. I thought I would find you in here dead." She laughed a little. "You never call in."

Indie thought furiously.

"I needed a . . . mental health day?" It wasn't like it was really a lie, was it? Marie looked at her shrewdly.

Well, Indie thought, she should love hearing *that*. Although she had always been pleasant to Indie, it was clear that she also wasn't entirely satisfied with her as the one who "took away her boy," and so unexpectedly.

Ugh. Indie hoped that *she* wouldn't be this way when Jake married.

I probably will be. No one good enough for my little son. She had to smile at the thought.

"A mental health day? What on Earth could be so wrong in *your* life that you needed to miss work?"

Indie did not miss the inflection. "Look, I'm just tired, and have a lot on my mind right now . . . I needed some quiet time."

"So what is weighing so heavily on your mind?" Marie pressed, leaning her petite frame against the kitchen counter.

Nothing I want to tell you about, that's for sure.

"Oh, I don't know. I think it's hormonal."

Marie paused. "I always forget your age. Maybe you're pre-menopausal," she offered hopefully. This would give her something to gossip about at the real estate office where she worked downtown. Indie could just hear her now; *"My daughter-in-law is going through menopause, can you imagine!"*

"Maybe so," Indie fed her, grateful for the offering. "Please, I don't mean to be rude or anything, but was there something specific that you were trying to reach me for? You never call my work."

Marie put forth her best wounded expression before answering. "Well, I tried to call Will first."

Of course you did, Indie mentally interrupted.

"They told me he was out of the office, and he hardly ever returns my calls, and . . ."

"So what did you need, Marie?" Indie interrupted aloud this time, in a most uncharacteristic show of impatience. She certainly did not want to hurt her mother-in-law's feelings, but she couldn't wait to get her out of the house.

"Well . . . *nothing*, really. I was just concerned because I haven't spoken to my son in a few days, and I wanted to make sure he was okay."

Indie resisted the urge to remind the woman that her son was not only thirty-five years old, but had a wife and children, all of whom had her cell phone number to call if any dark tragedy had taken place concerning Will. She should know he was perfectly fine.

At least for the moment.

Her guilt surged forward at the reminder that Will may be in for a rough evening, actually. But she was not about to broach that subject with Marie.

"Will is fine, of course Marie. He's just always very busy, as you well know."

"But too busy for his mother?" Marie pouted.

Don't feel so left out, Marie.

"You know he doesn't mean to neglect you. He just gets overwhelmed with work I guess. I'll have him call you, okay?"

Marie thought for a moment. "Yes, he does work awfully hard. Too hard, I tell him. Trying to provide for you and the kids."

This irked Indie, but she swallowed it down admirably.

"Yes, Marie. We *both* work hard to provide for our family." Indie looked over her shoulder briefly, still somehow feeling certain that Jackson was nearby and it made her uneasy. She didn't think that an introduction to Will's mom at this stage in the game would be such a great plan.

"Please, I think I need to lie down. I really don't feel right at all, so . . . if there's nothing else . . . ."

"No, nothing else. I was just curious, er, I mean *worried*." She smiled.

Indie smiled back. "Okay, then."

Marie hesitated, then finally gave up and headed out the door with a sigh.

Indie could tell that she wasn't at all satisfied with her quest for any information she could latch onto where Will was concerned, but it would just have to do for now. She said her goodbyes once more, thanking Marie for her "concern" as she shut the door behind her, and leaned back onto it, dismissing the woman instantly from her thoughts.

She allowed her mind to go right where it wanted to go.

My senses are not complete until I am joined with whom I belong?

Her head reeled with Jackson's words. Maybe she really did need to lie down. Indie went to her room, and threw open the curtains, so that the beautiful mountain view was visible. Beauty in nature was always a comfort to her, and she absorbed the familiar scene with a soft sigh.

She moved to lie down on the bed, facing the window and closed her eyes, feeling a fierce need to see this strange and beautiful man again. The man who was threatening to throw her entire life out of balance. She opened them again, and he stepped into view at the far end of the deck.

Indie wasn't startled, or even surprised. It was as if she had known he would be there. He stood, leaning back on the railing and looking at her, his hands crammed in his jacket pockets. She just let him stand there for a moment while she appraised him, his rich brown hair stirring in the breeze as he waited.

Indie's mind began to formulate an entirely self-centered form of reasoning, and dissected the situation in all the wrong ways. But she surrendered to her own mind's madness.

What would any woman in the world do in this situation? Her mutinous mind asked. *A man . . . the most appealing, attractive man that you've ever seen in your entire life shows up on your doorstep*, her brain argued, *and announces that he was born just for you!*

Indie snapped her head back and forth, but her thoughts continued to flow.

He wasn't just physical perfection either; there was more to it. He exuded an essence that told her he would be a true partner to her. This man, Jackson, soothed her parched soul, as dramatic as this seemed. What was happening? Did she finally actually fall asleep, and find herself in the middle of a dream? Or was it a nightmare.

In a sudden and blinding flash of insight, Indie felt a sick, suffocating realization wash over her.

She was going to hurt her husband.

And her children.

This had somehow just become an inevitable certainty, and it filled her with sadness. No one deserved to be hurt like that.

Her children! They loved their father just as much as they loved her, and she shuddered at the thought of the accusation she would see in their eyes. Cassidy especially.

Nevertheless, she was going to let it happen, monstrous as the thought was. She knew it, with a clarity that was without question.

Indie drew in a deep, steadying breath as she got up, and in a complete exercise of free-will, slowly walked her destined path to the door that led to the deck.

Without a pause, Indie opened the door to let him in.

CHAPTER 10

Revelations

Jackson followed her into the house on pins and needles. Surely Indie could hear the pinball action of his heart, pinging off his ribcage and spine. But an episode of full-blown tachycardia would not be good right now. He deliberately focused on slowing his heart rate.

"Are you sure you want me here?"

Ha. He didn't know why he had asked her *that* . . . as if he could possibly leave now. Well, maybe if she *really* wanted him to.

Indie turned to fix him with her own Caribbean blue gaze. He was wearing the expression of excitement mixed with pain once again.

"Tell me what you're thinking," Indie ordered him, and Jackson complied without hesitation.

"I know what this is doing to you. I'm not sure how I will bear this, but I don't know how else *to* do it. But I *am* going to do it, because . . ." his voice dropped to a seductive hiss, "because I must."

"Do what?" Indie returned the whisper calmly. "What are you going to do, Jackson?"

How serene she felt now, with the knowledge of the inevitable. Knowing, no matter how horrible, trumped ignorance.

Jackson's entire body stiffened at the sound of his name spoken in her soft voice. When he answered, his voice was raw with need.

"I'm going to bring you to me, where you belong!" He raised his head and looked her in the eyes when he said this, his own eyes clear and determined, yet troubled.

Indie felt a blush rising in the wake of his unrelenting gaze. He was rooted in place, watching her steadily, and his deep blue eyes were nearly the color of midnight now. She felt as if they were pools of life. Anything she could possibly want, she need only look there to find it.

"Indie," Jackson picked up on her emotions, "you will find what you are looking for. What you *need*. Because I have found *you*."

He spoke in his gentle but disconcertingly masculine voice; a voice filled with the longing that she had felt her entire life. Indie had been longing, but for what, she'd never understood. But she had an idea now.

She reached out her hand to him.

"Invitation only?"

Oh, by the Creator's will, she was going to let him touch her! Jackson's thoughts collided with themselves, threatening to overtake his reason. He quickly drew into his lungs a deep, cooling breath of air to bring himself down, and expelled it slowly, before answering.

"Yes, it has to be your choice . . . your *will*." Jackson's voice shook with anticipation in spite of his best efforts.

This spilled Indie completely over the edge.

"Take my hand," she whispered urgently, reaching further, and he slowly removed both of his hands from his pockets.

They were shaking violently.

Dismayed at his lack of control, he clenched them into tight fists and hesitated. Indie must have full disclosure.

"There will be no going back, you know," he warned. "Once we make contact, you may find yourself wanting me as much as I need you!" *I pray that you do.* "But it may make your future choices more difficult."

Those words, while shocking to Indie, served only to urge her forward. He paused once more, and stepped closer. Looking down, Jackson drew her into the depths of his stare.

"*I'll take your invitation, and you take all of me . . .*" He then broke into an uneasy smile.

"Nickelback. I tend to quote songs annoyingly often."

This caused a short huff of nervous laughter to roll from Indie's throat, and she couldn't help herself. "Uh . . . I think—that's actually Lifehouse . . ."

Jackson eyes sparked. "Yes . . . it is Lifehouse. Just checking to see if you're really someone I can spend forever with."

Indie didn't quite know what to say to this. The moment was so serious . . . so monumental.

Yet his humor still escaped. She also used humor to diffuse tension, and she felt an uptight giggle sneaking its way past her lips, only to become a soft gasp as Jackson's eyes suddenly turned deadly serious in their focus. They seized and held her own as he stepped closer still.

His features were calm as a moonlit mountain lake now, and he reached forward to curl his strong hands around Indie's small but capable ones, and a surge of something like an electrical impulse shot through his body.

Jackson's head snapped back and a low sound escaped his throat, echoed by a similar response from Indie. The sensations from both the current and the sound of Indie's shock made him feel faintly unsteady, and he gripped her hands tightly.

Indie felt a rush of strength climb through her frame. They were supporting each other now, and an immediate sensation of solid warmth flowed from his body into hers. She sucked in his scent now, greedily.

He smelled like everything warm and comforting; a cozy fire, hot buttered toast and cocoa, along with some kind of intense pheromone pull, like the scent from the top of your baby's head. The effect was close to an adrenaline high. Indie stepped closer, breathing in deeply. He stepped closer at the same moment, their faces inches apart.

Indie's head began to spin. Her thoughts clouded and she felt herself falling. Jackson wrapped his left arm around her, easily supporting her weight. He kept his right hand free, as he rested his fingertips on her forehead, tracing lightly now down her jaw line, and up to her lips. He dipped his head down and brought his own lips across her eyelid, and dragged them over to her ear.

"Are you okay?" he breathed into her hair. As Indie turned her head to look into his eyes, she started to speak, but lost her voice as she took note of the emotion on his face.

Oh God. It was *disappointment*. Jackson seemed distracted; looking for something in her that he clearly was not seeing. There was also a touch of confusion in his eyes, as if he had expected something . . . different.

No, please. She couldn't bear it. This was supposed to be different. She had been so sure. How could it be that he was losing sight of her already? Did she not meet his expectations? Indie choked back her tears.

Jackson's expression darkened and he spoke with such passion that it knocked Indie's oncoming sobs aside with blunt force.

"No, Indie." He shook his head. "Whatever you're thinking, if it makes you look like *that*, then you have it wrong!"

"You're," her voice cracked, "not exactly thrilled with me now, are you? I can see the disappointment . . ." She couldn't bear to go on, and struggled to break free of his embrace.

His expression softened at once, and he gathered her even more tightly against his hard unyielding body, easily resisting her escape attempts. When his eyes met hers once more, she saw laughter mingling with a look of wistfulness.

"Oh, Indie, if I could ever be angry with you, I would bet this would be one of those times! How could you possibly think . . ." he paused, shaking his head at her in disapproval. Before she could respond, he continued, but dipped down low to speak against her neck, and moving down her collarbone as he did, effectively silencing her ability to even think.

"Any disappointment you see, is simply the fact that I have been able to read your emotions and your feelings, but I *should* now be able to read your thoughts clearly, as we have made contact, and I . . . I don't." Jackson stopped, cocking his head to one side, thinking. He seemed to push the thought aside for the moment.

"There is also the fact that I thought that our bloodlines would be more closely aligned. Most *Equals* of Society Members from *my* particular genetics, are matched with *Equals* of the same ancestry, so that they understand our ability to do what we do." *He chuckled softly, before adding before adding, "And so there is no conflict* about leadership!" Jackson stopped his words.

He knew that Indie would have no idea what he was talking about.

"That doesn't matter. It was just unexpected. I'm sure there is a reason. We are meant to be compatible." He smiled reassuringly at her."
So tell me . . . what *are* you thinking, Indie?"

She was actually thinking that his voice should be dispensed like a narcotic, it was so dangerously addicting. But she decided to speak an all encompassing fact.

"Just that you're . . . perfect," she whispered, relieved by his words, and utterly amazed at the way the feelings obliterated any coherent thought for the moment.

She did wonder why he couldn't read her thoughts, if that's what he was supposed to be able to do, but kicked to the curb her natural urge to feed on this as another failure.

No. She was through with the self-doubt. She knew it, somehow. The deal was done, and she knew she belonged to this man from this moment on. How this could be, she wasn't sure, she simply knew that it was.

"I am meant to be perfect for you, and I *am* yours," he spoke in the most sure, calming voice ever to touch her ears. The whisper of his accent was pure seduction. He closed his eyes, and rested his forehead against hers, and Indie thought that she might pass out from the scent, the warmth and the need.

Moving with agonizingly slow caution, he kissed both of her eyelids now, gently . . . hesitated, and then moved to his target.

Tentatively, he sought her lips and brushed an exploratory kiss against them. Indie could tell that he was ready to allow her to pull away if she so chose.

As soon as it was clear that she wasn't going to do any such thing, his urgency took over, and he pulled her against his body with a soft groan of relief.

His kiss was filled with yearning—lips soft, yet firm. Firm enough to know that this was a man was kissing her, and that this man had needs. She felt his hips lock against hers, and her heart rate exploded into overdrive. Holding her in place with his carefully tempered strength, he pressed against her, just for a moment.

Indie had no way of knowing this little gem of information, but this was Jackson's first real kiss. The first that he'd actively participated in, at any rate.

Oh, he had been ambushed by overly enthusiastic females before, but this . . . this was what he'd been waiting for.

Saving himself for.

He stopped, clutching her tightly for a second and then stepped away with a sigh. She felt as though the sun had gone out. Or her air supply had been cut off.

"I know," he spoke, answering her feelings. "But I need you to break away from your"—he blanched—"from Will" He could not bring himself to say "husband".

He just couldn't. *That* reality made Indie flinch, too. But only at the thought of how to tell Will.

Jackson stepped back with a small groan of protest spilling forth inadvertently and took both of her hands in his, kissing each one.

"I will not truly have you as long as he still does, even if it's only in his mind." Indie moved toward the couch and sat, dragging him along.

"But how can I do this? I am sitting here with you; a stranger to me, but just because you *touched* me, I am ready to end my marriage? Divorce Will and run away with you?" Indie shook her head. "It's crazy . . . just . . . crazy. But I *know* I belong with you. It's like I've always known. Or am I finally just losing my mind, Jackson?"

"It's only crazy to you because you weren't raised in our world. You would understand why we connect this way, if only . . . ." He looked into her eyes with a return of the weary, exhausted look he'd sported when she'd first seen him.

"If only you'd been found right away, as you should have been." He threw her a quick smile. "But you are found now, and that is all that matters."

He curled his hand around the back of her neck, drawing her forward slightly. He raised his eyes to hers, his expression shifted back into sorrow. "Except that now, I need you to break free from William Taylor's claim on you, and I know I am asking you to do something painful to you."

Indie stared at Jackson without speaking for so long that he thought that maybe he asked too much. Something she was not going to be able to do. His throat began to tighten with sickness at the idea. Her words, however, when finally she spoke, were strong; filled with the certainty of her conviction.

"I know I have to do it. No matter how painful, I know it has to be done, if I want to find my 'happily ever after'. For Will too, I think. He's not happy with me either. Not really." Her eyes filled with pain.

"I just have to work up a way to do it. It will hurt my children, even if it won't really devastate him too badly. I don't think he . . ." Indie looked down at the carpet, and then forced the words out. Somehow, it was still painful. "I don't think he really cares where I go or what I do."

Jackson ran his hand through her hair and around her face before cupping her chin in his warm, strong hand. As he pulled Indie's face up to meet his gaze, she felt a forceful energy that seemed to originate from the very center of his body.

His eyes narrowed as he tried to read her, but his voice was soft. Even and controlled.

"You underestimate your worth in his eyes." Jackson's grip on her was strong, but muted with gentleness. "This will hurt him. Probably like nothing he has ever felt before, and by extension, it will hurt you as well."

He released her face, but caught her hand, and held it with both of his, looking at them thoughtfully.

"How can I say this the right way," he began, looking up at her. He tried to smile reassuringly, but managed only a painful grimace.

"I know you love him, and even though I know it is in a . . . different way, it will *kill* me. But I want you to understand, that this is my cross to bear, not yours." He held up one hand to stop her words, and ran his thumb across her lips, softly.

"You *must* love him for what you've shared, for what he's given you. He is the sire of your children, and they are the greatest gift of all. I am indebted to this man as well, for he has provided for you, and given you shelter."

His eyes were suddenly so clear, so blue, that Indie's breath caught, and a small gasp escaped her lips, washing over his skin as he continued to stroke her lips as softly as a butterfly's touch.

"I would have you know that I understand all of this, and you must never feel guilty for the love you have for him, but you must also know that your love is not a gift I will share well, so if you feel my struggle, my . . . darkness, you have to promise to leave me to it. It will be my problem, and not yours. It will never affect my feelings or thoughts toward you. You will care for him freely, and without guilt. You *must* promise me that. I need to hear you say it now, Indie."

He leaned forward, and speared her with his brilliant eyes when she made no response.

"I want your promise Indie, and in return, I will give you one as well. I will never allow harm to come to him, as far as it is within my power. I don't want him to suffer anything more than his sacrifice of you to me. That is one area in which I cannot compromise."

Indie's eyes began to burn with unshed tears. "I do have feelings for him, but . . ."

"No Indie. Please, do not explain yourself. It's only right." Jackson gathered her close, and held her tightly. She felt his warm breath in her hair.

"He doesn't deserve to be hurt," she spoke in a small voice.

"No, he doesn't," Jackson agreed. "Even for the crime he has committed in not fully appreciating the treasure that he has had right in front of him." He scowled in disapproval.

"But, what if he had," Indie asked, "what if he'd worshipped the ground that I walked on, and would never let me go?"

"I can't answer that," Jackson replied uneasily. "It would depend on how happy he made *you*. But he would never be your perfect match. That position has always been mine alone to fill."

"How does this *Equal* thing work, exactly?" Indie asked.

He pinned her neatly to the back of the couch, staring at her for what felt like an eternity before speaking.

"Your promise?" He drew out the "s" sound in a sinfully appealing way, setting small flying creatures free in her belly. She stroked his face and watched in wonder as he took his turn in a pool of new sensations, feeling his soft intake of breath at her touch.

"So, okay. I promise," she answered simply.

Jackson literally collapsed with relief at this, as if it had been of the utmost importance. How unbelievable was this? He didn't want her feeling guilty for the pain he would feel because she cared for Will. The selflessness of the act was touching her in all the right places. For the first time ever, someone was putting her feelings and her well-being above all else.

No, she would not cry.

Okay, not too much. The tears shimmered around the edges of her periphery.

Jackson hesitated, measuring her expression, and then acknowledged her previous question.

"The mechanics of *Equal* partnership is actually a pretty long story. There is truly a purpose behind Society Members coming in pairs." Indie started.

Society Members?

She had been so blown away by the revelation of this beautiful man being hers, and hers alone, that she had forgotten the other part of this story.

This not so very romantic part.

The potentially creepy update on her status. She looked back at him, eyes wide with trepidation.

"How about we take one thing at a time, my love," he whispered. She felt heat spread throughout her body at his words. His manner of speaking was somewhat formal and old fashioned, spiked with only the occasional contraction and modern slang. It was fascinating to hear, and something about it brought her heart home.

Men just didn't speak to women like this anymore.

The sweet endearments, the intense interest in *her* wellbeing were everything she had been craving her entire life. Indie was a goner. He was right. There was no turning back now. He stood, and she rose with him, immediately. A bright smile lit his face and eyes.

"You're sad to see me go."

It was a statement, not a question, and it seemed to make him indescribably happy as he pulled her against his chest.

"Yes. I'm not sure that I can stand it, actually," Indie answered against his shoulder. He lifted her face to look at him.

"Look, I want you to try something for me now."

"What is it?" she asked, nervously.

"I think the trick is focus and concentration. Your gift of *invisibility*, as Miss Maggie called it. You have an inborn and quite automatic ability to close yourself off from others. This may be why I don't fully get your thoughts as I should."

Indie had to laugh at this.

"I knew it was my fault!"

He gave her a gentle swat on her backside in retaliation as he corrected her. "Not fault, Indie. *Gift!* If you can focus, we will have the ability to communicate freely, without words."

What? "How can that be?" She asked, confused at the possibility of such a thing.

He pulled her into his mesmerizing gaze once more, and spoke to her hypnotically. "Open your mind, Indie . . . let go of your defenses and hear me! Relax. Listen. You'll have to turn away from the invisibility, and *let me in there!*"

For a moment, she was baffled, hearing only his soft breath, but then, it happened. She heard his voice in her head, as surely as if he had spoken.

I will never be far from you again, because I can't bear it, either.

His thoughts warmed her head from the inside. The most crazy part was that it didn't feel exactly . . . *crazy.* It felt right.

Normal.

Which in itself was insane. Indie's head was swimming. She felt all the swoon-y and sickly giddiness of a teenage love drama. This was all new. After ten years of marriage, and at age 40, who would believe she could experience first love?

The search has ended, and a journey begins for me as well!

She had to look to see if he had spoken. He had not, but his eyes shone brightly as he looked down at her. The lost and empty look seemed to have vanished from his eyes, replaced with a cautious joy and optimism. Indie wondered, briefly, if she too would see a different face the next time she peeked in the mirror. She had a strong feeling that she would.

He continued to stare down at her with a look of amazement stamped across his otherwise serene face.

"What?" She asked, embarrassed by the unfamiliar scrutiny.

"You are just so amazing, so . . . beautiful," he spoke reverently. Indie shivered, and whatever response she had in mind crumbled into dust.

The look on his face changed abruptly, replaced with resignation.

"I have to leave you now. I cannot help you do what you must, I'm afraid." A fleeting look of some sort of violent emotion shot across his face, then was gone. "My control is strong, but I know that I can't face Will with you. That would be . . . unwise, I think."

The idea of such a confrontation horrified Indie. "Oh my God, no . . . I mean, yes. That would be . . . no good at all, I am thinking." Ugh, Christ, what a vision that threw into her head. It was not a pretty one.

Jackson eyed her soberly. "You have a difficult job ahead of you."

"I know," Indie responded dully, and the sick feeling threatened to engulf her again. He leaned forward, and kissed her quickly, sending a spark of power surging through her.

"I deplore what causes you to suffer, and I know that this will. But you will be strong, because my heart will be with you. It's belonged to you for forty years, and now you finally have it in your hands."

He spoke with an enticing sweetness.

"That just might sustain me," Indie told him.

"I'm counting on it!" He stood for another moment, looking at her. He then leaped forward, pulling her into a criminally passionate kiss that left her panting, her hand pressed to her racing heart.

Jackson released her slowly, sliding his hands down her shoulders to her elbows, then to her hands. He clutched them firmly, then let go with a reluctance that was palpable.

He hesitated, and then whispered the words that left Indie's lips simultaneously: *"I love you."*

They both stiffened at the force of the declarations meeting one another's ears. On their faces were identical expressions of shock at the words they had each spoken so ridiculously soon. Oh, the feelings were more than clear, but to say the actual words out loud was another matter entirely.

Jackson's eyes recovered, then melted into Indie's. The smile that leaked across his face was achingly sweet and shy. With a quick wink, he turned and fled the room. The only evidence that he had been there, was the still open door, and the faint smell of yum, from where he'd been standing.

I love you? What was I thinking? Indie's belly was screaming as she tried to reconcile her brain with her mouth. Apparently she'd forgotten how to manage these two parts of her anatomy.

She stared at the place he had just vacated, committing this moment to her own personal history book, before turning to the mission that was soon to be at hand. Turning away, she allowed herself to feel an awful chill at the thought of what she had to do, and ran into the kitchen to begin to formulate the words that would emotionally destroy her family.

Jackson headed down the road on a high unlike anything he'd ever imagined. He'd connected with his mate, and the feeling was intense as he sang along with the radio, enjoying it for the first time as a joyful celebration, rather than something to simply blast the tension from his body.

He wanted to do something totally dorky and ridiculous, like tuning in to the "Delilah after Dark" show, and dedicating something appropriately embarrassing and sappy to proclaim his love for his woman.

But the car slowed unconsciously as a strange sensation crept through Jackson's brain, his vision clouding momentarily. At once, he began to experience a slow but certain downward shift in his elation at what his internal instincts were suddenly forcing through his head.

He felt an animalistic protective mode rising to engulf him, threatening to erase the civilized, rational being that he had believed he was.

His own gifts and abilities were trying to manifest, surging after the contact was made with his *Equal* and, although still weak, an undeniable premonition had driven itself prominently to the front of his brain.

Indie was the one about to be hurt.

Emotionally, and gut wrenchingly so, at the hands of her husband. Jackson was astonished at the fearsome reaction this knowledge generated within him. His inner warrior could not allow such a thing to happen.

Unfortunately, his vision also told him that for reasons yet unknown to him, he would have no choice but to allow it to play out. This filled him with a restless rage that shook him to the core. Society Members were not violent toward the Human Population.

They were guardians.

He was above such beastly tendencies, was he not?

Jackson had perfected the outward projection of calm collectedness to a fine science, but inwardly, he struggled. Wasn't it great that he had just shown Indie how to relax and move away from the barrier in her mind, and in the process, allowing her unlimited access into his own thoughts?

Nowhere to hide now.

He did not want her to know his carefully repressed dangerous side. Jackson thought it would horrify her if she knew he had such thoughts . . . such capabilities.

He had been taught well.

And trained to contain negative emotions, even though his body had been sent for tactical training. In fact, the contradiction had confused him at the time, but he had found he was a natural in combat operations, and most incredibly gifted in physical altercation.

He had totally enjoyed it, and it allowed him to burn off some of the unrelenting energy that kept him unsettled as a young man, before he had gained the upper hand on self-control. It had worked out very well for him.

Until now.

The idea of anyone or anything harming Indie in any fashion made him see various shades of crimson, and he felt a nauseating desire to kill and eat anything that dared to do so.

Jackson swallowed down the upsurge of his stomach contents that tried to come out and say hello at that happy thought. He wasn't one hundred percent sure that he could trust himself to do the right thing here, and knew that he needed guidance.

Making a quick decision, he turned his car southbound on I-89. His exit appeared before him, and Jackson burned a path toward Woodstock.

To one of the sacred places. He needed to ask, no, *beg*, for help from his Elders.

As he found the wooded area, semi-hidden in the brush, he parked his car and sprinted toward the cool darkness of Calendar II.

He took a position dead center of the small double-square space, facing outward and aligning his body toward the sun, and closed his eyes.

Contact was made nearly instantaneously, and Jackson began to plead for the strength that they would both need in order to survive the ordeal looming before them. The ordeal that he knew would begin tomorrow, in the very early hours of morning.

Taking deep steady breaths to calm himself, he allowed the resonation to take away his conscious mind, communing with the ones who gave him his comfort and his strength.

The rage died away, leaving only peace and the knowledge of what had to be done. Jackson knew that he would still have to battle with his instincts, but now he felt the reassurance he was seeking, that made him feel that maybe, just maybe, he was man enough to hold himself above the fray, and to allow fate to unfold.

God, he hoped so.

CHAPTER 11

Will down-shifted his trusty Ford Ranger, and slowed to a stop. The traffic light here was new, having cropped up just yesterday.

Another reminder of the slowly increasing population of what was once a very sparsely-peopled state.

The drive home was just over forty-five minutes, and as long as it wasn't during a winter storm, he was grateful for the distance, and the decompressing time it gave him.

Time to pull himself together and become just "Will" again.

Will, and Daddy.

And time to mentally assassinate the character of Special Agent William Taylor.

He never actually made it back down to the person he was when he woke up in the morning . . . always falling just shy of his goal. Like a computer trying desperately to back up its files and recover function after battling a virus.

Running better, but still not really okay.

The confrontation with the civilian today had been the usual. Fantastically successful.

And totally horrible.

The blast from the horn surprised him. The light was green. Grimacing into the rearview mirror, Will moved forward and turned onto the ramp to merge with the minimal I-89 traffic.

The monotonous strip of grey pavement ahead allowed his mind to wander back to the visit with one Mr. Richard McKinney.

Baker had been listening to his IPod and fidgeting restlessly on the quick chopper trip to the small New Hampshire town where the subject lived.

He lived for this stuff, and the part he played didn't require too much prep work, unlike Will's.

The data that he was able to gather in the twenty-minute ride to the heliport, then the next twenty-minutes in the air, was quite impressive. More than he'd expected.

Aside from the man's entire family tree, he'd found the jackpot of a recent transaction at a shoe store the night before. Will loved finding treats like that, because it gave them the opportunity to create the idea in the subject's head that he'd already been under surveillance; even before his face to face with a non-human life form.

What a lovely stroke of luck.

So Mr. McKinney had bought some cheap fourteen dollar shoes at Payless, and then swung by McDonalds for a number one combo meal, with coffee rather than soda.

And a happy meal.

Bingo.

The computerized ordering systems made his job so easy sometimes. Nothing more than a lazy game of "follow the debit card trail".

The limo was waiting at their destination, and the drive to the subject's home was brief. The guy lived in a small unobtrusive house in a neighborhood of mixed quality. Will already had ascertained that the guy was home, and on his computer, having hacked his way in through the firewall easily enough.

The subject was looking up different media contacts as they arrived . . . probably shopping for the outlet most willing to pay for his story.

And his video footage.

He'd called the radio show, Project Earth in the early morning hours. The show dealt with the supernatural, UFO's and conspiracy theories, ninety percent of which was crap, the callers nothing more than crackpots and whackos.

But then, there was always the rare exception, and so this was one of the million or so outlets monitored at all times. And they'd bagged a little fish in the big pond.

As the long black car slid to a smooth stop in front of the subject's home, Baker was out the door before it had altogether stopped moving. Will followed a few paces back, in possession of a briefcase that was well-stocked with paperwork and photos pertaining to the man in question.

Despite their personality differences, the two worked together flawlessly, each playing their role perfectly.

Baker always took the lead initially, getting things rolling in the traditional "bad cop, much worse cop" way that they operated.

He rapped out a friendly sounding series of quick knocks on the peeling wooden door as Will took his place several steps back.

Richard McKinney, sporting a bad haircut and a cocaine ring around his nose, answered the door with the suspicious manner of someone who wasn't comfortable with well-dressed visitors showing up unannounced on a weekday morning. He opened the door a scant inch and a half without a word; a surly, inquisitive look on his face.

"Richard McKinney?" Baker asked pleasantly. The man's eyes narrowed.

"He's not in right now. Sorry."

Without further comment, he began to shut the door. With the flat of his palm, Baker caught the door and pressed it open fairly easily, much to the dismay of the subject, and strolled in like he owned the place.

He wrinkled his nose at the scent of litter box, as he pushed his way past the now sputtering man.

"What . . . what in the hell do you think you're doing?" Mr. McKinney asked with a mixture of fear and anger very obvious in both his voice and expression.

"Nice place you've got here, Dick. You don't mind if I call you Dick, do you?" Baker grit his teeth, and then forced himself to sit in a casual sprawl on the man's newspaper and crumb-strewn couch.

The subject stared at him, outraged now.

"Hey, I don't know who the hell you are, but get the fuck out of my house!" He leaped comically in the air as Will appeared at his back silently. "You too! Get out of my house!"

Baker picked up a cup from the coffee table and sniffed it cautiously. "A little early to be hitting the Jack, don't you think, Dick? You ARE Richard McKinney, aren't you?"

"I told you, he's not here. And I'm calling the cops!"

Baker shrugged, and picked up a newspaper, seeming to scan the headlines disinterestedly. The man looked helplessly now at Will, who stood in menacing silence next to the front door after closing it with an ominous click.

"I mean it. I am calling the cops now . . . ."

The man stalked over to the end table and snatched up his cordless and dialed. Nothing happened.

He pressed the buttons with frantic frustration, trying unsuccessfully to get a dial tone. With an accusing look at Baker, he grabbed his cell phone off the couch, and paused as he looked at the small screen in confusion, the "no service" words displayed plainly.

"So," Baker began, as if he'd simply grown bored with the news articles. "I understand you had kind of an exciting night last night, huh? Up there camping on, what was it, Mystery Hill? Saw something pretty cool, did you?"

McKinney opened his mouth, but nothing came out. He glanced nervously at the guy standing in front of his door.

"How . . . how do you know about that? Did you hear my call this morning on Project Earth?"

He frowned. "But I didn't say where I saw them."

"That's right, Dick. You didn't." Baker rose from the couch and approached the man.

"We'd like to borrow your camcorder, if you don't mind, Dick. And your home computer. And your cell phone and digital camera."

He smiled pleasantly at the man's open-mouthed anger.

"If you would go ahead and get those for us now, that would be great."

"Who . . . what . . . I am NOT giving you anything!" McKinney sputtered, his face now flushed to a dull red. "What the hell gives you the right . . . ?"

"Why don't you like soft drinks, Mr. McKinney?"

Will spoke for the first time, cutting the man off with his softly spoken query.

"Uh . . . what?" McKinney looked baffled by the question.

"It's just that most people, when they eat a Big Mac, tend to go for a soda . . . but you always get coffee. I would save that for the pie."

Fear hit the man's eyes as he made the connection.

"I—I . . ."

"You let your daughter have soda, so it must not be a statement of health. Happy meals come with a choice. You could have gotten Skyler a milk . . . even a chocolate milk. But she got Sprite."

Will shook his head, as if he and the subject were fathers at the playground, discussing child rearing philosophies. "Oh well. At least it doesn't have caffeine. That's really not good for toddlers."

The man froze; his face a mask of horror.

"How are those new shoes of hers, Mr. McKinney?" Will's voice was now barely a whisper. "Do they fit properly? Sometimes it takes a day or two to break them in. We could call her mother . . . your former girlfriend, Theresa, and ask how they are working out for her."

Who are you?" Richard McKinney was now chalk white, and backing up toward the kitchen. He was shaking his head in an attempt to comprehend what was happening.

"You won't make it to the backdoor, Dick." Baker didn't step forward, but shoved his hands in his pockets and rocked back on his heels, fixing the subject with his still aviator-clad stare. The movement allowed his jacket to part slightly, exposing a fine leather shoulder holster; the heel of the weapon clearly visible.

"Who are you people?" repeated the man, his eyes darting rapidly from Will to Baker.

"We—" Baker slowly removed his sunglasses "—are the people to whom you are going to happily and willingly give all of your electronic devices." All trace of the lighthearted conversation was now gone. He fixed the subject with a terrifying glare.

Will's voice was cold as snow, and just as soft. "Do I need to break it down for you, or are you beginning to get the picture?"

The man stared back at him, riveted to the floor in his shock and fear.

"Go get those items, please," Will urged. McKinney stumbled backwards and fell, scrambling to get to the back room where he kept his computer, with Will on his heels.

"I'll get the video, man. Just don't . . ." *his voice tightened and broke off.* "Don't go near my kid, okay?"

"If you are wise, you'll have nothing to fear. You saw nothing out there on Mystery Hill. You thought you did, but when you got home, you realized that maybe you had a very vivid dream, that's all."

Will moved very close to the man who was frantically unplugging the modem and pulling cords from the wall, until he was right up against his shoulder. The man froze once more, breathing rapidly.

Will could smell the sickly sweet scent of alcohol on his breath.

"You will speak to no one about your experience. Not the encounter with the non-humans you think you saw, and most assuredly not from us. We will know. There are no means of communication that will be safe for you to use from this point in your life forward. We are always there, always watching, and above all, always listening. Your every move will continue to be monitored, as will the people most important to you."

He continued his assault on the subject's personal space.

"I sincerely hope you are absorbing this warning in the right way. The next move we make would be a visit with those you care about, and I don't want it to come to that. I am confident that you would not like it either."

"Not. At. All."

Will leaned closer still.

"Believe me, Mr. McKinney . . . we will know. And our reaction time would surprise you."

The man resumed shaking in his boots, and began literally throwing electronics through the bedroom door. He gasped as a huge man, also dressed all in black, entered the hallway with a large crate, and tossed everything into it, and stalked out of the house without a word.

Will gently steered the subject back into the living room and with a sudden and violently unexpected shove, slammed the man down onto the couch with such force that it scooted backward several feet.

Baker began to whistle tunelessly as he studied the man's cheaply framed photos hanging on the wall.

"I—I've heard about you guys . . . you're . . ."

"No." *Will gripped the man by the throat, and deftly sank something small, sharp and shiny into the side of Richard McKinney's neck.* "You haven't!"

The subject watched his field of vision shrink into a tiny pinpoint of light. The last thing he saw was the younger man, who produced a pair of dangling ear buds with a wink and a Vegas lounge-lizard style point and shoot of his right index finger as he turned toward the door. McKinney could just catch the sound of the music from the man's IPod; "Slow Ride," *he thought sleepily.* "I love Foghat."

He smiled for a moment before sinking into peaceful oblivion as the terrifying strangers faded from view.

Upon awakening, the man would find his house in perfect order, all electronic equipment in place and neatly reinstalled, minus any and all footage, documents or commentary relating to any otherworldly encounters. His memory would be foggy, but he would remember the fear, and the threat that came with the unwelcome guests that morning.

Will blinked as his exit appeared before him, and swiftly moved his truck down the ramp.

Thank God for his family, he thought with a touch of desperation. They were the only thing keeping him human.

He twisted his way through the winding back roads that led home, letting his truck lead the way. His mind was still filled with the look on the subject's face when he'd said his child's name.

Pulling into the driveway, he sat for a moment, mentally stuffing away his misery before dragging himself wearily from the cab; briefcase filled with homework in hand.

He closed his eyes and took a deep breath, and walked up the stairs.

CHAPTER 12

Indie flitted around the house, manic; doing nothing, but moving constantly. Max followed her uneasily for a while, before finally hiding himself under the couch.

She was terrified at what was coming, but it had to be done, and afterward, it would all be okay . . . right?

It had to be.

And she knew she had to be with Jackson, the sooner the better, but how to do it? Indie hated unpleasantness and confrontation, and this was about to be the worst of both worlds.

She looked at the clock. Two agonizing hours before the kids were due home, and fifteen minutes or so after, Will would be here too. She would only have a few moments with the twins before she had to face her husband.

Actually, she was more afraid of her children's reactions, regardless of what Jackson had said about Will's hurt. It was still impossible to believe that Will would be devastated by her loss.

"Maybe I could just sneak out the door tonight after supper," she thought dejectedly. He may never notice.

Well, not until he ran out of clean clothes and groceries, anyway.

Indie looked all around at the home where she had lived for the last two years. Her stuff, his stuff, mingled intimately.

She felt her throat tighten. She was going to start sobbing if she wasn't careful. Instead, she grabbed a small suitcase, and started placing the few items that she really cared about inside. The phone rang, and she ignored it. Indie had no wish to speak to anyone right now.

Well now, that wasn't quite true was it?

She tried an experiment.

Jackson, she whispered from the confines of her brain, feeling supremely stupid.

Yes, love? Was the immediate response. Relief washed over her, making her weak.

Where are you?

I'm not far. If you need me . . .

No, no, it's okay. This is just going to be so awful!

I know. I could try to do this with you, if you wish. Even in thought, he sounded doubtful.

Indie indulged in a fit of panic.

Oh sure. That would be swell.

Indie could just picture that little showdown.

"Hey Will, I'd like you to meet the guy I'm leaving you for. Jackson, William, and William, this is Jackson . . . so nice to meet you!"

Easy Indie, just stop! She heard his dismay. *You're getting hysterical!*

Oh? Does it sound that way to you?

The thought of her impending domestic demise *was* making her want to scratch the skin from her bones.

No, Jackson, I don't think that you showing up would be a good idea at all!

She could feel his sigh echo through her head.

I think you're right. I would hate for things to get . . . out of hand.

Indie shook with fear at the idea of Jackson and Will getting into some sort of brawl. Over her!

It was unthinkable. Her brain spoke to her again.

Hey, Indie, what's it like to trip and fall face-first into the rabbit hole? She gripped her forehead, covering her eyes as she tried to shut off her inner-sarcasm.

But she couldn't even begin to imagine that degree of passion coming from Will, although Indie knew he would be no pushover in the brawling department. He was a well-trained military man, and still in excellent shape. And Will was only thirty-five years old. It suddenly hit her that Jackson was older than Will.

It didn't seem possible.

In comparison to Jackson's youthful appearance, Will was definitely grown, and looked the part; right down to the few gray hairs beginning to sprout around the temples mingling with the blond, and the faintest beginnings of a receding hairline. He was still a very attractive man though, Indie realized.

But even so, how could he compete with someone born to be her perfect match? She had already determined that he could not.

Jackson, please . . . Indie began.

His response was instantaneous. *I won't listen to what takes place tonight, or rather, I won't hear the words. I will, however, feel the emotions . . . I can't escape that, and I will have to be strong enough to suffer your pain with you.*

Indie didn't know how to respond to this, so instead, she asked a question.

Jackson . . . when you said that my senses would not be complete until I was with whom I belonged . . . well, are they complete yet? Laughter.

No, not yet.

Why, then, she wondered to him, *can I hear your thoughts so completely?*

Because, he was responding slowly, *we HAVE made contact, and that begins the transition, but you won't have complete use of your senses, your . . . gifts, if you will, until after the commitment.* Commitment?

Like marriage, you mean?

His thoughts sounded like nervous laughter. *Something like that,* he answered mysteriously.

Okay, Indie thought into her newly discovered messaging system. *I need you to hang up now, because I have to figure out how I will get through this.*

Silence.

Are you there? Absurdly she panicked, even though she had just asked him to leave her thoughts.

I am. I was just thinking how I wish I could do this for you. I can feel your heart breaking, and it goes against every fiber of my being to allow this to happen.

This was too much. Indie was not used to anyone being concerned for her thoughts, feelings or her heart, for that matter.

I will be silent for now, he whispered breezily into her thoughts, *but I am always here.*

Indie heard the bus before it was visible, as it made its way down the street. She felt the squeezing pressure around her heart intensify, and enter into a lightheaded mode. Maybe she was hyperventilating. Consciously, she slowed her breathing.

The bus pulled up in front of the house, and came to a stop with a wheeze. Indie watched as the little feet of her children appeared, visible from under the bus.

First Cassidy's purple high-tops, and then Jake's brown Timberland's locked step as they made their way around, preparing to cross the street.

They walked together, the two blond heads bouncing in unison, backpacks heavy on their little backs. Moving steadily toward the house; toward the heartbreak she had waiting for them.

Some after school special this was.

Indie felt her stomach lurch.

She made an effort to compose her face into what she hoped would be an expression of nonchalance. Cassidy stopped directly in front of her.

"What's wrong, Mommy?" she asked at once.

Well, we're off to an immediate start.

"Let's go inside, baby, okay?" Her voice was shaky, and she coughed to clear it. The twins stole a glance at each other, and followed her into the house.

"All the way in!" She tried to speak in a normal voice. Both children had come to an abrupt halt right inside the doorway.

"Mommy . . ." Cassidy began once more. Indie held up her hand. "No, just wait and listen, okay? Everything is going to be okay, I promise." She pointed at the couch, and they both dragged their feet as they crossed the living room. Jake sniffed the air, and looked around uneasily.

Oh my God. Could they smell him, too? Indie wondered desperately.

Cassidy continued to look at her mother expectantly; her clear, intelligent eyes focused sharply on hers. Indie cleared her throat, and decided on a quick precision cut to open the subject. She would then focus on how to explain *why* Mommy and Daddy were not going to be together any longer.

"Daddy and I are going to be separated. He doesn't know it yet, but it has to be this way, and I will be telling him tonight, but I don't want you to worry, he will always be part of your lives".

Okay. She had thrown it out there in a mad rush.

Indie opened her eyes, not realizing until that moment that she had closed them.

Cassidy was now staring at the floor, but Jake was looking at her in the oddest way. Resigned? She couldn't be sure, but she was afraid to ask.

"Daddy will be very hurt," said Cassidy, in a faint voice. Indie bit her lip, hard.

"You know, I don't want that . . . but there is no other way. Even if I tried to stay with Daddy now, it wouldn't be fair to him." He deserved someone who was truly in love with him . . . or at the very least, someone who had not been swept away into full-blown love by a complete stranger.

"Couldn't you try?" Cassidy asked, miserably.

"No, baby," Indie shook her head sadly. "I can't do that to him." Or myself either, she thought selfishly.

Jake finally spoke. He addressed his words, however, to Cassidy. "You know she's been trying really hard to love Daddy the right way for a long time. Maybe she couldn't do it for a reason." He then looked at his mother.

"Daddy loves her," Cassidy whispered.

"He's never loved her the right way, either!" Jake retorted.

Indie felt the tears spring into her eyes, and felt a rush of overwhelming love for the little boy on her couch.

He knew.

To have the fact that she had never been loved "the right way", blurted out in confirmation to everything she had felt all along, was almost unbearable.

"He loves her more than you think," Cassidy said to Jake. Then looked at Indie. "More than both of you think." She sighed. "He's just not good at showing it, because he just doesn't . . . *see* you clearly!"

Whoa.

Indie backtracked. How did she get here in this conversation with her nine year olds? She had not meant to have a discussion on this level, nor about this sort of thing with them.

"Look, this is not your father's fault . . . it isn't anything he did or did not do." She hesitated. "It's not my fault either, really, but I am afraid that Daddy is not going to see it that way."

"But what will happen to us?" Cassidy asked in a small voice.

"You both will be okay. Daddy and I will have to work out an agreement on handling . . . joint custody arrangements."

This statement made her sick; as if somehow, it made it too real. Indie did not want to think about it. She wished that she could just pack up and run out the door without a second thought, but that wasn't an option with children involved.

Trying to soften the meaning of the words, she knelt in front of her children.

"What I am saying, is that you will not lose either of us. I will do anything I have to do, to make sure that you are still raised by both me *and* Daddy. He will always be a part of our family."

As soon as he can come to terms with that idea.

Indie couldn't bear to see their little faces, crumpled in pain. Mostly, it was Cassidy. Jake seemed sad, but more accepting.

"I just want you to be happy, Mommy!"

More tears.

Indie heard Will's truck pull into the driveway and her intestines twisted around themselves.

"Okay, guys, into your rooms until I call you, please." She hugged them both, and pushed them toward the hallway. Cassidy quickly glanced at Max, who had poked his head out from under the couch. The dog trotted instantly into her room.

Indie knew that Cassidy derived comfort from her pet, and was glad that she had him now. She was probably needing more than a little comforting right now.

Her heart began pounding violently. To shake it off, she drew a deep breath, and then walked to the door. Will walked in and set down his briefcase, looking up in surprise.

"I didn't expect to see you here," he said, looking around.

"Didn't you see my car in the driveway?" Indie asked in a wavering voice.

"Oh, sorry. I guess I didn't notice." He looked exhausted. Distracted. The usual.

Indie tried not to feel annoyed. Will had to be the *most* unobservant person in the history of mankind.

Does my vehicle now have the 'gift of invisibility' also? She thought, exasperated. Indie swallowed her irritation.

How could she be so cruel? She was about to blindside poor Will.

"I need to talk to you right away," she spoke quickly, before he could ask what she was making for dinner. She would start screaming if he continued to act as if nothing was wrong, although obviously, he couldn't know what was about to happen.

"Indie, please. Can I get in the house first?" He sounded tired and a little annoyed.

This hurt. Indie rarely imposed on his time.

Shouldn't he be able to look at my face; see the stress and tension there? Shouldn't he be asking me what's wrong? She thought with despair.

Indie pushed away the resentment. He couldn't help it, could he? He was just being Will.

Fine.

No problem. She could just suck it up, like she always did.

"Yes, put your stuff down and come into the living room, please." She decided that she was going to have to break out her "listen to me" voice.

He shuffled around her and she walked into the living room and sat down on the couch to wait. After a moment, she heard the sound of the shower and clutched at her temples in frustration. He had decided to take a shower while she sat; trying to figure a way to tell him she was leaving him. It was almost funny.

Almost.

Indie sighed, sat back on the couch, and continued to wait. *Jackson,* she whispered silently.

I'm here, was the instant response. She closed her eyes.

Just checking . . . and don't listen to this.

I won't, my love.

And don't leave me, either!

Tight laughter.

Leaving would be impossible, even if I were so inclined, which I am not. Be strong . . . I don't think he is going to take this well.

Don't you know? Indie asked, surprised.

No . . . I have an idea, but my senses are not yet complete either. Oh. Indie thought on that for a moment. She heard the shower shut off, and the stress plowed into her like a dagger thrown from across the room.

Will came into the living room, redressed in sweatpants and a t-shirt, smelling wonderful . . . Calvin Klein's Escape.

One of Indie's favorites. But the reason he owned it, was because she bought it, of course. His sandy blond hair was dark with dampness, and he disarmed her with a smile.

A real one.

"What's up?" Will's voice was light, more relaxed now.

What was going on? Why wasn't he being his normal, distant self? Oh, sure enough, he wasn't about to make this easy for her, was he?

"Um . . . God Will, I don't exactly know where to start," Indie floundered. It was a struggle just to find her voice.

"I guess just spit it out, huh?" he said, still in a good-natured tone. Indie recoiled internally at what she was about to do.

Okay. He was right, actually.

She tried to remember the tactic. A quick precision cut was always better than a slow jagged one, right? Or maybe like ripping off a Band-Aid . . . right before you throw it away.

She was going to die somewhere in the middle of this. She was positive. It was going badly already.

"Will," she had to clear her throat several times and begin again. "Will . . . I . . . I want a divorce."

Oh my God. She did it. Threw it right there on the table.

Will didn't move. He didn't say anything either.

"Did . . . did you hear me?" Indie stammered.

Will lifted his head. He looked confused . . . wary. "No," he said slowly, "I'm not sure that I did."

"I want a divorce," she repeated miserably, ducking her head down a bit, so that she could see his face. A look of wounded comprehension was moving across his features. He looked a little like he was going to be sick right there on his shoes.

It was awful to see.

"Why?" he asked in strained voice.

"Will, please!" Indie choked. Okay, this was a completely reasonable question. Who wouldn't ask *why*, but she didn't want to go there. He looked up into her face, his eyes searching. Disbelief clouded his features.

"*Why!*" He repeated. It was not a question. It was a demand.

"It's complicated." Well, wasn't that an understatement.

"Been thinking about this for a while, have you?" His voice was beginning to take on the thin edge of anger.

Okay, that was better . . . easier for her to deal with than his pain. "Yes," Indie lied awkwardly, looking at the warm tapestry pattern on the couch.

All of this afternoon. It felt like a while.

"And you didn't feel the need to say anything sooner? *Before* you came to this conclusion, huh? Maybe we could have worked on things. Maybe we still can!" Will reached out and grabbed her shoulders, pulling her toward him. He suddenly had a desperate look in his eyes.

Indie was now enjoying the combo meal of horror, with a side of stunned disbelief. She had never dreamed this man capable of feeling any depth of emotion, much less the amount that seemed to be building, right here in front of her.

"Will, no . . . please don't!" She pulled away from him, and stood up. This was rapidly becoming more than Indie was prepared to handle. It looked like Jackson had been right on the money about her husband's reaction.

Will remained seated, leaning slightly forward.

Without looked up at her, hurt glowing in his eyes, and reached his hand slowly in her direction. It felt like a test.

Indie swallowed hard. She lifted her hand shakily to take it, but she had hesitated too long. He dropped his hand to the couch.

"So . . . what, there's no love there at all?" he asked, now looking at the carpet. His voice sounded strange. Indie's heart ached.

"Will, I will always have love for you . . ."

"But not that kind. Right, I get it. Next, you can tell me we will still be 'friends'!" He looked so wounded that his sarcasm could not touch her.

"Let's face it, Will, ours never was a passionate love story, was it?"

"Is that the problem?' he asked roughly. "Not enough passion?" She didn't want to bring the dialogue in that direction, either.

"*Is* there someone else?" he asked suddenly, turning on her with new energy.

Oh, of course he would ask that question!

Funny though, she hadn't even considered the possibility of Will coming to that conclusion.

"I . . . I don't know what to say," Indie stuttered.

"Oh, okay," he spit out the words, "how about YES!" he growled. "Obviously, if that's your response!"

Indie continued to stare at the floor.

"Well, this has just gotten really interesting." Will hurled at her. "So how long *have* you been screwing around?"

"It's not like that!" she cried out hysterically, stung by his assumption.

"Really, Indie? I thought you had more class, but, hey, I've been wrong about things before!"

She couldn't bear this attack, his voice so full of sarcasm, anger and hurt. Telling herself that it was just his pain speaking didn't help.

"I have NOT been 'screwing around', Will!" she shouted. "Although why you would be so shocked if I was, is beyond me. It's not like you've shown any interest in that kind of activity . . . not with *me*, anyway!"

This brought him up short. She had never raised her voice to him, ever. Nor had she complained about their non-existent sex life.

"But you *have* met someone else?" Will pressed, sounding somewhat confused now, and oddly, not responding to the "no sex with me" part Indie had just tossed out there like a live grenade.

Indie sighed and nodded. What was the point of denying it now? And leave it to Will to still ignore important things regarding their relationship, even in the middle of an argument.

"So . . ." he was thinking, speaking slowly. "So, you've met someone . . . but you haven't been having a physical relationship with him?"

"NO!" Indie almost sobbed, "I have had *NO* relationship with him!" Will blinked, trying to understand. He put his head in his hands.

"So let me see if I understand this correctly. You saw someone on the street that you are interested in, and now you're going to dump me, and end our marriage, so that you can pursue a relationship with him?" Indie stared at Will, alarmed at how accurate this ridiculous statement really was.

"That's not . . . *exactly* what happened," she whispered.

"Well, feel free to clarify it for me, Indie," he demanded, exasperated. The odd hoarseness was back in his voice again, making him sound like a stranger. Indie decided at that moment, that she would just tell him, and let him make of it what he would.

"Okay," she took a deep breath. "I met him yesterday, and I fell in love, and I have to be with him!"

There. Insane or not, it was simply the truth.

"You're ending your marriage over a guy you met *yesterday*? I mean, are you fucking *kidding* me?"

Indie shrank back from his out of character use of profanity in her presence as Will fell back on the couch, looking as though he had taken a punch. He looked up at his wife and spoke miserably.

"Well. I guess you really do take me for some kind of idiot, huh?"

Indie sat down next to him, and spoke as gently as she could.

"I know it sounds crazy. I don't understand it myself, but it's true. I think the moment our eyes met, I knew."

"And are you telling me that this jackass feels the same way about you?" he asked in the same dispassionate voice.

Indie flinched at Will's word for Jackson, knowing how absolutely opposite of that description he was, but she could see where Will might feel differently.

"Yes," she answered simply.

"And he knows you are married?"

"Yes," she repeated.

"Jackass." Will confirmed to himself.

With a quick swipe of his hand, Will grabbed Indie's wrist, pulling her down to his eye level. He stared at her; his voice cracked in despair.

"Please, Indie . . . don't count me out . . . not yet!"

Indie's voice deserted her, and she was sickened by the desperate look on his face, but she shook her head sadly. She knew what had to be.

Will sat motionless for several minutes, and then began to shake. Suddenly, he threw his hands over his face and rolled over quickly, so that his knees were on the floor. He buried his face into the sofa cushions, hands crushing the fabric on the sides of the pillows. Indie was horror-stricken and speechless.

She had never seen him shed a tear. Not even at funerals. He'd never even seemed capable. Now, here was this big strong and always in control man, who seemed so indifferent to her existence, shedding tears.

Over *her*.

So Indie did the only thing she could think to do in light of the situation. She joined in by bursting into tears as well.

If I really am some kind of alien creature, she sobbed to herself, *now would be a great time for the Mother ship to send down a tractor beam, and suck me up in to the safe confines of the hold, and hyperspace away with me. Me and Jackson,* she couldn't help adding, guiltily.

Indie put her hand lightly on Will's back, and he startled her by rolling over again swiftly, grabbing her and pulling her tightly against his chest. He was still convulsing with silent tears, but it was slowing.

She allowed him to hold her, and after a moment, she allowed herself to hold him. She wanted to comfort him, and wanted to be comforted; the unaccustomed closeness of his body felt solid and secure.

They stayed this way, locked together for a long time.

Will slowly regained his composure, and sighed. He pushed her back a bit to look at her; the vulnerability in his eyes a completely alien sight.

"I just don't get it. How can you know this is what you want so suddenly?" he asked, brushing her hair out of her face.

"I can't explain it, but I know. I knew as soon as his hand touched mine, that he would give me exactly the kind of love I needed." Indie felt him stiffen instantly at these words.

"Wh . . . what did you say?"

Maybe she was being too blunt . . . too cruel.

He pulled back further and looked at her, seeming to study her in a way that he had never done before. His eyes narrowed slightly, and then widened, with . . . *what?*

Shock? Fear?

Indie wasn't sure.

Something significant had just passed through his brain, that was obvious.

Will stood up abruptly, nearly losing his balance and took a step backward, looking at her like she'd just turned into something coiled and poisonous.

"Oh God . . . maybe . . . maybe I *do* understand," he choked out the words. "Maybe even better than you do."

She didn't know what to make of this statement, and knew she was projecting confusion now. Will's face smoothly shifted expression, and Indie had a sudden, disorienting feeling of air shimmering, like an invisible cloud of something toxic.

She could actually see Will shrinking into himself, his emotions withdrawing inside until they completely vanished. Something similar to watching a leaf swirl around faster and faster until it finally slips down the drain . . . swallowed by a vortex.

For a nauseating moment, it was almost as if Will himself was shrinking, in the way that things get smaller as they move away from you. But it quickly became clear to Indie that what she was seeing was a perfect vision of his emotional retreat.

Warm blood and beating heart replaced with cold stone and crisp detachment.

"I hear you, Indie." his voice saturating her with its icy coolness. "I will give you what you want. Just stay here until we can get this thing . . . all of the details worked out, okay? It'll be easier on the kids, right?"

Suddenly overwhelmed by fear and exhaustion, couldn't argue with him now. She just wanted to crawl into bed and try to thaw.

And pretend to sleep.

"Sure, Will. You're right." Indie answered numbly.

"And Will, just so we're clear, I don't want to take the kids from you. I want you to stay in their lives just as much as you are now. We can work it out."

Will's eyes took on a narrowed glint that made her instinctively very uncomfortable.

"That's really good that you feel that way, Indie. Really . . . very good."

His voice was low and quiet, and set off every danger alarm she had. Indie's hand curled around her belly now, trying to hold everything in.

What was that Miss Maggie had said yesterday? She had the gift of "invisibility?" Well, wouldn't that come in handy right about now? If only she could simply vanish on the spot. How nice that would be.

"Go lie down, Indie. I'll get dinner for the kids."

She looked at him, uncertainly. Will blew out his breath, as if he had been holding it.

"Really, I'll take care of this. You go on to bed . . . I just want to think right now, okay?"

He wanted to think? Well, she didn't.

Indie wanted to sleep.

Therefore, she did the next best thing. She walked into the bedroom, crawled under the covers and closed her eyes, listening to the uneven racing of her heart. She replayed every word, every nuance of the awful scene that had just taken place.

Her entire body felt sore, as if she had gone a round or two with a prizefighter. As if her hammering heart had actually bruised her. She pressed her hand to her chest.

Indie was uneasy and sickened about how it had ended, with Will's abrupt emotional disappearing act.

Then his cold words spoken afterwards.

It felt like a tactical maneuver, meant to throw her off balance.

Well, it worked. Indie shivered.

She suddenly felt a little afraid, although she knew of no specific threat. Will was trained to be a very dangerous man, she knew, but she had never had the slightest fear that he would ever hurt her, under any circumstances.

Indie also knew, however, that you never *really* get to know a person until you try to leave them. Very normal people sometimes did very crazy things in the midst of a break up.

She had seen it. Hadn't she worked the ER enough times when an unfortunate girlfriend or wife was brought in, thanks to the handy work of someone who "loved" them?

Indie shook it off. Somehow, she just could not work up that kind of fear against Will.

Are you with me, Jackson? She threw the question out into the air, wordlessly.

Do you need me? He responded instantly.

No, please . . . . Not yet! She panicked again.

It's okay, he reassured her. *I'll wait. Please, try to rest.*

Indie was oddly comfortable already with this crazy means of communication. Even though if a friend had confided in her just yesterday, that she and her boyfriend just happened to communicate telepathically, Indie would have gently led her to the nearest couch, and then called to have her quietly collected by the guys with butterfly nets.

She heaved an exhausted sigh, and thought about how twenty-four hours can change a person's perspective.

And life.

Then the weight in her heart commanded her attention again.

CHAPTER 13

William's Gift

Indie continued to lie still for the next several hours. She heard Will in the kitchen, making dinner for the kids. The smell of cooking filled the air.

Hamburger Helper, she guessed. This was his one and only recipe. The kids did not like it much, but they would eat it just the same.

"Are you okay, Daddy?" she heard Cassidy ask, concern heavy in her sweet little voice.

Guilt took another bite out of Indie's belly. Will's hesitation was brief, but noticeable.

"Everything is going to be just fine, okay? Try not to worry, baby." "I'll try, Daddy . . . just don't . . ." Cassidy hesitated, doubtfully. Both Will and Indie waited for the rest of her words.

"Don't what, Cassidy?" Will asked.

"Nothing." It was softer than a whisper.

Indie heard no more conversation after that. Just the sounds of forks scraping plates, water running, and other insignificant noises that seemed incongruous after the emotional stress of the day.

So . . . I just told my husband of ten years, that I wanted a divorce. I told him I was in love with another man. A man I met yesterday! How ridiculous that must sound!

Indie agonized. Her whole world had just been upended. Funny how even when expecting the worst, one can still be surprised by its brutality.

My babies. My poor kids. How will we work this out? She wondered.

She knew it could be done.

Happens all the time. Joint custody, right?

Would she and Jackson move into a little house on the other side of town, and pass the kids back and forth on weekends? Somehow, she just knew this was not going to be the case. Indie had no answers, and wasn't ready to think about it now.

It just hurt too much.

The sounds in the kitchen began to taper off, and she heard bathwater running. Indie still hadn't moved when she heard the bedroom door open, but she knew it was Will.

He was being very quiet for a change, but she felt sure that if she opened her eyes, she would see him staring at her. She didn't move. He sighed, and she felt his movements as he walked around the Queen-sized bed, his shoes making creaking noises on the hardwood floors.

She heard a series of soft mechanical clicks, and wondered what he was up to, but didn't dare open her eyes. She couldn't talk to him again.

Not yet.

His heavy footsteps moved toward the French doors, and Indie wondered if he were looking out at the mountains, trying to find comfort. There was a blast of air exhaled on a heavy sigh as Will briskly spun about and walked out through the bedroom door, and he closed it softly behind him.

Indie could feel his emotions, but not his thoughts.

High stress.

Well, that was to be expected, right? She listened as he made his way down the hallway and into his office, where he closed the door. Now it was Indie's turn to exhale. She had been holding her breath again. She had to remind herself that air was a good thing.

She heard the kids get out of their bath, and moments later, the door opened again. Her senses immediately told her that it was Jake who came into the room first.

Warm and damp, he smelled of Paul Mitchell's "Baby Don't Cry" shampoo. He stood next to his mother, and she opened one eye. He smiled.

"I knew you were awake!"

"Good night, Little Son." Indie had called him "Little Son" forever. *My boy. My little puppy,* thought Indie, sadly.

"Good night, Mommy." He gave her hugs and kisses. Cassidy came in next, and looked at her with worried eyes.

"Good night, baby," called Indie, softly.

"'Night, Mommy." Cassidy hugged her mother tightly. She then gave Indie a long look, and seemed about to speak, but then, changed her mind. Both children ran out the door.

But Jake looked back. "I want to stay with you!"

"Don't worry, pup," Indie tried to smile. "We'll work it out."

He closed the door and she sighed. Yes, she really was going to have to deal with those particulars. *And very soon*, she shuddered. Indie rolled over and closed her eyes.

She lay there for hours, before opening them again. Knowing she was alone in the room, Indie glanced at the clock next to the bed. The green digital glow read 3:15 AM.

Will never stayed up this late. He left for work very early, and he had always been pretty needy about getting his "eight hours" a night. Something didn't feel right.

But what did she expect? Did she really think he would simply crawl into bed next to her, as if nothing out of the ordinary had happened?

Was he distraught, she wondered as she rolled onto her back? Maybe he'd just crashed on the little bed in the office. She should check on him.

An awful image of him hanging from one of his ties in his office flashed through her head. She sat bolt upright.

Jackson! Indie screamed, silently.

He hasn't hurt himself, Indie.

Are you sure? She asked, desperately.

He is very quiet, and contemplating something. Something pretty painful for him. Jackson responded. *His emotions are a wreck, but I think he's trying to reach a decision.*

Oh my God, Jackson, Indie wailed into her pillow. *Why did it have to happen this way?*

It took a moment for him to respond. *I . . . I am the reason that this has happened. I'm so sorry for what my presence is putting you through. I would never have intentionally caused others such pain, but I had no choice but to seek you out. You were always the missing piece of my life, and the most awful part was, that I knew you were out there! I didn't have the luxury of blissful ignorance!*

His thoughts sounded weary, exhausted even.

He continued.

I tried to be willing to let you go; to exist somehow without you, rather than destroy your world. But would you really have preferred to continue on with your life as it was, never knowing the truth . . . never knowing why you had to struggle all the time, just to get through each day?

The words had gained a little heat.

Great.

Just great. She was hurting him too, now.

No, no, please, don't think that. I'm so glad you came to me. It was the right thing to do, and it will all be okay in the end. I don't know how much longer I could have kept up the pretense, she pleaded silently. *Apparently I wasn't doing the job so well, anyway!*

Okay, love. Keep calm, Jackson whispered into her thoughts, *and go to him. He's just made up his mind . . .*

*   *   *

Jackson pulled his car up just past Indie's house, and slid it carefully to the side of the road. His hands were shaking, and the fury in him was stoked to an all-time high.

What would be so wrong, he ranted silently, *about just kicking the door into toothpicks, snatching up Indie and her children, and taking off with them?*

The man in that house was about to drive a virtual stake through the heart of the one he loved.

But I can stop this . . . I could get them all out of there to a safe place.

He would just love to see Will try to stop him.

Oh yes, he *really* would.

Jackson tried not to sigh with contentment as he visualized himself relieving the man of the burden of his head, and any other body parts that he could easily rip away.

He came back with a jolt.

That was sick. Sick and unprecedented.

As Jackson perched on the rear bumper of his car, there was not a single outward indicator that such violent ideas were joyfully tango-ing through his mind. His face held all the serenity that he knew he was supposed to be feeling on the inside.

I can control it. I can be strong . . .

He chanted his mantra, and swallowed a deep gulp of remorse.

The Elders knew best, obviously. How dare he even flirt with the notion of insubordination?

What made the whole thing that much more difficult, was the fact that Jackson was well aware of another factor in this unfolding drama.

The right to act of his own volition. The Elders would not move against him. He would simply have to endure the repercussions of altering someone's destiny.

Sometimes, the repercussions were not so bad.

And sometimes they were unthinkable.

Jackson decided that he did not have the gumption to spin that roulette wheel.

He remained seated, motionless now, listening and waiting for the moment he knew was coming. He would be there for Indie immediately. For now, all he could do was wait for her heart to be broken, and then do his best to mend it for her.

*   *   *

Indie climbed out of bed, and made her way down the hallway, listening for any sound coming from the office. She could hear the hum of the computer, and a scratching sound.

Pen on paper, perhaps? She tapped on the door, hesitantly.

No answer. The feeling of unease intensified. She tapped again, a little louder. Still no response. Slowly, she pushed open the door.

Indie found Will slouched in his chair, legs straight out in front of him in the cramped room, nearly disappearing under the twin bed that rested against the far wall. His arm was thrown carelessly onto the small oak computer desk.

With a pen in his hand, Will made swirling patterns on a notebook with no conscious thought.

He looked lost.

Indie pushed the door open wider, and then stepped inside. Will kept his eyes on the deep blood-red dust ruffle that encircled the base of the guest bed.

"Will . . . ?" she began, uncertainly. He slowly raised his eyes to hers. His expression was one of disbelief. Like he'd been told that a loved one, while just leaving his house, had died at the end of his street. Indie had expected him to be upset; confused even, but something here was all wrong. She could feel it.

He spoke lazily.

"What's up Indie, can't sleep?" There was a strange edge to his words, though he spoke softly. He didn't sound like anyone she knew. The voice was too cold . . . professionally detached.

"Well, no. Not really," she answered, confused.

Without moving, and in the same soft, disembodied voice, Will asked, "How *do* you sleep at night, Indie?"

She didn't know what to say to that. Did he want her to confess that her guilt would forever keep her up nights?

Okay. She felt guilty.

Mission accomplished.

Will watched her face as these thoughts scrolled through her head.

"It wasn't a rhetorical question. I mean, do you sleep okay at night?" She shrugged. "Okay enough, I guess."

"Really?" He spun his body around suddenly to face her, and looked at her with weary, but steady eyes. "Do you *really*, Indie?" he repeated.

A sense of unease began to build in her belly. What was he asking? It was becoming clear that this was not a random question. Will was not making polite conversation, she knew. He seemed to be on a mission.

—

"What exactly *are* you asking me, Will?" Indie crossed her arms, and looked back at him, trying her best to be strong . . . to hide the fear.

Will began a slow, hypnotic rocking back and forth in his chair, never taking his eyes off of her.

"Not a good subject?" He moved so that both hands were in front of him, and he held the pen between them, as though he were about to pull it apart, but his face was calm.

"Okay," he said, in the same soft conversational voice. "Let's talk about something else. Tell me more about this guy that you fell in love with at first *touch*!"

Indie didn't miss his inflection on the word "touch", and she winced. "Will . . . don't," Indie began.

"Oh yeah, I *really* want to know." Will's voice lost a little of the emotionless void he'd created. The anger seeped through his words, but he quickly contained them, and pulled back into neutral territory. "What's he like, Indie? Is he tall, dark and handsome?"

Yes, well, that did just about sum him up, didn't it? She shook her head.

"Just *stop* it, William!"

"What kind of work does he do? Where does he live? What kind of car does he drive? I think I have a right to know these things about a guy who may eventually become my children's stepfather, don't I?"

He was peppering her with his queries, and suddenly, Indie felt very foolish. It seemed as though Will knew that she didn't have the answers to these very basic questions; and the stepfather idea, well, that had not crossed her mind at all. She just had not thought that far yet.

"Let us take one thing at a time, my love," Jackson had said to her, and she was taking this to heart.

"I don't feel comfortable talking to you about this, Will." Indie's arms found themselves wrapped tightly around her belly again. "I don't even feel comfortable thinking about it right now."

"Oh, I'm so sorry. I don't want to make *you* feel uncomfortable!" His tone was solicitous. Will's eyes had still not left hers, and his focus was disconcerting. Indie shifted her own eyes to his computer, just to break the contact.

She noticed then, that on his computer screen was a very close photograph of her face. Her eyes were closed in the picture, and she realized that this picture had been taken very recently. Like, maybe earlier this evening, when she had heard the strange clicking noises when Will had come into the bedroom.

Indie moved toward the screen, and bent to examine it more closely.

Will swiveled around in his chair, as if to keep her right in front of him, still focusing on her intently. Indie glanced at him out of the corner of her eye, having gotten a strange but fleeting impression that Will did not want to turn his back to her because . . . because he was *afraid* to do so.

She shrugged off this ridiculous notion. What on earth could Will have to fear from *her*?

Uneasily, she returned to her image on the screen. Surrounding her picture was a complicated series of graphs, indecipherable to her.

"You've always been so pretty." Will spoke suddenly, watching her expression. "But you look too young, though. I've been noticing lately, that people are looking at me all disapprovingly when we're together. They can't decide if I've robbed the cradle, or if you are my kid!"

He laughed, harshly. "Wouldn't everyone be surprised to know that *you* are actually the cradle robber?

"I had almost decided that I was going to have to get a tattoo, or maybe have a special t-shirt made to wear when I was with you, running a disclaimer; 'she's the old one, really'!" His mouth smiled, but his eyes remained serious.

Focused.

"So, how old is your boyfriend?"

Indie groaned inwardly. Will was not giving up.

"Forty," she clipped out, crossing her arms again.

Her sympathy for him was waning, in light of his obvious determination to back her into some kind of corner. If he wanted to hear it, then fine. She was all in.

"Forty?" His eyes widened in mock disbelief. "Hell, he must look like your *dad* . . . maybe even your grandfather!"

Indie searched Will's face. He was building up to something, she was certain. However, he couldn't know about the Society Member thing, so what could it be?

"No, actually. He looks . . . like I do. Pretty youthful, I would say". "Really? That's a little unusual, don't you think?" Will asked, innocently.

"No, I don't!" She was starting to get frustrated. Did he really think she was such an anomaly?

A freak?

"Plenty of people look young for their years . . . it's not so odd!"

"When's his birthday?" he asked, sharply.

"*What?*" Indie sucked in her breath.

Now she was beyond uneasy. She was slipping into terror.

"Why . . . why would you ask me *that*?"

"When was he born, Indie?' His voice was softer now than it had been since she had come in, but he had a command in it that was compelling her to answer his questions.

"June 26th, 1968," she sighed.

"Wow," he responded, but obviously unsurprised. "Now why *does* that sound so familiar?"

She stared back at Will, and his eyes tightened on her face. Indie gasped as the realization hit her.

It was so obvious now. Why hadn't she caught on more quickly? Will wasn't playing games.

She was being interrogated, and by a master. Every question he asked was the foundation of a wall being built, her answers the mortar.

And every subject was carefully thought out, in order to flow to the next. Everything from his casual tone, calm manner, and nonchalant body language was a ruse. Here she had been thinking that this was just to get a little revenge for today . . . a chance to hurt her back and make her feel guilty and uncomfortable.

No, this was something much, much more. Indie's alarms earlier in the night had been correct.

Danger.

Her eyes remained frozen on his impassive face.

"Does he '*complete*' you, Indie? Is he your perfect . . . *specimen* of a man?" Will's voice was heavy with sarcasm.

She noticed another break in his emotionless façade as he spoke the words. He shook his head slightly, as if to knock loose the unwanted feelings and pressed on.

"Would you say it's like he was *born* just for you? A perfect match to you, physically? Emotionally? Intellectually? Maybe you could say he was your . . . *Equal?*"

He whispered the words as he leaned forward, eyes narrowing, watching her reaction.

Indie felt a reeling dizziness. Her legs vanished from beneath her, and she tumbled forward. Will's hands flashed out automatically to catch her, but then he very deliberately withdrew them, allowing her to collapse into a heap on the floor.

She couldn't move.

Or breathe. He could not possibly know this, and yet he'd said it—said the very word—*Equal!* What was happening?

"You know," he began speaking in a light and friendly tone, as if nothing out of the ordinary had happened. "you've never asked me about my work. I'll bet you've never even wondered to yourself, 'just what *does* William do all day long in that boring old office'?"

Indie didn't answer. She still couldn't speak.

Will continued in a pleasant conversational tone, talking to the pen in his hands.

"We have a kind of running joke at our office. We call it the 'Department of Myths and Legends', because what we do is investigate those kinds of things. And to top it off, we agents ourselves, have become something of a little mystery . . . the fodder of urban legends. It's amazing what a preference for a certain color in clothing, vehicles and choppers can achieve in the minds of the masses, isn't it?

"Men in black!" Will rolled his eyes in an exaggerated fashion, as if they were both in on some private joke.

"A lot of the other agents in other security branches think it's funny; at least the ones who believe we actually exist."

His expression returned to dead serious now. "But, we have a very crucial job. In the interest of homeland security, the Government is always conducting investigations. Sometimes on things that seem outrageous in their improbability.

"We follow up on every mythical beast sighting, strange lights in the sky . . . UFO's". His eyes darted down to Indie's for a brief second, as if to gauge her reaction.

She was silent.

"That part of my job is fascinating to me. I've always been interested in things like that. All mysteries, great and small . . . ghosts, ancient worlds, full of mysticism. Unfortunately, or maybe I should say *fortunately* for the world, most of what we investigate proves to be explainable in a very unexciting way. True proof of anything 'otherworldly' is usually very elusive. Sometimes, though, we get lucky.

"About five years ago, six agents brought in an old man. They insisted that they had captured someone who was not of this world. I flew out that day to see this 'person', for lack of a better word."

Will paused to drop his pen and pick up one of Jake's small, metal matchbox race cars that had been precariously balanced on the edge of the desk. He gripped the car tightly, spinning the rear wheels of the toy car with his thumb as he continued.

"This person . . . he just looked like an ordinary old man to me. I thought they were crazy."

As if by accident, he looked down at Indie, and her eyes shot to his. He looked quickly away before speaking again.

"It's funny. We didn't live here at the time, but the facility where he was kept is close to the Canadian border. I've been studying him for the last two years, as best I can."

Will shifted in his chair, displaying for the first time, some sort of discomfort with the conversation.

"It's horrible actually, the way they've kept him. He was continuously under a chemical restraint. It took ten times what should have been necessary to incapacitate him, but once he was under, the scientists took over. They took measurements of his facial features, and drew his blood . . . lots of it. They ran every test imaginable, and everything came back perfect."

He looked down at her again. "Too perfect. It was as if this person wasn't human, but *superhuman*. He was too strong. It had taken six of our hardest core agents to bring him down, when he looked like just an old man, albeit, an old man in extremely good shape.

"But the testing continued. We knew we had something truly unusual when we began examining his brain activity. He had extraordinary mental abilities. He was telepathic. He could read our thoughts, that much was clear. However, he was defiant . . . and would refuse to speak for months at a time, although we knew that he could. He was observed before capture, talking and laughing with a woman who looked similar in age; a woman who he made sure managed to escape by actively engaging all six agents while she fled.

"He used to sit, eyes closed for hours, with the encephalogram sensors attached to every part of his scalp.

"The scientists had shaved his head to fit him with permanent sensors." Will winced, as if the memory was difficult for him, but continued.

"The readings were off the chart. It was as if his brain was in overdrive; in constant conversation, but nothing we could hear."

Will suddenly paled at what he was about to reveal next. He stared at the floor once more as he spoke.

"They began more intrusive testing, opening him up for exploratory surgeries, needle biopsies to the brain . . . horrible things.

"We learned the hard way that he could also move objects with his mind when he used telekinetic force to hurl an entire shelving unit across the room, injuring several of the scientists. It was this that made them realize that they had to increase his sedation, and keep him disoriented. He was also under twenty-four hour armed guard.

"He began to speak, but was so drugged and out of it by this time, that what he said could never be trusted as reality. I questioned him myself, many times. When I asked his age, he laughed, and said that he had seen nearly three centuries!"

Will studied the computer screen now, as he spoke.

"Now, most people would dismiss this as nonsense, but in our line of work, everything is a fact, to be verified, or discounted later as fiction. I took notes on every single statement the man made. I listened as he called to 'her', someone he called his *Equal*. In his more lucid moments, he told me how the relationship worked, and that he and 'the others' were here to show us the way, and to prevent evil and negativity from destroying mankind.

"I learned that he believed he was descended from some sort of 'super race', although he refused to elaborate on his origins. This is why the government

Katherine Whitley

got involved, as legends make mention of beings similar to this man from the beginning of recorded history."

Will sighed as if repeating lines from a script that he had been forced to read a thousand times.

"Anything claiming to be of a super or superior origin has to be considered a threat, and that threat needs to be studied and evaluated."

Indie continued to simply stare at Will in a vacant trance; hearing everything, yet unable to react.

She didn't blink as he went on.

"At the very least, scientists are interested in studying their unusual immunity from disease and illness, and seemingly perfect function of all body systems, not to mention their mental abilities. Although he was the first and only . . . *one* . . . I ever saw, I later learned that there have been several captured in the past, all over the world."

Will leaned back in his chair, hesitating. His expression held in it his obvious distaste for the words to follow.

"The captive's mental state deteriorated rapidly, with the increased testing. He was, in essence, being dissected alive, and I suppose no one could endure that forever, although he lasted longer than I would have expected. He had been in what you might call a persistive vegetative state for the last few months, with no brain wave activity at all. That is, until yesterday."

Indie looked up at him suddenly. He had paused, quite deliberately, after he said this, and was looking at her again with appraising eyes. "Why," she whispered. "What happened yesterday?"

Will's eyes were burning straight through hers.

"Yesterday," Will leaned forward, "he spoke! He opened his eyes, and laughed, looking right through all of the people at his bedside. He just said something like 'speak now my darling, or forever hold your peace! Our time is near . . . '

"He said it like it was some kind of specific direction. Then he closed his eyes again. No one had a clue what this could mean, and he could not be compelled to speak or even open his eyes again. He died very shortly after."

Indie's thoughts shot straight to Maggie. It was becoming pretty clear that this had been her *Equal.*

Equals are born at the same time . . . and, it seemed, they died at the same time. How horrible, to think . . . to *know* that she had been forced to live without him for five long years, sharing in the pain inflicted upon him.

It made her sick.

Will was still staring down at her, and she slowly climbed to her feet.

She tried to pretend that this had nothing to do with her. Indie felt an instinctive need to try to protect the Society, even though she also knew that her efforts were pointless.

"Why . . . why are you telling *me* this?" she faltered.

"Still want to play games, do you, Indie?" He sounded so far away, that Indie felt compelled to look down at him, just to see if he was still in his chair.

Will gestured to the computer screen.

"It's all in the math, really," he shrugged. "It was right here in front of me, all these years, and I never saw it. I guess I *have* been a bad husband to you, never really studying your face, as a man should. A husband should have the map of his wife's face committed to memory, and in great detail."

Indie looked back at her picture on the screen. Miss Maggie's words floated through her head . . ."*It's as plain as the nose on your face* . . ."

Will spoke again, startling her out of her flashback.

"You might as well know that since our latest captive Society member has . . ." he paused, "*expired*, every agent has been given the priority assignment to capture another."

Expired.

How impersonal this sounded. Dehumanizing.

As if the man had been a gallon of milk, or a coupon clipped from the paper. Indie stared at him, speechless. "You . . . you wouldn't . . ."

She couldn't finish.

"No?" he asked, thoughtfully. "Why wouldn't I?" He looked past her as he spoke now, and focused on the wall behind her.

"I have to remain committed to my job, my duty to my country."

"What about me, Will? Am I meaningless to you? No commitment now, is there?"

Will struck her with his glare. "Don't you *dare* talk to *ME* about commitment. You do not want to go there, do you?"

Indie felt moisture seep into her eyes, and once again, there was a break in the impassive look that Will had kept in place throughout this ordeal. He looked down again at the toy car that had become one with his hand.

"What do you want me to do, then?" Indie pleaded in a whisper

"I want you to run, Indie," he whispered back, not meeting her eyes again. "I want you to grab what you can, and start running. Consider it a parting gift for you and your . . . *Equal*." His words were bitter, but his voice was calm.

A running start? Indie's mind raced. "But, the kids . . . I can't just leave . . ."

"Oh, but you will," he cut her off.

He was on his feet, backing her against the wall in one fluid motion. "You will always be looking over your shoulder from tonight forward, and with good reason!" He rested his hands on either side of her, speaking harshly.

"You will not bring my children into danger like that . . . how could you even want to?"

Indie felt the tears rush out. "No . . . no I wouldn't" she agreed in a broken voice. "I would never want them in harm's way, but," she choked on a sob, "they're my babies!"

She ventured a look at him again.

Will's face was hard, but as he looked into her distraught, tearful eyes, he seemed to soften for just a moment.

"Go tell them goodbye," he said in a slightly less angry tone. "I'll give you five minutes."

She drew a deep, broken breath. Five minutes?

To say goodbye to your children?

Indie felt the sobs rushing up into her chest, and her throat stretched as if she would never be able to speak again. She hugged her arms around her body as he opened the door and thrust her into the hallway. She looked back at him.

"Please, don't let them think that this was my choice, that I didn't want them!" Indie begged. "I can't bear it if they're hurt like that!"

Will nodded imperceptibly, but whispered again, "five minutes."

She turned and ran down the hall to Cassidy's room first. She sat up as Indie rushed in. Max, curled next her, looked up and growled softly. Indie scooped her daughter up into her arms, and buried her face in her silky hair.

She pulled down great lungfuls of her scent.

"I love you baby, and I will see you again, I promise, but I have to leave now, to keep you safe. I can't explain it to you right now, but I'm sure Daddy will answer all of your questions and I know he will take good care of you!" Her voice was choking, closing off.

Cassidy hugged her back, bravely hiding her tears, trying to comfort her mother.

"I know, Mommy. Don't cry. We'll be okay, and . . . we'll get to be with you soon, I know it!"

Indie stroked her hair, and laid her back down on the bed. Fighting for control, she kissed her forehead, and ran for the door. She looked back to blow one final kiss. Cassidy blew one back, and Indie caught it. "Goodbye, baby," she sobbed, and ran for Jake's room.

He was sitting up on the edge of his bed, his face streaked with tears. "Take me with you, Mommy, please! You're going to *need* me!" he pleaded. Indie's heart shattered into a thousand pieces.

"I want to take you with me so badly!" she said as she wrapped her arms around his tiny body. "And I already need you, but you have to stay here. It's not safe for you just now. Daddy can explain."

Indie had no idea what Will planned to tell them, but she was going to make sure that they knew that this wasn't her choice. She smoothed Jake's hair, and cradled his face in her hands.

"I don't care, Mommy, I can be brave!" cried her heartbroken little boy. The last shard of her heart dropped and hit her belly with a hollow sound that she could actually hear.

"I know you are brave, and that is what I am going to ask you to be . . . for me, okay?" He looked up at her, shaking his blond head.

"I need you to be here for Cassidy. What would she do without you? And . . . and take care of Daddy, too. You know he doesn't know what to do around this house."

She tried to smile, and ended up just clenching her teeth, in a frightening sort of way.

Jake sighed.

"Son . . . little Son, *please*," Indie begged him, "just look out for each other, okay? This will not be forever. I will find a way to be with you soon, just trust in that, okay?" She pulled his face up close to hers. "I have faith that this is going to work out, okay?"

He said nothing.

"Jake, you have to have faith with me . . . alright?"

"Okay, Mommy . . . but I love you!" He wrapped his little arms around her, and the tears fell fresh and hard.

"And you know I love you, my Son-shine." She heard Will's heavy step outside the door.

"Okay, now," she pushed him back down on the bed, and kissed his whole face again. "Be my strong Little Son."

Her voice broke, and she turned and ran out the door—forced to leave her whole world behind.

Will had her small suitcase in his hands. "I found this in the closet. I suppose you did plan ahead, a little," he said stiffly, as he held it out to her.

Indie took it and drew a deep shuddering breath.

"So, will you be coming after me, then?"

He shrugged, looking down at the floor. "All of us will be," he answered, in a flat monotone.

"You would really help them hunt me down, so they can dissect and study me, too?" she asked, icily.

Will didn't answer. He looked down into her eyes with a haunted expression, touched her face lightly, and then dropped his hand.

"Start running, Indie," he said softly, and pulled her toward the front door, never taking his eyes off hers. He opened the door, lifted Indie up into his arms for a millisecond, and gave her limp body a tight squeeze. She felt a shudder rip through his body, and he dropped her onto the front porch. He looked at her for one long moment.

Glancing around toward the road, his eyes hardened.

"Call your . . . *man*. I have some plans to make," he said in an empty voice, as he turned to shut the door. He looked back once, hesitated, and whispered, "Don't go back to your work again." Will slammed the door in her face.

The sound made her jump. The symbolism was perfect, as a chapter in her old life came to an abrupt end.

A chapter slammed shut, like what used to be her front door.

Indie stood for a moment, shaken and at a loss for what to do next. She had no purse, no keys . . . no phone.

Her hair was disheveled and her eyes were swollen and red. She knew she was more than the usual train wreck . . . more like a nuclear disaster. The sound of a car pulling into the driveway barely caught her attention.

A sleek bronze colored vehicle came into view, out of the rapidly dissipating blackness.

Come, Indie, let me take you home . . . The weary voice that entered her head was a balm to her torn and jagged nerves. She leaped into the car, and buried her face into the soft leather jacket that was covering Jackson's strong shoulders.

She let the tears flow, while breathing deep gulps of his warm and comforting scent. Her entire body was shaking, and Jackson wrapped his right arm protectively around her, as he drove with illegal haste, to where, Indie had no idea.

She couldn't bring herself to care now.

He kissed the top of her head, keeping his eyes on the road, as well as on the rear view mirror. Indie had no concept of time or distance. She was completely numb.

Only when Jackson turned off the main road, did she look around, becoming aware of her surroundings. The sun was starting to climb its way up from behind the mountains; a very faint purple aura beginning. They were in an area where the forest was thick, heading up a very steep incline.

The road finally leveled out and turned into more of a dirt path as they wound their way through the trees.

In what appeared to be a large clearing, and nothing more, Jackson slowed and parked the car. He leaped out, and came around to open Indie's door.

She didn't move. He dropped to his knees, taking both of her hands.

"It's going to be okay, Indie. Please, come with me." His voice was pleading. Indie stared at his beautiful face.

Of course. I would go with you anywhere, she thought, wearily. She tried to step out of the car, but her legs seemed to be missing. Jackson remained kneeling beside her, watching her with anxious eyes.

"Sorry," Indie spoke, wanting to reassure him. "I'm just waiting for my legs to re-form into a solid."

Wordlessly, he picked her up like a child and carried her forward. But being held so closely against his warm hard body was making her feel dizzy and out of breath.

"I think I can walk now, really," Indie panted, after a few yards, and extracted herself from his arms. She couldn't think straight when he held her that way.

"Where are we?" she asked.

"We are at my home, which is now also yours!" He was watching her carefully.

Indie looked all around, but could see no house.

"What, are you homeless . . . you live in the woods?" She laughed shakily, but really, the questions that Will had asked about him came into sharp relief in her mind. Indie really did not know. He smiled now, and took her hand.

"Walk with me," he said, in his most irresistible voice. They walked toward what looked like a sharp drop-off at the clearing's edge. She was surprised to see steps leading down the face of the cliff. These led to a level walkway where Indie saw two huge windows and a large wooden door built into the wall of the cliff.

Jackson opened the door and swung her up into his arms again. She yelped in surprise, and clung to him, aware of the cliff's edge being disturbingly near.

Indie closed her eyes in a panic; she didn't care for high places. He carried her inside, and shut the huge door with his elbow. Only then did Indie feel it was safe to look up.

She was set down lightly, and Jackson kissed her hand. He then narrowed his eyes at her.

"I'm offended. Do you *honestly* think I would ever let anything happen to you?" Indie looked at him anxiously, but he smiled at her, his eyes soft.

He did not look offended at all.

CHAPTER 14

The end of the pretense

Indie looked all around at the spacious, cabin-like great room where Jackson had brought her. It was beautiful, with the entire front wall facing out of the cliff constructed of some sort of light deflecting glass. There was no glare, but a perfect view of the valley below.

The room was warm and cozy, with large overstuffed furnishings. An enormous stone fireplace, complete with a walk-in hearth, was in the center of the room.

However, even as Indie was taking in her surroundings, noting that the house was stunning, the test of her inner strength overwhelmed her; an emotional hit and run. Without even realizing it, she began to tilt forward.

Like a cat, Jackson sprang, catching her in his arms, and dragged her to a suede chair that was oversized and indulgent in its comfort. He settled into it, tucking her tightly against his chest.

She could feel the fluid strength of his body as he arranged her into a comfortable position. Finally, safe and secure, Indie began to wail. The force of her sobs shook them both, but he just held on, moving in a gentle rocking motion, stroking her hair, allowing her to release the pent up emotions of the night. Her tears soaked his shirt, but he didn't seem to mind.

After a solid hour of sobbing, and having gotten past the hiccupping and shuddering breaths that followed, Indie became dimly aware of the sun's position in the sky outside his wall of glass.

It had burst over the horizon, unleashing intense fiery colors, and as it had the day before, it brought with it an unusual amount of heat for the season. She became aware of Jackson casting uneasy glances out toward the flaming orb, and was surprised at how late it had become.

—

"What time is it?" she asked hoarsely, sitting up in his lap. He held out a slim, silver rectangle.

"Time for you to give your resignation, effective immediately." His voice was quiet, holding back an emotion that it was obvious he did not want her to see.

"What's this?" Indie looked at the object he held out to her.

"It's a digital recorder. You will have to give your resignation via recorded statement. I will then transmit your recording to an out-of-state phone. It will be sent to your employer from there."

Indie met his eyes.

"So is this how it's going to be now? Life on the run?"

"Not exactly on the run," he answered reassuringly. "Just a different way of doing things. You learn never to leave a trail that leads directly back to you, when the men in mourning suddenly take an interest in you."

Men in mourning?

"The guys that like to wear black suits, all in the name of 'Homeland Security'." Jackson answered her thoughts.

He ran his free hand through Indie's hair, smoothing it down gently and studied her, his own eyes heavy with the weight of her burden. Indie fought down the choking need to sob again.

"Would you like some privacy, to formulate what you will say?" he asked. "No. I really don't want to move. Not just yet." He leaned back as she took the recorder, focusing his gaze on the expanse of glass in front of him.

Indie drew a deep breath, and pressed the button.

"Hi, this is Indie Taylor. I'm sorry to have to do this so suddenly, and in this manner, but I have to give my resignation, effective immediately. I obviously would have liked to give notice, but, unfortunately, it just was not possible. Thank you." She clicked the machine off.

"Good job." Jackson smiled, quickly returning his attention to her face. "Yeah, I thought I would keep it short and sweet," Indie sighed. His voice was soft, compelling.

"Yes, that is usually the best way to break things to people, so I've come to understand."

His face was serious. "When you are feeling more up to it, we will begin the question and answer session that I know you are dying to lead, alright love?"

His voice was sending shivers up her spine. She could barely focus on the words he spoke, simply because of the sound of his voice when he spoke them.

Indie frowned. She was going to have to learn to overcome her lack of concentration, because she *did* want him to tell her everything, and how could she absorb any information if she continued to swoon like an idiot every time he opened his mouth?

Looking up at him, she noticed that he seemed to be seriously busy trying to hide the fact that he found something very entertaining.

"Oh no!" Indie gasped, remembering that her thoughts were no mystery to this man. Well, this was going to take some getting used to. She hoped her dignity survived. She decided to ignore the issue for the moment, and just respond to his comment, trying her best not to act like such an emotional twit.

"Yes, I actually do have questions. A lot of them."

He allowed this change of venue, pulling her to her feet before suddenly pausing and speaking sharply.

"Hold that thought. I need to ask you, when was the last time you had something to eat?"

What? Food? Indie had not thought about food in God knows how long. She thought hard. When *had* she last eaten? Well, it had been too long then, she supposed, if the answer was not forthcoming.

Jackson scowled in disapproval as he flipped her back into the chair they had just vacated.

"I'll be right back." He pressed his index finger to her forehead for a moment. "Do not move!"

He disappeared into the kitchen, and Indie could hear him mentally growling as he moved around, opening and closing the refrigerator door. She could feel his stress because she had neglected her own needs, and it made him . . . angry! Indie had a crazy impulse to laugh at his extreme reaction to such a thing.

She closed her eyes and leaned back into the softness of the chair, working to absorb this new sensation.

Jackson taking care of *her*. Never in her life had she had this kind of experience and her need to laugh dissolved into a fresh round of tears, although quick and silent this time.

Indie had always found herself performing the role of caretaker and, although she did it very well, she had always secretly yearned to be the cared for . . . the protected.

Well, it was happening now, and it felt pretty darn good.

So right.

Yet she felt, out of habit, a little guilty. She struggled with the autopilot in her head . . . the voice that wanted to say, *"Oh no, you don't have to do that. I can get it myself!"*

She heard a snort from the kitchen. Jackson appeared in the doorway, with a plate of food in one hand and a glass of what looked like orange juice in the other.

"I'm going to need you to get over *that*." He knelt down in front of her. "Seriously, like, right away!"

Indie stared at him. Surely she had accidentally stepped into one of those wormholes you hear about . . . the ones that transport you into some parallel universe.

This unbearably handsome man was kneeling in front of her, telling her to get used to being cared for in this way. Well, what could she say?

She nodded slowly and said gravely, "I'll give it my best shot." "Yes . . . you do that," he replied with a narrow-eyed smile.

She looked at the square, white plate Jackson was holding. Of course, it was full of things that she loved.

Naturally. The man was uncanny in his anticipation of what she needed.

Indie loved things that were cool, crisp and fresh, and Jackson had assembled on the plate treats like star fruit and kiwi, giant red grapes, and slices of a milky white cheese.

Her belly roared. Suddenly ravenous, Indie took the plate and began to eat hastily, rolling her eyes a little. How good it tasted. He watched with amusement at first, but then flashed her a warning through his eyes.

"Don't ever go that long without eating again!" He spoke a little gruffly. In an instant, the look was gone and his gentle smile returned. "Now that I think about it, since it is now my honor to care for you, I don't think I'll have to worry about it happening again."

Indie shook her head in amazement, and continued to eat. He held out the juice and she took it, gulping it down greedily. Thank goodness he didn't stare at her while she scarfed her meal like a jackal.

Looking lost in thought, he seemed content to sit on the floor at her feet, leaning back against the base of the chair, one hand rubbing absently along the top of her right ankle.

A small remote control was on the arm of the chair where Indie was sitting, and he absently lifted and pointed it toward an intimidating sound system against the far wall.

Quickly, he lowered the volume on *Slipknot* from ear-shattering, to background noise. His mind was cluttered with a menagerie of emotions, and she left him to them for now.

Finally, Indie fell back into the chair, full and exhausted. Jackson took the plate and glass from her hands, and set them on the floor next to him. He turned on his knees to face her, and squirmed his way into the v-shaped space between her legs as she sat in the chair.

Placing one arm on either side of her, he looked into her face with a wistful expression.

Indie's heart began to flutter around her ribcage in an irregular rhythm.

He leaned in tantalizingly close, bringing his lips very deliberately to her ear before speaking.

"Feeling better?" he asked in a whisper that was as seductive as an intimate touch.

"Much," Indie whispered back, using all of the air she had reserved in her lungs.

He leaned back, ever so slowly and locked his eyes on to hers. His hands came up to cradle her face and he stopped, allowing himself to study her, as if committing the moment to memory.

"I can't believe it . . . that I've finally found you, and you're really here, right in front of me!" He spoke in a voice that conveyed all of his wonder at this feat.

Indie said nothing, mostly because she was out of air, but also she knew that he could pull the feelings that she could not speak directly from her mind. It just felt so right being here. So incredibly right, there were no words.

Her life had been like a puzzle that was put together, but was missing the most important piece; the one that made the picture complete. It was as if he had reached out and shaken awake her sleeping soul.

Now that she was aware of what she'd been living without, Indie knew that she would never allow herself to be in that condition again. *Welcome to existence.*

Jackson closed the space between them in one swift motion, his lips brushing hers softly, intensifying as she responded automatically.

Her hands came up to lock behind his neck, and then slid upward to tangle into his deliciously disorderly hair. A low sound of pure need snarled from deep within his chest, as he pushed Indie farther back into the chair, his hands sliding from her face to encircle her body.

He tightened his grip behind her, and abruptly Indie was swirled out of the chair on to the soft area rug in front of the fireplace. His lips did not leave hers during this daring maneuver, and she quivered with excitement at his strength, a force so controlled.

Jackson situated himself so that he could rest his weight on one arm, and pulled back to look at her. His fiercely blue eyes sparked with an intensity that took away all thought, and any trace of fear or despair. He traced her features gently, and his eyes gradually softened into a look of unconditional love.

Indie had the distinct feeling that if she cracked him in the head with the fireplace poker, it wouldn't shake him. She looked up, curiously.

"How is it possible . . . ?" she began. "How can you have such strong feelings for me, just like that?"

Jackson looked thoughtful.

"Hmm . . . well, tell me, how do *you* feel about *me?*"

"Pretty intensely attracted," she had to admit.

"Attracted?" he asked, wide eyed, but his tone light, teasing. "*Attracted.*"

He pretended to ponder the word. "So that's it, is it? You are *attracted* to me, huh? I'm just another pretty face, then?"

He bent and nuzzled her neck, his warm breath doing strange and wonderful things to her equilibrium.

"Maybe attracted isn't exactly the right word." Indie shivered.

"No?" he asked against her ear.

Okay, so they both knew she felt *love!* They'd already dropped the "L-bomb" on each other the day before, shocking her as it fell out of her mouth, just as it did hearing Jackson say it at the same time. However, that was just not rational. A person can't literally fall into actual *love* with someone instantly, can they?

"You may have to learn to set aside your ideas of what is rational, in light of the situation." Jackson whispered the words while stroking the side of her neck with his lips. He then pulled back slowly, closed his eyes, and took a deep, shaky breath, held it for a moment, then exhaled slowly.

Some sort of Zen-like attempt at self-control, she guessed. He opened his eyes, and Indie watched the color lighten and clear, and then he smiled.

In a flash, he was on his feet as though gravity had no effect on him. He held his hand down to her. Confused, Indie took it, and he effortlessly hauled her to her feet.

"I think . . ." he took another cleansing breath, "that we should talk . . . get more familiar with one another, backwards as that seems, before things go . . . further."

She once again took note of the fact that, while Jackson looked very young, he most definitely had the commanding presence of a man; authoritative and calm.

His wisp of an accent gave him the cultured air of the well educated.

Ah, he was too freaking perfect. Indie wanted to toss him back on the floor and savage his body in an extremely un-ladylike way.

She knew he read those thoughts, because he froze and looked down at her with a territorial stare that made her belly clench like a fist. Jackson looked torn for a moment, as if he was ready to surrender all pretense of control around her, and pounce on her with equal enthusiasm, but then Indie felt his surge of strength.

Shaking his head, he threw off that notion, much to her disappointment.

"Well, I don't know if I want to get to know you better if you're going to be all reasonable and stuff." Indie sulked.

Jackson's eyes laughed, but his brain was clearly longing to explore her alternative option.

Instead, he led her to a wide planked wooden table, smooth with age, stopping to pick up a pillow from the couch as they passed by. Before Indie sat down, he tossed it to her. She was startled, but caught it easily and tucked it in front of her body, wrapping her arms around it automatically.

"Your security pillow, right?" He spoke absently, his mind still working on pulling itself away from the previous thoughts.

Oh sure. Right.

Of course he *would* know all of her little quirks. Indie always liked to hold on to something when she was nervous, and right now she was feeling it. He sat down across from her at the narrow table. She could easily reach forward to touch him, so she didn't feel the agony of separation that she was afraid that she would feel.

Indie let herself stare at him.

He was the picture of masculine perfection.

Jackson leaned back in his chair casually, with the four fingers of each hand tucked into his pockets, thumbs resting along the waistband of his jeans.

He wore a pale blue t-shirt, that fit him very, *very* well, and over it, a long-sleeved button down shirt, though it was unbuttoned as she noted seemed to be his preference. It was embossed with thin white and blue stripes, matching the tee shirt perfectly. He remained motionless, as he allowed this blatant appraisal to take place, watching her through hooded eyes.

The muscles of his belly were like speed bumps rippling down his abdomen, clearly visible through the tight shirt. Her eyes lingered for a moment, and then continued their assessment, taking in the narrowing angles as she dropped her gaze further towards . . .

"See anything you want?" Jackson's voice was no more than a hoarse whisper, and Indie flushed nearly purple with embarrassment. He shut his eyes and drew in a quick breath.

What a completely asinine thing to say; he couldn't believe the words had come from his mouth.

When did I become totally deranged? He felt horrible that he had caused her embarrassment, but when he opened his eyes and his mouth to apologize, he saw that Indie had recovered very nicely, and was eyeing him with, if it was possible, even more hunger and appreciation.

Interesting.

It was also clear from her thoughts that she was going to shelve those feelings, and forge onward with her quest for more information. She was going to ignore his cocky little statement, for now at least.

And so could he.

He just wished he knew where it had come from. Jackson shook his head a little. He had never thought of himself as a particularly forward or sexually aggressive kind of guy. Maybe he had just never been properly inspired.

This is becoming just more and more bizarre, he winced, confused.

For a split second, the sexual tension in the space between them created an almost unbearable surge of hormonal waves. The air was thick with it, and the weight of the needing was fighting for his acknowledgement. Indie was feeling it as well, he was willing to bet, but he was a master of control, was he not?

Christ, self-control was kind of his thing. One of the things he did best.

Jackson allowed himself to dwell on the question of what other things he might do best. So far, he had no point of comparison, other than the fact that he was damn good at any kind of physical activity. And sex was quite . . . *physical*, was it not?

No.

He had to stop thinking now, or else he was going to figuratively rip loose his control, wad it up and hurl it out the nearest window. He focused on what he wanted to say.

Indie finally coughed a little, regaining his attention, and started to speak. He held up a hand to stop her.

"Before the onslaught of questions begins, I would like to tell you what I think I know, because I'll bet you have spent your entire life thinking you were somehow 'abnormal', and I want to show you how on track you have actually always been."

How could he know this?

Wait. Of course. He seemed to know everything about her.

Her curiosity raised its weary head and sniffed the air, hungry for information.

"Well, okay." She leaned forward and shrugged. "Go for it!"

He leaned forward as well, unconsciously mirroring her moves, and placed his hands on the table, clasped tightly together. He cocked his head to one side slightly, and looked up at her from under the lock of hair that fell forward, and smiled.

Indie sucked in her breath at this sight.

Oh sweet Jesus, but he's breathtaking! His comment about seeing something she wanted had almost made her wilt with heat, but she felt that she had hidden her nasty little thoughts well enough. She hoped, anyway.

"Okay," he interrupted her second virtual molestation of his body. Jackson hesitated, relieved that no further idiotic comments dropped from his lips, and then continued.

"You don't sleep much, if at all. You naturally gravitate toward healthy foods, organic if you can get it, and you have an instinctive aversion to anything unhealthy. You wouldn't smoke, can't drink alcohol, and tend to like physical activity." He paused, as though listening to a distant sound, then resumed.

"You have exceptional math skills, your body temperature runs slightly higher than 'normal', but you've never been sick a day in your life. You are mesmerized by music, and drink it in with an almost physical pleasure."

"How could you . . ." Indie cut in and he lifted his finger in a "one moment" gesture.

"You have an outstanding work ethic, compassion that is off the charts, although you try to hide it, to appear 'tougher', and finally . . . ," he narrowed his eyes at her mischievously, "you are very emotionally needy!"

He easily dodged the pillow that she flung at him.

"And defiant as well!" He laughed, and threw the pillow back.

"I know these last two things about you because of my own traits. I am a natural born caretaker . . . protector. But I also need a challenge, I suppose. I couldn't respect anyone who instantly capitulated to my wishes all the time, with no opinion of their own . . . how perfectly boring *that* would be!"

"You see, Indie," he spoke gently, "I am supposed to be everything you need, as you are to me . . . my perfect match!"

Indie was speechless, but for only a moment.

Needy? Defiant? Oh really? She crossed her arms and stared at Jackson . . . well . . . *defiantly.*

"I am not!"

Jackson looked thoughtfully up at the ceiling past her right shoulder, and then abruptly met her glare with a little smirk. "Hmm, I've just checked with my imaginary friends, and they've confirmed this as fact!"

He had to laugh at the look on her face at this idea. She sat with arms folded, tapping her foot, and waiting for him to recover. It took quite a long time, and her annoyance faded as she watched him trying to compose himself. His laugh was infectious, and by the time he had pulled it together, Indie was more dazed than stressed, and had to fight to keep from smiling.

Just a little.

"Well, Indie." He shook his head, a little out of breath. "Let me assure you, these are adorable traits to *me*. I am just assuming, but I believe I am spot on about these things." He sobered.

"I've been searching for you for so long, but had not had much luck until Miss Conner reported that she suspected that one of her nurses was an 'orphaned Member', and I was contacted at once."

"Where were you when they called you?" she asked, curious about the places he had been, and how far he'd come, just to see if she was the one. He shrugged.

"I was right here," he gestured toward the huge wall of windows. I was assigned as caretaker to the points of alignment, Mystery Hill, in New Hampshire and Calendar II, which just happens to be in central Vermont, just a little over two years ago. There are several others nearby that I keep records on, as well."

Indie frowned to herself as the thought occurred to her that it was just a little over two years ago that she had gotten the unshakable drive to move to this very state.

Coincidence?

Probably not. Perhaps she had the answer as to why this had happened, huh?

She pulled her mind back to Jackson's comments. "Points of . . . what?" she asked, wary at once. She knew she was about to hear a lot of disturbing information, and she didn't know if she was ready. Indie decided that she would ask cautious questions, determining as she went along, whether she could handle the answers.

Quickly, she asked a different question.

"Miss Maggie called me an 'orphaned Member'?" she began, absently rubbing her hands up and down her arms, beginning to feel a little chilled. "What exactly does that mean?"

Jackson frowned as he reached over to pull a small throw from the couch, and rose to his feet, seemingly distracted.

He wrapped the throw around Indie, as if without conscious thought, then returned to his seat. He rested his hands on his knees, looking down at the floor, for just a moment. He seemed to be preparing to tell a very long story.

"Just the gentlest, most abbreviated reply possible would be appreciated," Indie warned him. His head snapped up, and he gave her a tight smile.

"An orphaned Member is simply someone with the complete set of genetic markers, making them a pure descendent of the First Society . . . but one who was never identified and has had to make their own way. It is extremely rare, and most, if not all, end up institutionalized, medicated or treated to some other form of misery, because people think they're crazy, and usually, they believe it themselves."

She shuddered involuntarily. How easily she could relate to that.

"You see," he still spoke with great care, "The very few orphaned Members that there have been, haven't fared well, at all. You are incredibly strong, and gifted."

"And my love for music is . . ."

"Your love for music is universal among the Society. We all do, and most play some kind of instrument. If we don't, then we play the hell out of a radio or an IPod!"

Jackson's eyes caressed her as he spoke. "I suppose the reason for this trait is the fact that our original ancestors communicated mainly by song, and wordless notes. I guess we still feel the attraction."

Indie drank this in. The *original* ancestors?

"Miss Maggie spoke about my having the 'gift of invisibility'," Indie whispered. "What does that mean, exactly?"

Jackson stood, and began pacing, dragging his hands through his hair, as Indie had noticed was his habit when he was nervous. She tried to ignore the sensual movement of his muscles, evident even under his t-shirt.

"That would be the explanation for how you escaped notice while you were a child, indeed, until you were sighted by Maggie. There are few Society Members in the first place, but people born with the markers have a trigger, like GPS, if you will, alerting the other Members when a pure descendent is born. They then track that child, and observe everything . . . the family dynamic, formulating a plan to become part of that child's world . . . his upbringing, and once put into place, the child is told very early about how special he is, and what he cannot reveal to anyone but other Members. It is pretty much part of the natural defense mechanism of the genetic set, that children understand easily, and instinctively that survival depends on secrecy, even from their parents."

Indie tried to envision some stranger showing up at her door, telling her that they needed to be involved in her children's lives, and visualized what her reaction would be to such a thing.

"How on Earth do they do it?" she wondered aloud. "It must be pretty difficult to get people to comply with that sort of thing. I mean, if they don't, do you just kidnap the kids?" Indie felt ill at the thought. Jackson stopped pacing and looked at her, appalled.

"Indie, we are not evil beings, who run around kidnapping children from the arms of their screaming parents!" He sounded reproachful. "We have been around for a very long time, and our tactics are very effective and positive for everyone involved."

"Okay then," she challenged, "tell me how it's done!"

He walked around the table to stand behind her and bent down, placing his hands on the table. She could feel his warmth spreading across her back and shoulders, his breath in her hair. His close proximity made it hard to focus.

"The tactics differ from one case to the next, according to the family dynamics," Jackson began. "For instance, we would go about things differently for a child born to a single mother, or an unplanned birth, than we would a child born into a family . . . planned and wanted. Sometimes, it is as easy as adopting the child."

"We have legal teams all over the world, and truly, unlimited finances available. But at times, we must take a more finessed approach. We go to the family, bringing a team of attorneys and very detailed documents tracking ancestry, and show legal proof that this child is the heir to a massive fortune, but that it comes with stipulations about the child's education, and various other caveats, which most families are quite ready to meet, not wanting to risk this fortuitous inheritance."

He smiled now. "It's not usually that difficult to convince a family to take a large sum of money when in return, all that is asked of them is that they allow their child to receive the finest education in the world! Believe me, the families are generally overjoyed at their unexpected good fortune."

"So, then what, you take them away?" Indie still didn't like this.

"It's no different than any privileged child going off to boarding school," he rested his hands lightly on her shoulders. "We try to get them into some kind of academic boarding school at a very young age. Prior to that, we arrange home care or a nanny service, which is always part of the contract.

"The caregivers are specifically selected Society Members themselves, chosen by their ancestry. They have the patience and commitment, and sacrifice time with their own *Equals* during the term of care for their charges. They are invaluable, because they begin the process for teaching the children, preparing them for life."

He smiled, looking distant for a moment.

"My nanny came to me when I was born. My mother was alone and sickly. I never knew my father. She needed help so badly and was thrilled to have a live-in nanny for me, as well as financial support. She never had to work again. I was sent to Queen Ethelburga's from age five to eleven, then to the Queen's College from twelve to eighteen. At graduation, I took the National Admissions Test for Law, and then continued my studies at Oxford, where I earned my PHD.

Indie was dumbfounded. "You graduated from Oxford?" She shook her head with new respect. "That's pretty impressive."

"The Society has been sending members to Oxford for nine centuries," Jackson explained. "Our nannies are our first contact for teachings that are for Society Members only. We learn our origins, our history and purpose . . . and how to survive.

"After graduating from Oxford, I was accepted into the British Special Air Service, and served for six years."

Jackson did not feel a need to add that he had spent an additional year with the Master Simon Wong, studying the Yellow Dragon Fist unarmed combat techniques. He figured that the fact that he was former SAS was probably quite enough for Indie to deal with, although she seemed to take this in stride.

Yeah, actually when he thought about it, it was definitely no big deal compared to all of the other information she'd had rammed down her throat in the past thirty-six hours.

Indie looked appropriately awestricken, but made no comment about his affiliations. "And do you see your mother at all?"

Jackson looked out the great window as he spoke.

"No, she died when I was thirteen. She had the best medical care, but her health was never good, and she finally succumbed to an auto immune disorder." Indie's eyes and thoughts relayed her sympathy to Jackson wordlessly.

He started pacing again, and the withdrawal of his hands from Indie's skin was nearly unbearable. A soft involuntary whimper escaped her. He shot her an anxious look, hastily returning to stand behind her again; hands warm on her arms as he wrapped up his monologue.

"I've spent the last seven years running my own law firm, often as an absentee partner, while doing work for the Society; research, volunteering, and actively working to promote the values that are critical to the success of the Population."

Jackson knelt at her side now, and sought her hand, interlacing his fingers with hers. He stared at them while he spoke.

"I also have other duties that I am positive would be very . . . *distasteful* to you, but involve the protection of the Human Population." He briefly looked up at her from the corner of his eye again, as her caught her mental gasp, but finished his thought. "I can't explain my other duties to you until you know everything, and can understand."

Human Population?

Indie's mind latched onto the words, the implication something that she was not at all prepared to face. Not right at this moment.

And to Hell with his statement about "other duties." The only way she could continue having any conversation now, was to bring it back to her earlier curiosity about convincing parents to allow the Society's takeover of their children's' future.

Jackson read her abrupt change of mental status, and went back to the earlier topic instantly, to accommodate her.

"Occasionally, there is the parent or parents who want no part of this gift, out of either pride, skepticism, or whatever, and send us packing. In those cases, we simply bide our time. The child is kept under constant surveillance and when he is older, he is 'befriended' by another young member brought in for this purpose. They are then assigned to slowly educate and advise them.

"Young pre-teens are very easy to convince, because they are already feeling the awkwardness of not fitting in, and as it so happens, this age group is very eager to believe that they are 'special', and adapt very quickly to the Society Rules."

"And just what are the 'Society Rules?" she had to ask.

"You will learn the rest later, but one pretty important one involves keeping your status a secret. I can more fully explain the reasons, at some point," Jackson assured her.

"Well, it's not exactly hard to guess some of the major ones." Indie shuddered, remembering Will's description of the treatment of the captive Society Member.

"Yes, that would be the main problem with disclosure," he nodded seriously.

"Also, as soon as it is feasible, you must meet your *Equal*, which is not supposed to take as long or be as hard as it was for me." He laughed, and kissed the top of her head.

"The Elders find them . . . same date of birth for one, which makes it easy to narrow the possibilities. In addition, certain family surnames have more incidences of full genetic markers than others do, just because the genes all began in a handful of individuals, and the surnames tend to follow those individuals. Although expanded by marriage, there are still approximately fifty surnames that have a higher percentage of births, Allen being one of these. Then, they just follow the built in tracking signal, which *you* deemed unnecessary at birth, apparently!" He smiled a little forlornly.

"Although we do use aliases at times, we know our true root names, and try to use them in the Population for as long as we can get away with it. It makes life easier".

"So all . . . Society Members have an *Equal*; a mate for life built right in?"

"Mostly, yes." Jackson replied. "To clarify, we all have an *Equal*. Usually they are introduced at boarding school as soon as the matches are located, which begins the bonding process right away. It is a match that leads to the Commitment, and they become mates.

"The exception is a rare phenomenon. There are some born, who are direct descendents of the most powerful, most pure of our ancestors. They have *Equals* of the same lineage. There is nothing . . . *passionate* about their partnership, although their loyalty and commitment is just as strong, possibly stronger. They find and love one another for life, but it is a mental connection, never physical. They remain untouched by carnal thoughts or feelings. Their power comes from the classification of their ancestor."

Jackson knelt next to Indie, and sighed. "I think you'll need to understand more about *your* origins, before I can elaborate on these particular Members."

She clutched at his hands, intrigued by the idea of "classifications" of these ancestors, but willing to wait for the full explanation.

"Okay . . . but that still doesn't explain my 'invisibility' gift," she pressed.

"Ah, yes." He straightened and resumed wearing a path in the hardwood floor. "Well, the gift of becoming invisible to others, mentally. You aren't invisible in the literal sense, obviously, but you have a natural ability to block your 'GPS', so to speak, as well as to make people sort of . . . see *through* you, for lack of a better description.

"It can be done deliberately or, as in your case, quite inadvertently. I can see where it would make you very adept at 'blending in', and is probably one of the reasons you have functioned so well on your own. People tend to truly notice your presence, only when you make them, either by commanding them in some way or by doing something out of the ordinary that attracts the natural wariness of the Population."

Indie was enlightened by this revelation. But how awful she felt now. It was never Will's fault that he seemed oblivious to her existence most of the time.

Until she was leaving, of course.

Demanding a divorce had apparently "commanded" his notice. It was a good bet that this was also the explanation as to why Will had been her first and only boyfriend. Suddenly, many things about her life were becoming a little clearer.

She felt Jackson's gaze. He was watching her with a sympathetic look. "No, it's fine, really. Go on." She nodded encouragement to him.

"All Society Members have some sort of gift, or gifts; powers that have been somewhat modified as they have moved down through the descendents," he continued. "The gifts that a Member has, reveal what classification their ancestors fell into."

Indie shifted in her chair. That word again.

"Classification?"

"Uh, yes," Jackson spoke while eyeing her warily. "There was a hierarchy of ancestors, the ones who were sent by . . . er—" He seemed to catch himself. "—sent to teach and to eventually mingle with mankind. Different ranks possessed different powers." He shrugged as if this information should be common knowledge.

"Some are protectors, warriors, having acute senses in knowing the thoughts of potential threats. We all possess pretty awesome math skills, and technical ability." He ran his hands through his hair, sighing. "I wish I could drop *you* off at some sort of training center," he said, wistfully, "then just pick you up when you have heard everything, and have reconciled your mind to it."

Indie made an impatient noise at this.

"Hey, look, I have no problem with the truth. Well, for the most part, anyway. It's the unknown that frightens me, and so I want to hear it all!"

Jackson stood against the wall with a resigned look, and then walked around the table, taking her hand and pulling her out of the chair.

"Right. Well, then, we might as well get comfortable," he sighed, "because it's going to be a long day . . . and night!"

He led her along down a short hallway, and stopped at the entrance to a huge bedroom. Her suitcase was on the bed. She hadn't even noticed that he had carried it, along with her, into the house.

He retrieved a small duffle bag from behind the door, and tossed it on the bed as well. "I took the liberty of lifting a few personal items from your house while you were conversing with Will."

"You were in my house, while Will was there?" Indie was belatedly horrified at the idea.

"Yup. Afraid so." Jackson was unrepentant. "The door to your deck was open, and I could feel where Will's thoughts had led him. I knew you were going to have to leave rather quickly." He shook his head, a pained look in his eyes. "I saw the things you had already packed. Sentimental things, but I thought you could use a few more practical items like clothes, toiletries, a toothbrush . . . you know."

Once more, she had the shivery feeling of comfort. Her horrified feeling quickly hit the highway, replaced with the overwhelming sense of being cared for. It felt good. He pulled her close in his warm, strong embrace. Indie felt as though nothing bad could touch her while tucked into his arms.

She sighed and snuggled closer.

His response to her body pressing against his was instantly apparent, and it sent a thrill of anticipation through her. She now fought to control the thoughts that threatened to embarrass her with their direction. It was still difficult to believe it was possible that she affected him as strongly as he affected her.

Indie decided she had to try a little experiment, just to prove it to herself. This was all new; the feeling of being acutely irresistible to another person and she wanted to test the waters. Reaching up slowly, she sifted her fingers through his hair, and then linked them around the back of his neck.

Her gaze sank deeply into his eyes.

They were intense, wary and appraising, yet his starvation for her was there. Indie could almost smell it. She tilted her head back, and pulled his face closer. He was cautious, but did not resist.

Her lips touched his, and his caution vanished. Like a lightning strike, Jackson's hands shot around her, crushing her into him as though to merge into one being. He was making the most heart wrenching sounds, low and deep, revealing the depth of his longing.

She moved her mouth to his neck and shoulders, and found herself lifted off her feet, and carried toward the huge bed. Indie was barely aware of the soft thud of the suitcase and duffle bag hitting the wood floor as they were unceremoniously shoved aside.

There came a terrible moment of recognition for Indie, in the feeling of desperate need she could feel pouring forth from Jackson . . . because it reminded her of Will.

In those few and far between moments when they'd connected physically, she'd felt that same yearning. A plea for her to soothe him . . . to fix what was tormenting him.

But she never could.

Those times were nothing more than a short reprieve for Will's inner angst, and it was the same for Indie. Temporary shelter from the loneliness that surrounded them; locking her in some sort of emotional quarantine.

But with the recognition came realization.

This was different. Although the fierce need and longing were nearly identical, with Jackson, there was resolution.

Closure.

Satisfaction for all parties. Not necessarily sexual satisfaction, although Indie was willing to bet that this was going to be the case, but through her senses . . . her touch, there was the absolute promise that the need was finally going to be met. In addition, she was going to actually meet someone else's.

Will was like a cracked vessel that could never be filled. Not by her anyway. It was the same both ways, with her need to feel loved and wanted simply a never-ending void.

She was already feeling Jackson's desperation and longing temper into a joyful feeling of coming *home*. What remained was his overwhelming urge to seal the deal . . . to lose themselves in the sensations of the physical demonstration of their emotional connection.

Jackson's eyes narrowed at her slightly, as he picked up on the vague idea that there was some sort of comparison between himself and the false mate going on in his beloved's head.

He pushed her onto the bed like an animal, ripping away the white down comforter, and then froze, poised above her. Lifting himself on his knees, he tried to slow his breathing as he fought back against his need to claim.

"Okay," he panted. "You are simply going to have to behave! You're completely destroying what's left of my civility. Believe me, Indie, you don't want me to lose my control!"

She grabbed him again, and pulled him toward her. "Aw, go ahead and lose it!" she teased.

With another blindingly quick motion, he rolled onto his back, and now had her on top of him. "I have to control myself, Indie," he breathed unevenly into her ear. "All of my training—our teachings—have been about maintaining self control at all times." He looked up at her pointedly.

"Besides, our union has to be recognized by an Elder, before . . . well, before we . . . . uh . . . ."

Indie stared at him, incredulous as something began to dawn on her. Jackson, so collected, confident and in charge, and yet, he could not even say aloud any kind of euphemism for *sex*! She went a little dizzy as the implication began to sink in, but the idea was hard to imagine.

Could anyone as beautiful and appealing as this man be inexperienced with women? How curious.

Curious and electrically exciting.

"Before we *what?*" she pressed, being very bad, indeed. She wanted to hear him say it.

"So, okay. I guess you have gathered that I have, um, waited for you . . . my entire life!" He stroked her hair, letting it cover his face, hiding and looking very uncomfortable.

"Waited for me?"

Indie knew exactly what he was trying to say. "I can't believe that you're still a . . ."

"Don't say it out loud, please!" he pleaded, as Indie fought a smile. He rolled her off his belly, and sat on the edge of the bed, looking a little put out.

"Yeah, I know." He smiled a little. "I think they even made a movie about me, right? The Forty Year Old *Virgin!*"

That did it. She burst into a fit of giggles, succumbing completely. Her laughter continued while he watched patiently, arms crossed.

Indie thought she might never be able to collect herself, she was so taken by surprise, but eventually, she stifled her shameful laughter, which was totally at his expense.

"Do you think you'll be okay?" he asked, dryly.

"I'm sorry." She shook her head. "Really, it wasn't even like it was so funny. It just . . . shocked me I suppose. But, you *do* want me?" she asked, needing suddenly to hear it from him.

"That would be a big affirmative! Isn't it obvious that the flesh is most willing?" he laughed. "I want you nearly more than I can bear, and you aren't making it any easier, you know."

She was intrigued, and wanted to know more about how she made *him* feel.

"What do I *smell* like, to you?" she asked, suddenly.

What?

He looked a little caught off guard, as his mind was still distracted by the word "*want.*" Indie shifted on the bed to better look at him.

"Well," she began, "you always read in those corny romance novels about someone being drawn to a person by their scent, right?"

"Er, well, I haven't actually had much opportunity to notice such a thing, seeing as I so very rarely allow myself to be caught reading . . . what did you call them . . . 'corny romance novels'."

Indie snickered at the thought as she flushed.

"Okay, I guess that was a dumb statement. But anyway, I've always thought it was such a cliché, actually finding myself irritated by the over-use of the idea, but I swear, you have a scent about you that is warm, safe, comfortable and cozy; I guess that describes it best, and I was wondering if you noticed a scent like that from me?"

Jackson returned to rest fully on the bed, his back against the pillows.

"Let's see. I guess if I had to describe it," he said thoughtfully, "I would say that your scent is one of brightness. Of all things fresh and green. Like after a cleansing rain, the smell of honeysuckle, or of a freshly sliced apple . . . absolutely intoxicating," he added, dreamily.

"Really? And *green* has a scent?"

He looked at her with a confident smile. "Absolutely green has a scent! And it is *you!*"

Indie laughed now. "Are you sure it's not blue? Purple or red?"

This earned her a fluff to the hair as he informed her that the only two colors that have a scent, are green and orange, and she decided that she liked this idea. She wasn't sure what she had expected to hear, but was immensely pleased with his description.

She lay back on the pillows next to him and sobered. "Does it hurt you that I didn't . . . wait for you, as you did for me?" She really didn't want to hear the answer, but felt guilty about her experiences after learning of his untouched status.

"Don't be ridiculous, Indie," he shook his head, grimacing. "How could you be expected to wait for something, or in this case, some*one*, whom you knew nothing about?"

"That's true," she answered, "but not what I asked you." She could feel the answer in his head, and he tossed it suddenly, as if to shake her out.

"Look, I am not going to pretend that the idea of another man touching you doesn't make me feel a little war-like." He tried to smile. "But I don't blame you, and I feel no animosity, especially in light of what you gained from that experience . . . something that I could never have given you." He closed his eyes and sighed as he said this.

"What is it that I gained from Will that you could never have given me?" She could not imagine.

"Children, Indie." His whisper exposed his pain beautifully. As she stared at him, he picked up a small pillow and turned it over in his hands as he spoke.

"A funny thing about our genetics . . . our history," he explained, "is that the original ancestors had no ability or need to procreate. They were incapable of death, (he winced at her sharp intake of breath) and so, I suppose there was no biological need to make more.

"After the ancestors became flesh, and mingled with humankind, they were able to procreate with the people, as was the intention, in the process of improving the population. However, when the full set of genetic markers are present, making us the very same as the original ancestors, we are drawn to our *Equal*, another pure descendent, and together, the genetics do not allow the making of children.

The only way for a Member to be created now is through the genetic spin of the roulette wheel, and yet, there is always a matched set. This is to compensate for the inability to conceive together, as you will have a true and devoted companion for life."

"I see." Indie said, thoughtfully. "So, Society Members are sort of like . . . mules!"

Jackson blinked in surprise.

"Yeah . . . ah . . . *what?*" A small huff of a laugh escaped him as he looked at Indie.

"Like, in the way that you can only make a mule, by crossing what is in essence, two different breeds, and you get the hybrid, the mule. But you can't breed two mules, and get a mule. They are always sterile!"

He chuckled. "Well then, I guess that about sums it up." He laughed in earnest now. "We are like mules! Except," he added, "we are not the hybrid here. We are the pure bloods, and the rest of humankind are the hybrids."

Looking up at Indie again, he gestured toward her with a sweep of his hand.

"But even among Society members, there are those with the genetics of two different ranks of the ancestors and enjoy the traits of both. You, for example, bear the bloodlines of two of the highest ranking of our kind."

He then placed his hand over his own chest, and looked up at her with the nearly submissive look Indie thought she'd noticed back at her—at *Will's* house. "And then there are those as I am, with the bloodlines of only one type. Pure, but one of the lowest of the hierarchy. But none can procreate together."

"Interesting," breathed Indie. "So you *know*, somehow, that I have the genetics of two ranks, I gather?"

"Upon our contact, I could sense your ancestry."

"But you say you are low-ranking, and I—I am of the highest? So I, um, *out-rank* you?" She couldn't help but smile at the thought.

"Yeah, but don't get all excited about *that!* Society Members have a very deep-seated instinct to follow our hierarchy, but I am also a fighter. And very strong willed about protecting you, so it should be very interesting to see how this plays out.

That is what I was so surprised about, when we made contact. Members of my rank in particular, are pretty much always matched with the same bloodlines." He narrowed the blue eyed stare in her direction. "Although there has to be a reason, it doesn't matter anyway. I will happily do your bidding, unless I see a strong need to take your leadership from you!"

"Oh, really? Well the idea of you *trying* sounds a little exciting, actually," Indie tossed back at him, just to watch him squirm.

But higher-ranking?

Hierarchies? What did it all mean?

And she'd just found another reason to thank God for Will; her children.

She shot a guilty glance over at Jackson at the thought, and she felt him tense. But his words for her were gentle. Sincere.

"Understand, Indie, that I consider your children a blessing and a part of you, which makes them very important to me as well."

Her face crumpled at the thought of the twins. She missed them with a physical ache.

"This is why I think you need time, Indie." Jackson spoke softly, winding his arms around her. "I would have you know everything, and have time to accept and adjust, before I seek your commitment, and before I think of being with you in the . . . physical sense."

Indie turned to face him. "I know that I haven't heard everything yet, and I still have a lot of questions, but honestly, Jackson, I have to be yours!" Her words came in a sudden rush so she wouldn't start sobbing.

"I'm letting go of everything I know, and placing myself in your hands. I am, as of this moment, homeless, jobless and—she nearly retched—*childless*. You are all I have." This was an indisputable fact in Indie's mind, but Jackson *was* disputing this.

"You are absolutely none of those things!" he stated, a little roughly. "What is mine is yours, so you are not homeless . . . you have need of a non-Member job only if you wish, and furthermore, your children are still your children!"

She tried not to allow her voice to break. "But I don't *have* them!"

"Regardless," he lifted her face with his hand, "they are yours, and they know it as well as you do. I swear to you, Indie, it will not be like this always."

Indie couldn't help but be comforted by Jackson's words. He was so totally calm and self-assured. She thought more about his statement. "I can have a Society Member job?"

"Yes, your 'higher purpose!'" He smiled, relieved that for the moment at least, she was okay.

"My true job is not what I appear to do for a living. Those sacred places around the world, some that are here in this area, are all about tracking and monitoring the sun. Not just to mark summer or winter solstice, as people believe, but to keep track of the age of this planet, and how long the sun will sustain it. And then I have those other duties that, as I alluded to before, are more . . . difficult. He looked very serious as he said this last sentence. Then his easy smile returned.

"This falls into the category of more information, and you were supposed to be having a bath, and getting refreshed and comfortable, before your evil attempt to seduce me took over."

His eyes gleamed down at her, and she felt the blush burn. She was *truly* not accustomed to attempting such tactics.

He laughed out loud, pulled her off the bed, and sent her with a little push, to the bathroom.

"You get yourself ready for a day in pajamas," he stated firmly. "I have some things to attend to, okay?"

"Right. Okay." Indie had to admit, the thought of a hot bath sounded delightful all of a sudden. His hands stroked down her back, and he kissed her forehead. "Come out whenever you're ready," Jackson told her, his eyes appreciating everything he saw in front of him, and very willing for her to see it.

Yep, she thought, lost in those eyes.

I'm doomed!

CHAPTER 15

The interrogation of Jackson

The bath was ridiculously well appointed. Indie looked around, taking in the sight of the huge round garden tub, with a small rectangular window alongside, facing down into the valley below.

Now that's a million dollar view! She thought to herself.

She began exploring the cabinets, and found a stack of big fluffy white towels, then turned to see a super soft robe hanging on the hook behind the door. It was pink. She had to laugh.

Did he run out to Bed, Bath and Beyond, as soon as he caught a glimpse of me? she wondered.

There were also a number of potions and oils in a basket next to the tub. All organic, soothing scents like lavender and jasmine. Indie picked up a small bottle, and smiled. Honeysuckle.

Perfect.

She turned the water on, and plugged the tub, drizzling a thin stream of the scented bath oil into the water. The scent filled the air; sweet, but not overpowering. She shed her clothes hastily, and looked around. There was an empty hamper by the linen closet, so she dumped her stale and crumpled garments into it.

Does he do laundry, too? She wondered with a snort. Somehow, it was hard to imagine his manly perfection, sorting and pre-soaking the laundry.

Of course, if he did, he would probably make it look like some sort of sensual fantasy.

Stepping into the steaming tub, Indie gingerly lowered herself into the very hot water. Her body nearly convulsed with pleasure, and the heat began to smooth out her knotted muscles instantly.

Jackson was right. I did need this, she thought gratefully.

She closed her eyes, and sank down as low as she could into the soothing water, feeling the stress of the past forty-eight hours begin to ease. She allowed herself to think of her plight for a moment.

How would it play out? What was all of this going to mean, in the scheme of her life. And, how on Earth did she merit the love and devotion of a creature like Jackson?

Jackson. *Jackson.* As Indie thought of him, she could hear the voice of Miss Maggie. *"Shall you tell her, young Jackson, or shall I?"*

I need to create my own name for him, Indie decided. *To hear it from my perspective only.*

Jax will do just fine! His suggestion broke into her thoughts. She jerked her head around, startled. He was nowhere in sight.

"Hey, get out of my head!" she complained.

Laughter.

Sorry, he sent his voice into her mind. *But it was a little hard to ignore my name, repeated so many times in your thoughts!*

She could hear his smugness at the idea that her thoughts seemed to be consumed by him, and a diabolical thought occurred to her.

Indie very deliberately gazed down at her body, softly distorted, but clearly visible through the deepening water, and heard his agonized groan echo through her head.

Indie smiled, although hotly embarrassed by the reaction that she precipitated.

That was just ever so wrong, Indie! He scolded.

Yeah, well, that's what you get when you spy, she thought back. *I thought you had things to attend to, anyway.*

Well, maybe you could stop distracting me! He shot back with a chuckle. Indie was once again alone with her thoughts.

She suppressed a deep sigh. She *was* ready, in spite of what Jackson . . . *Jax,* thought. More than ready to give herself over to whatever fate awaited her. In truth, Indie knew that there was no alternative. Whatever he told her that she was part of, whatever she was, she also knew that she was his.

She wanted the Commitment, whatever it meant. To Indie it could only mean that he would be hers, finally, and that she could be truly his, in every sense.

She shivered, despite the heat of the water. She had come this far . . . given up everything. There was nowhere else to go but forward. In spite of the uncertainty that lay ahead, Indie was oddly serene . . . content. Apart from the Jake and Cassidy-shaped holes in her heart, she felt quite complete.

She flipped herself around in the tub, washed her hair, and then pulled the plug. Grabbing a towel, she dried herself slowly, and then wrapped up in the pink fluffy robe.

Indie was warm and drowsy, and knew that she needed to rest her body and mind. She padded back into the bedroom, and climbed up onto the giant bed, where she lay on her back and glanced around at the expanse of mattress.

What size was this thing, anyway? It was ridiculously huge. She loved it. Indie rolled across from end to end, then back again. She couldn't explain her unexpected rush of happiness.

It was completely out of place; as if she were participating in a word association game, and the therapist had given her the word "kite", and she had come back with "jackhammer".

So wrong and disturbing, considering the circumstances.

But for the first time in her life, she felt like she belonged. Moreover, belonged to someone, truly and completely, who assured her that she was not a freak or an oddity, and she could not contain her joy at this new sensation.

She exhaled and closed her eyes.

Indie opened them an hour later, having experienced the closest thing to sleep she ever had. The house had been utterly silent, and she wondered, briefly if she were alone.

No, she could feel his presence. She wandered back out into the living room, only to find it empty, then retraced her steps back to the hallway, and ventured farther down to find a smaller bedroom, used as an office.

Jax was sitting at the desk, head bent over some paperwork that looked important. He jerked his head up instantly, and smiled.

The effect was startling. Did he honestly have no idea how breathtaking he was? He looked like a Hollywood movie star preparing his taxes or something. Indie tried to speak, but had to cough a little to clear the way for words.

"Um, hello," she croaked.

His smile broadened. "Hi, back at you! Do you feel better?"

"I feel wonderful, physically," she confessed. Jackson's eyes appraised her knowingly.

He hadn't missed the implication that emotionally, she was not all together perfect. He stood, and moved toward her. The breath caught in her throat, as she took in his effortless, fluid motion. Indie locked her knees in order to remain upright.

"That robe looks pretty good on you," he said, a little weakly.

"Oh, yes, thank you for stocking up on the 'girly' items," she gushed. "That was so thoughtful." He moved closer, and breathed deeply.

"Ah . . . honeysuckle," he murmured. "Oh sure, I was thinking only of you, of course!"

His eyes sparkled with humor, but then he looked back over his shoulder, and they grew serious. "Listen, I was working on some papers that are actually for you," he began, "but it may be way too soon for you to think about . . . about, well, these details."

He looked troubled now, and uneasy.

"What are they?" Indie asked, nervously.

"Uh, well . . . they . . . they are divorce papers." He closed his eyes, and she could feel him in her head, anxious, trying to see her true thoughts.

She froze, but just for a moment. Then gave a resigned shrug. It *was* too soon to think about it really. Less than twelve hours had passed, since Will had tossed her out of the house, but what did she expect, though? Had she not told him that she wanted a divorce?

That she was in love with another man? There was no sense in dragging it out, was there? This WAS what she had asked for, after all, right? So what right did she have to feel sadness or shock?

"Indie, it would be weird for you not to feel sad," Jackson assured her. "The end of a marriage is just not a happy event."

"So, how are *you* working on these papers?" She looked at him, confused.

"Well, you did wonder if I was gainfully employed, did you not?" Stepping back to the desk, he reached down and plucked a small white card from a little drawer in the top, and handed it to her. It read "J. R. Allen—Attorney at Law, and gave an address in Montpelier.

She stood, looking at it for a long moment. "That's right, you're a lawyer." She spoke a little breathlessly.

"Are the details of my life so forgettable?" he scolded, gently, but with a smile. "I think I indicated that I had a pretty decent education, remember?"

"Right." Of course she remembered.

"I'm not part of the main legal team for the Society, but I am more than qualified to write up a no contest divorce document, be assured.

"You don't have to look at them, or even think about them right now, I just thought I would get them ready." He put his hands in his pockets, and rocked back on his heels.

"I'm afraid that we do kind of need to move a little quickly though, and catch Will off guard, because, believe me, he is not a happy guy right now, and that could lead to real problems. I want to drop these papers off, legal and already signed by you, so that it is filed and official."

Indie looked back at him, and spoke, numbly. "Well, that makes sense."

"Of course, if you need time . . ." he began.

"No!" She shook her head. "The sooner this is done, the sooner I can move forward, right? I mean, we can't really have a Commitment until I am divorced, can we?"

Jackson reached out slowly, took her hand and led her back down the hallway to the comfortable living room, and sat down in the suede chair. He pulled her down onto his lap, without answering.

Encircling her entire body with his taut, muscular arms, he rested his head on her back. Indie squirmed around to face him. "Am I right?"

"Not . . . necessarily," he hedged. She waited.

"You see," he spoke in his slow, cautious voice again, "the Commitment has nothing to do with marriage, although we would do that as well, when you are legally able, for compliance with the laws and customs."

Indie kept still, bidding him to go on, silently.

"We bond with our partners for life, and it defies the realms of the created legal status of marriage. It goes way beyond the contract of a marriage, which can be broken by divorce." He looked at her and sighed.

"There is no divorce after the Commitment is made, but then, I know of no situation where any *Equal* wanted to break away from their partner." He grew thoughtful for a moment. "I'm not even sure that it's possible."

Jackson made strong eye contact with her now. "But the Commitment fully entwines our destinies. We are born together in time, but the Commitment seals the connection. We will share the same date of *death*."

Jackson shrugged in an attempt to lighten the words. "It's just something to think about, when you are making your decision."

"My decision was made a long time ago, Jax. Probably before I met you." Indie was blithely unconcerned about that detail. She already thought that it was that way anyhow, so it was no startling revelation.

"So, our ability to make a 'Commitment', as you call it, is not related in any way to the legalities of divorce?" He shook his head, watching her face. "So, why the urgency?" she wondered.

"Because, legally, he would be your responsible party and could speak for you in an emergency, or if he could convince someone that you were, oh, I don't know, *insane*, or mentally afflicted in some way. He could cause trouble, Indie.

"We need to limit ways that he can do that, although Will strikes me as a pretty resourceful guy. We've found that it helps our cause to follow the letter of the law, whenever possible." He forced a thin, hard smile.

"We don't need anyone to have the ability to put you at the mercy of any Federal agents. The government isn't able to slap us all on America's Most Wanted posters, because what are our crimes? As I told you, we have top notch legal teams, and unlimited resources, ready to come to the aid of anyone being stalked by the Feds, as well as a great many media contacts.

"It's all about the government's desire to control information and public knowledge. The last thing the government wants is publicity about their hunt for any kind of other worldly' beings, shouted out from every newspaper. Their biggest liability is their desire to keep our existence a secret, in order to avoid what they fear would be panic, chaos or some other form of anarchy, the top fear of every governing establishment."

He looked out through the glass walls, at the valley spread out beyond the confines of the living room.

"No, they have given up cornering us, trying to trump up some kind of charges against our Members, in an attempt to *detain* us in the normal sense. They now employ the 'stalk and snatch' method, which works well in isolated places; if they can catch us alone, we simply disappear like so many people do, without a trace.

"That's when they begin their 'research', and the torture of our members can take place in the secret rooms of government labs." He rested his head back on the chair with a look of disgust.

Glancing up at Indie, the look vanished nearly instantly, as he continued his thought. "It's all in the name of security for the country, so they say. But in reality, it is to quench the curiosity of scientists, who are baffled by what we truly are."

Indie finally spoke, but her voice was so small that she couldn't be sure that she had really spoken aloud. "And, what exactly are we, Jax . . . ? *Aliens?*"

He cringed a bit at the word.

"Really, I wish you would uninstall that word from your vocabulary. It's truly inappropriate." His reproachful tone made her feel guilty, although she wasn't sure why, exactly.

"Why? Why is it so 'inappropriate?'" she demanded.

"Well, two reasons, really. For one, you are so terribly off track with your suspicions, and secondly, there is nothing 'alien' in the universe. Almost everything is part of nature, and has a reason for being, so I think to call anything 'alien' is a misnomer."

"Look," she began, a little impatiently. "Enough with the mysteries. I want to know, once and for all, what are you trying to tell me? *What* am I . . . and what are you? Are we talking semantics, here, all in the name we call ourselves? Just spit it out!"

He crushed her tightly to his chest, and she could feel his body, rock hard with tension. Indie pulled away and looked at him in disbelief. "Is it really that bad?" she asked, suddenly afraid.

"I am just so afraid that it will be more than you are ready to hear, more than you can accept. It's pretty out there," he admitted, with a rueful smile.

She stared at him for a long moment. "Okay," she sighed. "Tell me about it your way."

"Just ask me questions, and I will answer, and you may come to the conclusion on your own," he suggested, eyes closed.

Indie closed her eyes as well, for a brief moment. "Okay then. Miss Maggie was obviously a 'Member', right?"

Yes. The word sifted into her mind.

"She recognized me, and reported my existence to . . . someone, right?" He nodded, opening his eyes, and resting them on hers.

"They then contacted you, and told you that your '*Equal*' may be right here, in this little town."

"Something like that," he agreed, cautiously.

"Okay, so why didn't you just skip on down to the nursing home, and present yourself to me?" she wanted to know.

"Well," he paused, then continued in a rush, "your husband presented a problem. First of all, in the fact that you had one at all, and two, his job just happened to be somewhat incompatible with our kind. I was asked to be very cautious, to bide my time, and to try to happen upon you, away from your home, and your work place. I was allowed, if I saw you, to approach you, and speak to you, but not to touch you." He shivered, suddenly.

"But," he went on, "when I caught the very first glimpse of you, I have to say that the emotions that hit me were so unexpected, so powerful, that I was rendered quite literally incapacitated for several minutes, and you were so quick; you took off before I could react!

"I decided at that moment, that I had fulfilled the request of the Elders, and now, I was going to approach you wherever you were going, which happened to be at your work. I didn't realize that Miss Maggie was about to move on."

Indie looked down at her hands.

Move on. That was an interesting way to phrase it.

"When I was in her room, and she was relaying the story to me, she . . . she stopped time, somehow!" Indie's voice broke at the absurd sound of this accusation.

"No one can stop time, Indie. Not even the Creator. Time marches on. It is meaningless to Him. Miss Maggie happens to have the gift that allows her to alter people's perception of time. It is a mind trick of the most complicated type. She could have held us there, had she not been dying, speaking as long as she liked, and only moments would have truly passed."

He shook his head in admiration. "It's one of the greater gifts, and speaks of her ancestry . . . of . . . of the *Virtues*." He glanced at her from the corner of his eye, allowing her to absorb this information.

Indie saved the last word he spoke, to ponder later.

"And what are your gifts?" she asked, a little shakily.

"Well," he looked around, as if trying to find moral support from the furnishings. "I do not know the full scope of my gifts, but I have a small idea . . . I have the gift of knowing the mental words of others, but it isn't fully developed as yet, seeing as I have not had the Commitment of my *Equal*, but this is not special among us . . . we can all do that little trick, though some more fully than others. None of us can *fully* know the thoughts of Man . . . but many of us can get pretty close. Close enough to perfect for our purposes." He lifted his shoulders.

Hmmm ... the thoughts of MAN.

Indie filed the word in her mental scrapbook, but said nothing, busily tying every nugget of information together to form her conclusion.

"I have quite the capacity to learn as well as teach and have a photographic memory. I sometimes have quick flashes of potential future events ... not quite a future-sight, but along those lines.

"People are naturally drawn to me, and I am unusually persuasive, which I have used shamelessly in my life, and I seem to be able to channel positive energy, and help others achieve their goals. I am classified as a warrior, although I *try* to hate the thought of violence." He paused.

"Part of my Society job includes ... well ... things I will go into more detail about later. But I also know that I will fight to the death to defend what is in my charge, and that I stand loyal to the Creator, and ready to give myself to whatever purpose is asked of me."

Wow. Indie thought to herself. *That was one heavy statement.*

"I guess it was," he sighed. "But, really, although I am well trained and famously good at what I do, I'm not sure that I am *extraordinarily* gifted in comparison to some of our kind." He continued to look sideways at her.

"Are you freaking out, yet?"

"A little," she admitted, "but I think I can take more."

Jackson leaned back in the chair with a bemused expression. He pushed back the now dry wayward tendrils of her hair. "You are really something, you know?' he whispered.

She stiffened at his words. "Yes, but *what*?" she whispered back. "What am I? Am I ... human?"

"You are human-*ish*." He spoke the word with a small smile, although she knew he wasn't thinking anything slightly resembling humor at this moment.

"*Ish*? What in the hell is that supposed to mean, Jax? Human-*ish*?" Indie was trying hard to control her horror, but losing the battle.

"Indie, please ... don't lose it. Retain your senses. You said you could handle anything, as long as it is the truth, right?"

"I know I said that, but ... oh my God. Not ... not *human*?" She was beginning to take on a greenish hue.

"Listen, Indie. You are more human in some ways than our charges. We were the first of *this* form; life on this Earth did not look like this initially. *We* brought the image of our Creator ..." Jax looked as if he'd spoken out of turn, and turned the thought aside.

"When the Ancestors were instructed by the Creator to come down, to teach and assist the life that was forming on Earth, they came down into the flesh.

They became the life form . . . *this* life form, only we came as the life form was always meant to be. You could say they were human beings, *perfected*."

Indie's eyes narrowed. "Perfected in the Christian Biblical sense?" she asked. He shook his head.

"No, perfected in the flesh. Immune systems able to stop any kind of invasion by bacteria or virus. Strong, healthy with an unlimited capacity to learn, and to love. The ability to feel and enjoy pleasures with senses that made the other life forms pale in comparison." Jackson clutched at her hands in a pleading gesture.

"We are built to last. Our lifespan are much longer than that of the Human Population, but we have been trying to infuse these qualities into humanity. If you pay attention, the human life-span is ever increasing. The medical field can only claim some of the credit, but the dominant factor is the gradual infusion of the genetics from the short supply of Society Members.

"In short," he summed it up, "we are what humans were always meant to be."

"They came down . . . into the flesh?" she whispered. An idea that was so unbelievable, so incredible, that it threatened to shake the very foundation of her sanity, was beginning to take shape in her mind.

Jax held her tighter, as if to prevent her leaping up and running away.

"Yes," he softly answered the question she wasn't even sure was fully formed, in her mind.

"Jax . . . who is 'the Creator'?" Indie choked out.

"He is simply that," he answered. "The Creator of all that is, all that will ever be."

"Are you speaking of *God*?" Indie was no disbeliever, but to have this set in her lap was nearly more than she could comprehend.

"That has always been an assumption of Man, the human authors of the Bible, and tales of all cultures, that they believe in God, or Gods. He himself is the Creator," his voice was soft, reverent. "Or *God*, if you will."

She inhaled sharply, and began to shake, violently. "And he sent the Ancestors down, to take form among the life here?"

"Yes," he answered simply. Quietly.

But then felt a need to elaborate.

"The earlier forms of life knew what they were seeing, and listened and learned quite readily. Modern day people . . . they have a much less accepting attitude, preferring to attack and demonize what they can't understand."

"Who are the Elders?" Indie whispered numbly, simply to clench what she already knew to be the truth. Something that was about to engulf her, and sweep her into a spiral right out of reality. Jax answered with a resigned reluctance, afraid for her sanity now.

"They are those closest to the Creator, rarely leaving His side. They relay his wishes to . . . the messengers . . . the *Principalities*."

His eyes darted toward hers as he spoke this word, in time to see them widen with full comprehension.

"Principalities . . ." Indie's head began to feel as if were detaching from her body, and floating away.

"The fallen angels?"

She thought, for a moment, that she might be sick, and took deep gasping breaths to attempt to maintain the contents of her stomach.

Jackson swung her around to face him fully, pulling her up against his chest.

"No, no," he insisted hoarsely, "*We* are not the *fallen!* Not at all! That is a myth written by *people* out of fear and ignorance in Biblical times. *We* are and have always been here on Earth at the direction of the Creator. Our Ancestors lay with the daughters of man, *as was His will!* To improve, guide and perfect the lives of humankind.

"We are to teach and to *protect* the sacred elements of Earth. But we are not to interfere with free will, except by the direct wishes of the Creator." His tone lightened, becoming gentle once more.

"We also have free will. That is why I was directed to approach you and to plead my case to you verbally, not to touch you . . . not until *you* asked me to do it, so that it was your choice to know."

He stole a glance at her, but she had frozen against his chest. "*Please*, Indie, keep your head with me!" he pleaded, giving her a little shake. Indie was nodding her head, slowly.

"The Elders . . . *Seraphim* . . . ?" She was reaching deeply into her brain to pull out all she had ever learned about Theology.

The Seraphim . . . angels of the highest rank. Those closest to Divinity, closest to God, always chanting threefold perfection . . . *Holy, Holy, Holy!*

And Jackson . . . the warrior genes; the bloodlines of the Archangels . . . of course . . . Miss Maggie, daughter of the Virtues . . . *my God!*

Indie shut her eyes and clung to Jackson, trying to stop her descent into stark raving madness.

"I believe," he sighed into her hair, "that you have just hit your limit!"

Indie's shaking suddenly stopped. In fact, she felt unable to will her body to move in any way. She tried desperately to rationalize with herself, to allow what she was hearing to take form, while retaining her sanity.

It's so strange, she thought to herself, *how those of us who claim to believe in a God by whatever name we call Him, cannot fathom any real confirmation of His existence. If anyone ever claims to have seen or spoken to God, that person is automatically a nut. Is it because actual knowledge of His existence is simply too much for us to bear?*

And the belief in the angels? People say all the time, 'oh yes, I know an angel is watching over me!' but what if they really saw one? They would run, screaming in circles, terrified . . .

Inexplicably, she began to laugh, sounding slightly maniacal. Jax pushed her away from his body, in order to look at her, eyes full of anxiety.

"*Indie* . . . ?" he began, his fingers wrapped around her forearms tightly. It took several long moments for coherent speech to return.

"No, no, really, I'm okay. I just have to let this seep into my pores, for just a moment," she gasped. "Although I have to say, I think aliens and spaceships would have been easier to reconcile my mind with, you know?"

Jackson frowned, but said nothing, and pulled her close again. Indie could feel his mind racing, trying to decide what to say next. "Don't say anything just yet, Jax, just let me absorb this, please!"

"Yes, of course," he agreed, worriedly. He held and gently rocked her in silence for what seemed an eternity. She took a deep breath after the prolonged silence, ready to speak again.

"So," she exhaled the word. "I am an . . . angel?" Indie felt an appalling need to giggle at the word escaping her lips.
Jackson struggled to conceal his look of nervous amusement.

"Perhaps in *my* eyes, but in reality, not exactly. You are a direct descendent of those first two hundred angelic *beings*, made in the flesh."

She was confused. "But . . . I thought you said . . ." she stammered. "No, Indie, I am telling you that once the"—he stumbled over the word—"the *angels* came into the flesh, they became human forbearers."

He spoke patiently, carefully.

"It just so happens, that when one inherits the full and completely aligned set of genetic markers, he or she is genetically identical to the first angelic *beings*. You are a true descendent of the first beings of human *form*. Only upon the death of this body, (he gestured toward her with a sweep of his hand), will you re-gain the true status of angel."

Human form . . . perfected. She had to focus. Certainly, she never would have put herself in *that* category. How could this be? She had wanted to hear this, right? Whatever it was, Indie had wanted to know. But now, she wasn't sure that she could accept it. Jackson was silent, as he allowed her inner struggle to take place.

"We have unusually long life spans?" she asked. It seemed Indie *was* a glutton for punishment after all.

"Longer than the Human Population, yes," he spoke into her hair.

"Like . . . ?" she let the implied question hang in the air, but then suddenly wasn't sure that she really wanted to hear the answer. However, he spoke first, in a rush as before. "Like, perhaps, several centuries, as long as nothing takes us prematurely," Jackson revealed.

"Centuries!" she gasped, her head buzzed with the implications. *Preposterous.*

But then Indie knew without a doubt that it was true. What had Miss Maggie told her? She had said she was three centuries old. And she'd thought Miss Maggie was going for a walk down the dementia-freeway.

"This would explain our youthful appearance, then," she guessed. "That would be correct," he answered, in his low, soft cadence. "There are more than enough accounts in the Bible about the longevity of certain men at that time . . . men touched by the Creator." Jackson elaborated.

"Noah. Methuselah, Moses . . . many others. There is fact, and men's amplified version of fact to be found in the Book.

"We begin our lives aging fairly normally, and then the process begins to slow. By age thirty or so, it slows significantly," he explained further. "Usually by the time a Member nears forty, they have to gain new legal documents, adjusting their ages, and have to move on to a new place." He looked at Indie, pointedly.

"You would not have been able to pull off your true age without adjustment for too much longer, that's for sure!"

"Oh?" Indie gestured back at him. "And you think people can really swallow *your* age?" Smiling now, he shifted in the chair, and drew out his wallet. With his arms still encircling her, he flipped it open, and slid out his driver's license.

Jackson Riley Allen, date of birth, June 26th, 1983.

"You made yourself twenty five?" she demanded, feeling suddenly and quite ridiculously too old for him. Oh, and wouldn't you just know it, his driver's license picture was flawless. It was completely unfair!

He laughed. "I felt like I could pull this off for a while. Physically, I could have entered an even younger age, but I don't like to waste my education, and even twenty five is pushing *that* envelope. I do *so* enjoy being a very young attorney . . . child prodigy and all that!"

Indie smiled at his words, and then grew serious again. "I still can't fathom the idea of such a long life, and having to move around to keep people from knowing. From realizing the truth. It seems sad . . . *lonely* somehow." She sighed.

"That's true, but, don't you see? This is why we are given a companion for life. One who can make you truly complete. You will always have someone in your world to share everything with," Jackson replied in a soft, comforting voice.

"But my children!" She shrank back against him, horrified, as the realization hit her. "How on earth can I keep this from *them?*"

He breathed a heavy sigh. "That," he spoke sadly, "is not something that Members have had to face before, as far as I know. I have no answer for you, at the moment."

Indie sank her stare into a spot in the far corner of the room, her mind unable to take anymore of the conversation. She was done, at least for the moment, and Jackson read this instantly from her overwhelmed thoughts.

He took her face in both of his hands, and stroked the hair away from her eyes. He looked into them deeply . . . studying, seeking to reassure. "I am going to make you an early supper," he spoke finally, "and while you eat, I have to go out for a very short while."

Indie nodded, mutely. Jackson lifted her over to his side, rising to his feet smoothly, and headed down the hallway.

He returned in an instant. In his hands were the papers on which he had been composing. "My divorce papers," Indie realized with a small twinge. He knelt down next to her, taking her hand.

"Are you truly ready to do this?" he asked in his deep silky timbre. She said nothing, but held out her hand for the papers, and glanced around for a pen. He produced an exquisite one, made of a nearly black polished wood, and passed it to her, wordlessly.

Indie hesitated for only an instant, then signed in all of the appropriate spots, and handed the papers back. Jackson gave her a grim smile. He leaned forward to kiss her forehead.

"Thank you!" he whispered, voice heavy with relief.

After surveying her face once more for just a moment, he rose and ambled into the kitchen with his particular style of heart stopping grace . . . masculine and sensual. Indie closed her eyes, and listened to the sounds of a mini feast being prepared again, just for her.

Returning with impressive speed, Jackson carried a tray loaded with salad and some sort of pasta dish. It looked wonderful. And somehow he'd managed to sneak off to the shower too, without her realizing it. The black t-shirt, sporting graphics from the band Oleander, and the well-fitted Levi's made him look insanely young.

And obscenely hot.

The scent of Kenneth Cole wafted gently in his wake, and his hair was damp and disorderly. Suddenly, the dinner he'd prepared for her was no longer the most appetizing thing in the room. Indie felt she had to look away from him to avoid retina-damage.

It was like looking at the dangerous beauty of a solar eclipse. He grinned down at her as she struggled to compose her thoughts.

"I will be back in a flash," he assured her with a quick squeeze of her hand. "But please, Indie, I *am* going to ask that you stay inside while I am gone . . . just as a precaution," he added seriously.

"No worries." Indie promised. "I have no desire to walk out that door anytime soon!" He planted another soft kiss on her neck and shoulder, and pulled away reluctantly.

"In a flash," he repeated, and was gone.

CHAPTER 16

Will's Darkest Day

"Cromwell, I charge thee, fling away thy ambition: By that sin fell the angels; how can man, then, the image of his Maker, hope to win by it? Love thyself last: Cherish those hearts that hate thee . . ."

William Shakespeare
King Henry VIII, Cardinal Wolsey; Act three, Scene two

Will spun the cylinder of his old service revolver without seeing anything in particular. Nothing except the scene on his computer screen, that had played out a hundred times so far today. He was not feeling suicidal.

Homicidal, perhaps.

He shuddered at the dark thoughts trying to push their way to the front of his mind.

I am not a killer, he snarled to himself.

Not that he hadn't killed before. But killing someone when it was unavoidable, in the line of duty didn't count, did it? Whenever it happened, it made him sick for days. He certainly didn't *enjoy* killing, even an enemy, as some of his team members pretended. At least, he tried to tell himself they were pretending.

No, Will had never had an *urge* to kill.

Until now.

And he was not at all comfortable with the thoughts rolling around in his head, screaming for justice.

He clicked "replay" on the digital recording once more, and watched again as this . . . *creature* came into the house—"*My* house," he growled, furious—and sat on the couch, telling his own wife, that she actually belonged to *him.* Will's eyes narrowed as he watched the stranger slide off the couch and sit, crouched on his knees, in front of Indie.

"*I was born . . . for you!*" he heard the stranger say.

Again, it caused his stomach muscles to contract with rage. He clenched his hand tightly around the handle of the revolver.

Thank God, he had gotten his mother to pick up the twins today, he thought, relieved. It had been an awful and uneasy morning. The kids were unnaturally quiet and he could not bring himself to meet their eyes, fearing the accusation that he might see there.

Why in the hell should I feel like the bad guy here? He thought to himself, defiantly. *She's the one who made her choice.* His thoughts were fraught with anger and disbelief, and he heaved a sigh and placed his head heavily into the palm of his right hand, covering his eyes.

He was glad it was Friday, and his mother was keeping the twins for the weekend. He needed time.

Time to continue torturing himself with the images that he replayed across his screen repeatedly, apparently.

Being the good agent that he was, Will had arranged to have several "nanny cams" installed throughout the house, back when they had to hire a babysitter to watch the twins when Indie was starting her new job at the hospital.

He'd seen no reason to trouble Indie with this information, and he'd simply checked the digital images randomly during that brief time. He had never had the motion activated cameras removed, and simply cleared them once a month or so now, without even looking at them. But now, they'd come in quite handy.

Will took a long, deep swig of the beer he had perched on the edge of the desk, savoring the cold, bitter bite from the hops. He held the liquid in his mouth for a few seconds before swallowing. Yeah, so he'd had a few. Indie was not big on drinking, and he had always limited himself, to keep the peace.

With more than a touch of defiance, he sucked down his fifth. The way he saw it, a few beers were definitely in order. Only the good stuff, though. Will hated cheap beer. He liked it dark and strong.

He took another deep swallow, and returned to his private viewing of Purgatory, watching and listening to every detail again; pausing to make sure he got the full taste of the parts that caused him the most pain.

One of the leading contenders for favorite scene was perhaps the one taking place now: "*William Taylor is not your Equal,*" the one called Jackson said, and Indie had barked out a laugh.

"*Like that's supposed to be news to me!*" she'd blurted out, before covering her mouth, looking embarrassed. Oh, but the damage was done.

Yeah, he had *really* liked that part. It was like a physical blow every time he heard it, and yet, he couldn't stop.

—

He fast-forwarded to the place where Indie *invited* the son of a bitch in, to . . . to *touch* her!

Then the kiss. Let's not forget that.

Will could not contain the expletive that that shot out of his throat, yet again, as it had for each ghastly viewing.

"*Bastard!*"

Will stood and smashed his fist through the office door, rage consuming him. He focused the full force of his anger on this Jackson *thing*. This human-shaped monster. This freak was one of *them*!

The alien or whatever-the-hell-they-were, creatures that his government paid him to find, help capture and to interrogate.

They were considered a threat to society. "Super-human" creatures, they called them.

Human, hell!

These beings had not been totally figured out, because no real information as to where they came from, or their origins had ever been obtained. However, he did know that the unknown constituted a danger. The agenda of these *things* was unknown, and one of them had marched right into his house and taken his wife.

Will allowed himself to dwell for a moment on the idea that, apparently, Indie was one of *them* too.

Right under his nose.

Closing his eyes tightly, he suppressed a sob.

What an unobservant jerk I am. I really never studied her face . . . or paid much attention to her at all, I suppose, he thought, with a shot of guilt.

"She just never seemed to need it," he defended himself angrily, and out loud to no one in particular. "She always seemed to have a handle on everything . . . things just got done, and I never *had* to think about it."

The truth of this slapped him hard across the face.

Time to wake up, jackass.

Indie *had* done everything for him, and he had just . . . let her. He had taken her for granted for years.

Will stalked into the kitchen and ripped open the refrigerator door, grabbing another beer, roughly.

No more after this one, though, he told himself. He couldn't allow himself to get wasted, no matter how justified he felt. He had to remain in control of his faculties.

As he sought to open the dark brew, he realized he still had the revolver welded to his left palm, and shoved it hastily into the back waistband of his jeans. He resolved to get the thing back into its holster as soon as possible, because cold beer and loaded weapons seldom make good party favors when they are too close to one another.

Will despised anything he construed as weakness, and getting drunk and out of control was definitely weak. He sat down heavily at the kitchen table, taking a break from the torment he was inflicting upon himself.

In all actuality, he *had* indulged in a small act of weakness today; he had taken the day off from work. Not because he was weak, or to wallow in self-pity, he told himself, but to take care of business . . . figure out his next move. Yeah, that was it.

"Jesus, Max, would you shut the hell up!" The dog had not stopped pacing and whining restlessly all morning. Max folded his legs underneath himself, and dropped to the floor with an indignant huff.

Will's head whipped around at the violent knock that shook the room. Frowning at the unnecessary force used, he walked briskly to the door, and yanked it open.

A kid, maybe fourteen or fifteen, stood on the porch, headphones on; the tune from his IPod clearly audible to anyone within twenty feet.

Fall Out Boy.

Will ground his teeth in disgust. "What do you want?" Will barked out, in his most drill sergeant-esque voice, irritated at the sight of the teen. The intruder jumped at the sound of Will's command, which cut neatly through the music blaring into his ears.

"Uh . . . um, are you William Taylor?" the boy stammered, clearly uncomfortable. He was shifting his weight from foot to foot, fidgeting. "Who wants to know?" demanded Will.

"Er . . . uh, I have something I was asked to deliver to him . . . to you?" The boy looked at him questioningly, and Will's eyes dropped to the manila envelope the kid held. Sighing, he held out his hand.

"Yes, I'm William Taylor," he growled impatiently. The kid tossed him the envelope, and turned and fled, quite obviously in a hurry to get the Hell out of sight.

Will stared after him for a moment, and then shut the door, shaking his head. After a careful examination of the envelope in question, he ripped it open and withdrew the papers inside.

It took only three seconds to comprehend the type of paperwork he was holding in his hands, as he scanned the words on the first page. It took another ten seconds for his body to react. Dropping the papers, he tore open the front door, and sprinted out into the road. No sign of the kid, anywhere.

Violently, Will kicked at a chunk of asphalt, to release the sudden rush of fresh rage and fury, sending it bouncing to the end of the street.

Divorce papers? What, not even twenty-four hours had passed, and he was getting divorce papers? His body seemed to lose all function at that moment.

He sagged to the pavement at the end of the driveway, and sat, trying to wrap his brain around the events taking place. How had things devolved into this sorry state of misery so quickly?

This was crazy.

As Will groped around mentally for something solid to latch onto, a movement in the wooded area across the street caught his eye. His body reacted instinctively, in full motion before his brain engaged, Will's hand caught the revolver from the small of his back and leveled it directly at the figure across the street from him.

Only after the target was caught in the sight of his weapon did Will's mind catch up. It took every single fiber in his muscular make-up to hold himself back from unloading the weapon as he recognized the . . . *thing* standing near the trees across from his house.

"*You!*"

Jackson held his hands away from his body as he stepped forward, partly annoyed at Will's unexpected bolt out of the house, catching him off guard, and partly impressed at Will's keen senses and rapid response.

"What in the hell could possibly have possessed you to come here? Come to gloat about your scoring of my wife, did you, asshole?" Jackson's respect for the other man's abilities dried up quickly.

"Not at all, William Taylor. I wasn't planning a face-to-face with you, actually. Who knew you'd come stumbling out of the house like that?" He looked around stealthily to make sure no neighbors were nearby doing any dog or power walking.

"You *really* don't have to hold me at gun point . . . not if you don't want to." Jackson spoke with a wry laziness that Will found instantly infuriating.

"Well you know what, I'm kinda gettin' off on it right now, so I think we'll keep things as they are." He gestured with the handgun in an up and down appraising manner. "So this . . . *this* is what my wife found so appealing? I don't get it. You look like a punk. I didn't realize she was so into little boys!"

Jackson cooled his own fury at the insults directed toward Indie with agonizing effort. He didn't care what Will said about him, but putting down his love was a hazardous sport, and Will seemed up for the game. He tried to remember that Will was rightfully hurt and angry, and that he was even one of the Population he was charged with protecting. This helped just enough so that he could speak without gagging on his rage.

He crossed his arms and stared back at Will coolly.

"I think I can handle the fact that *you* don't find me attractive." He shrugged slightly before adding vindictively.

"As long as Indie does."

He winced as the unaccustomed nastiness tainted his mouth like poison.

Will's finger twitched on the trigger. "What are you doing here at my house again, you fucker?" His voice was now deadly cold.

"You kiss your kids with that mouth, William?" Jackson grimaced and shook his head.

This was *so* not part of the plan. He needed to get out of here before he was forced to engage with this man, and he truly . . . *truly* did not want to do that.

Not really.

"Look, I only came to make sure that the boy delivered the papers to you. I didn't want a confrontation."

"I'll bet you didn't," Will threw back at him with a sneer. "So what did you *really* want, oh high Society Member? Did you come for pointers on how to pleasure my wife? I can give you a few tips on the likes and dislikes if you want."

Oh my God. I am going to kill him. Keep it together . . .

Jackson worked valiantly to avoid launching himself at the man's throat. "Actually, William . . ."

"Stop saying my name, God damn it!" Will interrupted with a bark. "Okay. Actually . . . *Agent,* I'm willing to lay down odds that I already know more about that subject than you do."

"Fuck you!" Will all but screamed.

"Fuck *you.*" Jackson returned evenly.

"You kiss my wife with that mouth?"

Jackson's stomach burned. The whole exchange was like nothing he'd ever participated in before, and it was making him physically sick. The flow of negative energy pouring out of him now was almost *visible* to his eyes.

But he couldn't seem to cap off the anger and jealously that kept him here, playing this ridiculous game of "tit-for-tat" with Will.

"She's . . . no longer yours . . ." Jackson whispered, taking deep breaths to contain his urge to either vomit, or kill this man. These two things were demanding that he surrender to the impulse to do one or the other, and damn soon.

Will heaved a deep gulping breath as well, that caught in a near sob at the end. It made an odd, almost heart wrenching sound, and Jackson's fury left him, instantly.

This man was really hurting.

More than that. Jackson could read from him that Will was distraught beyond measure, and on the edge of a desperation he had never encountered in a human before. And, somehow, it didn't seem to be precisely *all* about Indie, although losing her had been the tipping point.

He could now taste the bitter sting of bile on his tongue, as sympathy for the man's pain caused his inclination to want to kill him, to tilt suddenly and violently in the opposite direction, which meant he was now in danger of soiling the front of his favorite t-shirt.

Shifting slightly to the right, Jackson decided that enough was enough. He was getting the hell out of here.

Somehow, his desire to hurt the man with either words or actions, had dissolved like flesh dropped in acid. As if sensing his thoughts, Will snapped the muzzle of the handgun upward.

"You aren't going anywhere. You know that, right? Actually, I'm surprised that it was this easy."

"I beg your pardon?" Jackson looked genuinely offended. "Did you think that you . . . *had* me?"

"Well, let's see. Here's *me*, holding a *gun* . . . pointed at *you* . . . ." Will looked around briefly. "Yeah, I'm thinking I have the upper hand here, you'd have to . . ."

Will was suddenly talking to no one. He'd seen the man move, but before he could conceivably even think about reacting, the guy was simply . . . gone.

He looked around frantically, and thought he may have heard the crashing of underbrush as something tore through the woods at top speed. But he could sight nothing, and swore in frustration.

"Shit. Just . . . *shit!*"

The alcohol in his system must be clouding him, just a little, he had to admit. He'd rolled up into a very professional-looking crouch, from his seated position at the end of his driveway, and now, he sat for a moment, adrift in his thoughts.

Divorce papers?

An opportunity to bag the bastard who stole Indie from him, missed. Having to look into the face of the . . . the *thing* that was now probably happily banging her. Well, it was simply too much.

Hate, anger and jealousy obliterated Will's normal capacity for calm, cool function, and penchant for thinking through any and all actions, before actually taking them.

Resolutely, Will jumped to his feet, and jogged back up the steps and into his house. He kept going until he could launch himself onto the bed and lie face down in the soft, dove-gray comforter.

It smelled like Indie.

He lay without moving for a good hour, his mind swirling with images and decisions to be made. Abruptly, he flipped over onto his back. Hurt and rage ignited in his head, turning everything inside William Taylor's mind smoldering black in a flash.

His eyes were narrowing, as he drew close to forming his thoughts. Suddenly, the decision clicked into place in his head. Will's eyes had the cold, calculating look of a hunter closing in on his prey, as he slowly reached out his hand to pick up the phone next to the bed. He dialed with one hand, using his thumb and lifted the receiver to his ear.

"Shawn Baker," he stated softly into the phone, and waited as his call was transferred.

"Baker," announced the somewhat flippant voice on the other end of the line.

"Baker, its Taylor. I need your help!"

"What the Hell's going on, Taylor?" he asked, instantly on edge. "Is everything okay?"

"No, it is not." Will began. "How fast can you get here?"

There was the sound of paper shuffling in the background. "Are you at home?"

"Yeah."

"Give me an hour, okay?"

"One hour. Got it. See you then." Will hung up the phone thoughtfully, unsure of where to take the idea he was pulling together.

Will did not believe Baker was any true friend to him, exactly. Truth be told, he had no special love for the guy either, although they had hung out once or twice. Baker always seemed just a little too eager for the wrong kind of action.

Nevertheless, he owed Will.

During one of their missions to question a local man, tucked into the wilderness of Cabot, Will just happened to save Baker's life.

The man was someone claiming quite publicly to have been "abducted by aliens". It so happened, he also had a few warrants out for his arrest. The guy had not come quietly, and only Will's keen eye, catching the slight movement of the blanket that the man had hung for curtains, had saved Baker's ass when Will threw him to the ground.

A shot echoed through the mountains, and a nice chunk was missing from the tree behind them where only seconds before, Baker's head had been.

Will had brushed off his gratitude, saying brusquely, "hey, it's my job, right? We're supposed to look out for each other." Will hoped that Baker's debt to him would encourage a little loyalty tonight.

He stood and began pacing as he refined what needed to be done. *Okay, Jackson Allen . . . you want to play? I'm ready . . . I hope you are!* Will shivered a little as he planned how to present this to Baker. He had to be very careful, if he wanted to protect Indie.

He was beginning to regret all of those extra beers, needing a perfectly clear head. "Maybe some coffee will help," he thought distractedly.

His thoughts went back to *Jackson*, and his stomach contracted. The name was poisonous to him. This creature was going to pay.

Big time.

And Indie was going to have nowhere to run . . . except back into this house. Yes, he decided. He was going to get her back.

His rage had centered on the man who had so boldly come into his home, and as good as kidnapped his wife. All with some kind of hypnotic mind trick, for all he knew. The beings had all the earmarks of some sort of sinister cult.

Will managed to conveniently brush aside the fact that he had practically thrown Indie out into the street himself.

Her Equal! He thought, scathingly.

It wasn't Indie's fault, he reasoned. It was all the *Society Member*. Get him out of the picture, and maybe life could go back to normal.

Well, not just like before.

He would try to be a better man for her. Yes, he just needed the chance, and the only way that was going to happen, was to eliminate the obstacle in his path.

And that obstacle was Jackson.

Will's eyes caressed the revolver as he placed it on his desk.

"Yes," Will whispered. "Enjoy her while you can, *Jackson!*"

Will went to the refrigerator and helped himself to another beer, cracking it open furiously, quite forgetting, for the moment, his thoughts of needing a sober outlook on things. He then moved into his office and set to work while he awaited the arrival of his partner.

Chapter 17

A Friend in Need

"Betrayal. Next to suicide and the wasting of good chocolate, the *most* unforgivable of the unforgivable sins."

Katherine Whitley

Twenty-six year old Shawn Baker was a company man; career focused to the extreme, and he enjoyed his job immensely.

All parts of it.

He even liked the boring parts, when nothing new or exciting came his way for weeks. Computer games or simple internet surfing placated his restless mind when those times hit.

The way Homeland Security worked in his particular division, was lots of busy work, which involved gathering intelligence on persons of interest, and following up on leads and tips.

Then, there was his favorite part; the excitement of a confrontation with someone who needed convincing that they simply had an over-active imagination, and had *not* had any close encounters that they originally may have *thought* they'd had.

The job was punctuated by short spurts of intense action, and separated by intervals of zero activity. Shawn had seen his share of excitement, so downtime was cool by him, although he lived for challenges thrown in his path.

And the harder the better.

He, like Will, was a proud graduate of many of the Gryphon Group's toughest combative courses, completing his last class in the Melbourne Florida location, just prior to accepting his current position here in Vermont.

—

Although not thrilled to relocate to what amounted to Hooterville, from the Green Acres series, in his opinion, he decided that the nice fat promotion and raise that it earned him would allow him to someday return to his native California a pretty wealthy guy.

He dreamed of retiring young and early to a cool bachelor pad in L.A., because he sure as hell was not returning to the Napa Valley where he was born. That place was a snore.

A snore and a bore.

Besides, he had walked away from that life of white-collar Hell, hadn't he?

Every now and then, he allowed himself an uncomfortable bout of missing his mother. It was amazing how love mixed splendidly with hate sometimes. And yes, his mother loved him, he knew, but never enough to make up for her uncanny talent for marrying exactly the same asshole over and over again.

The name and the person changed, but the character always remained the same, like a nightmarish version of Darren Stevens, from "*Bewitched*". Except in Shawn's personal show, the guys all seemed to enjoy using small things as punching bags.

Usually, one of those small things turned out to be Shawn.

From his earliest memory, his only recollection of the men in his mother's life, were measured by how hard they hit.

He wondered sometimes, if his real father had been violent toward him. He could only assume so, but the guy had taken off when he was six weeks old, so it was just a guess.

At first, he was sure that his mother must be unaware of these ugly character flaws in her favorite brand of "man". But when Shawn eventually found the courage to tell her, after a particularly brutal round with her latest fiancé, he was horrified to find her continuing on with her wedding plans, pretending nothing was amiss.

It was a lot to come to terms with for a twelve year old, especially since he had been suffering along in silence from the age of three, and had thought that spilling his guts to her would mean liberation from the abuse.

Unfortunately, it had meant no such thing, and Shawn developed ulcers at this very tender age from the near constant stress of trying to either avoid or recover from the latest pounding.

His mother apparently thought that the way to make it up to him was to indulge Shawn in every material thing she could purchase. There was never a shortage of money, which a now older Shawn strongly suspected was the motivation behind his mother's ability to turn a blind eye from the fact that all of the men in her life were using her kid as a living kickboxing target.

Well, at least he could credit her for exposing him to all of the finer things in life. She definitely enabled his brand name lust. When he and his mother went shopping together, at least he didn't have to worry about receiving a surprise and totally random clock to the melon.

As things happen, boys grow taller . . . and stronger, until one typically bright and sunny California afternoon that Shawn remembered as clearly as if it happened yesterday, his mother's latest husband had drunkenly challenged him to "take the first swing" at him.

This was one of Bobby Tilman's favorite intros to an ass-whipping, only this time, seventeen-year-old Shawn decided that today, it would be just too rude not to accept the invitation.

He'd grabbed the man's half-empty beer bottle and used it to racquetball Daddy Dearest across the face. It didn't take Mr. Tilman long to recover from his shock, and just before being carted off to the ER for some very necessary stitches by his hysterical wife, he had engaged Shawn in one hell of a battle.

At least this time, Shawn felt pretty good about the fact that he had given just as well as he'd received.

After all, it's only the courteous thing to do.

In spite of the short-lived joy this had given him, Shawn decided that the camel's back had been officially nuked, and so he laced up his "*fuck-you*" boots, and burned pavement down to the Army recruiter's office.

He filled out every paper he could that didn't require a legal guardian's autograph, and put himself in the delayed entry program. He slept at friend's houses, sneaking back home to round up enough belongings to get by for the three months before he became legal.

Shawn decided bright and early on enlistment day that he was going to be a professional badass, and the baddest dudes he could think of, were Army Rangers.

He told his recruiter he wanted in the 75th Ranger Regiment, and almost immediately following Basic Training, moved out for Airborne training. He was then assigned to the Regiment, and had the pleasure of completing the Ranger Indoctrination Program.

It was during this time that he discovered his mother's men had actually done him one really big favor; Shawn could take a punch.

A whole hell of a lot of them, as a matter of fact, and just keep on ticking.

It was just home, sweet home to him, after all.

Taking on a fight became somewhat of a specialty for Shawn, and it didn't take long for people to learn not to fall into this kind of pointless venture with him.

It wasn't that his fighting skills were any better than the other guys'; it was the fact that Shawn was damn near impossible to take down. Many had tried, and been driven to near madness by his resilience.

After fiercely kicking his way through all of the required training schools, Shawn was sent to Headquarters, where he served with obsessive devotion until the day a mysterious visitor came to speak to him personally.

A visitor with more security clearance than Shawn had ever seen bestowed on any one individual. At least anyone he had met personally.

This visitor told Shawn that he had been watching him, and that he had a job offer. Shawn had been both intrigued and uneasy at the idea of people "watching" him, but the man had made him a career offer he couldn't refuse.

It had everything. Money, power and the feeling of belonging to an elite group of individuals that had drawn him into seeking a Ranger position in the first place.

One honorable discharge later, Shawn Baker was on his way. Nothing remained of the seventeen year old who had endured a lifetime of abuse at the hands of others. The only remaining scars were internal; cynicism and an inability to get emotionally close to women. Physically close, absolutely, and as often as possible.

But he couldn't trust them . . . no way.

He kept track of his mother, but not in touch, only sending her official forms so that she would know he was alive, and that she was his beneficiary. It surprised him that she was now single. The divorce was no shocker, but that fact that she had not immediately moved on to the next jackass was puzzling.

Oh well. Maybe since she no longer had a sacrificial lamb to offer, the kind of guys she went for just weren't interested any longer.

Yeah, that really sucked for her.

Shawn ignored all communication attempts from the woman who gave him life, and then allowed that life to become hell. The part of him that still loved her, wanted to protect her from the larger part that hated her, and would probably say or do something very hurtful, so it was best for all parties if he stayed out of her reach.

For now, anyway.

There was always room for the tearful reunions down the road, but this was definitely not the time.

As an official member of the badass society, Shawn felt he had finally arrived. He was now Secret Service certified and as dangerous as they came.

He had worked with Will for the last two years, and respected him as much as he could respect anyone. Hell, he even owed him his life, but Will had downplayed his role in the official report. Shawn went right along with Will's story that they had both simply hit the deck to avoid the shot some dumb fugitive had taken at him, mortified that Will had been more on the ball than he, himself was.

It didn't flow with Shawn's self-image, to be shown up by someone he considered somewhat of a middle-aged has-been.

Not that he didn't *like* Taylor. He really did, for the most part. Shawn was simply suffering from the smug superiority complex that so often dwells in the minds of the young and powerful.

He played his part as a team member well, but really, these days it was *all* about Baker. He did not attempt to hide his Machiavellian beliefs, and spoke confidently about the righteousness of the end justifying any means.

Whatever it takes, to get the job done.

And Shawn Baker always got the job done.

"So," he wondered to himself, "just what could possibly rattle our little William's cage?" Will was usually so collected that it was just too unnerving at times. "Wife troubles, maybe?" Shawn speculated. Will had called out of work today for "personal" issues. If that were the case, what could he possibly need *his* help for, Baker wondered.

"It's not like I'm an expert in *that* field," he thought with a sharp laugh, having three broken engagements under his belt already. This was impressive, for his young age.

There was no doubt; he had serious trouble in the fidelity department. On the subject of getting up close to the fairer sex, too much was never enough, in Shawn's humble opinion. Temptation was everywhere, and he was not accustomed to denying himself a little pleasure now and again.

He seemed unable to stop himself from succumbing to the abundant female attention he attracted, and it was much worse in this area, where the pickings were mighty slim for both the ladies and the men.

But Shawn always had a shot at the best available.

This was spurred by the fact that he still had his basic training six-pack, and wore his golden brown hair a little longer that the upper management cared to look at. He loved to work out and it showed, earning the sarcastically respectful title of "PT Stud" from his co-workers. It secretly got him off whenever he heard it.

The man had also retained his penchant for fashion, and loved to look the part of a classic "Fed".

Growing up, he'd had a super-sized man-crush on the fictional character of James Bond, and modeled himself quite deliberately after 007; his closets full of black Tom Ford and Brioni suits, with narrow ties, topped off with his ever present Tom Ford single-bridge aviators, that he had picked up for a cool three-hundred and thirty dollars.

Perhaps this enhanced his womanizing ways as well. After all, Bond was a ladies' man, was he not?

Off duty, he was a brand-name junkie as well. Nothing but the best would do. Only a lack of funds kept him from tooling around town in an Aston Martin DBS 1. This was still slightly out of his reach, but he was saving up. For now, he suffered along with a candy-apple red, Nissan Sentra.

—

Oh well. One can't have everything.

But he was getting there. The personal weapon he carried was the 7.65mm Walther PPK. Something he had decided was necessary after seeing "Dr. No" for the first time. Shawn Baker was very detail oriented, and this acquisition was one that he was particularly proud of. No one was allowed to touch his gun.

No. One. Period.

His mind focused again on the ridiculous notion of Will asking him for relationship help. Will *had* to know better.

Obviously, Shawn had no problem attracting the females of the species. Keeping them was the one challenge that he apparently was not even really interested in meeting. No, he could not fathom Will looking to him for any kind of advice on that subject. Well, he would find out what the problem was soon enough.

He made a few phone calls, finished the report he was filing and hurried to his car. Shawn pulled into Will's driveway less than forty-five minutes after hanging up the phone. Punctuality was another one of his strong points.

He looked around as he sprinted lightly up the stairs leading to the front door, with his typical long-gaited and decidedly self-assured saunter. Something that always kept him moving just ahead of Will's casually deliberate stalk.

"Nice little suburban plot," he thought, a little sarcastically. He had been here only twice before, and both times at night, for a little after work hanging out.

He and Will shared an interest in motorcycles, and all things military. They had discussed endlessly the various battles of nearly every war in history, and then moved on to an argument about the motorcycles of British heritage, verses American made.

"Yeah," Shawn mused, "I guess I should try to help the old guy out." Anyone over the age of thirty was old, as far as he was concerned. It occurred to him every now and then that he was headed that way in only a few short years, but Shawn was positive that he would be different.

In spite of his fearlessness in performing his job, Shawn was terrified of death, or rather, what came after. He wasn't sure what the afterlife held, but the horror of lying underground and rotting like the corpse of a family pet buried in the backyard was revolting to him.

His bravado came from the typical mixture of youth and the feeling of immortality that keeps its company. Surely if he remained youthful, in good shape and tragically hip, he just might elude the grim reaper altogether.

At least he had his delusions to keep him warm.

No, he would never become some old, settled down, suburban plot-dweller.

Will jerked open the door before Shawn could knock.

"Hey man, thanks for coming!"

"No problem, Taylor. What's going on?" Shawn smoothly hid his irritation that the man had taken him by surprise. His partner was probably the only person in the world ever able to catch him off guard, and it bothered him greatly.

Will hesitated for just a moment, and then sighed. "I, uh, am not sure exactly where to start." Shawn created a frown of concern for his partner's benefit.

Will, suffering uncertainty and self-doubt? This should be good, he thought, with a slight touch of satisfaction mingling with anticipation.

"Well, hell, why don't we start with the very beginning, and see where we get?"

Will drew a deep breath. "Indie is gone. She ran off with another guy . . ." Shawn shook his head. This was not as interesting as he'd hoped, and damn it anyway, Will *didn't* know better than to come to him with this kind of bullshit, did he?

"Wow, man, I'm . . . uh, sorry to hear that, but . . . what do you want *me* to do?"

"You've met my wife, haven't you Baker?" Will asked. "You remember?"

Shawn sighed and thought back, pushing through his urge to roll his eyes. He'd rushed over here for this kind of crap? Jesus Christ, what a let-down!

Yes, he recollected, she had been here when he was over, but he had no clear memory of her. However, now that he thought about it, Shawn vaguely remembered dark hair and a generic idea of attractiveness.

"Yeah, I guess . . . I mean yes, I did meet her."

"What did you think of her?' Will pressed.

What in the hell was Taylor getting at, Shawn wondered, although now that he'd been asked, he could not remember thinking *anything* specific about her, which was pretty bizarre actually. Noticing females was one of the other areas in which Shawn Baker excelled. But the query was an odd one.

"Is there some reason you're asking me weird questions, man?" Shawn demanded, somewhat suspiciously. "No, no. Just forget it . . . come into the office. I need to show you some surveillance video of what happened here yesterday." Will led the way down the hall to the small room. As he followed, Shawn pursed his lips thoughtfully as he spotted the slight unsteadiness of Will's gait.

A dog watched him walk by on his way to the office, the fur on its back raised. He snarled when Shawn reached down to pat him.

"Nice dog," he said dryly as he snatched his hand back, tossing a glare at the animal. Max showed all of his teeth in response.

Will was distracted, and did not answer.

Shawn took in the fist-sized hole smashed into the office door, and the small collection of beer bottles stashed neatly in the trash bin next to the desk. His interest was returning as he instinctively felt something bigger was lurking in Will's bag of angst.

The mental memo pad was out, in full operation, and Shawn took excellent notes. He swiveled his eyes around to the coat rack where a shoulder holster, minus the weapon that it was supposed to house, was hanging.

Very little escaped Shawn's shrewd notice.

"Have a seat," Will gestured to a small stool next to his office chair. He sat as Will opened a file on the computer. While waiting for the show to begin, he looked curiously at Will.

"So there's more to this than just your run-of-the-mill, cheatin' wife story, isn't there?"

"You could say that," Will answered glumly.

The video was loaded and Will clicked "play". Shawn watched as the video showed some guy talking urgently to Will's wife, obviously making a play for her and then made its way to the grand finale'; the kiss right in Will's own bedroom.

Shawn blinked. "You've got no audio on this?"

"No," Will lied. "It wasn't working." Shawn looked at the keyboard, then back to the screen and narrowed his eyes briefly.

Okaaay.

"So," he turned in his seat to look at Will. "Who is this jerk?"

Will did not answer right away. He had a slightly frantic look in his eyes, but was calmly clicking and enlarging a still shot of the wife thief. "I don't know him, but I have managed to track down a name; Jackson Allen, and I have a P.O. Box in Montpelier for a Jackson R. Allen, attorney at law." Shawn looked back at the monitor, incredulous.

"Attorney! Are you kidding me? That guy looks like a senior in high school!" He laughed, then qualified, "Well, maybe one who failed a few grades, anyway."

Will leaned forward. "Yes!" he hissed through clenched teeth. "What else do you notice about him?"

Shawn crouched down to get a closer look at the computer screen. The guy was likely a lady-killer, that's for sure. Probably had to beat them off with a bat. He squinted at the image in front of him. There was something definitely very appealing about the man Will had captured on camera.

I guess Will's wife didn't put up much resistance, he thought caustically. Then, there was something else . . . something didn't quite seem right about this guy's features. They were too . . . perfect.

Shawn glanced up at Will.

"Something *is* a little off with this guy, Taylor."

Will nodded slowly. "The old man, Baker. Remember, he called himself a Society Member? We've questioned him several times. The one that just expired?"

Shawn's heart stopped. "The one we just had the meeting about . . . the one that the entire CIA and every Federal agent in the country have been instructed to be on the lookout for another . . . *being*, just like him?"

"That's right," Will answered pointedly.

Shawn's eyes widened, then narrowed with concentration as he studied the image more closely.

"But, why?" he asked. "Why here . . . why your wife? I thought they had some kind of built-in lover or companion . . . whatever!"

Will shook his head. "I can't answer that Baker. All I know is that he was very persuasive, and she left with him willingly." Shawn jerked his head around.

"Where are your kids, Will?"

"It's ok," Will assured him. "They're with my mother. There are no potential eavesdroppers around."

He spun around suddenly to look at Shawn, rage seeping out of his carefully arranged facade. "I want to get this bastard, Baker, and you're going to help me do it, understand? But I don't want Indie harmed in any way. This was not her fault. He . . . *conned* her, in some way!"

Shawn's eyes glittered with excitement.

"Do you know what a career high this would be if I brought this guy in? He's a young one too; in good shape. They could probably keep him alive for years, as long as he could withstand the slicing and dicing of the mad scientists down in Research. We could learn *everything* about his kind!" Will blanched, and then forced a smile. "That's exactly what I was counting on; your youthful enthusiasm!"

Shawn stood and glanced around the office. He noticed the framed school portraits of the twins hanging on the wall.

"Must be tough for the kids," he said thoughtfully, as he examined the pictures. "I mean," he continued, "they must be pretty upset by all of this, huh?"

Will narrowed his eyes at him warily. He did not entirely trust this man, but for the moment, he needed someone, and Baker had seemed like his best choice. Then he shrugged.

"They are, but they're pretty strong. I think we will all pull through this, okay. That is, as soon as we get this freak out of the picture and into captivity where he belongs!"

"Huh? Oh, yeah. Absolutely." Shawn turned and faced Will.

"It seems we have some plans to make." He smiled in a way that caused an uneasy chill to curl around the base of Will's spine.

No, he really didn't feel good about putting his trust in this man. Mutely, Will nodded in agreement.

"Time to launch our own private, Operation Overlord!" Shawn spoke with obvious glee. This was going to be one sweetheart of a deal, if he could pull it off and he had no reason to doubt himself.

His brain was already ticking off a list of things that he needed to do to make this work. He had a plan forming in his head.

All he needed now was to figure out how to put it into play.

He hoped to keep Will on board for as long as he could. It would make life easier. Shawn left with assurances that he was on top of things, and headed back toward town. He drove slowly, thinking.

It hit him in a flash.

Shawn knew just the person who would be perfect as his co-conspirator. He fished out his cell phone and dialed, glancing quickly at the clock.

He would so hate to interrupt Lockhart in the middle of her nightly fang-sharpening ritual or something. The woman had all the charm of a pit viper, and was twice as irritable. Exactly the reason she was perfect for this kind of stuff. Moreover, adding in the fact that he knew she had a thing for him, well, he had a home run.

"You are not going to believe what I am about to pull off," he spoke coolly into the phone. "Yeah, meet me at the Wayside in twenty minutes . . . I have a proposition to discuss with you!" He hung up, and threw the phone down into the console.

In full business mode, Shawn shook off the momentary feeling of guilt when he thought of Will.

After all, they *were* partners.

But, hey, he reasoned, *Will began this thing with a lie. How could he think I wouldn't notice the film footage had been edited?*

Oh, he knew how all right.

"Yeah, drink another one, Buddy!" Shawn laughed.

Not that he blamed him. If anyone had an excuse to get his drink on, it was Will.

However, that's how mistakes are made. He could guess what was on that audio that Will didn't want him to hear.

"No sound, my ass!" He would bet his mother's right kidney that there was plenty of audio, but for some reason Will was holding back, and he had a pretty good idea why. Then he sighed.

"Taylor, old buddy, I hope you understand. It's just business!" He accelerated sharply, and disappeared into the darkness.

*   *   *

Cassandra Lockhart hung up her awkwardly large, princess-style phone, carefully containing her excitement.

Shawn Baker was the only man alive for whom she would jump through hoops.

Big burning hoops of fire.

However, this was only for her own selfish reasons.

The cold truth was, that Cassandra cared for nothing and no one, and slithered through life with an extremely inflated sense of how appealing she was to others. Agent Baker was nothing more than something she wanted.

She found him to be very much to her liking, and his womanizing ways simply made for better sport, in her eyes.

She liked his sarcasm and his quick wit, not to mention his magnificent body. And she was determined to have him; at least for a tryst or two. Cassandra was smart enough to know that holding on to this man was improbable, to say the least, but that was okay.

She didn't give two shits about winning his heart. What in the hell would a heart do for her? There were other parts of Shawn Baker that she could find very useful, she thought with a smirk. He had been the subject of her increasingly rabid and explicit fantasies for over a year now.

Shawn was young and exciting. Much better than his boring old office partner . . . what was his name . . . Will?

Ugh, she thought, making a face. Of course, Will *was* somewhat hot in a way, but he was such a rule follower; all calm and stoic.

Men who were rebellious and volatile were more her speed and Shawn beautifully fit that description. Her hungry need to be around him brought her around to their department much more often than was necessary, with obviously contrived excuses.

She worked on another floor in a much larger unit, but not for much longer, she hoped.

She'd been trying to get a promotion to the top-secret elite team on which Shawn and Will were players, for a very long time, and not just because she wanted to jump Baker's hard, handsome body.

It was mostly that, yes, but the idea of being a member of this very special group was appealing as hell.

But for now, the one she was fixated upon had called and said that he needed her. What a breakthrough.

Shawn had said be there in twenty minutes. She would make it nineteen. After she put on her best face. This was her chance to flaunt her off-duty-true-beauty.

Cassandra perused her reflection in the huge, gothic mirror that hung on the wall adjacent to her bed, liking what she saw. She was proud and vain about her appearance. Little did she know that the world viewed her in a somewhat less flattering light.

Oh, most men found her attractive in their peripheral vision, but a closer look revealed something faintly repulsive.

Off-putting.

It was nothing they could name specifically, but it made most of them keep their distance, unless enough alcohol was involved.

Hell, after a few drinks, she wasn't all that bad. Nevertheless, the light of day brings good sense back to the foolish, and they always made a break for it, when the princess slipped off to the shower.

Her physical description sounded good; petite, thin and blond. Her arms and legs were deceptively boney and frail looking, but she was a highly trained and vicious fighter. Everything about her was pointed and sharp.

Cassandra was all elbows, knees and sharply filed nails.

Even her hair, in its dated, seventies feathers, looked as if it could impale; the combed back wings stood out, the tips looking like shards of glass. Her eyes were the only thing round on her body. They were large and dark, always looking on the verge of spilling over with liquid, giving her the appearance of a Japanese anime drawing.

Just under her alarmingly large eyes was set a thin, pinched nose; a beak in the middle of her face. Her lips were thin as well, with sharp points at the top. On these lips, she quickly painted on a wet, pink gloss, carefully tracing and enhancing the sharp points, and fluffed her hair.

She turned her head left, then right, appraising her look. All she needed now was her lowest cut top. She might as well take advantage of the fact that this was an after-hours meeting, and she wasn't locked into the frumpy restraints of any stuffy dress codes. The female agent shimmied into her formfitting outfit, and re-checked her face.

She then grabbed her keys and a slightly mashed pack of Marlboros.

As Cassandra darted to her car, she was giddy with curiosity. What was her bad boy Baker up to now, she wondered. Whatever it was, he had called the right person. Everything about Lockhart that made her a bad human being made her a great agent.

She was ruthless and fearless, with more than a touch of a sadistic nature.

She hated other women, could not stand children, and had contempt for most men. They had their uses, but that was about the extent of it. Baker was something entirely different. She was certain that they shared some sort of warped kindred spirit. *If only I could make him see . . .*

However, he seemed oblivious to her advances, which had gotten less and less subtle with time as she grew more impatient.

Well, maybe he was beginning to come around, she thought hopefully as she leaped into her P.T Cruiser with a horrible grin.

CHAPTER 18

A Day of Firsts

Jackson was gone for nearly two hours, and Indie busy was doing an awful lot of nothing, while rejecting her brain's demand to exercise its right to panic. The awful feeling of separation was pressing thumbtacks into her belly, and she had nothing left to serve as a distraction.

She had already horrified herself by peeking into every drawer, cupboard and cubbyhole that she'd found like a nosey neighbor, but she was hungry for any bits of information she could glean from her shake down of Jackson's home. Indie wasn't sure if she should be happy or disappointed when her Mrs. Kravitz impersonation turned up nothing Earth shattering.

She wandered through his bedroom, and inhaled the cologne that smelled delicious and sensual, like him. Indie stroked the silky softness of the cotton button-down shirts that he seemed to favor, which she found hanging in his closet.

She brushed her fingertips across the acres of CDs that were neatly lined on small shelves purchased just to hold them, noting with surprise that the majority of his music collection was made up of high energy heavy metal, and very ramped up alternative.

Killswitch, Blink 182, Disturbed . . . *Bullet for My Valentine?* And what was this, White Zombie?

One CD was facing the wrong way so that the title wasn't displayed, and stood out from the perfect order of the others. Seeking only to fix this imperfection, Indie slid the case out of the row and looked at the cover.

ABBA's Greatest Hits.

She covered her mouth with the back of her hand to smother the laughter that escaped at this discovery. It was probably turned the wrong way for a reason,

Indie decided. What self-respecting male would want to be caught with *that* on his playlist?

Finding this was the best. After all, *everyone* likes ABBA. You just don't want anyone to see it proudly displayed in your collection.

It would be like getting caught jamming to "*Copacabana.*" With an evil little laugh, Indie carefully slid the CD back into place the correct way, title facing the world, and sat back on her heels as she surveyed the rest of the collection.

She wasn't sure what she had expected. Choir music? Gospel? Chanting monks? Really, even a little *Train* would have seemed in order.

Can one stereotype the descendants of the angels? Apparently so.

She was finished admiring every corner of the house, which was decorated by someone with taste eerily similar to her own. Now Indie was restless. She longed for his return and was a little more than anxious about his main mission, which was to present Will with divorce papers.

Her heart ached as she pictured Will opening the envelope and finding what was inside. She wondered how they would reach his hands. Would Jax deliver them himself? Somehow, that didn't seem likely.

He surely was not one to go looking for a fight, which his close proximity to Will with such paperwork staring him in the face would certainly prompt. Although Indie was gaining a sense that Jackson would have no qualms about leaping headfirst into a battle that was necessary, she knew that he was not cruel by nature.

Trying to smooth the worried crease between her eyebrows with her ring finger, Indie retraced her steps through the house once more, reaching the large bedroom where her belongings were still in the suitcase on the floor.

She rummaged through the duffle bag Jackson had packed and retrieved a pair of softly aged pajamas, pale pink and girlie. Indie was feeling girly for the first time in . . . well, pretty much her whole life. She had felt obliged to take charge and take care of others from earliest childhood.

Indie had warm and clear memories of her mother, in spite of the fact that she had died when Indie was so very young. Car accidents are an especially cruel trick fate can play on people, tearing away loved ones with no warnings, no chance to say goodbye.

You watch your mother get in the car, simply to run to the market to buy a forgotten ingredient for supper, and that's that. You never see her alive again.

No closure, whatsoever.

Her father was a Marine lieutenant, who, although Indie had considered him a strong man, never recovered from the sudden loss of his wife. He'd sent Indie from family member to family member, and visited occasionally, until the alcohol finally overwhelmed his system. Indie was fifteen when she'd become a full-fledged orphan.

She then finished out her years as a minor living with an Aunt who was never home. Indie got herself to school and took care of the house, while her Aunt pursued various men, constantly changing careers and money-making schemes.

Indie filled her time by volunteering at the animal shelter, and the local nursing home. She didn't mind helping out those that were truly in need, although she always tried to put forth an exterior facade of nonchalance and tough humor, to hide the insane fragility of her heart. When she was a child, anything could make her cry, and her sobs made people take notice. She was teased mercilessly for her easy tears whenever the facade slipped.

She decided early on that she should work in a field that let her care for others, and nursing fell into her lap with a scholarship and money from her father's insurance. That was when she discovered her funny little gift for knowing the magnitude of a person's illness or injury simply by touch.

This scared her at first, but then, people's reactions when she wasn't careful, began to scare her more. It seemed she could ease some people's pain through her touch alone, which Indie initially attributed to the power of any touch having the ability to comfort, calming the "skin hunger" that people have naturally when sick or hurt. It didn't take long, however, before she began to see that her peers didn't have quite the same effect on the suffering of others.

Indie was glad that she had this gift, but at the same time, it furthered her sense of isolation, and of being different. It fed her unnamed angst; her sense of need that she could not calm. She felt obligated to swallow it down, and focus on being like everyone else.

Indie thought that love could save her. When she met and eventually married Will, she had secretly hoped it would put to bed those restless aches that followed her around, nipping at her heels.

Unfortunately, the similarities between her marriage and the intense passionate connections that she read about in her multitudes of romance novels, fell somewhere between none, and less than none.

She finally decided that she must be delusional, or even greedy to think that there was more . . . a different kind of fierce and unconditional love that a man and a woman could feel for one another.

But was it so wrong to need true passion, tempered with fun, humor and compatibility? A partner who inspired pride and respect?

Yet she wanted no one to misunderstand; Will was perfectly deserving of respect, and he did have that much from Indie. She *was* proud of him, in the way that he provided well for his family, had a strong work ethic and was well thought of by others.

Indie resigned herself to choking back the irrational feelings that surfaced nearly every day of her life. The feeling that somehow, she was missing a very important part . . . like *lungs*, or something equally necessary, but survived on a portable ventilator of sorts, that allowed her to walk around, continue to function, but on a much lower level than she knew she was capable of.

Indie was restless, but resigned until she saw *him*. She shuddered at the memory of her first glimpse of Jax, and how it made her feel. Indie sat on the bed, absorbed in her thoughts. She heard the front door open.

*   *   *

After Jackson's mad sprint through the woods to get away from Will, he'd had to do a little deep meditation, gathering himself together before he could start his car. He'd rifled though the glove compartment, grabbed a small roll of Pep-O-Mint Lifesavers, and crammed two of them in his mouth at once, in order to scald out the acrid taste left in his mouth from the obscenities he'd inexplicably uttered during his verbal smack-down with Will.

Although Jackson was far from perfect, and had definitely dropped the occasional oath here and there in his lifetime, the "*f-bomb*" was one of the few that had never crossed his lips before, and he wasn't feeling it.

Nope. Not feeling it *at all*.

Now, Jackson knew that words are exactly that, and were created and given their meaning by man. Therefore, swear words didn't particularly dismay the Elders, nor the Creator either, but *still* . . . .

By Jackson's understanding, the only thing verbal that goaded the Creator was any and all suggestions on who or what to submit to eternal damnation. He kept his own counsel on that subject, and was not impressed with input from humans on that note.

But the whole meaning and use of the "f-word" was distasteful to Jackson as a matter of principle, and swear words in general were simply discouraged by the Society teaching as a matter of using your education. One should have a decent enough vocabulary to be able to express one's self without relying on crutches such as obscenities.

He had really almost lost it . . . until he'd gotten a glimpse into Will's head.

Feelings only, but they'd hit Jackson like a truck. He was just happy he'd ended up not succumbing to the horrible urge to hurl, and his t-shirt remained unspoiled.

Finally, after impatiently crunching up the mints, and feeling the cleansing breeze of peppermint sear through his sinuses, Jackson fired up the engine. He carefully cleared his thoughts. Not to hide or deceive, but he knew Indie would be upset by the unintentional confrontation, and he sought only to spare her this sorrow.

Stopping only once, to commit a quick, violent act against a creature that had no business mingling with the Human Population, Jackson headed home feeling somewhat vindicated.

*　　*　　*

Indie!

She heard the anxious call in her head before he spoke aloud. "Back here, Jax . . . in the bedroom," Indie called out, relief audible in her voice. He appeared in the doorway in a remarkably short time. She had to wonder with a little laugh to herself, if he had run through the house.

"Maybe we could call it a brisk walk!" He smiled down at her. She looked up and caught her breath as his calming eyes met hers. It took a second for her speech to return. He reached out and gathered her hand in his, pulling her off the bed to stand in front of him, then hesitated, and pulled in a deep breath.

"On second thought . . ." He pulled her around suddenly back to the bed, and took her down with him, wrapping the arms that were now Indie's addiction, around her tightly. They stared at each other for a moment, and she felt her face begin to feel hot under his unwavering gaze. Indie started to pull away, but his arms tightened in protest.

"Please," he pleaded softly. "Not just yet. I need to hold you." He closed his eyes now, and buried his face in her hair and breathed deeply, his lips managing to graze her neck and ear, making Indie whimper involuntarily. She felt him sigh.

Rolling her to the side, he looked down at her, his eyes serious. "I accomplished what I set out to do today." His face was taut with worry.

Indie tried to suppress the sick feeling that washed over her, as she again pictured Will's face, contorted with humiliation and pain.

All of a sudden, she had a split-second image of complete and utter desperation pouring forth from the man, as the memory escaped Jackson's thoughts, guilt twisting his gut once more. The sharp tightening of her throat burned, and tears stung her eyes. She tried to curb them, knowing that this would make Jackson feel even more anxious and guilty, but they could not be stopped.

As he pulled her up into a sitting position, and dragged her onto his lap, the tears became sobs. Indie curled into a tight little ball against his chest, overcome by her sorrow for Will's suffering.

"I am so, so sorry, Indie," he said softly. "Tell me what I can do? Your compassion for the suffering of others is your strength. Can you believe me when I say that I take no satisfaction in Will's pain?"

"I know that. I really do." Indie sobbed, "And I know *this* hurts you as well."

He sighed deeply once more, crushing her tighter, and he shivered a little. She looked up at his face. His eyes were filled with her pain, as he looked back at her for a very long moment before finally speaking.

"It is too much? Was this worth it for her? And the man, Will . . . I think I've destroyed his *humanity*. What have I done?"

Jackson's voice was nearly inaudible, as if in prayer. He was barely speaking aloud, but his eyes were no longer focused on Indie.

"Did I simply destroy her life, rather than save her? Look at all I have cost her." Indie tried to meet his eyes, but they looked past hers, as if he were seeing another place.

"I could take her back," he whispered, closing his eyes. "But I've put her in danger. William knows now that she is Society born . . ."

She stared at him in shock.

You would choose her path for her, young Jackson? A soft, yet powerful voice seemed to come from every corner of the room. Indie looked around for the source, and found no one, but immediately sensed an august presence.

It soon became clear that the voice was coming from inside her head, yet seemed as though anyone in the room would have heard it. She clung tightly to Jax; not fearful, but overwhelmed by the idea of the origin of this voice.

The voice laughed gently, full of love and smooth as silk.

William Taylor would take her back, even as he plans his revenge upon you, my Brother!

"I would take her back, and leave her in peace. I will turn myself over to officials, to take away the heartbreak I have brought to her . . . and her children," Jackson spoke, misery overcoming him. The voice caressed the corners of Indie's mind.

Ah, but there begins the conundrum, does it not? The pain inflicted upon you if you are captured and harmed, will be simultaneously enjoyed by your Equal. She would share in your torment, as well as your death, should it occur. Are you prepared to offer her this fate?

Jackson shook his head fiercely at this idea, and snarled in a nearly bestial fashion, before dragging himself away from the rising outrage at the very thought.

"Not if I forgo the Commitment. And I will. In a heartbeat, to free her from her pain! There is *nothing* I will not offer for her happiness." The abrupt shift in his expression and tone from murderous to distraught was astonishing.

Indie pulled herself out of his clutches.

"What are you *saying*?" She gasped the words, feeling, suddenly as if she were speaking in a vacuum.

"Who are you talking to?"

He didn't respond, but continued to look through her, his expression one of devastation, desperation.

"Jax, *PLEASE!*" she shrieked at him now, truly terrified. The whispery voice filled her head again, soothing yet commanding.

Our young Brother is fighting a battle within himself at the moment, and he is looking to the Elders to give him the strength to take himself away from you, if that would ease your pain. The voice sounded amused, in spite of her rising panic.

"Are you—?" Indie already knew—"you are an *Elder*?" Indie gasped, awestricken.

That I am, my precious one, the voice confirmed. Indie was reeling. She grappled with the knowledge that the voice she was hearing, belonged to one who was part of the reality-shaking concept that Jackson had presented earlier.

She also realized that she had not had time to allow this knowledge be fully accepted, in spite of the fact that here she was, *hearing* the voice of one of the highest order. It was impossible to shake away the feeling that she was somewhere outside of her body . . . a fascinated observer of the whole scene.

She turned to face Jackson, and planted herself on her knees in front of him.

"Jax!" She shook him. "Listen to me, please! In spite of the fact that this is painful for everyone . . . I can't regret this. I just *can't!*" Indie shook him again, and his eyes looked slightly more focused.

"You say you have waited your whole life for me, but I also, have waited my entire life for you! How can you not see . . . how can you not *know?* I was half a person, simply existing for the sake of others before you found me. I didn't know why I was lost, I just knew I was. I need you now with every ounce of my being, and I *won't* be without you, do you understand?" Jax turned his eyes fully on her, tortured and almost the color of the night sky now.

"No. I *can't* do it, Indie, and I *won't* bear your suffering!" He placed both of his hands around her face, and brought his forehead down to rest on hers. But Indie pulled back and spoke firmly.

"Just *stop* it! Shake it off, warrior! If you say that you can't bear my suffering, then how will you live if you leave me?" she demanded. "That will be suffering that neither of us can bear, and I will not allow you to do that to me . . . to *us!* You would *not* take away my free will, would you? I heard somewhere that you can't do that!"

Soft laughter filled the room. The disembodied voice of the Elder swirled around her.

Your Equal rejects your heroic attempt to rescue her from the path that destiny has set before her. Do you hear her? Will you honor her vote in the decision of her own fate?

Indie seized Jackson by the shoulders and got all up in his face before speaking again. "Let me put it to you this way, Jackson Allen; I will not tolerate separation from you. Period. What do you have to say to that?"

The stereophonic laughter deepened, and Indie could feel the rumble deep within her chest.

Are you stating your Commitment, Indie, to your soul mate . . . your Equal?

"Yes!" Indie spun around wildly, trying to face the origin of the voice that seemed to come from everywhere. "I am! I will make the Commitment, right here. Right now!"

These words had the effect of knocking Jackson free of the numb sickness that he was allowing to consume him. His head shot up, eyes snapping as he tried to turn her toward him.

"Indie, wait. You have to stop . . . to think!" he pleaded, his voice hoarse with misery. "You cannot rush into this decision."

Your partner has chosen her path, Brother. You should respect it. She makes her choice with full knowledge, and free will. Would you truly deny her this?

The voice was gentle, but faintly disapproving.

"But does she?" Jax looked up fiercely. "Does she really know what this could cost her?" Jackson still sounded broken. Indie opened her mouth to give Jackson an earful for being so stubbornly obtuse, but before she could respond, the voice of the Elder rose to fill the house with its sound.

Does anyone know in advance, the consequences of their actions? One may have an idea, but the true outcome is an unknown. Your Indie has very clearly indicated that she is prepared to face any situation, except for the removal of yourself from her life. These are the words of your worthy Equal, and I have seen, and now accept her Commitment to her life with you . . . her partner, her Equal, for all eternity. The question now is, do you accept her will, Jackson?

He brought his eyes down to meet hers. They were wide with uncertainty.

"How can you be sure?" His voice was strained. "Can you know in such a short time?" He shook his head. "*Eternity*, Indie! Did you hear what he said? And the danger. You can't forget, there will be danger!" Indie caught both of his hands in hers.

"I knew it from the beginning. I knew from the moment of your touch. I will not be without you . . . *ever*! You *have* to know this. You can *see* into my thoughts and find your answer!" She lifted his warm hand and placed it on the side of her face.

"Weren't you the one who told me to learn to put aside what I believe to be rational? When I asked you how you could have such love for me in an instant?

Well, I know what I want; what I need and you . . ." She kissed his palm and met his eyes defiantly. "You *are* going to give it to me. And you're going to do it *now!*" Indie's words carried a direct command now.

Jackson moved so that he was on his knees as well, facing her.

In thought, he tried desperately to challenge her authority over him. *But for the fact that your word, is my law!*

His face was a perfect picture of this internal battle. Indie could clearly read fear, longing, love and desire, and finally, a grudging acceptance of her words. With that acceptance came hope. He stared into her eyes for a very long time, not speaking, his thoughts slowly becoming focused.

Speaking softly, hesitantly pushing the hair away from Indie's face, Jackson spoke in a whisper, barely audible. "Then I—I accept your Commitment, Indie. And *most definitely* give you mine, for eternity!"

"For *eternity,*" she echoed, fervently.

The voice of the Elder encircled them both in warmth, and a feeling of tangible love.

You are, by the blessing of the Creator, fully Committed, and Recognized. Your union will always be. Each of you will share in the others' triumph and sorrow, until the end of your time in this life, after which you shall move on together in the fulfillment of your future. I leave you now, in the care of one another.

They were alone. The intensity of the moment made her want to cry. She also experienced an unexplainable sense of loss at the withdrawal of the voice of the Elder.

She shed now, not tears of sadness, but tears for the sudden, overwhelming feeling of total love and acceptance. Indie tried to swallow the lump in her throat . . . the emotions that she couldn't quite grasp.

She peeked out through her hair to look up at Jackson. Her earlier inexplicable claim to her higher birthright over him, had run off somewhere, and left her feeling uncertain.

This was her life now.

Her world.

Jackson's eyes conveyed the same unspoken feeling. As she studied him, taking in the curiously unique color of those eyes, they suddenly darkened with another emotion. One that Indie recognized, and shared instantly.

With a speed and strength that left her gasping and disoriented, Jackson lifted her toward him and brought his lips to hers in a commanding kiss that threatened to ignite the fabric on the bed.

She could feel the need and purpose in his hands, as he brought them up to stroke through her satiny hair, then down the length of her arms, and up again. With a quick motion, he scooped her up and back, pushing Indie deeply into the soft blankets as his hands left a trail of searing heat all over her.

Indie felt his body flatten out on top of hers, as if he were reaching for something. She heard the sound of a drawer opening and Jackson spoke in her ear with an urgent and seductive masculinity.

"There is something I must do first, my love . . . at long last!" She could detect an undertone of held back emotion, as if his excitement could burst through his vocal cords.

For a moment, being the modern-day woman that she was, Indie thought that he was reaching for a condom, and a soft chuckle escaped Jackson's lips as he picked up on the idea. Before she could respond, she felt something cool and smooth slip over the middle finger of her left hand, to take up residence next to the very place vacated by Indie's wedding ring, which was now in the bottom of her duffle bag somewhere.

With a gulp of surprise, she lifted her hand to examine what had been placed upon it, and drew in her breath at the beautifully inscripted, sparkling band that now rested with a solid and proud presence on her finger.

As she was still staring at this lovely piece of artwork, she spied Jax moving his hand surreptitiously, and noticed that he was about to shove something onto his own finger, and she stopped him with a shriek and a smack.

His eyes flew open in surprise, and then sparkled mischievously as he handed Indie the slightly larger mate to the ring he'd placed on her hand, without a word.

Indie took the ring in steady hands, and looked Jackson directly in the eye as she carefully slid it home in a gesture that increased her desire for him threefold. This, he also read with no trouble at all, and his own hands trembled as he glanced at the symbol of their Commitment, at rest on his finger after waiting so very long for the honor.

Jackson stretched, full length over her, not allowing his weight to crush her, but the evidence of his need was impossible to ignore, as he allowed his hips to lock naturally into place with hers. She felt him begin to slow, the furious kisses softening, though his breathing was uneven. Indie felt him pull back, and come to rest on her side, as he turned her to face him.

He pulled her very close, and closed his eyes, trying to slow his breaths and regain some control.

"Are you really okay with this?" he asked, reluctantly. In answer, Indie rested her lips on the curve of his neck before kissing her way south. "No," she murmured against his skin. "Are *you* okay with this?"

Okay?

Jackson's heart was beating so violently against his ribcage that his brain almost responded with a terrified *"no!"* But his body was busy putting out the *"hell yes"* vibe, all without his help, and a feeling began to build in him that was all *too* okay.

The feeling was powerful, and dragged itself up through his belly; beautiful, except . . .

"Stop!" he ordered, his voice unsteady, "or this will be over before it starts!" Indie had to laugh, softly against his throat.

"Really, Indie . . . *is* this it?" he persisted. "Are you wanting to continue? It's okay if you need some time."

Indie clutched his shoulders impatiently. "Look Jax, it's a done deal! I've made my bed, pardon the pun, and now I fully intend to roll around naked in it!" Jackson looked a little uncomfortable.

"You aren't . . . *nervous*, are you?" Indie suddenly felt the acknowledgement in her head, and wanted to comfort him immediately. In spite of the cocky statement he'd made to Will earlier about his confidence in his ability to "pleasure" Indie, it had been mostly for effect. He *wasn't* sure about it.

Not at all.

He was afraid of not living up to her expectations, and afraid of any regrets she may have later.

"I am under the impression that I *have* to be able to make you happy, because I *am* supposed to be perfect for you." He looked so vulnerable now, so different from the calm, strong and confident man she had seen thus far. Her nurturing instincts kicked in, and she gathered him even more tightly into her arms.

"There is no possible way that you can't make me happy, because I am already there. The only thing that can improve this moment is to get even closer to you. I *want* you, Jax, in a way I have never felt before in my life."

He stared at her, uncertainly. Finally, he smiled.

"There's nothing I want more as well, but truly, you need to take it easy! You're kind of making me crazy, and I don't want it to end in like, ten seconds!"

Indie had a short fit of soft laughter. "That's okay. We get unlimited 'do-over's'!"

"Perhaps so," he acknowledged. "But only one 'first time,' and I mean to make it count!" he explained with a little growl.

"I don't think I'll fight you about that." She mused over this sentiment.

She closed her eyes, and began to give herself over to these unfamiliar but wonderful feelings taking over every corner of her body as a slow shift in power occurred; Jackson began to take charge.

There was not an inch of her that he did not give his attention, in his quest to bring her up to his dangerously peaking level of excitement.

His warm hands slid around her body, maneuvering her where he wanted her to lie with ease, his kisses growing more urgent, more intense. As Jackson moved to grip her wrists, he hesitated, and then lifted them suddenly over her head, breathing fire into the shivery, sensitive places around her collarbone, and then slowed again.

"I—I am *trying* to be gentle, Indie . . . ." His voice was incredibly male; raw and raspy.

"Do you feel like being gentle?" Indie moved her head to get to his neck, whispering in to what was apparently quite the sensitive area for Jackson, judging by the sound of air being pulled through his clenched teeth.

"I *want* to be gentle for you. I want to do this the *right* way."

Indie's response was spoken in small nips down his neck, and he began quivering all over. "That's not what I asked. I asked if you *feel* like being gentle."

His whisper was like satin. "No . . . no I don't"

"Then maybe, it would be okay if you weren't . . . so *very* gentle!" Jackson shuddered again as she continued.

"I'm thinking that if you are supposed to be perfect for me, then you need to go with what you want to do, understand? Because guess what? I don't think I will mind being, um, *ravaged* by you." She dug in her nails and felt his entire body stiffen.

The idea had suddenly come into her head that maybe, for the first time, she was going to be able to let loose with her full strength. There would be no need to hold back, for fear of hurting someone. She knew that whatever she dished out, Jax could take it.

And the idea that he might meet her with equal enthusiasm!

Oh, she could hardly wait!

"I am not fragile, you know," she whispered in his ear. "Not physically anyway. I find the idea of you losing a little of your self-control . . . interesting! What do you think about that?" Indie bit down gently on his ear, prompting a very ferocious sound of approval from her mate.

"I think those thoughts are quite . . . *inspiring!*"

His hands suddenly moved with even more purpose now, his passion nearly explosive as his body seemed to blast into overdrive. Indie went limp with pleasure. He was every inch the man, and she was ready to receive anything he chose to do for her.

More than ready.

As Jackson went all out, she was pleasantly shocked.

Whoa, he was really into this, she thought breathlessly.

Well. The civilized gentleman had stepped out for a bit of fresh air, leaving behind a simply raging beast of desire. Which was perfectly fine by Indie.

It crossed her mind briefly that the books that she loved, maybe, just maybe, had a little competition now.

As Indie felt her own desire rise, the passion building, she inexplicably thought of Will. Not in a wistful or desirous way . . . just the fleeting thought that with him, it had never felt like this. With Will, the rush of need, the tightening below her belly, screaming for release had never manifested. Will had never . . .

Jackson abruptly tore his lips away from Indie and took her face in his hands, pulling her up to look in his eyes. Eyes that were blazing fiercely, with an almost violent emotion.

Not at all afraid, Indie watched in fascination as the fierce look gradually softened into one of rueful apology.

His breathing steadied, and he leaned forward to kiss each of her eyelids, then her cheek, and finally, ever so softly, her lips.

"I . . . ah, I am thinking, that maybe we could do this without quite so much *"Will"* in your thoughts?"

Busted. Oh how horrible, that he thought . . . .

"No, I don't mean to intrude, but his name was kind of hitting me like a spike through the forehead, and I just couldn't . . . I mean if you want to stop . . ."

"No! Oh, no I do not! And, just so you know, the only thought I was giving to . . ." she felt Jackson tense, "to *him*, was how completely different this was, and in only the best of ways."

Indie met his eyes and silently commanded him to read the truth in her thoughts. "I was simply thinking that I finally get to feel how it is *supposed* to be, and it makes me so very happy!"

Jackson's beautiful eyes cleared as he acknowledged this revelation, and he began the assault on her senses once more, with even more enthusiasm.

He was relentless as his lips left trails of fire down her belly, and he hid his lack of experience amazingly well, as his tongue masterfully traced tantalizing patterns of sensation in exactly the right places.

She felt a torturous need to have him inside her when she experienced the release that she knew was coming, but no matter how hard she tried to dictate the pace of things, Jackson held her fast to his own schedule, defying her impatience with maddening strength and complete control now.

At precisely the moment that Indie truly feared for her sanity if he didn't give himself to her fully, Jackson pulled upward and turned to lay on his back. He lifted her body, aching with need, down to his own, completing the union; his hands locked down behind her, and his triumphant whisper in her ear kicked her straight over the edge . . . .

"So much for your leadership . . ."

When the promised reward came, she felt a shock of relief, joy and pure love that was almost unendurable as they finally crested in the most primal of physical acts. Physical, but with more emotion than Indie had ever imagined could exist between two people.

When her heart rate finally returned to within normal limits, she felt as though every bone, every muscle in her body had turned to liquid.

A warm, soothing liquid. and she was unable to move.

"And who *wants* to, anyway!" Indie thought, completely dazed, and grateful that the house wasn't on fire or anything, forcing her out of her state of blissful paralysis.

Jackson surfaced somewhere behind her, in a state of new-found physical disorder.

"Unbelievable . . . that was . . . ." His words trailed away. Speaking seemed just too difficult a chore, somehow.

He was floating, and his joints and muscles had little function, and so he decided that collapsing in a heap next to Indie was all he could manage, although his hand kept contact with her skin.

Indie was dimly aware of Jax's hand, softly tracing patterns across her shoulders and back. It felt so soothing.

So loving.

She sighed contentedly, and allowed herself to be engulfed in the clouds of swirling emotions. She knew that the difficult realities that lie ahead were still there, tapping their fingers impatiently, waiting for them to recover. However, for the moment, she was going to ignore them.

But it soon became clear, that something was different.

As she lay quietly, she noticed the clear sound of Jax's heartbeat; steady, strong and regular.

"How strange," she thought. "It's not as if I have my ear pressed to his chest." Actually, she had ended up on her belly, face pressed into the pillow. Her hands had always been warm, but now she could actually feel heat pulsing out from her palms.

Not a sweaty, nasty heat, but a powerful warmth she somehow knew would bring a more impressive healing comfort to the suffering than she had previously given. There was also now a strong sense of serenity within her; a confidence from knowing with certainty her true destiny.

She felt Jackson roll over fully, to shape himself to the curve of her back, and he pulled her close.

Well, I suppose the days will be full of surprises for the both of us, as we become privy to the full range of our gifts!

His thoughts were now moving fluidly into her own, while his lips trailed kisses from her shoulder to the bend of her elbow. Indie's brow creased in concentration. She could feel her heightened senses. Her hearing, amazing before, was amplified further.

From the skin-to-skin contact she shared with Jackson, she could sense his perfect health. A complete lack of inflammation or disrupted cellular growth. She was also slowly gleaning an uncomfortable feeling coming from the mind of her *Equal.*

A sharp instinct, warning of something horrible swirling its way toward them both. She cringed, feeling the hair on her body rise, goose bumps appearing everywhere.

"Jax?" Indie spoke out loud, her voice strangled with a sudden unnamed fear.

"It's true." Jackson responded reluctantly. "I can feel a danger. A plot building that will bring about . . . unpleasant events."

Indie spun around to face him. "What is it, then? What can we do?" "Nothing, for the moment," he answered, speaking with deliberate thought, cradling her close to his chest. "This plot is still unfolding, and we must bide our time until we understand it fully."

With a swift kiss, he moved her back, and brought his head down to look her in the eye. "Know this. Whatever happens, I will not let any harm come to you, and I will battle for those that you love!" he reassured her.

Indie stared back at him, swallowing the sudden terror she felt. Placing her hand to his face, she nodded her head.

She did trust in his vow to protect her. She reluctantly pulled away, leaving the bed. Jackson followed. They showered and redressed in casual comfy clothing. The afternoon was ending, and they had no need to leave.

They spent the next several hours locked together in the big suede chair, communicating silently, and adjusting to their own unique new feelings. The warnings of danger were set aside for the time being, as Jax was certain that they were safe for the night, at least.

Indie mentally prepared herself for the next day's challenges, as Jackson regarded her in worshipful silence during this transitional time.

As the sun began to set, Jackson disentangled himself from Indie's grip very gently and stood, pulling her up along with him.

"Come," he spoke aloud. "I have much to tell you, and even more to show you. We should begin at once!" Indie's eyes were clear, bright and expectant as she looked at him with complete trust.

"Yes." She whispered softly. "I am ready!"

CHAPTER 19

Shawn pulled his car into the parking lot of the diner. In keeping with her typical scofflaw ways, Lockhart's car was parked in the handicapped space near the front door.

He closed his eyes and shook his head.

"Yeah, real classy, Cassandra!" He exhaled with irritation.

The woman disgusted him, although he couldn't put his finger on exactly why, aside from her blatant disregard for anyone other than herself. It wasn't as if Shawn had never seen less attractive women in his life, but for some reason, looking at this one for too long made him nearly physically sick.

Her infatuation with him was no secret either, in spite of his continued act of ignorance. It was the main reason he had decided that she should be the one to help him hatch this plot. There wasn't much Cassandra wouldn't do to improve her chances for a little game of one-on-one, Shawn was willing to bet.

He suppressed a shudder of revulsion. Not that there was any chance of that happening, *ever!*

There wasn't enough tequila in Tijuana to get him near that.

Stepping from his car, Shawn cursed as he sank ankle deep in the muddy parking lot.

March, in the great state of Vermont, was a truly awesome experience. Otherwise known as mud and black fly season.

Sweet. No wonder Lockhart had parked practically on the walkway.

He extracted a small roll of Tums from his pocket, as he prepared himself for both the brutal assault on his senses from Agent Lockhart, as well as the rare treat of diner food that he was going to indulge in for supper tonight.

Maybe a little greasy, but good.

If any of his snobby friends found out, he would deny it to his dying breath, but Shawn loved their Sheppard's pie. It was killer here.

210

It should be worth the extra hour it would require at the gym to work it off.

Shawn tossed the small pink tablet into his mouth and worked at grinding it into the dusty-tasting paste that was a part of his every waking hour. He tilted the cylinder-shaped roll and squinted at the wrapper.

Cherry flavor.

Right.

Shawn's sensitive stomach was about to be put through a hellacious ordeal; diner food in tandem with Lockhart.

Good God!

Meeting with Lockhart was an unavoidable necessity right now, but Shawn couldn't help thinking how much he'd rather be out doing his usual Friday night thing; cruising the clubs of Stowe, and disturbing the peace of every female around, by his very presence. He paused, thinking wistfully of all the activity he was likely to miss out on, all in the name of duty.

But it will all be worth it in the end, won't it? Just think of it as a working tribute to mashed potatoes and gravy, right?

He just hoped that he could still enjoy the treat while looking at her bulging eyes, watering at him suggestively. Shawn took one more, just to be safe.

As he picked his way carefully through the mud, Shawn heaped silent curses upon the head of the plow-guy for this establishment. You would think after being in operation for almost one hundred years, they might have found a way to scrape the slush, mud and melted gunk off of the damn parking lot.

Pausing at the front door, he scraped as much of the mess from his shoes as he could manage. He spied her, waving from a booth near the back of the restaurant, and rolled his eyes. Yeah, good thing she was back there with the hand gestures. God knows, he never would have found her otherwise, in that tiny little dining room.

Shawn buried his irritation, and fixed a grin on his handsome face. He knew how to work her.

"Hey there, Cassandra. Lookin' good, sweetie!" He restrained his desire to laugh at her obvious "come hither" outfit.

Agent Lockhart had transformed herself into something resembling a pole dancer on break.

"Yeah, eat your heart out, Baker," she purred, tossing her head, but looking pleased. She smiled a big toothy smile at him, and Baker winced. There was pink lip-gloss on her teeth.

Shaking off his revulsion, he took a steadying breath and reassembled the sincere looking smile as he slid into the seat across from her. She reeked of cigarettes and a potent amount of a sharply unpleasant perfume.

As Shawn struggled not to gag, he reminded himself how important she was to his plan. Cassandra Lockhart was his candidate of choice not only because she would bleed just to get closer to him, but also because of her nonchalant attitude toward rules and the law in general.

She got off on using her status for bullying the good citizens of Earth, to get out of speeding tickets and most especially to intimidate local law enforcement. For reasons Shawn didn't understand, Lockhart seemed to have a real problem with cops.

But she would have no problem going along with the most unthinkable of plans, if there was something in it for her. Or if she thought there was.

"So." She got right down to business. "What is this career making coup that you're about to pull off?"

"Well brace yourself," he replied, grateful that there would be no need for small talk. "I have found us a few *Society Members!*"

"Society Members?"

Cassandra drew back her lips in a grimace, which Shawn guessed meant that she was digesting this information. She did not work in his department, and wasn't fully educated about these creatures, but he knew that she had heard about them, and no doubt, the direct instructions to find another.

"Are you sure about that, Baker? I thought that they were, like, really rare. We only got the word yesterday about looking for another. And, what did you say . . . *a few?*"

"That's right." Baker replied casually, picking up a menu in an effort to deliberately keep his eyes distracted from the woman across from him.

"Where—when . . . ." she began excitedly, looking around and spotted an elderly gentleman looking at her curiously from the next booth. "What are you staring at, Methuselah?" she snapped, rudely.

The old man shrugged.

"Keep your nose at your own table, then!"

"Yeah, okay. You've got lipstick on your teeth . . . ." the old man shot back, before returning to his coffee and paper.

Shawn coughed quickly to hide his laughter at the old man's moxy. Cassandra snarled, enraged, and suddenly, he was a little afraid for the outspoken senior citizen. He decided to get her back on track, quickly.

"Listen, we don't have time for you to play with the locals, okay? I need you to help me with a plan. A plan that will get them all together where we can snap them up fairly easily."

Palms down on the formica table, he leaned in closer, fighting his facial features to avoid having a lip-curling look of disgust accidentally pop up while he was looking at her. "I don't want anyone else in on this, understand? You and me, that's it. We don't need anyone one else horning in on this haul!"

This idea quickly recaptured Lockhart's attention. "What do you have in mind?"

"Well." Baker drew another head clearing breath. "First you should know, there are children involved."

"So?" she returned, harshly.

"Will's kids."

"Will? As in your partner, Will?" Cassandra demanded, incredulous.

"Yeah. It's his wife who is one of the things we are hunting . . . his wife, and her boyfriend, who she ran off with yesterday!"

She grinned her nastiest grin. "Kinky!"

Baker swallowed down the acid rising from his stomach. It was true, he was willing to do whatever it took to get what he wanted, but damn, he didn't take the glorious pleasure that she seemed to get out of the thought of bringing down one of their own. The unethical feel of the idea did *bother* him, at least.

That had to make him better than she was, didn't it?

"So." She was speaking again. "Where do the brats fit in with the plan?"

"They will be the bait; the incentive to get them out of hiding. This will be where you come in. Will's mother is keeping the kids for the weekend. You are going to go pick them up, telling her that you were sent by Will."

"And suppose she doesn't let me take them, without talking to Will first?"

They paused the conversation as the waitress appeared to take their order. After another furtive glance at agent Lockhart, Shawn decided that he did not trust his stomach after all, and ordered only coffee and a slice of pie. Cassandra ordered a small side salad.

Oh yeah, whatever! He thought to himself, thoroughly annoyed now. Like you're not just going to go home and down a pint of Ben and Jerry's!

There was nothing worse than the chicks that pretend they don't eat, around guys.

They kept the conversation stalled until the she reappeared with the pie, coffee and the tiny bowl of salad and left them alone again.

"So, okay," Baker began again. "You leave that to me. I will take care of the Will angle, if she gives you any trouble, but I doubt she will. I have met Will's mom a few times and she's kind of an airhead. I know Will has complained about how Indie was never really comfortable with his mom watching the kids, because she's just not a real cautious person."

"Good. Then what?"

"You will take the kids somewhere, to a motel or something, but listen, it's important that I don't know the location."

"Why should it be secret from you?" Cassandra was confused. This reminded Shawn that she didn't know much about these creatures' abilities.

Okay, this was always the hard part.

Shawn thoroughly understood the difficulty people suffered when confronted with the alternative realities that he had come to discover dwelled within this world. Things that most citizens were not inclined to believe.

He leaned forward and whispered urgently. "They can read *minds*, Lockhart! If they get near me, I can't know where those kids are, until I'm ready for them to know!"

"Read minds?" She guffawed, skeptical.

"Yes. Do not blow this off, Cassandra. Remember, I have dealt with them before. They have all *kinds* of abilities. We don't even know exactly what we will be dealing with, but they can all dig into your brain, and I want to control the amount of information they can get this way, understand?"

"Whatever you say," she smirked, still unconvinced.

Well okay, fine.

To hell with it then. At least she wasn't afraid, and he knew that she would do what he told her regardless, even if she was not a believer.

"Okay." He sighed. "Bright and early tomorrow morning, you will go to Marie Taylor's house, grab those kids, and hit the road. You don't have to go too far, but definitely get out of town. I will contact Taylor and tell him that we have a plan to catch the male . . . the guy Indie took off with. This will keep him in the game because he wants his little wifey back. He thinks that I don't know that she's one of *them*, too."

The waitress strolled by, refilling the two coffee cups as she passed. Shawn doctored his with cream and Splenda before continuing.

"Will unfortunately had a few too many when he brought me into this. He wanted me to help him get this dude out of the picture. I guess his plan was to simply welcome Indie back home. He thinks that he's been very clever and kept this little interesting fact from me." He laughed his famous Bart Simpson-like evil laugh.

"There is no way I am not capturing the two of them. At least the two!" He cut his eyes over to Lockhart, pausing dramatically.

"What do you mean, 'at least'? What else do you have up your sleeve, sugar?"

Baker recoiled mentally from her endearment, but forged on. "I mean that I have reason to believe that when I . . . I mean *we*, bring down Indie and her boyfriend, that we just may have a shot at a couple of others, okay. Let's just leave it at that, shall we? I'm not 100 percent positive about it yet, so let's just see what happens!"

Cassandra narrowed her spherical eyes at Baker for a millisecond, and then smiled.

"Alright then baby, let's go for it!" She reached across the table and grasped Baker's hand. Involuntarily, he shrank away from her cold and bony fingers, but quickly hid his shock with the pretense of checking his cell phone for messages.

They proceeded to go over all of the details, in preparation the next morning's misdeeds, finally leaving the diner after many more cups of coffee, with plans to meet up again at eight AM.

As they left, Cassandra climbed into her car after snatching the ticket she had earned, straight off her windshield, tossing the crumpled wad down in the mud.

Baker watched her from his own vehicle until she drove away, tires screeching as she pulled recklessly out into traffic.

Yes, he had definitely chosen the right person for this job. He just hoped that he could keep up the facade of civility toward her until the job was done. He sighed.

It was going to be a challenge.

Feeling a rush of adrenaline, Shawn hastily dug for his cell phone to make an impulse call. For some reason he knew he couldn't be alone tonight.

The lighted curser scrolled down his contact list until he found a likely candidate, and Shawn hit the "send" button as he started his car and pulled out of the parking lot.

CHAPTER 20

There were approximately eight hundred and sixty two thousand dots on the textured ceiling in his office, by Will's best estimate. He came to this figure, having been in the supine position on the small twin guest bed for the last five hours.

First, he counted them in rows lengthwise, then across, in sections. Anything to distract his mind from reality, and to allow the pounding feeling of the unwise amount of alcohol to evaporate from his aching brain.

Sobriety and the passage of a little time were one hell of an eye opening combination.

It was slowly beginning to dawn on him that he might have had a critical lapse in judgment; that he had allowed jealousy, an emotion that he had never believed himself capable, to mix with his rage, his hurt and more beer than his body was accustomed, to form a potentially deadly combination.

The thought had grown persistent, creeping through his brain despite his attempts to keep his mind benignly occupied.

He also felt another rapidly growing emotion—one that he'd had more experience with, but not in many years.

Fear.

No, not fear. Terror.

Terror, sparked by the realization that he had possibly set in motion something that could potentially have horrible consequences. Something that once put in motion had become unstoppable.

Will sat up, a little too quickly as the feeling began to grip him in earnest. He sat for a moment on the edge of the bed, allowing the room to stop swirling around him. He pressed his fingers to his temples, moving them in hard circular motions to try to dissipate the lingering throb ricocheting inside his skull.

Baker.

The guy was a snake. Just what the Hell had he been thinking? How could he have involved this man?

Will stood, a little unsteadily and made his way through the now darkened hallway and into the kitchen. He flipped on the light, and filled a glass with icy water from the tap.

Cursing his stupidity, he rummaged around in the cabinet looking for some Motrin.

He shook four of them out of the little bottle, having triumphed over the pain in the ass childproof cap, and tossed them down his throat. He chased them with the ice water that suddenly, he could not get enough of. As he lowered his glass, his eyes dropped to the shadow that had slinked down the hallway after him.

Max came into the kitchen and sat next to Will, staring up at him with mild urgency.

"Need to go out, boy?" Will asked. Max responded by leaping up and racing toward the door. Will ambled after him, and opened the heavy oak door, watching the dog bound out into the yard and disappear into the darkness.

Will gripped the doorjamb with both hands, and leaned to rest his forehead onto the frame. He considered his situation for a moment, wishing that he could press some sort of "undo" button, to rewind the events of the day.

Make that the last two days.

Or ten years.

Will was now forced to face some realities that he never had before.

He was selfish. He was inconsiderate to his wife. She had not been happy, and he had paid no attention. Not to her feelings, not to her . . . nothing. He had just done his thing, and thought of little else, and he had gotten away with it for all this time.

She had deserved better, whatever she may be.

Will's rage had left him, and he was in a much better position to look at things more clearly. Indie was not bad, or evil. On the contrary, he had never met a kinder or more compassionate person in his life.

She was dependable, hardworking and took care of him and their children without complaint.

It was odd that now, suddenly; it was as if he was able to see her more clearly than he ever had before. Moreover, what he saw was a condemnation of himself as a man.

He felt an overwhelming sense of nausea as he found himself hurtling down a spiral of shame and remorse.

How had he never noticed that she had always seemed on the edge of despair? Suddenly, he could picture her beautiful blue eyes, always touched with a sadness and longing.

Had he ever inquired about this? No, he had not. It was like he had never seen it before, but now it was impossible to ignore.

His mind, against his will, was playing back ten years of little scenes, times where it seemed she was trying to reach him. Trying, and failing. How could this be?

The other thought fighting for attention, was the idea that if Indie *was* one of them . . . then how could they be bad? Or a threat?

If Indie had any "super powers", she would use them to save the world, not harm it, of this he was sure. In addition, from what Will had learned about these beings, if Indie was indeed a Society Member, she had no choice but to follow this man, Jackson.

She—Will choked on the very thought—*belonged to Jackson!*

In order for Indie to have the life and the happiness she deserved, he had to let her go. He was coming to the realization that he had never really had her. She was physically there, but never in spirit, and it was not her fault. He could see that now.

But how could he fix this? He himself had set up the very foundation of her destruction. Whatever Baker was planning, it was going to hurt Indie.

Even if he didn't suspect the truth, which Will now thought was highly unlikely, having reviewed his drunken video editing job. Baker was many things.

Stupid was not one of them.

Will felt, for the first time in his life, that the same could not be said about himself. He had never felt more idiotic, and he knew suddenly, that there was going to be a heavy price paid for his own ignorance.

Exactly who was going to pay that price was also becoming painfully clear. All of them were . . . his entire family.

He, Indie and God help him, even his children.

He whistled for Max, and tried unsuccessfully to stop the shaking of his body, which had started deep within his belly, and was now spreading outward with alarming speed.

As Will shut the door behind the dog, he glanced at his watch. It was nearly ten o'clock. He debated as to whether or not to call his mother. He felt a great longing to speak to his children, but he decided with a sigh, that he had better wait. His mother was always early to bed, and besides, if he called her now, it would alarm her.

He did however, dial Baker's cell number only to have it go immediately to voice mail. This did nothing to calm the tension growing like a cancer in his core. He felt strongly that Baker would move very quickly to act on this chance to look like a champion, the best agent in the department.

Baker was extremely career-minded, and would take no chances that the prey would escape while he sat around perfecting a plan. No, he would be on the move tomorrow. Probably bright and early if Will read him correctly.

"This could work to my advantage," Will thought. "If, in his haste, he leaves himself open to mistakes."

Will's mind was beginning to clear, and he got down to business doing what he did best.

He was something of a computer-hacking genius, and an accomplished profiler who paid close attention to the habits of those around him.

Everyone but my wife, he reminded himself with an anguished moan that he freely allowed to escape, taking advantage of the fact that he was alone.

With a valiant effort, he threw off his guilt and remorse, determined to save it for later, when he could more freely indulge in a nice long session of self-loathing. He returned determinedly to the task at hand.

Will made a fresh pot of coffee, and returned to his computer on a new mission, now. He paused for just a moment, thinking, and then began to type.

"Okay, let's see who Baker has spoken with since our visit, for starters."

It took Will exactly two and one half minutes to break into the T-Mobile account of Mr. Shawn Baker, and retrieve his latest cell phone records. His heart quaked as he cross-referenced the first number that Shawn had called as he left Will's house. Its listing was private, but this was no barrier for Will, and he quickly found the name of the owner for that number.

Cassandra Lockhart. This was no good. No good at all.

"Jesus Christ, Baker . . . *Lockhart?*"

Will was shaken. She was one scary ass female. Well, there could only be one reason that he would call her, and that would be for business. He knew for certain that Baker despised the woman, as did virtually everyone.

If ever there was a person that Will could describe as pure evil, Cassandra fit the bill. Her involvement could only mean disaster. His fear intensified.

Whenever Cassandra went on even the simplest of missions, people had a nasty habit of ending up dead. Amazing, everyone always tried to attack her, or whenever a man was involved, she would claim he had tried to sexually assault her, and she had no choice. Self-defense, clear-cut as always. She was trouble, most definitely.

He noted that the phone call had lasted less than two minutes, and deduced that he had probably arranged a meeting with her. He would need a place to speak to her and not be noticed, overheard or rushed. There were three options, Will decided.

A nightclub, which, luckily there were a precious few in this area; easy to check. A restaurant or just a simple meeting in his car.

He though carefully. Nightclubs were good places to avoid notice, but were loud, and not good for discussing important details. A restaurant would be perfect for a quiet, intimate discussion, would it not?

—

Where would Baker go on a Friday night in this area, dragging along Cassandra Lockhart? Nowhere that he would normally hang out, Will guessed. He would never allow himself to be seen publicly on what would be perceived by all as a date, with that woman.

Baker was very much into appearances, and would make sure that no one he knew would see them. Besides, running in to friends would infringe upon his ability to cook up a plan. There would be interruptions. This cut down on the possibilities dramatically.

Will briefly considered the car theory, but quickly rejected the likelihood of Baker closing himself up in a vehicle with agent Lockhart, parked in a quiet and intimate location for privacy. He knew Baker had an ulcer, what with his desk drawer full of Zantac and Tums, which he popped into his mouth like candy.

His stomach could never take it.

Besides, who would want to give Cassandra an opportunity like that? She would probably get the wrong idea, and try her luck in that scenario. No, Baker wouldn't put himself in an uncomfortable position like that. It almost made Will gag just imaging it.

Will decided to zero in on the restaurant angle. A good possibility came to him in an instant.

The Wayside.

Baker was not a regular, but enjoyed it infrequently. In addition, no one Shawn knew would be caught dead in there. Especially at five-thirty in the afternoon, when it would be filled with a few early-bird special seekers, and that would be about it. It would be easy to sit in there for hours, incognito, as many of the old-timers did, just drinking coffee and socializing with the waitresses.

Will made a quick phone call to the diner, describing the two of them, and the approximate time they might have been in.

Yes, the cashier answered, she remembered them all right. Especially the woman.

She and her date had hogged the table for hours, and then split the check. At least the man had tipped well, to make up for it. The woman had left nothing.

"What a surprise," Will thought, disgusted. He frowned as he hung up. Yes, they were clearly hatching a plan.

He returned his attention to the cell phone records and saw that after he had left the diner, Shawn had made two more calls. Will recognized both names that came up as former girlfriends of Baker's. The first call lasted for only one minute, and the call concluded on her end first. Will had to laugh a short humorless laugh.

"Got shot down on your booty call, didn't you, jerk?"

He noted that the second one lasted longer. Nearly fifteen minutes, and both callers had hung up simultaneously. After another quick hack job, Will noted that the location function was "on" for Baker's phone, and he was able to ping his whereabouts precisely at the address of Jessica Kiel, the apparently successful back-up call that Baker had made.

Oh yeah. Baker was on a high, full of excess energy and excitement for his upcoming feat, and had decided to burn off some of that excess with a recycled girlfriend.

At least Will knew that he would not have to worry about Baker tonight. He carefully set the GPS tracker he fished out of the drawer, to alert him when Baker left this location.

Armed with this new knowledge, he knew he probably had all night, because Baker had no problem sleeping over, usually scoring a free breakfast out of the deal as well.

He rounded up another cell phone that he used for fieldwork, when he needed to make calls. It was programmable to show any name and number you entered to come up as the caller id.

Working quickly, Will plugged in the name of a local dive, and then dialed Lockhart's home number. It rang three times before it was snatched up, and her wheezing voice shrieked into the phone,

"This had better be important!"

Through the shriek, Will could detect the thickness of sleep, and smirked bitterly as he hung up on her. She had obviously not had the same kind of luck as Baker.

The phone rang back immediately, and he answered with a heavy Spanish accent. He held the phone away from his ear as Cassandra spewed forth a stream of obscenity laced fury, and then hung up abruptly.

"Always a lady," Will thought as he turned off the phone. He held it tightly gripped in his hand as he considered how to approach this from a professional angle.

Pitting his skills and abilities against others with much of the same training was going to be a challenge. But Will had no choice but to take on this challenge.

He had started it, and now, he was going to end it.

He glanced once more at the GPS, noting Shawn was still busy in his location. This fact, coupled with the knowledge that Cassandra was safely tucked away in her crypt, encouraged Will to get a little rest. He needed to be at the top of his game in the morning. His mind was calmer, now that he had focus.

He felt more like himself.

Stretching out on the small bed, he closed his eyes and promptly fell into a light sleep, listening for the telling "ping", alerting him to Baker's movements.

—

His dreams were strange, filled with images of some hideous sharp-toothed beast with the body of a man, and the sounds of his house, as his ears remained on alert.

He awoke with a start at five A.M. God, what the hell was *that* about, he wondered as his eyes snapped to the GPS automatically.

Baker was still at his ex's house. Will stretched and peeked out the window. There was only the faintest hint of a lightening sky toward the East. He leaped to his feet, alert and on edge.

The dream left him uneasy, but he was ready to move on from that little freak show his mind had invented for him.

Max needed to go out, so Will opened the door for him, and afterward, jumped into the shower.

He decided that a surprise visit to Baker was in order. Normally, Will didn't like to tip his hand so early, but he decided that the best approach with Baker was to put him on edge. The guy was cocky, and needed unnerving. He was more apt to slip up if he were just a little rattled. Will was going to stick with him like glue today, starting with the instant he emerged from his little love shack.

He held his head under the bracing stream of water blasting through the shower head.

Calm focus was what he needed today. Will watched the suds swirling around his feet circle the drain, destined for a rendezvous with the septic system, and then lifted his head.

In his eyes was a deadly calm, the grey stillness before an approaching monster of a storm.

Stepping out of the shower, he toweled off roughly, and then stalked naked to a locked chest at the back of his office closet. He dragged it out, and then threw on a pair of jeans with cargo pockets, a button down shirt and a denim jacket, which was for function today, rather than fashion.

He then unlocked the chest and threw back the lid, rifling through the contents on a hunt for exactly what he needed.

And he had everything.

Will could have led a war against a small third world country with the items at his disposal.

He gathered a small arsenal of weaponry, attaching them to nearly every part of his body, ending with the fully loaded 9mm, and several extra clips, just to be safe.

Will glanced longingly for a moment at his S&W X-frame Model 500, of which all fifteen inches were restlessly reclined in a wooden box at the bottom of the trunk.

At four point five pounds; five fully loaded, this was a weapon that you didn't just pick up . . . you had to lift it.

This sweet thing would blow a hole in your chest the size of a dinner plate, but even if you didn't plan on actually firing it, the bastard was just plain intimidating as hell; especially if you happened to be unfortunate enough to get an introduction from the wrong end.

Or maybe he should just go old school with the classic forty-four. After all, it seemed to work for Dirty Harry.

Will opened several more boxes, placing the contents carefully on the bed.

Hell, maybe he'd go gangsta, and pack his Sig.

He had no desire to use any of these things on his fellow agents, but he knew what this could mean to them, and he was sure that at least one of them would not mind if anyone was hurt or killed during this little operation. Will was going to make damn sure that it was not going to be himself or Indie.

He grudgingly realized that he also had to include this Jackson person in his protective thoughts.

For Indie.

After a brief hesitation, Will lugged the 500 out of its resting place, and stood for a moment, at a loss as to where he would stash the thing. With a sigh, he replaced the beast back into its box, and impatiently snatched up the forty-four. The thing would put holes in whatever needed shooting just fine.

After making sure that he had every possible gadget and piece of gear at his disposal loaded into his truck, Will pulled himself up into the four-wheel drive Ford, and found his way to the little house where Shawn had spent the night. Baker's Nissan was still parked conspicuously in the driveway.

Will looked around quickly, and found an area to the side of the house that was thick with small saplings and bushes. He backed his truck into the midst of this, concealing it very nicely, then crawled out through the back window, as he could not open the door without the echoing sound of it shutting again. This neighborhood was very secluded, and the sound would draw notice if anyone were awake.

Will crept carefully to the side of the house, and sat down to await Baker's departure. By his watch, it was now nearly six thirty. He was willing to bet that he wouldn't have long to wait.

Sure enough, by seven o'clock, Baker was exiting the front door. Will waited until the kisses and promises of a call later were finished, and the door closed again, signaling that the girl was out of the way.

As Baker strolled to his car, Will moved behind him in complete silence. Baker swung open his car door and sucked in his breath as Will threw his arms casually over the top of the window, inches away from him.

"'sup, Baker? Got an early day?"

Shawn recovered quickly. "Jesus, man, you scared the crap out of me!"

"Did I? Christ, I'm sorry buddy . . . are you okay?" Will's voice was heavy with deliberate sarcasm. "I just couldn't help wondering where you could be going at this time of day."

"Well, you seem to be out and about a little early yourself," Baker replied stiffly. He was instantly suspicious, noting Will's tone.

"I'm not sleeping well these days," Will replied steadily.

"Yeah, man. I told you I was on top of the situation. You know I don't mess around. I've got a plan." Baker spoke carefully, determined to play along.

"I appreciate how seriously you're taking this, Baker. It means a lot to me." Will's voice held a mocking edge. He could play too.

Shawn looked uncomfortable. Unlike the drunk and careless man he'd seen the night before, he knew *this* Will.

Dangerous Will.

In control Will. In spite of his tendency for bravado, Shawn was unnerved.

"Uh, what are you doing here, dude? How did you know where I was?"

"Oh, I know a lot of things, Baker. I just thought I'd come out to see what our plans are for today. You don't mind, do you?"

"Well, actually, I had planned to work alone on this part of the plan, Taylor."

"Is that so?"

"That's right. Now if you'll excuse me . . ." Baker's eyes were narrowing.

Will was obviously there to let him know that he was on to him, but he comforted himself with the knowledge that he couldn't know his entire plan.

"Sure, Baker, no problem. I don't want to mess up anything you've got going on. I'll just hang back until I hear from you, right?"

"Right. I'll be in touch. See you later, man." Shawn sat down in his car and slammed the door, scarcely controlling his fury that Will was already being the cog in the wheel. He thought he would have some time today, before Will got all antsy.

With a barely concealed glare out the window, he cranked the engine and roared down the road, leaving Will standing in the driveway.

Will watched him drive until he was out of sight, then turned and walked casually back to his truck, using the door this time. He retrieved a small device from his pocket, and switched it on.

The small magnetized tracking tool that he had deftly slipped under Baker's wheel well was working perfectly. He started his car, and followed, keeping out of sight for now.

Guess what? I'm not so easy to double cross, Baker, Will thought.

Now let the games begin.

CHAPTER 21

Baker was on his cell phone immediately. Cassandra answered on the first ring.

"What's the problem?" She asked at once.

"It seems William is having an early case of buyer's remorse. He thinks I might be planning something he won't like."

"Hey, Will's smarter than I thought!" laughed Cassandra, which caused a fit of smoker's cough to incapacitate her for a moment.

Shawn listened with distaste.

Apparently, Lockhart used her mornings to hack a clearing through her blackened lungs.

"So," she continued, the fit over. "You wanna proceed as planned, or what?"

"Yes, but do it now, don't wait. Get those kids out of town and we'll maintain the upper hand."

"Got it. I'm already there!" Cassandra hung up the phone without another word. She'd gotten dressed and ready earlier, and was ready to roll, but gave herself a moment to think over the situation.

She drummed her pointed nails noisily on the black laminate side table that supported her ridiculously heavy and outdated gold and cream enameled phone.

The sharp tacking sound seemed to help form her poisonous thoughts quickly.

Yes, she would go along with Baker's plan, but with a few modifications of her own. This was too big to let anything blow it. Cassandra wasn't sure that Baker was heartless enough to do whatever it might take to make this work. She knew that she did not have that problem.

Not in the least.

After a deep moment of concentration, she snatched up her purse and her handgun, tucking it into a modified holster that clipped on to the back of her skirt. She was dressed in her regulation outfit, skirt and jacket, having decided it would be beneficial to dress the part of the professional federal agent that she was.

Best to look official. She slipped on her sunglasses, and walked briskly out the door.

CHAPTER 22

What Man sets in motion
I can put right
For I am the Sun
The dark and the light
I slay the shadows
My fury, profound
The claws, they're extended
My rays pierce the ground
So spew forth your hatred
Your evil, your fright
The last of my fire
Brings eternal night

"Final Warning"
Katherine Whitley

    Indie stood looking out of the huge picture window, not seeing the beautiful view sprawled out before her.

    No, she was seeing something else entirely. She knew that what she was viewing was second hand, from Jackson's mind, and it wasn't giving her a good feeling.

    Jackson was in the shower, but apparently, his mind was busy evaluating the visions playing across his mind, although they seemed to be in an unusual form.

    Vision without pictures, only feelings. He appeared to be working on decoding these feelings.

    They had discovered many surprises from yesterday afternoon and throughout the night. For one, Jax, who had thought himself only marginally gifted, had discovered that he was able to "see" plots against them, and the level of danger to expect. Jax had told her before their Commitment that he thought himself able to know the thoughts of potential enemies and threats, but not to what extent.

This seemed to be an extraordinarily handy gift, given the circumstances.

What she did not know, because Jax could not see it yet, was from whom the threat was coming. They had assumed the problem would be Will, and his promise to come hunting them down, but there seemed to be more involvement, and on a more personal level.

Apparently it was *not* just a bunch of armed government goons on a random witch-hunt. But Indie left those thoughts to ponder other things now.

She had learned much in the last 20 hours. Jax had given her every detail that he knew about the Society in a quick condensed version, and she found that her already good memory was now flawless. Better than photographic, it was *audio* graphic. If she saw it or heard it, it was locked in forever.

She had also learned how to throw off the cloak that she had wrapped around herself, concealing her from the notice of others . . . her gift of "invisibility".

Before this, Indie had been unaware that she herself was responsible for others' inability to see her clearly, but she now realized that it was not entirely an unconscious act. Had she not always tried to be as small and unobtrusive as possible, struggling to blend in?

It had worked, and splendidly.

Indie now understood how to allow herself to be seen and thought of by others through nothing more than an act of will. A simple relaxation of her mind, letting go of the fear that she *would* be noticed and seen as an oddity. She also knew that her ability to retreat into the safety of concealment remained at her disposal, should she ever feel threatened.

The veil had been lifted, for the moment.

Jackson and Indie had taken a little field trip down to Woodstock to visit the Calendar II stone chamber. She had sat on the cold damp ground within, felt the vibrations of the Earth, and the power of the sacred geometry.

Indie had also been given incredible lessons regarding the Society, linking legends from all over the world, about beings "from the sun."

Of all the lessons, the one that had touched her the most, remembered as if it were a favorite bedtime story, was about Society Members who were Equals most pure, descending from that powerful single Elder, the Seraphim who came, separate from the rest, sent to infuse a select few with his divine perfection in the completely sexless union.

His children, these descendents, were equally pure, sent by the Creator to begin the Incan dynasty.

Not the first, but one of many accounts of "Children of the Sun." The legend captured her imagination, and was one of the most well documented. Ironically, it was also the most factual, despite having been brushed aside by the modern world as mythical nonsense. Nothing but a good story.

Jax explained how Equals Mallku Kapuc and Mama Ocllo, were given a second life by the Creator, after the end of their first incarnation, and arose from Lake Titicaca where they began their journey to find the land that would become the cradle of Incan civilization.

They settled on the highlands of Huanacauri, and drew people to them, encouraging them to abandon their barbaric ways, and embrace true community values. They formed two more centers for teaching in Cuzco and Vilcashuaman.

Indie loved the legend's suggestion that the learning centers' locations were decided upon by the rays of light that the pair carried with them, selecting the first places where the sunbeams sank into the Earth, rather than reflecting upwards. It was not part of the factual story, but it was intriguing to her, just the same.

These Equals began the first simple teaching of "Society Rules"; *ama suwa*, *ama quella* and *ama llulla*; translations, do not steal, do not be idle and do not lie. More rules were to follow, regarding self-reliance and accountability for ones' own actions.

They taught the Inca rulers the laws of energy and the secrets of the sun.

Indie wondered about the partnership of this particular brand of Society Member, and if they suffered any sense of loss, not marrying, and never having more that a "spiritual" relationship.

Jax had explained that what these beings shared transcended any other sense of connection and love. They were completely engulfed in one another's minds, and partners in the truest sense.

Definitely, no one needed to feel pity for these beings. They bring light to those around them, so perfect is their serenity and limitless patience and love. This was the reason they were chosen to bring light and civility to this particular future dynasty.

The genetic combination culminating in such beings was beyond rare, Jax told her, re-stating the fact that he had never come across any or anyone else who had. He, himself, had only heard the stories of their existence.

Indie drank in this knowledge, as well as the legends from every culture since the beginning of time referencing the people of the sun. Jax had told her about the rules of energy, negative and positive, how it affected the energy of the Earth, and how this, in turn affected the energy of the sun.

The secret to survival of humankind was always the sun, aside from the obvious way. Of course we need the light and heat . . . but the *energy*. Negative energy weakened the sun, hastening its aging, its demise. And a sun that was dying burned more intensely, pouring forth the last of its fire before the end.

The supernova.

Global warming. The scientists were so misguided.

No amount of tree planting and light bulb changing would affect the increased amount of solar flares, and building pressure in the core of the sun. Negative energy caused by the acts of evil in the world was what had to be controlled. These simple emotions and actions severely affected the energy flow from the Earth to the sun.

Positive energy soothes the raging core of fire, reducing the frantic energy expended. Negative energy opposes positive. These opposing forces create conflict, and the sun burns hotter.

Imagine, Indie thought.

Emotions causing such a thing.

Callousness, apathy, greed and misery.

She had also learned that there are those among humankind who thrive on creating chaos. Those behind the drive for the end of humanity. It was terrifying to learn, but it stood to reason.

The simple fact that there were angels . . . and a Creator . . . meant that there were, conversely, demons.

They stalked humankind. Indie had been struck mute with horror by this revelation.

And the fear she'd felt from finally learning Jax's job, and the feat he'd performed while still a teen that had made him famous among the Society, had left her; rational thinking showing Indie the necessity of things that were monstrous in their distastefulness.

The horrible fact was that one of Jax's jobs was to kill.

This fact had shocked and confused Indie. Aside from the very idea of it, she had seen not a single weapon anywhere in his home, and she'd been very thorough in her nosiness.

"I am obliged to use only organic weapons, those that I pick up in nature . . . or my own hands to dispatch our common enemies." He'd told her.

"Gun's . . . ." he'd shrugged. "I am well trained to use them, and carried those weapons in my duties with the SAS, but I may not use them for Society purposes. The things I . . . kill—" Jax looked at her nervously as he said the word, but Indie was stoic, "—do not belong in this realm and the organic nature of the weapons help me destroy them."

He then showed Indie the only real "weapon" he owned, which was a four inch long hilt, fashioned from an ancient-looking stone, with the very tip ending in a sharply pointed curve.

Indie gulped. One would have to get very, *very* close to whatever you were trying to kill to use this weapon.

This, Jax acknowledged was true, but he caressed the weapon reverently, and informed her that it had served him extremely well in the past. It was one of the first weapons fashioned by the first descendent of the Archangel bloodlines, and was given to Jackson upon his completion of his Society training.

Jackson had explained that when the truly Fallen One, once an Elder himself before his tumble from grace, saw the Angels turning into the flesh, instructed to infuse their angelic perfection with the daughters of man, he was outraged, and sent several of his Dark Soldiers down to do the same.

Only the seed of these evil ones did not perfect the human form . . . the human *soul*. It decayed it, from the inside out.

It turned all that was good in the Creator's world into distorted versions of beings in human form.

As their spawn reproduced, they also created the random synchronization of the genetic make-up of those demonic ancestors. When they came together, it meant nothing but chaos. These being were like hideous caricatures of the Society Members. They were not warm, but like ice.

The only powers they possess are the power to ruin and destroy. They are shrewd enough to sense and avoid danger, but usually unable to read minds. One must be able to open one's self up, and to *coax* the mind to reveal its secrets, in order to read the thoughts of another.

Evil does not coax. It demands. The human mind instinctively protects itself from such invasions.

It was during this discussion that Jackson revealed the reason for his infamy.

His words had left her speechless, his confession unfathomable; He'd killed *Satan* himself.

And with nothing more than his crudely fashioned, hand-me-down weapon.

Now this, of course, was *technically* impossible, as the Fallen one is actually immortal, but in his jealousy and need to be worshiped, the Fallen takes the flesh, and becomes The Speaking Man.

He'd done it numerous times throughout history, and the method was sickening; the literal high jacking and possession of a human embryo.

Jackson had explained how the Fallen One, Satan, was incapable of true creation . . . of becoming the flesh, and this infuriated him. Oh, he could possess a *body* for a short time, but it took so much effort for him to remain in a body that instinctively rejected him, that it was all he could do to remain anchored.

As Jackson wryly put it, in the end, all he could do when possessing a body, was make a lot of disgusting noises, and make the unfortunate one possessed seem to have incredible anger-management issues.

Not exactly the power trip that Satan was actually seeking.

"But," Indie had asked, confused, "you said that the angels were sent down into the flesh, to spread their genes, and that the Fallen sent his soldiers to do the same, right? So they could become flesh then?"

"When the Creator chose to send His selected few to become flesh, he created a pathway from The Kingdom to the Earth. As *His* angels passed through this path, they became flesh and blood. The Fallen sent his soldiers through this same pathway. Only a few got through before it closed. Enough to create a few perverted and deviant unions."

"So, it was an accident? The Devil snuck in a few of his own, right under the Creator's nose?" Indie sounded incredulous, and Jackson had to laugh.

"I am inclined to believe that He allowed this, for reasons unknown by us, but I bow to His infinitely superior wisdom. This is an easy conclusion, because nothing—but *nothing*—happens which the Creator cannot stop or control, if he so chooses."

Indie had then made the mistake of demanding to know how the Fallen was able to make himself the Speaking Man, as Jackson called him. True in the flesh.

His answer had disgusted and horrified her, sending her to the comfy chair to recover quietly by herself, as Jackson paced around her anxiously.

The Fallen One.

Satan.

The Devil . . . or *Sobek*, as Jackson told her was his favorite name, taken from the Egyptians who inadvertently bestowed upon him the name, and the status of a God. He really got off on that, apparently.

Whatever you called him, the method he used when he wanted to become the Speaking Man was obscene.

He would find a newly impregnated woman . . . within twenty-four hours of the union of sperm and egg, and invade the forming fetus. Only the rapid cellular development of the embryo allowed the matter of the Fallen to become incorporated and finally intertwined with the new life forming, and the spirit or soul of the destroyed infant was unceremoniously shoved out of the cells, and sent home to the Creator, as the Fallen takes over.

He is then forced to go through the entire process of development, birth and growing up in human form, and every time he'd done it, he'd been a person of note in history. Because he'd only done it to seek pleasure, power and in the end, attempt to be worshiped as the God he wished to be.

The evil deeds always were such that the world was forced to notice.

Twenty-one years ago, a very young Jackson had come across The Man himself, and seen the evil in the making. Satan was so amused by the idea of one so young challenging him, that he'd been caught completely off guard by Jackson's skill and ferocity, which was atypical in most Society members, and was taken down in a bloody battle.

This sent the Fallen back to square one.

Assuming he set out to grab a new human form right away, which was very likely since his plans had been cut dramatically short, that would put his newest incarnation at approximately twenty years old. Perhaps too young to have achieved evil of note, but probably very busy cutting his path of destruction. He'd not been pinpointed yet.

It was just something to be on the lookout for, Jax soothed her.

He would not be able to avoid notice for long.

In the meantime, since his stolen mortal body was cumbersome, the Fallen placated himself with his dream-like mind travel, projecting his image around the world, nosily investigating anything catching his attention.

Humans could not see his image in this form, but the Society Members could. This was what had so unnerved Indie at times in the past; catching glimpses of this, as well as other things that don't belong in the company of humankind.

The revelation that the "Gator-Man", as she'd named the thing startling her throughout her life was, in fact, the favored image of his persona of *Sobek*, the crocodile-headed god of ancient Egypt.

Jax flatly refused to call Satan by this name of Sobek, as a rule, because he would not flatter the Beast with a favored title. He preferred to call him nothing more than The Fallen, as this matched just exactly what Satan had accomplished; getting himself booted out of The Kingdom.

Jax claimed that this actually *was* a feat worthy of recognition, as The Creator was nearly limitless in his patience and tolerance. To finally goad Him into such a response was, in Jackson's opinion, quite amazing, and indicative of the truly evil nature of this Fallen One.

Jackson also took out other lesser demons and entities who would occasionally find themselves on the astral plane of this world. He made sure they understood that they were not welcome.

Indie herself had finally learned that the scary things she'd seen throughout her life had been these things . . . things unseen by man. But the true danger was from the Fallen Angel.

The Fallen One, the self-proclaimed keeper of darkness, hoped for the destruction of humankind, and the world along with it. He'd felt from the beginning that the human experiment was an affront; an insult to the angels, and should be eliminated from creation.

The Creator, however, had no intention of giving up his world, or the creatures that inhabit it. Not yet, at any rate.

And He wished the great plan to continue to unfold, striving to move toward the Perfection of Being.

This argument with the Creator is what led the banishment of the Fallen One, and along with him, those who believed as he did. They became his soldiers, following his bidding, most likely because of their comfort and familiarity with the natural tendencies of the angels, even the fallen ones, to follow protocol.

———

The Fallen ruled in his dark kingdom, and the other outcasts still bowed to the Elder, even though he'd been stripped of that title. Of course, this pleased Satan immensely, allowing him a taste of what it could feel like to be a God himself. And he liked the flavor.

He liked it a *lot*.

Satan took great pleasure in the antics of his Dark Soldiers' offspring. These creatures had no guidance such as the Society had given their own, creating a network of love and support for *their* descendents.

No, the Children of the Fallen were abandoned, left unleashed upon the world, going mad and committing the unspeakable crimes that are rabidly reported by news teams everywhere.

Indie could not stop herself from feeling sympathy for these creatures, evil though they may be; sympathy for the fact that they wandered, lost and miserable, with no clue as to whom or what they were, or why they suffered a relentless and restless fury, existing in a state of perpetual chaos and disorder.

She could almost relate; just not to the way that they responded to their angst.

Jackson, however, felt little sympathy for these beings, having never suffered the lost feeling of not knowing one's true self, as Indie had.

These demonic descendents were genetically pre-disposed to create misery and increase the anger and destructive feelings in our collective world. At times, they seemed to be winning.

Society Members were to counter such forces. It was The Creator's only concession to his rule of allowing destiny to unfold, the rationale being that He had sent the ancestors before to help human kind, and so would allow the descendants to continue working toward the same goal.

The Elders were committed to the care of The Society.

With an effort, Indie pulled her thoughts back to the moment at hand. Jax had emerged from the bedroom dressed in jeans and yet another well-fitted t-shirt topped with a long-sleeved button down; the sleeves rolled halfway up.

She watched his carefully controlled facial features. He was toiling madly to project an outwardly cool facade of confidence, while simultaneously trying to block the frightening images in his head from Indie. She would have laughed at his struggle, if her body wasn't so heightened with tension.

His words were deliberately light and teasing as he sought to distract.

"Do you plan to run a brush through that lovely mane of yours today?" He reached out and tousled Indie's uncharacteristically tangled hair. Her hair generally was not too knotted since she did not sleep on it, truly.

"Oh!" She put her hands through her hair and felt the wildness.

"Look who's talking!" She had to smile. His hair, it seemed, had a life of its own. "Has that mop of yours *ever* lain down?"

"Only once." He forced a short laugh. "My mother shaved my head when I was four, she was so exasperated. My nanny was horrified!" Indie tried to picture Jax with some sort of buzz cut.

No, she decided. His out of control hair was most definitely him.

Jax followed as she walked slowly to the bedroom, and then rummaged through her bag to retrieve a large paddle brush. She began to detangle her hair, but let Jackson know, silently, that she was aware of the coming danger. He sighed, and shoved his hands into his pockets, regarding Indie with some uncertainty.

Funny, but he'd been so sure that as the fighter . . . the protector, that he would be the more dominant in the relationship. He had actually been afraid of coming off as too controlling toward Indie, whom he'd seen as fragile and needing rescuing.

However, it was becoming clear that just the opposite was true. Indie had a command over him that he simply could not resist. Little things, maybe, but when she spoke and really meant it . . . well, it became all about whatever his *Equal* wanted. The hierarchy remained intact.

Simple enough, huh?

It intrigued him, and made him want to laugh all at once, except that the visions of danger were a problem right now. One that had to be faced soon.

"Just spit it out," Indie spoke calmly, defying the quaver in her voice.

"There are changing enemies, at this point . . . sometimes one and sometimes two. It's very strange," he exhaled finally, "and oddly, three or four friendly entities. I don't entirely understand this, but I know it to be true!"

"Friendly entities?" Indie pondered this information. Who could be helping them? This seemed to be a very private battle, known to no one except by those most intimately involved.

"Is it possible that the Elders or some other Members could be coming to our aid?" Indie asked. Jax hesitated, thinking carefully as he spoke. "I think not. Things are usually left to fate. Stepping in and changing destiny is not something that the Elders do, as a rule."

"What do you think our next move should be, then?" Indie felt a strong compulsion to act, although she didn't know where to direct her energy. Jackson reached out and pulled her into his arms, resting his chin on the top of her head.

"How do you feel about a little preemptive activity? I am feeling like we need to check on Will's activities . . . see what he might be up to. We don't have to confront him, just some careful reconnaissance, if you will."

Indie nodded her head in agreement. Yes, she felt that this was the right move as well. She pulled back and looked up at Jax.

"What about these "friendly entities?' she asked, still a little baffled by the idea. Jax pushed the hair back from her face.

"I honestly have no idea," he confessed, "but I am damn grateful for them, whoever they might be!"

Indie's mouth dropped open, a little shocked by the profanity. Jax grinned at her, impishly, and pulled her back to his chest.

"Sorry," he said with a low chuckle. "I told you I was no angel!"

Her shock evaporated and she had to smile back. She was discovering that he could be somewhat incorrigible, and though she didn't like to encourage it, she found she loved him even more for his spirit.

She took his hand. "Come on then, let's go and take the bull by the horns."

Jackson scooped up the car keys, stopping to spritz a light spray of the delicious cologne that was in a small bottle on the dresser, in spite of Indie's protest that he didn't need it.

"I had no idea you were so metro," she teased. He didn't respond, but let his eyes sparkle down at her as he checked his look in the mirror, raking his hands once more through the dark shiny mess.

"And you said I was the defiant one!" She once again had to laugh a little, in spite of her anxiety. He always seemed able to make her smile, even through her fears.

They walked hand in hand through the door to confront the unknown.

Chapter 23

Cassandra Lockhart slowed her vehicle to a crawl before finally stopping on the road, a safe distance from Marie Taylor's tiny cottage located a mere two miles from the home of her son.

She studied the cheerful pale yellow exterior, and the whimsical dark purple shutters framing every visible window, each underlined by window boxes stuffed to overflowing with flowers leaning determinedly toward the rays of the early spring sun.

The front door was also purple. Hanging on a brass hook was a wreath of still more bright and colorful flowers.

The place looked like something from a fairy tale, thought Cassandra, lip curling in disdain. She felt a sudden and unreasonable surge of contempt for the woman who would live in such a house. "An old hag in the throes of dementia," she thought, venomously.

This was going to be like shooting fish in a kiddie pool.

Lockhart reached into her purse without taking her eyes off the house, and dug out a pack of Marlboros. She slid one of the cigarettes out of the pack and lit it, drawing deeply.

Leaning back into the seat, she considered how to approach the situation in a fashion that would cause her the least amount of irritation.

Oh, she was taking those kids; there was no question about that. Lockhart was perfectly ready to simply storm the house, shoot the old lady and take them. The only trouble was, Lockhart knew that this would scare the kids; not that she was concerned for their feelings, but she knew from observing life around her that children who were frightened tended to make a lot of noise.

No, she did not want to be trapped in the car with a couple of sniveling whining brats. Not even for five minutes.

She briefly considered just taking them all out.

Did the kids really need to be alive?

They were only bait, after all. Will's wife and her alien boyfriend need only think that she had the kids, right? It wasn't as if those two were ever going to see the light of day again, so what did it matter?

And Will, if he caused any problems, he was going to become collateral damage as well, so why keep the kids around?

They would only be shuffled around to state agencies, raised by strangers. She clenched her teeth.

She knew what *that* was like. She would be doing them a favor, to keep them from that fate.

Cassandra wondered what Shawn would think of her plan, and laughed. She was pretty sure that he would be less than enthusiastic about it, and she wasn't ready to piss off Baker.

Not until she got what she wanted.

Lockhart made a few quick phone calls, and ascertained with glee that Marie Taylor had never gotten a landline phone, relying solely on her cell for communication.

This was great luck.

She pulled out a black box, plugged it into her car's cigarette outlet, and switched it on. Instantly, an electro-magnetic current was generated, effectively disrupting any cellular device within a full mile radius.

"We wouldn't want Will's mom making any phone calls to verify anything I tell her, now would we?" she thought smugly. Taking a last hard drag on the cigarette and tossing it out the window, she made her decision. She would try using diplomacy first. Shawn wouldn't be upset with her, and, hopefully, the kids would be quiet.

Ugh. She hoped they weren't all chatty, like some she had been around. The thought of trying to make polite conversation with them was almost more than she could stomach.

Inside the little house, Marie watched the children finish their breakfast.

The twins were certainly funny little things, she thought, with a pang of fondness. They were eating their favorite breakfast of whole-wheat toast, lightly buttered and sprinkled with fragrant cinnamon, then cut into strips and dipped in honey.

Indie really had those kids brainwashed, she thought a little cattily. They never touched sugar, or soda or even candy, like any normal kids would. Marie guessed that Indie had convinced them that they would burst into flame if anything "unhealthy" touched their little lips. Honey seemed to be their only sweet weakness.

She continued to study them, looking so like William had in his youth, with their corn silk blond hair, and deep, natural tan skin tone, and so *unlike*

Indie's alabaster coloring. In spite of this, Marie knew that the kids never stepped outside without at least 40 SPF. Their mother was diligent about her kids' health; Marie could say that for her.

She caught Cassidy peeking up at her questioningly, feeling her scrutiny. Their eyes. So odd with that skin color.

They definitely were Indie's startling pool water blue.

The children were a perfect mix of their parents, physically.

Their behavior, too, was always beyond reproach. Marie could never remember having to scold them. They were sweet, respectful, and never left messes. She didn't like to use the word perfect, but that is what they were. She never minded keeping them.

She noticed that their usually sunny dispositions were somewhat dulled. However, this was to be expected, was it not?

Marie still could not believe the sudden departure of their mother.

It was incongruous.

Marie knew that Indie loved those kids fiercely. She suspected that there was much more to the story than Will had shared hastily with her, about marriage troubles, and Indie "taking off for a while."

It made absolutely no sense, but she had agreed to take the kids for the weekend, to get them out of the house and keep their minds off the domestic issues.

She could see their sadness, but they did not bring up the subject. Marie felt a little squeamish about being the first to speak of it, and so the elephant in the room was pointedly ignored, for the moment.

The children finished their breakfast in subdued quiet, and Marie paused to stroke the silken strands of their hair, saddened herself, by the burden that they were forced to bear.

The knock at the door startled her. She looked at the old schoolhouse-shaped clock that hung on the wall opposite the little window over the sink. It was still quite early and she was not expecting company.

She cautiously approached the front door, half expecting to see Indie standing on her porch, on an impulsive quest to reclaim her children. Marie hoped not. She was ill prepared to be thrust into an uncomfortable custody tussle with her daughter-in-law. Though Marie knew Indie to be a good mother, and believed that the children needed her, her loyalty, of course, had to remain with her son.

She stole a glance through the long glass that ran the vertical length of the door and frowned. She did not recognize the woman standing on her porch, shifting her body about with quick jerking motions, clearly conveying a sense of impatience.

As Marie opened the door, the woman's face shifted into a mask of cool, professional nonchalance.

"Marie Taylor?" she asked.

"Yes?" the affirmation contained a question.

"I'm special agent Cassandra Lockhart," she answered, flipping open a small leather case, thrusting her identification at Marie's face.

"Will sent me to do him a favor. He wants me to pick up his kids for him, and bring them down to the New Hampshire line. But then, I'm sure he's spoken to you about this already?"

"No, I haven't heard from Will today. He's told me nothing like that. He wants you to bring them down to New Hampshire?"

"He didn't call? That's odd. He told me he would clear it with you before I got here." Cassandra projected a perfect replica of a face stymied by confusion.

"He wants them brought to New Hampshire?" Marie pressed.

"Yes, he is working overtime on a case down near Bethel, and will be wrapping it up soon. I told him that I have a meeting scheduled in West Lebanon this morning, and he asked if I could swing by and pick up his kids. He said something about taking them to the Montshire Museum, or something."

"Daddy's taking us to the Montshire Museum?" Jake came running toward the door, eyes eager. He stopped short when he looked up at Lockhart, and fell silent. Cassandra looked coolly at the little boy.

"Yep, that's the plan, kid." She leaned toward Marie in a confiding manner, although she did not bother to lower her voice. "I think he wants to take their minds off of their mamma running off with that other guy!"

Marie drew a sharp breath, bringing a hand up to cover her mouth. "*Indie?* Running off with another man?" she gasped in disbelief and shock. Her eyes shifted down to Jake, still standing motionless at her side. She flashed with a quick anger.

"What in God's name are you thinking, saying something like that in front of my grandson? It was very inappropriate!"

"Oh, so sorry!" Cassandra was the picture of insincerity. "I didn't know it was a secret!" Her eyes were impossibly round with false innocence. Marie was instantly repelled. She did not like this woman at all, and found it nearly impossible to believe that her son would send such a person to collect his children.

"I'm calling William!" Marie announced icily.

"Oh, go ahead, for sure. You can't be too careful these days." Cassandra spoke to the rough edge of her fingernail that had apparently seized her attention.

Marie left Lockhart standing on the porch, and retrieved her cell phone from her shapeless, faux leather beige handbag. Jake remained in the doorway, seemingly mesmerized by the woman on the porch. Lockhart fidgeted restlessly.

Marie reappeared with the phone pressed to her ear, a frustrated look on her face. "I can't seem to get a connection. I've always gotten a great signal here!"

"Oh, here, try mine," Cassandra offered graciously, before adding, "sometimes those cheap cell phones will crap out on you at the worst of times!"

Marie stared at the woman, rendered speechless by the sheer tactlessness of this creature. Cassandra was holding out a very complicated looking device toward her.

Marie hesitated, not sure if she wanted to touch anything that had come in contact with this agent Lockhart.

With barely concealed irritability, Cassandra exhaled loudly, and made a great show of dialing Will's number, pressing "send" and handing it off roughly to Marie, who took it reluctantly.

"It still won't go through!" Marie was becoming worried, although she could not help shooting a smug glance over to the woman. Even her expensive model was having problems.

"Well I know it works. I was using it as I pulled into your driveway. You know, now that I think of it, I did hear something about an abnormal amount of solar flare activity today, and that it can affect cellular service, and even cable T.V."

Cassandra knew that the electro-magnetic surging device that was plugged at this moment into her car's lighter outlet also would cause mild picture quality issues with her cable. Marie turned quickly and snapped on her television. It was working, but having constant episodes of pixilation.

"See!" Lockhart smiled.

Marie pursed her lips, uncertain what to do, while Cassandra dramatically lifted her arm, and looked at her watch.
"Listen, I hate to rush you and all, but I can't be late for my meeting. I told Will I would do him a favor, but I didn't expect it to be this big hassle!"

Marie shook her head. The woman was grossly uncouth.

"It's up to you," Lockhart continued, "I really don't care either way, but Will is gonna be pissed off if he has to drive all the way back up here to get them, for no reason!"

Will's mother tried to reason through the situation. Cassandra had hit all the right buttons. Marie never wanted her son upset with her. The woman *had*, after all, showed proper identification—it looked just like Will's—and she did seem privy to the details of Will's marital woes. "More than even *I* know, obviously," she sniffed indignantly to herself.

The woman *had* encouraged her to call Will herself to verify the story, even offered her own phone. The woman could not possibly have known that the phones were not going to work, after all.

As Marie directed this internal dialog, Cassandra was becoming more agitated by the moment, finally deciding, as the fury began to rise in her belly, that the old woman had exactly thirty seconds to cooperate, or she was simply going to unload her weapon into her face.

—

241

Her hand twitched toward the pistol sheathed in the holster at her skirt's waistband. Cassidy appeared in that instant, eyes wide as she reached up to place her tiny hand on Marie's arm.

"I'm sorry, Grandma. Daddy told me that he might send someone for us, if he had to work today. I . . . I forgot to tell you!"

As she spoke, Cassidy covered her eyes with her free hand, looking as if she had committed the most grievous of crimes.

Marie relaxed at once.

"It's okay, honey, I'm just relieved that now I know that it's alright for you to go!" She looked up at Lockhart. "I'll just go and get their bags." Cassandra simply looked confused. Could Will have planned to have someone get them? It was certainly possible. If so, she decided, it was even more reason to get out of this place quickly.

"Why don't you go help your Granny get your stuff together?" She spoke, looking at both kids. They moved at once.

"Hmmm, well, at least they do what they're freakin' told," she thought, relieved by this knowledge. They returned so quickly that she was almost impressed.

"Bye, Grandma," Cassidy hugged and kissed Marie, her expression one of complete misery. Marie knelt by the little girl's side. "Don't be upset, Cassidy, about forgetting to tell me . . ."

"No, Grandma," Cassidy interrupted her, hastily, shooting an uneasy glace at Lockhart. "I'll just miss you!"

Marie shook her head at the drama, and laughed. "I see you almost every day, honey!" Cassidy simply nodded, effectively hiding the slight tremble of her little lips by pressing them tightly together, and picked up her backpack, then walked toward Cassandra's car. Jake followed, looking back once to blow a kiss to his grandmother.

"Alrighty then." Cassandra turned her back on Marie, and trotted down the steps onto the walkway, carelessly stepping on several of the young purple tulips, newly emerged from their winter's slumber.

"Get in!" she snapped brusquely at the children, the mask of civility already slipping in the wake of her victory.

The children obeyed instantly, while Marie was momentarily dumbstruck by the woman's nerve.

Just you wait until I *do* speak to Will, Thought Marie angrily. I am going to give him a piece of my mind! What on Earth could he be thinking?

She folded her arms, watching the black P.T. Cruiser back quickly out into the road.

To send a person like that for his kids!

As the car prepared to speed away, Marie saw the clear images of her grandchildren, peeking out at her through the window. Their small faces were pinched with misery, causing a sob to catch suddenly in her chest. She swallowed as her throat tightened with a feeling of apprehension, and she closed the door, determined to reach Will as soon as possible.

She sat down on her sofa with her phone in her hand, deciding resolutely to press "redial" as often as necessary, until she reached her son.

Chapter 24

Will pulled his truck into the parking lot of the convenience store, and quickly scanned the rows of mud and salt encrusted vehicles. Baker's bright red Nissan was hard to miss, but Will sure as hell didn't see it now.

The tracking monitor was screaming its insistence that the target was nearby. Will forced himself to slow and look again, more carefully now, but a distinct feeling of resignation was blanketing his shoulders that were now hunched over the steering wheel wearily.

Baker had shed the tracking device. He was certain of it.

Heaving a small sigh, Will steered into a parking spot, and turned off the ignition. He pulled himself out of the truck and dropped to the ground lightly, bringing the monitor with him.

It led Will directly to the magnetic tracking bug, now neatly stuck to the metal paper towel dispenser that was hanging between the gasoline pumps. The magnet was pinning a small scrap of paper to the metal container, which Will retrieved with annoyance.

The note simply read, "Try harder, old man!"

Will laughed softly to himself as he crumpled the paper in his fist, and flung it into the trash container. Baker had also recently had the brilliant idea of turning off the location function of his cell as well, which was unfortunate.

Will walked slowly back to his truck, hands crammed in his pockets, thinking furiously. He had known that this was not going to be easy. He wasn't crossing swords with rank amateurs here, this he already knew. Baker was a punk, yes, but a smart little bastard all the same.

He climbed back into his truck, and then rested his forehead on the steering wheel. He had a real problem right now. Having spent many long hours orienting eager and young new agents to the field, he repeatedly had to remind them that in spite of what they might have learned from watching "24", or the Jason Bourne movies, it's usually best to stick with the herd when facing an adversary.

But sometimes, what is best and what is possible are so far apart, they can't even see each other.

He couldn't bring in anyone from his work, he knew, nor did he want to involve any other outsiders, simply because it was too dangerous with Lockhart lurking around the edges of whatever Baker had up his sleeve. Besides, the status of the Society had to be kept top secret, and Will could not risk that little factoid getting out into the public view.

But he had to catch up with Baker, and soon. He wished he could simply put out an APB for a red Nissan Sentra. There weren't many in this area.

He suddenly jerked his head up, a hopeful glint in his eye. Maybe there *was* someone he could call for help; someone who would understand his situation, and not demand any explanations.

He pulled his phone from his pocket and dialed.

*　　*　　*

Captain Nick Broccato was a twenty-two year veteran of law enforcement, continuing a long family tradition of first completing a prerequisite stint in the military, followed by enrollment into the police academy.

Seventeen years were given to the NYPD, and the last five in faithful service to the Vermont State Police.

Nick steadfastly refused to move into any desk or office position, preferring to spend his time outdoors, even if it meant viewing it mostly from the slightly darkened interior of his cruiser.

He didn't mind taking the promotions, though, and his only requested perk was Sundays off. Saturdays he would work any time they asked, but Sundays were for family.

He was born in the Bronx, and had that certain rhythm that comes with the classic accent, making him sound exactly like an extra in a mafia soundtrack.

Nick also unwittingly carried the attitude; that genuine and absolute confidence in your own willingness to act, coupled with the unshakable belief that you will prevail against all odds.

This, combined with his formidable six foot six inch frame, surrounded by two hundred and seventy pounds of pure muscle, made Nick a force to be reckoned with. He was a forty-year-old masterpiece of strength.

A man who could make even the hardest of criminal minds back up, and think really, *really* hard about whether crossing him was worth the potential outcome.

Nick's coal black eyes could either melt with concern and sympathy, sparkle and shine with humor, or burn black with an intensity that had made more than a few evil doers come very close to needing new pants after a confrontation with him.

His wavy hair was still dark, with no sign of gray pushing its way forth to give away the passage of time. Nick's big secret however, known only to his boisterous family and a very few close friends, was that he was a gentle giant.

Good natured and kind, he had endured being dressed up and used as a living doll by his seven sisters, suffering this with a saintly and indulgent patience.

Classical music was another passion, and he blasted it throughout his home while cooking huge feasts for his family on Sundays, which were often day-long events.

No one, but *no one* knew his very deepest secret, however; and he feared that his image might never recover from its exposure.

Nick loved flowers.

The bulbs he'd carefully selected, one by one and with the greatest of care from Boulevard Gardens last fall, were just starting to peek through the muddy soil around his home, and Nick was ecstatic. He couldn't wait to see how his careful orchestration of colors and breeds played out in full bloom.

He kept a small and well-abused copy of The Botanical Encyclopedia in the glove compartment of his cruiser, carefully concealed in a black zippered cloth case. Identifying plants and learning their correct Latin names kept him occupied, and he practiced . . . liking the sound of them as they flowed from the lips, much like his beloved classical music.

The fact was, there were very few things that could make Nick genuinely angry, and they all involved breaches of trust, or any dangerous disregard of the law. If you were someone who put others in danger, then Nick took great pleasure in becoming your worst nightmare.

He had seen so much in his career that had threatened to harden his deceptively tender heart, but the terrorist attacks on 9-11 had overshadowed any kind of horror he ever could have imagined. Many police officers and firefighters lost life-long friends that day, in the line of duty.

But Nick had lost more than just friends.

Candace Lowry.

The shy and quiet girl had become the love of his life, and worked in the restaurant on top of the Twin Towers. She was lost as well. He'd planned to propose to her, and in a magnificent way that would have truly exposed Nick for the sentimental man he was. He'd had the whole scenario mapped out in his head. He was playing host for the upcoming Thanksgiving holiday, and planned to make his intentions known to Candice, on his knees and surrounded by those he loved the most.

But the opportunity was lost, forever.

Although Nick struggled on for another year, his mental state declined to the point where he had created an unending state of sullen depression. A sharp contrast to the joyful soul he once was. He continued to descend until finally, alarmed, his friends and family staged an intervention. Only with their insistence did he consent to seek help.

"A head shrink!" Nick had barked, angrily at the time. "How can they fix *this*? What's going to make it better?" But, the sight of his mother and sisters' tears convinced Nick to give it a try.

Just for their sake, he told himself. He had promised that he would go, and he was a man of his word. But to his surprise, he found that it *did* help him to finally release his repressed grief and suffering, as well as the guilt he held, for a secret known only to himself and his shrink. In the end, a change of scenery was just what the doctor ordered.

Literally.

He knew he could never move far, because he couldn't bear the thought of his family not being close to him. However, Nick need not have worried. As he stopped by his sister's house to borrow more packing tape, he was shocked to see her little studio apartment in the process of being packed up by a couple of burly and competent-looking men.

"What's up with this?" he demanded.

"What, did you think we were lettin' you go alone? We're movin' too, Nicky! Pretty much all of us, 'cept for Uncle Manny. Says he's gotta retire, first."

Nick had been moved to tears by this news. A good Italian family always tries to stick together, but this kind of sacrifice was totally unexpected. The family up and leaving the area where they had made their home and built their lives for so long?

Uprooting everything. For *him*?

And so the entire Broccato clan made the pilgrimage over to central Vermont.

His mother was a true matriarch, and had chosen the location of South Burlington, based on her declaration that "at least there are some decent supermarkets here!"

Nick was snapped up immediately by the Vermont State Police, and felt an instant acceptance. He also felt the beginnings of peace and serenity that had eluded him since that dreadful Tuesday in 2001. It was a new beginning, so different from where he'd come.

He had the respect of everyone he worked with, and his years of experience as a New York cop served him well.

Nick could size a person up in less than thirty seconds, and could read one's intentions like a book. He formed his opinions and his loyalties quickly and unflinchingly. The fact that he was a multi-generational, dyed-in-the-wool law enforcement officer to the bone, made him trust his instincts completely.

A natural-born cop, and proud of it.

During his time in central Vermont, he had worked with William Taylor exactly twice, forming an instant liking to the guy. He knew him to be honest, ethical and full of integrity; traits he valued above all, and Nick always made sure to embrace those very values himself in his every action.

The two veterans had formed a tight friendship, speaking often by phone, trouble-shooting together, although neither had the time for a quality "hang out" very often.

The officer was parked in his cruiser this morning, pulled into a quiet corner of a supermarket parking lot, half-dozing in the sunbeam warming the interior of his car. His beloved and dog-eared book of botanicals was open in his lap, along with a half-dozen or so leaves he had picked up, not recognizing their shape.

He jumped at the sudden command of his cell phone, and sighed as he picked it up, looking regretfully at the leaves as he set them aside for now. Much to his surprise, the call was from Will Taylor. Answering quickly, Nick greeted his friend warmly.

He instantly detected the traces of strain in Will's voice, and felt his body slip into a cop's natural alert mode automatically. "What's wrong, Will?"

"Hey, Nick. Are you on duty this morning?" Will asked.

"Yeah, man. What do ya need me to do for ya?"

Will sighed with relief. Although he'd known he could count on this man, just hearing his reassuring voice, offering up his assistance blind, made him sure he'd made the right call.

"Listen, Nick, I would really appreciate it if you could help me find a red Nissan Sentra, two-thousand six model, but off the books, man. The driver will be a male, by himself, most likely. Twenty-six years old, and just so you know, he's a Fed. He works with me."

"Well, yeah, Will. I mean I can help you, but what's the problem with this guy? I'm guessing he's armed, then?"

"Oh, yeah, he's armed. But Nick, I don't want you to do anything but find him, and give me his location. Then I need you to just back away, ok? I don't want to bring you into anything dangerous."

Nick was already on the road, speeding back toward town. He choked back a laugh. "You don't want to bring ME into anything dangerous? Gimme a break, bro!'"

"No, I mean it, Nick. I am surveilling this person, because he is a double-crosser. I think he's about to throw his partner under the bus, and that partner would be me. I'm not really into allowing that to happen, if I can help it, but this has to be off the record. No one at the department knows about any of this right now, and it has to stay that way. He's got a female agent helping him, but she's not with him now."

Nick listened carefully, all trace of humor gone. He did not like people who would screw over one of their own.

Especially your own partner.

"Can you at least tell me what it's about?"

Will hesitated. He didn't want to lie to his friend, but he couldn't tell him this story. Not now. "Nick, I—I just can't . . ."

"Say no more, buddy. I know you got your reasons, right? You don't need to tell me nothin'. We'll get this guy, and then you can handle it your way." Nick's Bronx-laced words of confident assurance were oddly soothing.

Will choked out his thanks, and gave him Shawn Baker's last known location. He once again warned Nick just to find him, and nothing else.

"Yeah, well I'm gonna hold him in the place I find him, 'till you get there, so know that! I'll speak to you soon Will, right?" And he hung up.

Will shook his head as he folded his phone shut with a click.

Nick was going to do what Nick was going to do. He just hoped that he would back off and leave Baker to him, when the time came. He pulled into traffic, searching the side streets as well, as he waited to hear back from Nick.

It took Nick less than six minutes to find Shawn. The town was small, and Nick had phoned two of his buddies who were also on duty, taking care to avoid the police radio. He had asked them to casually look for the described car, for an "unofficial" reason, and they had happily obliged.

As soon as Shawn Baker was spotted barreling down US 2, Nick phoned Will and then flipped on his lights and siren. After all, the guy was legitimately speeding, and looked as if he could use a fast driving award. He watched with a little perverse pleasure as Shawn glanced into his rear view mirror, first in disbelief, then frustrated anger.

Nick smiled. He might even enjoy this.

Shawn pulled to the side of the road with an impatient snatch of the wheel, and then broke all protocol by immediately leaping out of his car and storming towards Nick's patrol car.

Captain Broccato's brow darkened in disbelief at the sheer audacity of this move. He looked out of his window, outraged, as he grabbed his clipboard and ticket pad. Shawn was shouting furiously at the still closed door of the car, when Nick abruptly flung it open and hurled himself out and into the much smaller man's face.

Shawn took two long steps back as the police officer towered over him in a most intimidating fashion.

"You got a *problem*, pal? Don't you know better than to approach a police officer in a threatening manner? I coulda blown your friggin' head off! You get the Hell back in your car, Jack, and you stay there until I come to *you*, you got it?" Nick bellowed, furious now.

Nick had to acknowledge that perhaps knowing that the guy was a traitor to his partner had gotten under his skin.

Maybe just a little. But, still, to rush his cruiser like that was not going to be tolerated.

Shawn suddenly felt very small. His usual cocky manner deserted him as he tried to find his voice. He jumped as Nick barked out again.

"Did you hear what I said, guy? Get back to your *CAR!*"

He felt his legs turn and begin to carry him very quickly back to his vehicle, and he sat down behind the wheel, a little shakily. Damn, but this was easily the biggest dude he had ever seen. He took deep breaths as he waited, feeling some of his fear begin to evaporate.

How could he let this cop talk to him like that? Just wait until he showed him *his* credentials. Then the shoe would be on the other foot, by God. He would have *him* shaking in his boots.

Crossing his arms, he tapped his head on the back of the seat and waited impatiently. What the hell was taking so long? He ventured a look back, and the cop instantly looked up and met his stare.

Shawn looked quickly away.

Nick was on the phone with Will. "I'm just writin' this guy up a nice two hundred and fifty dollar speeding ticket. The ass was driving like . . . well, like an *ass!*"

"Fine then. Hurry up and nail him," Will chuckled. "And Nick . . . thanks man. I owe you!"

"Yeah, you can bring me some of that snobby beer of yours. I think a twelve pack should cover it!"

"If I make it through this, I'll bring you a case, and you can party with your sisters." Will spoke with feeling.

Nick was silent. He didn't like the feeling he got from Will's words.

He then spoke soberly. "Ok, Will, just park it out of sight right around the bend, here. The curve is good. You'll be able to see us, but we can't see you. You pull out as soon as you see me get back in my car, right?" He paused, uneasy with the instinct that flooded his gut.

"Are you sure you got this? I don't feel so good about leaving you to something that might . . ."

"I got it, Nick. There's no way around it. I have to handle this one on my own. I promise, I'll tell you all I can about it one day."

"Alright," Nick sighed. "But if things go bad, you got my number, right?"

"Thanks again man. I really appreciate that." Will so wished that he could confide in Nick right now. He had never felt so alone.

He pulled up to the curve in the road and stopped. Sure enough, he could see Nick's cruiser parked to one side, and the tail end of Baker's car just ahead.

Will watched with mirthless humor, as Nick strode to the side of Baker's car. He could just make out the muffled sound of Baker's blustering protests, and thinly veiled threats, something to the effect of the classic "do you know you I am?" routine.

He cringed just a bit as Nick's voiced clearly bounced off the mountains as he shot back at Baker. "I don't care if you're the friggin' Pope, *Agent Baker*! You don't speed down my roads, right? You could kill someone!"

Will snorted into his coffee cup, spraying liquid everywhere. He sure hoped Baker had brought some extra underwear with him today. No doubt, he probably needed them just about now.

His cell phone rang sharply, and he snatched it up quickly, not wanting the sound to carry. It was his mother.

Will groaned. She always had the worst timing. He knew he should answer, though. She had the kids. What if one of them was hurt?

"Hey, Mom, what's up?" Will answered, keeping a sharp eye on the tantrum-throwing agent up ahead. His face froze in horror, as he decoded the shrill and angry voice of his mother, chastising him for sending "that horrible woman" to pick up her grandbabies.

Will's voice was like ice. "When did she leave with them, Mom?"

"I guess about fifteen minutes ago. I tried to call you before they left, but the phones wouldn't work, and I wasn't going to let her take them, but then when Cassidy told me you said someone might get them, I figured it was ok, but I don't like . . ."

"Cassidy told you *what*?" Will cut her off, confused.

"She said that she was supposed to tell me that someone may come get them for you. Is that not true, Will? Why would she lie to me about a thing like that?" Marie was beginning to sound hysterical.

"Calm down Mom, it's ok. Don't worry, I will get them. I have to go now. I'll call you." Will's throat was stretched so tightly with fear, he was amazed that he was able to complete his last sentence. He didn't want his mother to suffer guilt and terror along with him, but for just a moment, he felt that the series of events in the last forty-eight hours had suddenly become just too much to bear.

His life, as he had known it, was over.

Indie was gone, and he knew he would never have her back, no matter what happened. And now, his children were in the clutches of a psychotic monster, who, for some unexplainable reason, Cassidy had told her Grandmother that it was ok to let them go with the beast.

It made no sense at all, and Will felt himself beginning to sink into despair. Karma, as it turned out, *did* in fact exist, and was exactly the bitch it was reported to be.

The echoing sound of a car door slamming jolted him back to life.

A defibrillator to his stopped heart.

He saw that Nick was back in his car, and Will felt a sudden surge of furious and righteous energy as he started his car and pulled into the road.

He came around the curve just as Shawn was preparing to pull out, and with a quick decision, Will accelerated swiftly and slammed his truck into the Sentra, avoiding the driver's seat area, aiming for the front of the car.

Will had just enough time to note the matching shocked expressions on the faces of both Nick and Shawn, just before the airbag exploded in Shawn's face. Will tried to jump out of his truck, but found that his door was jammed, and would not fully open, pressed as it was, into the Nissan. Undaunted, he leaped out of the side window, taking a moment to note that his truck was barely injured by the impact, and was most certainly still drivable.

The same could not be said of Shawn's car. It was going nowhere under its own power. Will looked back at the stunned face of Nick, and shouted. "Go Nick, you've got to get out of here, please! It's okay, trust me!"

Nodding speechlessly, Nick started his car, suppressing a sick feeling of foreboding in his belly. He did trust Will, and decided to keep his promise in spite of his feelings, and pulled out into the street and drove away, much to the dismay of Shawn Baker, who had finally beaten back the airbag and was struggling to climb out through the passenger door.

He opened it and felt himself slammed to the ground with an astonishing force, then quickly flipped over onto his back before he could form coherent thought. All he could see was Will's face.

"WHERE ARE MY KIDS, YOU SICK SON OF A BITCH!"

CHAPTER 25

Jackson carefully guided the Mercedes down the winding, twisting road that led down the mountain. He released the hand that he clung to so tightly, after giving it a reassuring squeeze, so that he could block the searing beam of sunlight from his eyes. Out of the corner of his eye, he saw Indie holding out his sunglasses, and he took them, gratefully.

Reclaiming her hand, he lifted it to his lips to brush a soft kiss against her wrist.

He was struggling valiantly to sort out the unfamiliar barrage of information forcing its way into his brain, like an overwhelmed inbox. Most Society Members get a very early start in learning their abilities, and how to use them. However, he, at the ripe age of 40, had only just been exposed to the full scope of his gifts, and he still had a lot to get used to.

It was most unfortunate, Jackson decided, that a somewhat urgent situation had shown itself so early in the process.

Yes, he had been told what to expect and had all the teaching, but the actual experience was something altogether different.

He still wasn't sure how crazy he was about the open book that he once called a mind, fearing that Indie would pick up on the fragments and images coming to him, and read too much into his reactions, before he could sort them out. Jackson wanted desperately to protect her from some of the more disturbing things that had begun to push their way to the forefront of his thoughts.

Cutting his eyes to the right once more, to sneak another peek at her, he felt a rush of overwhelming love for Indie that made his breath catch in his throat. She was staring out the window silently, no sign of stress in her posture.

She, at some point, had locked herself back up into her protective cocoon. Her thoughts were silent. He also knew that she had done this quite inadvertently, and wasn't even aware of the fact at this very moment. There was a small twinge of envy felt for her particular gift, only for the fact that he could not protect her from his own knowledge.

Indie turned to look at him and covered their intertwined hands with her free one, and spoke firmly; "I am forcing myself not to intrude on your thoughts uninvited, because I can feel your discomfort, but you simply don't have to protect me from your thoughts, Jax."

He looked at her, and spoke thoughtfully. "You are so strong. The fact is, *I* am the one with the training for focus and control. *I* am the one who had thought I'd mastered my emotions, and yet *I* am the one struggling. But there you sit, so calm and so sure. How is that possible?"

"Because I trust you implicitly. Whatever comes our way, I know that you and I will deal with it. And believe me, I was trying to work myself up into a state of terror, but my body just won't cooperate. Therefore, I give up. I have put myself into the hands of fate and Jackson Allen, wherever that takes me."

"Well, I guess I *should* be happy to hear that," he laughed to himself. "I just hope I don't let you down."

"You won't. I won't let you. Now, what exactly is our plan?" Jackson let go of Indie's hand and gripped the steering wheel tightly now, as he answered.

"I just want to start at Will's house and have a look around. I just have a feeling that this should be our starting point. But if Will is there, we will ditch the car and I'll see if I can get close to the house and find out what he may be planning."

Indie looked out the window once more before speaking. "Jax, I don't want a confrontation of any kind . . . ."

"Oh, not to worry. I don't fancy Will having a go at me either!"

"Is that Brit-speak for 'I don't want to fight him?'" Indie smiled in spite of herself. She loved his way of speaking.

"Yeah, that would be the translation. Will's in good shape. I might not be up to the challenge!" His voice clearly conveyed the fact that he did not believe that he would have any problem taking on Will at all

. "Don't worry, because this is not going to happen, understand?"

"Yes, ma'am. And don't *you* worry." Jackson relaxed just a little. Indie's calming influence was pulling him in. Making him focus.

"Do you have the same feeling that I do? That Will is not actually after us at all?" He asked, suddenly. Indie didn't answer immediately, gazing intently at the pointed tops of the blue spruce trees breezing past.

"Yes, I share that feeling," she answered, finally. "I'll even go you one step further. I think he wants to *help* us. I know that sounds a little crazy, but I feel a threat from your mind, and I know somehow it is not from him. I think Will knows where the threat is coming from, though. Why he would want to help us, I can't explain, and, obviously, you can't figure it out either, am I right?"

"Unfortunately, you are exactly right. However, things are getting clearer. I think either the gift is evolving, or maybe I am just finally beginning to learn how to use it!"

"Two enemies and three friendly entities?" Indie spoke aloud, thoughtfully. "Could Will be one of the three friendlier?" Jackson stared straight ahead, eyes on the road.

"Three or *four* friendlies," he corrected her. He lifted his shoulders in a weary shrug. "It seems a reasonable assumption, although, I'm not generally big on making assumptions."

The road began to level out, and the surrounding area was becoming the familiar suburban outpost that Indie, until two days ago, had called home. She looked out at the small subdivisions and cul-de-sacs with a detached interest. This was no longer her world.

It never really was at all, she'd finally realized.

Not until Jackson turned down the street that led to what she now thought of as "Will's house", did she begin to feel a sense of apprehension tugging at her heart.

"Come now, where's all of that confidence you were showering me with just a bit ago?" Jackson gave her a quick smile and mussed her hair teasingly, in an attempt to soothe.

"It's still there, I promise." She smiled weakly. "It's just sort of weird to be back here, you know? But I'm sure this is the thing to do."

"Good. Then you and I . . . we're right here!" He held up two fingers and pointed them first at his own eyes, then at hers, which made Indie break into tense nervous laughter. She shook her head at his attempt to keep her spirits up.

Jackson slowed as they found themselves in front of the house. Will's truck was not there, and the house looked quiet and empty. "Hmm, I wonder where everyone is, on a Saturday. Will's usually off, and the kids would be home." Indie mused aloud.

"Maybe Will took the kids somewhere for the day?"

"Maybe. He was never one to spontaneously suggest family outings before, though. Let's go in." Indie was suddenly seized with a strong desire to look around inside the house.

Jackson hesitated, then pulled the car up the road several yards, where it was somewhat concealed by a large box hedge. Will would not recognize this vehicle anyway, so he wasn't overly concerned about hiding it. They both exited the car and, Jackson stood at the end of the driveway, feeling for any eyes upon them.

Finding no inner warning that they were being observed, he looked around with his eyes now, and noted that the street was quiet as they made their way up the driveway. Indie stopped short. "Do you hear that?" The eerie sound of moaning and whining was coming from inside the house.

Indie raced to the front porch and tried the front door. Naturally, it was locked. She quickly darted around to the back deck, and triumphantly opened the French doors that led to the bedroom. "I've been asking Will to fix that lock for six months," she muttered.

"Yeah, too bad he never got around to it." Jax stepped in and looked around, warily.

He was overwhelmed momentarily by the memories of the first and only other time he had been here. This is where he had brought Indie into this life. This was where it had truly begun.

Indie reached out to him and took his hand. "I know," she gave him a little tug. "Come on!"

They moved cautiously through the house, following the mournful howls that Indie now recognized as Max. They found the dog sitting in the middle of Cassidy's bed, yowling anxiously. Indie noticed that the windowsill had been scratched to pieces, as if the dog had been desperate to get out.

"What's the matter, boy?" Indie was incredulous. He had never done such a thing before. She was also certain that he didn't howl like this when he was left alone. They would have heard about it from the neighbors, surely.

She knelt by the bed, trying to comfort the dog, who had leaped to the floor and jumped into her arms, shaking with his excitement.

"Indie, I think you should come see this." Jax's voice came from the small office across the hall. As Indie rose, the dog began whining urgently, and looked at Indie expectantly.

"Just hang in there, Max. I'll be right back."

She walked into the room and gasped in shock. The small guest bed was covered with boxes of ammunition, emptied of their contents, several holsters, and various other containers that she know housed much of Will's small arms and investigative tools stash. Things she had hated even knowing that he owned, but conceded that they were probably necessary in his line of work, at times.

Will was obviously prepared to go to war, but where had he gone? Moreover, on whom was he planning to use this arsenal? Could they have been wrong about Will not planning to hunt them down? Indie felt that she might begin hyperventilating.

She consciously pulled back her panic, and slowed her breathing as she looked questioningly at Jax.

He was picking up the boxes, examining the labels as he spoke. As Jackson heaved the S&W X-frame Magnum 500 into his hands, he grimaced and looked up at Indie.

"Well, I would *really* hate to be the prey, if this is what our hunter would be using. This is astounding!"

"Do you think our assumption was wrong, about Will wanting to help us?" Indie's head was beginning to clear as the shock wore off. "Because, for some reason, I still think don't think we're in danger from Will. Does that seem naive?"

"No, but we have a much more urgent threat. It is becoming clear to me that we are about to have our hand forced. We are going to have to meet it, head on. We will have no choice. And by the way, I think your dog is desperately trying to tell you something!"

Indie turned in time to see Max pulling and tearing at a small white sweater that belonged to Cassidy.

"Max, No! What's the matter with you?" He had never destroyed items in the house, ever. Not even as a puppy had Max been a destructive animal. He'd always stuck close to Cassidy, and she'd trained him with remarkable speed and ease. This was behavior far outside the norm.

As Indie carefully tried to pull the sweater from the dog's teeth, she suddenly recoiled in fear.

Jax was instantly at her side. "What is it? What happened? Did he bite you?" Indie shook her head, eyes wide with terror. She slowly picked up the sweater again, and looked at Jackson.

"Lift up the veil, Indie! You've got yourself closed off from me!" Jax spoke urgently as he pulled her closer.

Almost immediately, he heard the sounds of children calling out for help. It was heart wrenching. As Indie had touched the sweater recently worn by her daughter, she could clearly hear the voices of her children crying out for their mother, and now, so could Jackson. His reaction was instant. He moved at once, pulling Indie to her feet.

"Where would Will take the kids so that he could go off on an adventure that would require all of this firepower?" he asked as he began pulling her at top speed down the hallway.

"Marie . . . he would take them to his mother's." Indie spoke in a hoarse whisper, as she tried to keep her feet under her, now nearly numb with fear. Who would want to hurt her children? She couldn't fathom it.

"Then that is where we are going. Now!"

Jax shot through the house practically dragging Indie behind him, pausing only to unlock the front door, which provided faster access to the car out front. Indie's eyes fell upon her cell phone on the counter, still on the charger where she had left it the night Will had made her leave. She quickly snatched it up as Jackson pulled her through the front door and down the steps, not bothering to shut the door behind them.

As they made a run for the car, neither noticed the terrified dog bolt out the door and streak down the road as fast as his legs could carry him.

CHAPTER 26

Cassandra alternated her stare between the road in front of her, and the rearview mirror, watching her little captives closely for any sign that they were going to begin sobbing or some other annoyingly audible sign that they were afraid. So far, they had been completely silent, only their faces conveying wide-eyed fear.

This was fine, as far as she was concerned. She just hoped they kept it that way. She briefly took note of the fact that the boy was clutching his sister's hand tightly, and she would stare at him pointedly now and then.

Weird kids.

She was chain-smoking, on an exuberant high from the near-altercation and eventual victory over the old woman. The windows in her little car were up, save for the thin crack at the top of her driver's side, to allow a small amount of cigarette smoke to pull its way through.

Cassandra enjoyed the feeling of the unreasonably hot March sun baking the entire left side of her body through the glass. She didn't mind the heat, and always wondered cynically what the big deal was, with everyone bitching about the winters getting milder, and the summers getting hotter. These were good things, as far as she could tell. She enjoyed her mental picture of all of the old people down in Florida roasting to a crisp. *Vermont could just become the place to be*, she smirked to herself.

She blew through the back roads leading her toward the interstate, wondering if she should call Baker now or wait until she reached a safe destination. She decided a little bragging was in order, about just how effectively she had done her part of the job, and that it didn't need to wait until later. Cassandra pulled her cell phone from her purse and dialed. It rang until it went to voice mail.

"What the hell, Baker!" She was disappointed. He should be expecting her call, shouldn't he? What kind of unprofessionalism was this? She dialed again, with the same result. The phone was thrown into the passenger seat with exasperated flip of her wrist, and she pulled another cigarette from her pack.

She heard a small sigh from the back seat, and her eyes snapped back to the mirror.

"You got something to say, missy?" Cassidy hesitated, and then spoke in a quavering voice. "It's just that the smoke is kind of choking us. Can you open your window a little more, please?"

"Aw, I'm sorry the smoke bothers you. Of course I'll fix the window." Cassandra pressed the automatic window button, and the small crack in the driver's side window disappeared altogether.

"Is that better, honey?" Cassandra laughed hysterically at her own cleverness, and lit up. Jake's eyes filled with silent tears, as Cassidy stroked his hair, fighting back tears of her own.

Naturally, Will's kids would be all wimpy, Cassandra thought caustically, as she watched the scene through the rear view.

Probably never had a moment's hardship in their lives. They looked like the kind of kids that had always been worshipped by their parents. Always to bed by eight, teeth brushed, bellies full of a nutritious supper, followed by a nice dessert of some kind. Typical spoiled upper-middle class snot noses. She had convinced herself that she was glad of her harsh upbringing.

Abandoned at age two, left in a bus station in Michigan, she had endured abuse at the hands of the first people who had found her. A couple of teenage boys had tormented her for hours before finally being discovered by the security officer. He had taken her to the police station and from there, it had turned into the nightmare of a series of foster homes, each seemingly worse than the last.

Cassandra had long ago stopped crying. She knew it didn't help. No one ever came for you, and no one cared if you suffered. In her opinion, the world sucked, and the only recourse you had was to seek out your own pleasure and to hell with the rest. In fact, causing as much trouble and unhappiness for the others you met along the way, simply enhanced the journey. No one deserved happiness just handed over to them. You should have to work to make your own, and screw everyone else.

She was lucky enough to find herself an opportunity to join the police force, and took some classes to obtain the required Bachelor's degree to land her first federal job. They required a B.S. in any subject. She chose philosophy, because, after all, can one actually fail philosophy when there *are* no wrong answers?

This would be, she'd decided, a philosophical conundrum.

At any rate, she passed, and worked her way up the ranks with a vicious diligence. She knew she could never have made a better career choice. What would she do without the official ability to provide government-sanctioned bullying to the masses?

She stole a look back again, as the two children tried to comfort one another, and sniffed disdainfully. In Cassandra's warped and twisted mind, these kids represented everything that was wrong with the world, today.

Everyone had it too easy. A little suffering, or in her case, a lot of suffering, makes you stronger. Worrying about everyone else made you weak and vulnerable. If you care about anything or anyone, it can always be turned around and used against you.

Take kids, for instance.

If she herself ever found herself tied to a bed, pregnant and forced to give birth, (she shuddered at the horror), she was one hundred percent positive that she would be concerned only with Numero Uno, still. Let them take her kid, if she had one.

See if she cared.

She was glad that she had no such weaknesses.

But these children were treasured and valued, and such was the reason for the brilliance of Shawn's plan. Both parents would move mountains to save their precious little offspring. No sacrifice by themselves would be too great, if it just saved the poor, poor children. The innocents.

Cassandra hated the term, and people used it all the time to describe children.

Please. No one is innocent. Everyone is born guilty, and everyone should have to pay. She had. Now, she made it her business to share the experience with everyone she could.

After all, it was only fair.

She looked at the phone on the seat and snatched it up again. Patience was not one of Cassandra's strengths. She dialed Baker's number once more, received the same generic voice mail prompt, and decided that she would have to make do with a text message, and then wait for his response.

As she began typing into the phone with her thumb, while still speeding down the two-lane road, she heard the small sound of a child's voice clearing.

"What now?" Cassandra snapped, irritably.

"You shouldn't text while you're driving. It's not safe." Cassidy spoke miserably—afraid, but obviously more afraid of the car careening off the side of the mountain. Cassandra stared at the child through the rear view, incredulous.

"Thanks for the public service announcement. I've never heard that one." She then returned to her task, which was to send an alternately crowing, and irritated message to Shawn Baker.

It happened in the blink of an eye.

Cassandra had only enough time to make out a blinding white flash coming from the left-hand side, before she felt the impact that shoved the car off its course and into a deep ditch on the side of the road.

After a stunned silence, she looked around, unable to find the source of her near death experience from her nearly nose-deep position in the ditch.

Both children had already scrambled from the car, and were climbing up the steep bank that held the car prisoner.

"Don't either one of you kids try to take off, you hear me?" Cassandra screeched from the front seat, finding that she was unable to open either of the front doors. She climbed deftly to the back seat, and out.

When her head reached the level of the road, she could see the culprit. A large, snow-white deer lay in the middle of the road, bleeding copiously from an obviously fatal wound. It was writhing in pain; its back leg twisted at an unnatural angle.

As she pulled herself up the embankment, she pointed at Cassidy who was standing by the road, looking at the deer.

"Not one word, kid, if you know what's good for you, understand?" She turned her attention to Jake, who was now kneeling in the middle of the road next to the animal. His small hands were stroking the bleeding creature, which was obviously in the throes of death.

"Out of the way, boy!" Cassandra barked, and pulled her pistol from its holster. Jake gasped with terror, but stayed where he was.

"What are you *doing*?" cried Cassidy, horrified. Cassandra looked back at her impassively. "I'm putting that damn thing out of its misery. Besides, look what it did to my car!" Her fingers tightened on the handle of the pistol as she raised it and took aim.

"Stop!" screamed Cassidy. "Please don't *kill* it!" Cassandra looked back and narrowed her eyes at the small girl standing on the side of the road, both hands covering her face.

Fine, she decided. *Let it suffer*. Its movements were slowing and it would probably be dead in a minute or two anyway.

Yeah. It deserved to suffer for hurting her beloved vehicle.

"Whatever, kid. Who cares? If you want it to suffer, far be it from me to deny you the pleasure of watching!" She shrugged, and turned her back on the deer. She had bigger problems right now, because her car was most definitely stuck, whether or not the impact had caused a lot of damage.

"And you, kid. Get away from that damned deer!" She turned to yell back at the boy. "Don't you know enough not to sit in the middle of the freakin' . . ." The rest of what Cassandra had to say trailed off to nothing. The deer was no longer in the road, and was just disappearing into the woods.

Jake was still crouched in the road, next to a huge puddle of the animal's blood.

There was no way that deer had been able to get up. Its leg had been nearly severed by the impact, and yet, there it was, now bounding through the trees.

She lowered her eyes back down to the boy, who was watching the deer run away with a small smile on his face.

Her own face become stone cold.

"You two, over to this log, NOW!" She spoke in a whisper, but sounded all the more malicious in her lowered tone. The children obeyed, and she stared at them with new interest. "Do not move, do you understand me?" The children nodded in unison.

Cassandra made her way back down and retrieved her cell phone, to attempt once more to reach Baker. No answer.

She pondered the circumstances for a moment. There was no one else she could call. She sat down on a large rock jutting out from the side of the woods, very close to the children, and proceeded to send a text message to Shawn, with a slightly different tone.

He needed to call her at once.

Cassandra crossed her arms and prepared to wait. Baker was going to feel the wrath when she did reach him. She looked over at the kids once more as they huddled together on the fallen tree, and repeated her warning.

"Not one word, and do not move so much as an inch. Got it?"

The children nodded their heads once more, and clung to one another.

The sun burned brightly, high in the midmorning sky.

CHAPTER 27

Shawn Baker was much too preoccupied at the moment, to notice his cell phone vibrating madly in his coat pocket. His mind began clearing in seconds, even as he felt himself dragged violently to a standing position. Will's fists were clutching the front of Shawn's shirt and jacket in a painfully tight grip.

It seemed just a little obvious that William had become aware of the plot in progress, and that Lockhart had taken his children, but more than that, Will could not possibly know.

Shawn himself didn't know much more than this.

In the span of a millisecond, Shawn's mind began to race. He wanted to stall Will for as long as possible, to allow Lockhart to get to her destination unencumbered. Taking a deep breath, he decided on his tactic.

It required him to swallow down his fury that Will had deliberately wrecked his car. It would also require him to feel a little pain, which he was not looking forward to, but hey, he could take one for the team if he had to.

Go team Baker and Lockhart, he thought, wearily.

Here we go. Shawn stifled a sigh, and then carefully relaxed his facial features into a well-contrived look of innocent confusion.

"What the hell, Taylor? Why did you smash up my car, dude?" Will swung Shawn around, and into the side of the bent Nissan.

"I asked you a question, Baker. Where are my kids?"

"Hey, I don't know *what* you're talking . . ."

The rest of Shawn's sentence was lost, as Will's fist connected with the left side of Shawn's face with a force that snapped his head back onto the roof of the car.

"Jesus, man, not so hard! You nearly broke my neck!" He continued his maddening game of passive evasion.

Will, still gripping Baker tightly, dropped his head and closed his eyes. He breathed out slowly as he recognized the tool that Baker was implementing. He was very good at it too, he knew, having seen him put it in action many times.

It was used to either infuriate a person into blurting out details that he might not want to reveal, or to stall action for whatever purpose, and to put your adversary on the defensive by mocking and provoking. It was very effective, and usually caused the person on the receiving end of this treatment to completely lose all reason as their fury is stoked.

The trouble was, Will wasn't sure that he wouldn't accidentally kill Baker if he didn't tell him what was happening with his children, and very quickly.

"Baker, I take the safety of my kids somewhat seriously. Are you sure you want to go down this path with me?"

"Honestly, Taylor, I *don't* know where your kids are." Shawn struggled to sit up, still pinned to the hood of his car by a coldly furious Will.

A young man wearing a bulging backpack and filthy clothing appeared suddenly from the dense woods, momentarily distracting both men. "Um, everything okay here?" the hiker asked nervously, looking back and forth between Will and Shawn. He was definitely concerned, but the modern-day fear of getting involved in something he shouldn't was clearly etched upon his face.

"Yeah we're fine." Shawn spoke up first. "Do you mind? We're kind of having an intimate moment, here!"

The young man seemed confused, and then shook his head, looking at Will for confirmation.

"It's okay, man. Just a little disagreement between friends. Nothing to worry about."

With one last uncertain glance, the hiker plodded back into the woods on the other side of the road. After a moment of hesitation to make sure the backpacker was out of earshot, Will swung Shawn around again, and gave him a violent shake.

"Start talking, Baker, God Damn it! I want to know what you and your psycho-bitch girlfriend are plotting, using my children!"

"Ok, first, let me run the disclaimer that Lockhart is *not* my girlfriend. I just enlisted her help so that we can catch your wife's boyfriend. That's what you wanted, *right*?" Shawn was wide-eyed and innocent.

"So help me God, Baker, I am going to blow your brains out, right here and now, if you don't tell me the truth!" Will hissed through clenched teeth.

Shawn wrenched himself free with a quick backwards motion, and stepped a safe distance away before answering. "Now, you wouldn't want to go and do that, old buddy, would you? How would you ever find out what's going on that way!" His voice was mocking, now.

Will lunged forward, driving Shawn backwards against an old sugar maple tree, knocking loose a bucket someone had secured to its side, and began battering him with blows to the face.

Baker responded with a kick to the gut, knocking the wind out of Will for an instant. Will leaned forward, hands on his knees as he struggled to recover his breath.

Shawn laughed.

"Sucks gettin' old, doesn't it bro'? Kinda hard to keep up, sometimes!"

His eyes widened as his legs were briskly knocked from beneath him and he went over backwards, landing hard on his back. Will stood over him.

"Yeah, it can suck at times."

He reached down and snatched Baker's weapon from its custom shoulder holster. "But that's ok. I'm glad I'm not still a stupid kid who thinks he's invincible. The trouble with punks like you is that you think you have the world by the tail. Maybe you do, but you don't realize that things with tails also have teeth, and it can turn around in an instant and bite you in the ass. It takes a little growing up to figure that out, I suppose."

"Aw, hell Taylor, I feel less cool just hearing you say that!" Shawn eyed his precious gun worriedly, as Will tucked it into his waistband. A sharp kick brought his attention back to the issue at hand.

"Where are my kids?"

Shawn hesitated, wondering if he had given Cassandra enough leeway. This brought about several more sharp blows, courtesy of Will's Desert Storm boots. "Once again, what is happening with my kids?" He delivered another nicely aimed kick to Baker's ribs as he repeated the question.

"Well, maybe when you're through kicking my ass, we can talk like mature adults, huh?" Shawn gasped. "Isn't that what you old folks like to do? Maybe we can reach some kind of common ground."

Baker held up his hand as he said this, as if requesting assistance in sitting up.

Will frowned, and stepped back. Yeah, right. *Sure* he was going to give him his hand. He was pretty damn positive the guy could sit up on his own, and was immediately proven correct, as Shawn abruptly sat up, resting his arms on his now crossed legs.

Will was amazed; aside from his crumpled and muddy clothes, Baker showed no sign of having participated in any kind of physical confrontation, with the exception of the rapidly swelling area under his left eye, which he noted with satisfaction.

"Ok," he spoke gruffly. "Start talking!"

"Well, ok, how about we start with you thanking me!" Shawn spit out at him.

"*Thanking* you? Are you *kidding* me, fool? I trusted you and you double crossed me!"

"Oh, really, Taylor? You trusted me? No, you lied from the start. I am *saving* your ass. How about the fact that you are required by your job description as the task force leader, to report, and or capture these Society Members? You did neither. You just wanted *ME* to catch your wife's boyfriend for you! How do you think the bosses would feel finding out that their golden boy has been harboring one of them right in his own house, for what is it, ten years or so?"

Will's stomach contracted. Yep, Baker had figured it out all right.

"I didn't know about Indie. Not until that day that I showed you the tapes. Not until I realized what the other guy was."

Shawn's sarcasm was thick. "Oh sure, dude. They'll believe that, no problem. Their most skilled profiler had no idea he was married to an alien, living in the same house with her for all those years!"

"But it's true!" Will was fierce, but confused himself at how this had escaped him. "I can't explain that myself, but it's a fact."

"Not even during your most intimate moments?" Shawn was working the provocation angle thoroughly. "You noticed nothing, even while you were busy fathering children with a Martian? Or maybe she's from Venus. She *is* kind of hot!"

With a howl of rage, Will hurled himself at the seated man, flattening him, and spoke inches from Baker's face.

"She isn't an *alien*, God damn it!"

"No? Then what is she, Taylor? Do you even know? Or maybe you don't care. Maybe you knew all along, and things were great, but apparently, you couldn't keep your little woman satisfied, so she hooked up with one of her own kind. Maybe they have some kind of special freaky outer-space sex, huh?"

"Shut your mouth, you little shit!" Will was reaching the breaking point. He consciously pushed back against his natural instinct to react to Baker's intentional baiting.

"She was gonna run away and leave you, wasn't she? And you got your feelings all hurt, so you got drunk, and decided to call up your partner, hoping I would do your job for you! Only you thought you were so clever, and could keep your wife's status from me, but guess what Taylor, I noticed right away!"

Will cringed as he thought about the fact that he had been so stupid, as well as again trying to absorb the idea that he had blithely lived in the same house as one of the beings that he was well trained to recognize, without ever having the slightest idea. He couldn't begin to fathom how this could be.

Baker was right. No one would believe that for a minute.

Shawn used this opportunity to wrench himself from beneath Will, and again move a good distance away. "You're lucky I don't have you arrested as a traitor. You totally blew off the security of your country, and over a woman! How classic."

Will narrowed his eyes at him.

"Maybe you're right, Baker. But I swear to you, I didn't know, and when I found out, sure, I was stunned; but I loved her. I still love her, and I don't want her hurt.

"But *you!*" Will growled now. "Don't you know there's an extra-special, dark corner in Hell for people who fuck with *children!*"

Shawn barked a laugh. "Oh yeah? *Well, follow me down, buddy!* How many people have *you* terrorized with the threat of violence towards their kids? Are you immune to this rule, partner?" He kicked at the pile of leaves at his feet in disgust. "Maybe we can carpool to Hades."

Will shook his head desperately. "But I would never . . . ." He was having a very hard time not gagging at the memories. His voice tightened and dropped. "I would never, *ever* have done it!"

"Oh. So I guess that makes it okay. Except for the fact that the subjects definitely believed that you would." Shawn crossed his arms and stared coldly at Will, who suddenly wasn't looking so well.

"Baker . . . ." Will could barely breathe from the weight of his guilt.

And his fear.

"I just want to take my kids and go home. And I want Indie to go her own way, and have the happiness she deserves. She is not evil, and definitely not a threat to anyone!"

Shawn shook his head in disbelief. He really couldn't understand, because he had never had very deep feelings for anyone in particular, and felt sure that he would always put his duty first.

As he stared down at Will for a moment, another realization hit him. Will truly *was* clueless. Yet, Shawn *knew* that Will was one of the most observant, clever people he knew.

It was simply incongruous.

"You really *don't* know, do you?" Shawn's voice was soft . . . thoughtful.

"Don't know *what*, Baker? Please, are we through wasting time here? I *need* my kids, man. Tell me they're not in danger from that . . ." Shawn came forward and knelt down in front of Will.

"Dude, did you even *live* in the same house as your family, or what? You truly have no idea, do you? I'm thinking that even if anyone in the agency believes that you didn't intentionally harbor these fugitives in your home, you'd probably be fired at the very least, for being the most stupid and unobservant guy to walk the planet!"

"*Fugitives?* What the hell are you talking about, Baker? I sure as hell never let that Jackson person in my house. I'd never even seen him in person before . . ."

"*Your kids, Taylor!*" Shawn interrupted him, reaching out to give him a shake. "*YOUR KIDS!* They are Society Members, too! Honest to God, Will, you really didn't know, did you?"

Will felt his mind begin to shrink, pulling away from the sides of his skull and detaching from his body. The oddest feeling of disorientation was engulfing him, and he could feel blackness closing in around the edges of his peripheral vision. Curious.

He had never passed out in his life. Only sissies and women fainted from the delivery of shocking news, didn't they?

A tight squeezing sensation was radiating from the center of his chest, localized and persistent. He was unaware that he was staring back at Baker with a detached, unfocused gaze, as he attempted to reconcile his mind with reality.

Will began sweating profusely.

Maybe Baker would be merciful, and just put a bullet through his head right now. He allowed Shawn to pull him to his feet, although he couldn't feel them. He couldn't feel any part of his body.

As he continued to stare at Shawn, he was faintly aware that the man's lips were still moving, but he could hear nothing above the rush of blood and his slamming heart, which seemed to have filled the vacant area in his head.

"*Taylor!*" He felt the blow to his face with a dull realization, but no pain. The second blow was sharper, jolting him ever so slightly from his out of body experience. He looked around as he tried to reach out and pull the parts of his brain back into place.

"My kids?" he whispered. "But they're just ... *kids*! Baker, why are you saying this? What are you doing?" The sensation in his chest was lessening, slightly.

He drew in a deep breath.

Shawn was looking at him with a pitying expression, and in that moment, he knew it was true. Now, he was going to lose them too.

He felt his body suddenly snap back together with a painful force. Well, he decided, it was going to have to be over his cold dead body! With the speed of a striking cobra, he had his forty-four out and under Shawn's chin.

"Please Baker, don't think I won't kill you. I really do not want to, but I want my kids, and I want them now."

Shawn was very still, looking at Will thoughtfully, seemingly oblivious to the gun screwed into his throat. Something very hard in his heart was beginning to soften. He didn't know why, exactly, but he was starting to feel, well ... *bad* for Taylor.

After all, how much could the guy lose before he went insane? He had to concede that Will had done nothing to deserve what was happening to him right now.

"Cassandra picked them up from your mother's house."

"I already know that, Baker!"

"She was going to take them somewhere out of town, and then call me. I don't know where she was going. I told her to keep it to herself so I wouldn't know."

"Because Indie and the guy could read your mind, I suppose?" "Yeah, that's right. Hey, look, Will, we don't have to take the kids. I didn't say anything to Lockhart about them being Members . . . ." Baker's mind flipped backwards trying to remember if what he was saying was actually true.

"My kids . . . ." Will's voice nearly broke. "They're all I have left, Shawn!" He felt his throat constrict as a sob threatened to break out of his chest as he pictured the sweet and loving faces of his children, so helpless and small.

He didn't care what the hell they were, they were still his kids. The twinge of pressure in his heart fluttered back to life, for an instant.

Shawn cleared his throat. Will never really called him by his first name before, preferring to use the standard military last name titles. This was fine with Shawn, as he did the same, but somehow, Will breaking protocol and using his first name brought everything down to a personal level. He felt a need, for perhaps the first time ever, to explain himself. Justify his actions.

"I hear you, Will. I . . . I'm not a bad guy, okay? I was just doing my job. We aren't planning to hurt your kids, we were just . . ."

He swallowed hard at the sound of his words. They sounded so vile, spoken out loud. "Using them as . . . bait."

"Using them as *BAIT*?"

"Uh, yeah," Baker looked thoroughly uncomfortable. "We thought it was the best way to lure your wife and that guy out of the shadows. I was never sure about turning the kids in, Will. Honest. I was mainly going after the others."

Will quickly reeled in his torment, shaking off the despair in order to function. Getting his children to safety was the priority right now.

He could have his wimpified breakdown later.

"Yeah, well I've had a change of heart. I don't want any of them captured, and I've just decided that I really don't care what I have to do to keep them out of the hands of you and our government, Baker. I might just have to kill Lockhart, you and myself, but hey, we all have to make sacrifices, don't we?"

"I got you, man! Move that damn cannon out of my throat, dude. Let me call Lockhart, then we can figure out what to do, okay?"

Will appraised the man in front of him, warily. He didn't dare trust him, but he knew that Baker needed to make the call to Lockhart. He lowered his weapon slowly, watching for any sign that Baker was going to try to regain the upper hand.

Will knew that in the frame of mind he himself was in, he was far more deadly than Baker could ever dream of being. He had made the decision that he was ready to die to save his kids, feeling the coldness of his fear drip through his torso and into his extremities.

Ready to die, but also sickened, because he couldn't fathom a way out of this mess though, that was not going to require him to take the lives of his fellow agents.

He did not want to kill Baker. He didn't even really want to kill Lockhart. Hurt her very badly, perhaps, but not kill. Unless she hurt his kids, or traumatized them in any way. If that happened, he might accidentally enjoy blowing her apart, starting at her toes and working his way up to her head. He felt a wave of nausea shoot through him at the horror of knowing that he was actually capable of such thought. And such a deed.

He stepped back and gestured for Baker to make the call. Shawn pulled his phone out of his pocket and squinted at the screen. There were six new text messages from Lockhart. He read the first, and rolled his eyes.

"Lockhart's in a ditch, just off of US 2, right across from Highgate Cemetery. She hit a deer!"

"Are my kids okay?" Will's stomach could not take much more. He stubbornly ignored the odd sensation in his chest. There was no time for whatever was ailing him now.

"I guess. She doesn't say anyone was hurt. Let me call her, alright."

"Yeah, go. That's what you were *supposed* to be doing, isn't it?" Baker threw him a withering look, and dialed. Lockhart answered before the first ring was completed. Baker held the phone in silence as he allowed Cassandra to release her pent up fury at her situation, finally cutting her off.

"Sorry, honey, I was a little *busy*, okay? I'll be right there. Where are the kids?" he asked, responding to Will's agonized expression. "They're fine," he mouthed back at Will. "Ok, give me ten minutes. I'm headed that way. Oh, yeah, I'll be in Will's truck, so don't freak out, okay? Yes, I have everything under control. 'Bye!"

He looked up at Will. "Okay?"

"Yeah, let's go. You're driving!"

"And Will? I really am ... well, sorry for bringing your kids into this. I guess I was just focused on the job, you know. Doing whatever it takes to get it done!"

"Yeah, well, I guess we've all been guilty of that," Will replied, not letting his guard down for one second. "Let's get out of here."

They climbed into Will's truck, and Shawn backed up, his Nissan disentangling from the truck's grill with a sickening metallic sound. He winced as he looked at what was left of his car.

"Did you really have to destroy it, man?"

"Just be glad you aren't in the same condition," Will retorted darkly, wiping away the perspiration now dripping down his face. He leaned against the window, keeping his eyes trained on the younger man, his fingers tightly gripping the handle of his 9mm in his pocket ... just in case.

Baker looked at him curiously, then simply nodded and pulled out into the road in the direction of Lockhart and her prey.

CHAPTER 28

Jackson and Indie flew at ridiculous speeds through the back roads leading to Marie Taylor's house. They made the two-mile trip in record time, and contemplated in silence how to approach Marie in a way that would not endanger anyone or upset the woman.

This was still unresolved when they reached their destination, and Indie decided, as she fell out of the car before it had completely stopped, that they would just have to improvise.

She nearly bumped into Jax, who much to her surprise, had beaten her to the walkway, and was leading the way up the path. "Jax, maybe I should speak to Marie. You are a stranger to her. At least she knows me."

"This is true, but she is going to be wary of you now, in light of the circumstances. I'm not sure if it's going to matter much, but you go ahead."

They reached the porch and Indie rang the doorbell. Jax stepped back a respectful distance as Marie answered the door. Much to Indie's surprise, Marie reached out and pulled her into a tight embrace, and began sobbing.

"Oh, Indie, I don't know what's happening, but I think something terrible is going on! The kids . . ."

"Marie, it's okay." Indie spoke soothingly as she pushed the older woman gently back into the living room, and down onto the couch. She sat down next to her and took her hands. "Now, tell me what's happened."

"Well, Will had asked me to keep the kids for the weekend, because of, well, you know . . ." Her eyes fell upon Jackson for the first time, and she gasped. "You brought this, this *person* here, to my house?" Marie's voice was choked with outrage.

"Was this your doing, Indie? Did you send that dreadful woman here to pick up the kids, because you won't get away with it. My son will get custody, and I'll testify in court about this!"

"Marie, please!" Indie spoke beseechingly. "I had nothing to do with what happened. Nevertheless, the kids might well be in trouble. The woman who picked them up . . . do you know who she was?"

Marie looked at Jackson with accusing eyes, and then back to Indie. She had to admit that Indie seemed genuinely afraid.

"She showed some identification that said she was a Federal agent . . . a Cassandra Lockhart, or something. She said she worked with Will, and that he had sent her to get them," Marie sobbed.

"I wasn't going to let her take them, but then Cassidy told me that Will said he was sending someone for them, and that it was okay. She has never told a lie in her life, so I let them go. Then when I spoke to Will, he sounded like he knew nothing about it! I have been sitting here so worried; I didn't know what to do. I almost called the police!"

"No, don't do that, Marie. Will is going to have to handle this. We will help him if we can."

"Why on Earth should I not call the police?" asked Marie, suspicious once more. "I mean, if someone has kidnapped the kids . . . ."

"No, Marie, you don't understand. You will put them in grave danger if you involve the police." Marie continued to look back and forth between Jackson and Indie, unsure of what to believe.

"Honestly, Marie, regardless of what you may think of me, do you really think I would ever put my children in danger, or scare them to death with some crazy kidnapping scheme, just to steal them away from their father? I would never do that to them, or to Will!"

Jackson spoke suddenly, startling them both.

"Mrs. Taylor, I am so sorry for causing distress to you and your family." He spoke softly and compellingly as he stepped forward. "We will certainly explain everything to you about the situation between Indie and me at some point, but right now, our only concern is for the safety of the children. Can you believe me when I say this to you?"

Jackson's voice held the tone of a master hypnotist, casting a spell over the woman. Her eyes became soft and unfocused.

"Yes," she breathed. "I understand. I believe you."

Indie watched in disbelief, as the older woman became ensnared in Jackson's gaze. He knelt before her and spoke again, his voice soft and persuasive.

"Tell us when the woman left with the children, Mrs. Taylor. Please help us find them!"

"It was about an hour ago," she answered in a dazed whisper. "They were headed north, toward the interstate."

"Thank you, Mrs. Taylor." Jackson's voice was barely a whisper. "There will be no need to involve the police, don't you agree?"

"Yes, no need at all," Marie answered, dreamily.

"Just stay here and listen for the phone. We will call you when we have the children safe and sound; will that be okay, Mrs. Taylor?" Jackson's voice was like silk, mesmerizing.

"Of course, you're right," she agreed, a little sleepily. "I'll just wait to hear from you." She settled back into the cushions of the couch and closed her eyes, as Indie looked on, fascinated. Jackson looked up at Indie and nodded. "Let's go!"

They quickly made their way back to the car, and after they were on their way down the road, Indie looked at Jackson questioningly.

"Don't ask!" He shook his head. "I didn't know it would work like that, but I've always been fairly persuasive. Especially with the fairer sex, for some reason!" He shot a glance at Indie; the look on her face could have been funny if the situation were not so dire.

"What?" he asked, squirming with just a slight amount of discomfort at Marie's reaction. "I felt that it just might be possible that my funny little ability may have become more pronounced now that we have fulfilled our Commitment. Looks like I was right, huh?"

"I would say!" Indie still wore her look of amazement at the way Marie had capitulated without protest. She decided that this was a good thing after all, as they were on their way without further incident.

Her face darkened as she thought of her babies, terrified and in the company of a stranger. She also thought of Will, and felt a surge of sympathy for him. What must he be going through, she wondered, knowing with certainty that he also had no part in the abduction of their children.

How she knew this, she had no idea, finally deciding to just accept her knowledge as the evolution of her gifts. She would not question herself any longer. Jackson reached out with his right hand and gripped her shoulder hard enough to break through her internal terror, and spoke with feeling.

"Indie, I swear to you, we are going to get your kids back. We will take them with us, and then we are going to grow very, very old together."

Indie swallowed hard and nodded, gripping her seat tightly as he accelerated and shot down the road toward the interstate. She glanced down at the console and noticed her cell phone, and snatched it up, looking at Jackson.

"Go ahead, call him." He answered her unspoken question, his voice gentle.

"We need to all get on the same page if we want to be successful, don't we?" Indie impatiently wiped away the tears that inexplicably surfaced at Jax's words, and nodded.

She dialed Will's cell phone number, and put the phone to her ear, waiting for him to answer.

CHAPTER 29

Out of the mouths
Of babes, it is said
The truth will surely out
I feel no dread
I answer your call
A Savior, so faithful
We serve at your whim
Your summons will lead us
On a journey, most fateful

"The Alpha"
Katherine Whitley

He whimpered as he ran, limping along, alternating his right and left foot; front and back, to lift and hold high above the rough, abrasive and salt-covered asphalt. This, however, slowed his progress only slightly.

The pain was nothing. The pain could be ignored. He felt a drive to reach his destination that even he could not understand.

All he knew was that he had to keep going.

Even as he felt the rubbery pads of his paws shredding, allowing the thick, dark blood to leave small droplets wherever his feet touched down, he kept an even and steady pace.

Max paused at a set of railroad tracks, tongue swollen with thirst, and hanging from his mouth. He must not be careless. His call was to come, and he was determined to answer that call. It would not do to be crushed to death by a car or a train, never to complete the bidding of his mistress.

The poor dog was riddled with anxiety. The call had come early this morning, hours ago, but one of the more unfortunate aspects of being a dog was the fact that you were slightly limited in your ability to come and go at your leisure.

Not that he hadn't tried.

Were his claws not bloodied before this journey, with his attempts to tear his way through the window? Well, there was nothing to be done about that now, was there? He was on his way, and he was going to let nothing stop him.

He carefully looked both ways before crossing the railroad tracks and then bounded forward again with all of the speed left available in his weary little body. He could ignore the fatigue as well. Nothing was more important than reaching his destination.

Then, he must remember to use stealth and caution. He was warned not to show himself until he was told. He must remember, although he knew that it was going to be hard not to throw himself into the arms of the one who called.

He would be patient, and await her command.

First, though, he had to get there. He finally reached the main highway, and from here it was a straight shot, although he had several more miles to cover. Panting mightily, Max urged himself forward with a burst of reserved energy.

He would not let her down.

CHAPTER 30

Absolution, redemption
Is it one and the same?
Will salvation come
If I call out your name?
K.W.

Will remained propped upright, but leaned heavily against the truck door. The right side of his face, he kept pressed against the glass window, which retained the remnants of the cooler early morning.

His left eye was locked unflinchingly on Baker, who was silently steering Will's truck expertly down the twisting two-lane road.

The sensation of pressure within his chest had become impossible to ignore, yet that was exactly what Will was doing. Really, what were his options? Beg Baker to make a quick swing by the E.R.?

One medical evaluation to go, please.

Leaving Lockhart and Baker free to do God knows what with his kids? Would he let the hospital tie him to a gurney with IV's and wires, while his entire family was left to fend for themselves?

Nope. Not a chance.

Will had already decided.

He just hoped to remain upright and conscious long enough to see this through. Then he could die.

Although he was sorely out of practice, having uttered not one single earnest prayer in many years, Will gave it a shot.

Please, God, just my family . . . just let *them* get out of this unscathed, and let them live in peace. They all deserve it. I have done bad things. I have taken the lives of others, but they . . . they shouldn't suffer my punishments. Let them go, please, and I will come quietly. Honest!

He steadfastly maintained control of his body; neither his face nor his posture betraying anything out of the ordinary. There was nothing he could do however, to stem the persistent and rapidly increasing flow of perspiration from every pore in his body.

Hopefully Baker would simply attribute this to the obscene amount of heat radiating through the windshield, although Baker himself showed only minimal discomfort, having shed his muddy and destroyed suit jacket.

He was busy mourning the demise of his favorite Brioni suit, as well as his car.

Will shifted in his seat, passing his pistol from his left hand pocket to his right, with a smooth sleight of hand that would have impressed even Cris Angel. He was beginning to feel numbness in the fingertips of his left hand that made him unwilling to trust his ability to act quickly if Baker tried to misbehave.

Baker had thus far shown no sign of plotting an attempt to overthrow his command but regardless, Will was taking no chances. With his weapon now securely in his right pocket, Will repositioned himself slightly, to have a clear shot.

Just in case.

He was amazed at how much effort this simple maneuver had taken, and was suddenly very nearly overcome with fear, and a horrible feeling of impending doom. He clenched his teeth tightly, now defying the emotions as well as the physical evidence that something was very wrong with him.

A heart attack. Well, wasn't this rich. As much as Baker had enjoyed taunting him and calling him an old man, this had never really bothered Will. He knew he wasn't old. Thirty-five was still pretty young, for God's sake, and he was most definitely still in his prime. Baker was just being a cocky jackass.

Now, his body was going to betray him by succumbing to something that Will would assume could happen only to someone, well . . . *old!* And out of shape.

This so cannot be happening to me! Will protested, silently.

Yet it was happening. He could no longer deny it.

He was still absorbing the absurdity of this fact when his cell phone rang shrilly. With a supreme act of will, he pulled the phone from his pants pocket with his left hand. He kept his face non-committal as he noted the caller ID.

The only visible sign of Will's surprise was a slight tightening of his eyes. Naturally, Shawn noticed immediately.

"Who is it?" he asked in an almost convincingly casual voice.

"Shut up and drive, Baker!"

"So answer it, why don't you?" Shawn returned with an infuriating grin.

Shawn was very confident that, somehow, everything was going to work out, and was obviously not feeling the fear that was almost paralyzing Will. Having never had children, he was completely unable to relate to the kind of terror that Will was suffering. In his mind, Shawn couldn't understand Will's continued worry.

Had he not as much as told him that he was no longer interested in capturing his children? And furthermore, he had no doubts as to his ability to control agent Lockhart, so what was the problem?

Taylor should just relax, Shawn thought with an exasperated sigh.

Baker just doesn't get it, Will thought to himself, after noting his expression. He stared at the ringing phone in his hand, and then sighed too.

The idea of Indie in the same space as Baker, even over the phone, was unthinkably disturbing to Will. On the other hand, what he wanted more than almost anything in the world was to hear her voice—to know that she was, at least for the moment, okay. He answered, hesitantly.

"Will? Oh, *Will!*" Indie's voice was agonized . . . distraught.

Oh God. This was a mistake.

The moment he heard the sound of Indie's horrified voice, shaking with fear, Will felt his throat constrict. Now the unnatural pressure in his chest was joined by an altogether different kind of tightening.

Oh no.

Uh-uh. No way.

He was absolutely *not* going to do something so humiliating as burst into tears, right here in front of Baker. The guy already thought him a moronic old fool. Now he could label him a crybaby too. Oh holy hell, talk about the last straw.

The last remnants of Will's dignity were slowly being shredded into so much confetti. Maybe later he could piss his pants . . . or worse, he thought morosely, fighting back against his overwhelming need to vent his despair.

Having never shed a tear since he was a baby, with the exception of the night Indie told him she was dumping him, Will was completely out of his element. Where in the hell was his self-control? He could only rationalize this new and inexplicable tendency to want to cry like a child, to be the direct result of the distressing feeling that Will had been struggling to come to terms with.

The feeling that he was about to die.

Maybe in a blaze of glory, attempting to save his loved ones. Or maybe of a massive myocardial infarct. That idea in itself was a little humiliating.

It wasn't actual death that Will feared, precisely. He had faced death squarely and without fear numerous times in his career, always with courage, fearless in the knowledge that his wife, then later, his children were safe at home, and would be very well provided for in the event of his demise. It was nothing that a million dollar insurance policy hadn't taken care of.

No, his fear today was mired in the horror that, should he die prematurely, he would not be assured of the outcome. How could he die not knowing that his family was safe, if his mission was accomplished? It was unthinkable.

He became aware of Baker's eyes on him, and he resolutely decided that he most definitely could not give in to the infantile bawling that was trying to push its way out.

Absolutely not.

Will inhaled deeply, forcing the breath through the catch in his throat. He shut his eyes and swallowed the football-sized lump that lodged in his vocal chords at the sound of his wife's voice.

His *wife*.

She was still his wife, right? Even though she was no longer . . . *his*?

"Will!" Indie's voice was pleading now. "The kids . . . ."

"It's going to be okay, Indie." Will spoke steadily, turning his head slightly from the phone to clear the thickness from his throat. He tried again.

"I've got it under control—please, you . . . you have to . . . stay away. Get . . . get your . . ."

God, could he stop stuttering, *please*? "Get . . . *Jackson* to take you away, out of town somewhere. I will get the kids, Indie, I swear to you." Will gulped at the lump once more.

"And Indie, I . . . I will bring them to you. To you and Jackson. They'll need to go with you."

Will felt as if he were suffocating, between the feeling that his throat was collapsing, and the crushing pressure in his chest.

"Will, what are you saying? And what's happening with you? You're—something's not right with you. You're . . . not . . ."

Indie's voice trailed to a whisper. "You're not okay, are you?"

"I'm fine," Will lied. "Don't climb all through my head, okay? Right now, I need you to promise me that you'll stay away and let me handle this. Please."

Silence.

"Indie, *promise me*!"

"I can't do that, Will. I'm sorry. I know you want us safe, and I cannot even begin to tell you what that means to me. But you; you're not . . . *well*. You won't be able to . . . ."

Indie stopped. She couldn't complete her sentence.

"*Please*, Indie!" Will repeated, grinding out the words through gritted teeth. "I won't be able to function very well if I have to worry about you, too!" Will decided to ignore Baker, who was staring straight ahead at the road, but no doubt listening with great interest.

To hell with him.

"Will, listen to me. Jackson and I—she hesitated after saying this, feeling Will's mental cringe at the words—we're on our way to where you are headed, because . . ." she faltered again. " . . . Because I have a bad feeling that you are not going to be able to function much longer, regardless."

Her fear was heavy in her voice.

"Then I'll just have to prove you wrong." Will breathed deeply, fighting the curtain of weakness descending over him, growing heavier by the moment.

"So, this woman who has our children is on US two? By the cemetery?" Indie asked, suddenly. Will did not answer; his silence confirming what Indie had already pulled from his mind.

"Then I guess we'll see you there, Will. We will be coming from the south in a bronze Mercedes—she paused again as Will snorted at this—and will come around to the cemetery on foot. You're in your truck, right?"

"Why ask?" Will spoke dryly. Indie ignored this.

"And, Will . . . you have a friend with you?"

"*Friend?*" Will snorted again. "Yes," Indie spoke softly now. "I think you do.

"Will, please take care of yourself as best you can, and don't be afraid for us. The children are all that matter now. Always remember, I do still love you."

The call ended with Will left numbly frozen, the phone still held against his ear.

Her last five words had warmed him, but not enough to thaw the deadly chill that the rest of what she had said instilled in him. Her goodbye sounded like something you would say to someone who was going away on a very long trip.

Someone you think you might never see again.

The iciness washed over his skin, yet had no effect on the drenching sweat still cascading down his face and soaking his clothes.

Shawn's voice cut through his morbid thoughts. "So, that was your wife, huh?" Will didn't answer, feeling that a response was wholly unnecessary.

"Sounds like she and her . . . *friend* are coming to join the party!" Will turned in his seat to face Shawn fully. "Don't you worry your pretty little head about what my wife may or may not be planning."

Will tried to make his voice sound convincingly mocking and self-assured. He hoped he was successful.

"Hey, don't worry, Will. I thought we had a truce!"

"Did we?" Will responded. "I don't remember. I somehow don't recall you actually convincing me that you were no longer on a mission to snatch up *any* member of my family. Or anyone else important to any of them," he added reluctantly.

Now it was Shawn's turn to be silent. Will was right. He hadn't promised that he would not still go after Indie and her boyfriend, although the Indie part was becoming distasteful to him too, now. Growing a heart as well as a conscience was hard work for Shawn, and it was kind of pissing him off.

Things were so much easier when he really didn't give a damn.

There was still a small part of him that was scheming of ways to at least pick up the guy. He kept telling himself that it was for Will's benefit, as well as his own career. Maybe Will had been right the first time, Shawn justified.

Maybe his wife would return to him, if her *Equal* was hauled off to some unknown location—*"and tortured to death!"* The horrible sound of his newborn conscience added.

He let a small growl of irritation escape at the sound of this new and unfamiliar voice in his head. This visibly startled Will, and unbeknownst to Shawn, very nearly cost him his life, as Will's finger snapped around the trigger of his weapon.

Shawn stole a look at Will.

Jeeze, the guy didn't look so good. He was white as a sheet, and soaked with sweat. It wasn't *that* hot out, was it? Could it really just be the news about his kids that had him like this? Shawn had never seen anything get under Taylor's skin before. The man was the perfect poster boy for nonchalance.

Now, the guy was falling apart, right before his eyes. In fact, if he had observed correctly, he could have sworn the man was about to freakin' *cry* when he was on the phone.

It was incomprehensible.

Will gave a sudden and violent shake of his head, sending a spray of sweat to every corner of the truck's interior, and, unfortunately, all over the fastidious Shawn Baker.

"Ew, Taylor, that was sick, man!" Shawn whined, wiping the spatter of sweat from his face with the back of his hand. Will didn't answer. He was beginning to look a little grey around the edges.

Something was definitely going down with Will, and it looked like it was a kind of something that could actually take him out of the game.

Alarmed, Shawn reached out toward Will, only to have him shrink back more tightly against the truck door, and shake his head ever so slightly in warning.

"No, Shawn . . . don't." Will whispered.

Shawn stared at him for a moment, feeling almost sick. He remembered thinking what he now realized was a childish and pretty shitty thought, about wanting to see Will really freaking out about something.

Well, he'd gotten that wish, and then some. The sense of "over the edge" despair radiating from the man like heat from a furnace, was suffocating. And nauseating.

It seemed so very clear now to Shawn that Will had been swallowing down some serious unhappiness for a long time, and now he'd simply gone off the cliff. And he, Shawn Baker himself, had done the pushing.

What the fuck did I do? He felt the question ring through his head.

"Ok, Will. Take it easy, man. We're almost there, and this will be over. Then . . . I think you might need some medical attention."

"Yeah," was all that Will could manage in response.

Shawn now wore a look of genuine concern.

He and Will might not have exactly shared the same goals, but he felt no ill toward him. He was still coming to terms with the idea that he was an ass, when his brain added in the additional fact he did, in fact, also owe Will his life.

This whole situation had pretty much become total bullshit. He just wanted to call the game on account of humanity, and go home. Preoccupied with these thoughts, Baker pressed down harder on the accelerator of the heavy truck, urging it forward to the place where Lockhart awaited.

She would be disappointed, no doubt, with Baker's change of plans, but she would just have to get over it. Maybe he would even—Baker swallowed hard at the very idea—have to *sleep* with her, to placate her. Aw, holy shit . . . . Talk about taking one for the team. Could he even get it up for that? Couldn't he just take another ass kicking instead?

Shawn took a nice, deep breath as he began to organize the sweet talk he was going to have to put into action soon. He looked around, remembering that he was not in his own car, and there were no Tums or Zantac readily available.

Oh hell. How will I ever get through it, he wondered with a groan.

CHAPTER 31

The imprint from Nick's cell phone was clearly visible in the man's palm as he grasped it for perhaps the four hundredth time—squeezing it in his hands while glancing uneasily around outside his patrol car. With a sigh, he laid it back down on the seat next to him, just as he had done for the last three hundred and ninety-nine times.

Anxiety was chewing holes through the walls of his usually calm belly, as he tried to decide what course of action, if any, he should be taking.

He was still shaken by Will's sudden and violent demolition of the car that he had pulled over and detained for him, although he was sure that the driver was unharmed. Driving away and leaving Will alone in what he was now sure was a potentially lethal situation was just wrong on so many levels.

He was confused, afraid and uncomfortable right now.

Emotions that he didn't care for at all, and had moved a whole state over, simply to get away from that sort of thing. Yet, he had given his word to Will. Nick had broken a promise only once in his life.

Terrified, and seeking only to comfort, he had promised his girlfriend that she was going to be okay. He told her that she would be rescued, even as he watched in horror as the upper third of the Tower became engulfed in flames.

Candace was trapped on the top floor, every possible exit, every way out obliterated by the jet fuel-driven inferno.

Her desperate call to him came only minutes before the building had collapsed, right before his eyes. It haunted him still, every night in his dreams.

But those weren't dreams. They were nightmares. Every day he pushed it aside, got up and got on with his life. Really, he was okay now.

Except for at night.

He had confessed this sickening event finally, to his shrink. Not even his family knew about this little detail; the true reason for his short descent into bottomless depression. However, thanks to the good doctor, he had learned to shake off the guilt.

The shrink, as well as the change of location, had truly given him his new lease on life. Now, the only after-effect that remained from his personal horror story, was his absolute refusal to ever break a promise again, under any circumstances.

This brought him back around to his current dilemma.

It went flatly against his nature to sit idly by, knowing that someone could be in trouble. Big trouble by the look of things.

Nick was more than convinced that Will was potentially in some kind of seriously bad scenario.

At the very least, Will was attempting to take on a situation that should require back up, but he was performing as a solo act. Always a very dangerous position to put oneself in, Nick knew. Of course, Nick also knew that he wasn't aware of all the details about what was taking place, but he couldn't fathom why a backstabbing partner situation had to be kept so . . . so *hushed*.

Why? He wondered, somewhat sullenly.

He didn't like it. Frustration, irritation, fear, concern and back to frustration. The carousel of emotions playing across his face would have been comical; a real scream, had anyone else been around to enjoy it. He snatched up the phone in his fist again.

How could he break his own rule?

But really, isn't it true that the most beautiful part of rules are all of the exceptions? There are no such things as absolutes are there? Not on this Earth, anyway. His own internal argument was making his head hurt. He glanced wistfully at the police radio, which was squawking out a steady stream of uninteresting and meaningless chatter.

Living in a state filled mostly with small, sleepy communities was a mixed blessing. Yes, he was happy not to live in a circus of violent crime and constant calls, but on the other hand, downtime gave him little to do but remain focused on his mounting uncertainty and frustration.

Normally, this was all well and good, but right now, he sure would appreciate a little action of some kind. Just enough to occupy his thoughts and allow him to lay aside the tug-of-war within himself. At least for a little while.

As if in answer to a prayer, he heard the roar of a powerful engine. Nick looked up to see a car approaching, and joy upon joy, it was traveling at a speed that he could easily discern, without the use of any radar equipment, was well above the posted speed limit of fifty miles per hour.

He could just now see the make of the vehicle.

A Mercedes, gleaming bronze in color, shooting towards him at a fast, but not obnoxious speed. Well, this was perfect. *Something to do!*

Maybe he would just let the driver off with a warning, since they weren't driving recklessly fast. Just give the person a little reality check, right? As the car passed him, the woman in the passenger seat met his eyes directly, but briefly.

Uh, wow! Nick shook his head.

What a very . . . pretty lady, he thought, but her face was slipping away from him, like the trailing remnants of a dream. He tried to pull back the thoughts that were just with him, but couldn't quite grasp them now.

The officer sat for a moment, stumped.

An odd lethargy settled over him, and his mind felt a little cloudy. He shook his head once more, feeling it clear a bit. What had he been doing? He looked down to see the cell phone still wrapped in his hand, and thought. Oh, yeah. He had been trying to decide if he should call Will. Or someone.

With a grunt of surrender, he threw the phone back down once again, a little more forcefully than was probably good for the little electronic marvel. He now felt restless and unnerved, absurdly positive that something had just tampered with his mental function.

Why had he been about to pull out into the road?

Nick sat with his hands clenched into duel fists, then forced himself to relax them. He made a conscious effort to open his hands and to shake loose the tension.

Now, he attempted to stretch his legs out in front of him—moving his seat back as far as it would scoot. He still couldn't unfold the full length of his lower extremities, but it was an improvement. He decided to put into action some of the relaxation techniques that the psychologist had recommended to him, for times when the stress began to rear its ugly head.

Deep breathing. He would start with that one.

He reached down to his left and felt around until he found the small lever, and tugged it upward. Sighing, he rode the seat as it tilted back into an almost lying position with a smooth gliding motion. He folded his giant hands together and rested them on his belly, and closed his eyes.

Nick drew in a deep breath through his ample nose, inhaling the familiar warm and slightly grassy scent of the interior of his patrol car. Green and grassy from the near constant presence of some sort of foliage that Nick always dragged into the car.

As he slowly blew out his breath through pursed lips, he felt his body begin to respond by becoming almost limp in the seat.

The intrusive blast from a car horn cut through his serenity, causing him to jump and bang his right knee painfully into the steering wheel. He popped his head up to look outside, annoyed and now rubbing the offended body part as he let down the window.

The sound of the horn had come from a Chrysler Cordoba, circa nineteen seventy-nine. The culprit guilty of honking it, was an elderly woman, most likely in her eighty's, who was glaring at Nick from the driver's seat with a matching annoyed expression.

"It's nice to see my tax money so hard at work!" She spoke dryly, with the trembling notes of an aging voice. Nick grimaced; a mixture of pain, embarrassment and irritation flowed across his face.

"What can I do for you, lady?" He tried not to sound rude.

The old woman stared at him, and began a series of har-umphing noises, to show her indignation, Nick supposed.

"Well," she spoke finally. "You might be interested to know that there is a car in a ditch, just up the road a couple of miles."

"Is anyone hurt?" Nick asked, instantly concerned.

"How should I know," the old woman scolded. "I didn't see anyone around, but I certainly wasn't going to climb down into a ditch to look! That's what we pay you people for!"

"Yeah lady, that's right." Nick's annoyance returned. "That's what I'm here for!"

He rubbed his eyes and tried to start over. He should not take his frustration out on this person. *Even though she started it*, he thought a little childishly.

"Okay, Ma'am, thanks. I'll check it out. Did you happen to notice what kind of car it was?"

"I have no idea," she sniffed. "It was one of those new-fangled kinds—you know—not just like a *normal* car!"

Nick stifled a grin.

"How about the color, then? Did'ja notice *that?*"

"It was black. After you check it out, then I guess you can go back to your nap!"

The urge to smile faded. He sighed now.

"Yeah, thanks. Maybe I will. You drive careful now, y'hear?"

The woman pulled away in her Battlestar Galactica-sized vehicle in a huff. Nick watched her go, relieved now to have something official to do. His body suddenly went rigid as he remembered something . . . almost.

He *had* been about to do something official just a few minutes ago, hadn't he? He paused, and then shrugged. Couldn't have been that important then, could it? This car in a ditch would occupy him now, and relieve the impotent helplessness he felt as he worried about his friend.

Nick pulled a neat Vermont turnaround, and began to drive North, on US two, but as he turned, the full force of the sun hit his eyes, blinding him. He put up his hand to block the sudden burst of light in his face, and looked over the top of his fingers.

He felt the shock of foreboding hit him squarely in the gut.

The sun.

Had anyone else noticed how odd it looked, he wondered. It was raging, and a perfect orangish-red, and somehow it looked . . . well . . . too *close*.

Of course, that was ridiculous, right?

But, damn, it just didn't look *normal*.

And the heat. Jesus, man. The *heat*.

The fire waving off the surface of the orb made it look deceptively soft and furry, like a kitten. A very deadly kitten. Nick laughed uneasily to himself. "What am I, crazy or something? I must really be hell-bent on freaking myself out." He flipped down his visor impatiently, and continued down the road, shaking his head.

CHAPTER 32

"But Jesus said, 'suffer the little children, and forbid them not, to come unto me: for such is the Kingdom, of heaven'"

Matthew 19:14

Over the near deafening sounds of wildlife; birds chirruping, squirrels chattering, and whatever the hell else was living in the woods making all that racket, Cassandra was enjoying the faint rasping sound that her sharp metal nail file was making as she scratched letters into the back of the ancient headstone in front of her.

Jake and Cassidy sat on a lichen-covered log only a few yards away, watching in awe. They seemed quite impressed by Lockhart's fearless blasphemy.

This was an outstanding display of Cassandra's ability to amuse herself at the expense of others, even if that person didn't happen to be alive to know about it. The late Mrs. Nora Walker surely wouldn't mind her little joke, would she?

On the back of Mrs. Walker's simple stone marker, dated 1890-1918, Cassandra had scrawled the faintly visible letters that spelled out S-h-a-w-n B-a-k-e-r.

She thought this was hysterical, especially in light of the fact that right now, she rather wanted to wring his handsome neck for putting her through this miserable morning.

Not that she didn't still believe it would all be worth it in the end. Oh, yes. She was sure it would be.

It had better be, she thought, with an extra hard jab at the crumbling stone, causing a large chunk to fly off.

Damn it—now she would have to re-do the "r".

She doubted that Shawn would be as amused by this as she. It was well known that he was a little squeamish about things such as cemeteries, and probably headstones as well.

So much for his tough guy rep.

Cassandra had no such fear. A cemetery was just a place. It just happened to have some dead people lying around underground. So what? And a headstone. Well, it was just that; stone.

Whether large and fancy, as some of the more elaborate granite ones were, with the huge sculptures, statues and crypts, or the older ones made of softer stone, like poor Mrs. Walker's here, whose marker she was now defacing.

It was just rock. Nothing more. She was not sentimental about such things.

Cassandra was simply killing time now, having moved her quarry across the road and deep into the cemetery after the third nosey do-gooder had stopped to ask if she needed help. She had sent all three packing with her ungracious thanks, and made a silent vow to make the next Good Samaritan very sorry that he'd stopped.

She was a little disappointed though, because from that moment on, not another car had happened by at all. It was a pretty weird, actually. The road was just visible from where they sat, and the lack of traffic was conspicuous in its absence.

Cassandra had herded the children ahead of her through the maze of old and new monuments to the dearly departed—the children respectfully following the old brick path, nearly obscured by weeds and muddy debris—unlike agent Lockhart, who walked a ruthlessly unswerving path, regardless of who this required her to trample.

They'd reached the far end of the small and sporadically maintained graveyard, whose heavy cover of trees gave the place a dark and slightly sinister air. Even in the light of day, with the hot sun shearing neat holes through the foliage, it was a little dubious . . . or would be to most people.

The children had watched as Lockhart's moods had swung like a pendulum; shifting wildly from fury and irritation, to a cackling giddiness and back again.

It was fascinating to observe.

She would seem the picture of triumphant serenity for short intervals of time, only to have her anger flare, bubbling to the surface and exploding like a pyroclastic cloud of toxic fumes.

She was actually maintaining quite well for Cassandra, considering that practically everything that could possibly go wrong, had done exactly that, ever since she had absconded with these kids.

It started with the deer collision, and from there, every freaky thing under the (oddly hot) sun seemed to be attempting to thwart the good agent, making the morning quite difficult for her.

Shortly after abandoning the car, while Cassandra had been pacing the road and irritably texting Baker, the heel of her left shoe had inexplicably separated from the sole. This left her to wobble unsteadily along in her uneven footwear until finally, in a rage, she had removed her right shoe, and with much clawing and swearing, managed to rip the heel off of that one as well.

Then, there was the bizarre feeling that unfriendly eyes were spying upon her. It seemed to be coming not from the kids, but the very trees themselves. They appeared to be trying to stare her down.

In addition, it seemed as if she were being pelted with small objects, such as acorns and little pebbles.

The trees were noticeably over-populated with squirrels, birds, and other creatures and she could swear they were purposefully hurling these objects in her direction. It didn't hurt, of course, but it was unsettling and annoying as hell, to boot.

For the moment, she was on her manic high, and blowing off these events, convinced that these were nothing more than the imaginings of a bored and restless Federal Agent. Now that she suspected that these were no ordinary kids, she was working very hard to keep a tight lid on her excitement.

She was imagining the looks on the faces of all of her fellow agents, when they heard about her and Shawn bringing in the mother-load. Not one, or even two Society Members, but *four of a kind!* Two matched sets at that, she was willing to bet.

A winning hand, for sure, she gloated.

No one would ever beat that... not as long as the Homeland Security office continued to exist, would she ever be bested. It would be legend, and the stories told to everyone. She frowned for a moment, as she lamented the fact that this wouldn't be one for the history books.

No, the average American citizen would never know her name, because none of this could ever be made public. It was all top-secret activity.

That was the bitch of this kind of work. No widespread glory.

Oh well.

She straightened herself, having completed her engraving project; At least everyone in the department will know. And Baker and I will have something to toast, over an intimate dinner, maybe at my place! She drifted off into her fantasy, while still keeping her eyes on the kids. *Mustn't let them get away, hmmm?*

Cassandra allowed her mind to play out her cozy little scene, letting it veer sharply into dangerously x-rated territory.

The sound of embarrassed snickering pulled her from her reverie. The children were watching her with their heads close together, whispering and squirming uncomfortably.

"They can read minds, Cassandra!" Baker's warning words that he had spoken at the Wayside came back to her. She had scoffed at this at the time, having never encountered anything outside of nature before, but now, she was all but certain that they were spying on her passionate interlude.

"Just what is so funny?" Cassandra crossed her arms and glared at the two cherubic faces, now red with embarrassment.

"Nothing," coughed Cassidy, looking pointedly away. She prodded her brother with her elbow, and he looked away as well.

Cassandra moved closer to the children and perched on the edge of a large above ground crypt. She spoke softly, but menacingly. "I think I'd better tell you, that you two are worth almost as much dead, as you are worth alive, to the people I work for." The children went pale with fear.

"So that means, you'd better not piss me off," she continued. "And intruding on my private thoughts will definitely piss me off! Don't do it again." She spoke coldly, staring only at the girl.

There was something about her that brought out something close to . . . well, not *fear* exactly, but some other strong, unnerving emotion in Cassandra; something that she did not care for at all.

The boy was simply a wimp, she thought nastily, allowing his sister to be the obviously more dominant of the two. He looked almost constantly on the verge of tears, except when he was too busy looking terrified, then he would be comforted by the girl.

Cassidy disappointed her by simply tilting her head in acknowledgement to this direct threat. Cassandra attempted to stare the little girl down as Cassidy looked back at her steadily, although her eyes were touched with fear.

Satisfied by this for the moment, Cassandra broke eye contact, and whipped around to look behind her.

She could have sworn something had darted past her. She almost saw it, but not quite.

Something in her peripheral vision.

Cassandra narrowed her eyes as she scanned the thick tangle of brown grass and small trees, then around to the tree-crammed forest surrounding the little cemetery. She heard the rustling sound of leaves and dried grass being trampled by some unseen thing, just at the edge of the clearing.

Probably a raccoon, or something, she thought. God knows the place was crawling with them. She returned her gaze to the children, and repeated her warnings, before standing up to stretch her arms above her head.

Damn it, where is Shawn? She felt as if she had been here for hours, and it was *hot!* She had never felt such heat this time of year in Vermont. It was bordering on the ridiculous, she whined to herself, quite forgetting her earlier rant about enjoying global warming.

This sucked.

She snapped her head around. There it was again, only this time, whatever it was had been closer. The shadow of something just about knee high was slinking around just out of her field of vision.

Cassandra spun around, rapidly becoming exasperated with her failed attempts to catch whatever this thing was that seemed to be taunting her with its presence. As she searched the clearing, she noticed the girl looking toward the area where the woods became impossibly thick and dark. Her light brow creased with a small frown, and she shook her head ever so slightly.

Cassandra tried to follow the child's gaze, seeing only the clumped overgrowth of vegetation.

"What is it?" she demanded. "What do you see?"

"An animal," Cassidy whispered, now looking fully at the woman. An unnatural chill shivered through Lockhart's body at the child's unflinching stare.

What was up with this, Cassandra wondered. These kids might be the so-called Society Members, but they were still small children, and thus far, had shown her only properly respectful fear. She wasn't afraid of them, that was for sure . . . but still.

She remembered Shawn also telling her that they were not sure exactly what abilities these creatures possessed.

She absently patted the Beretta 92 F that was housed in the holster behind her skirt's waistband, as if reassuring herself that it was still there. She felt her anger beginning to resurface.

Damn it! How *dare* Shawn leave her to baby sit here in the middle of a freakin' graveyard? He had better have a really good excuse for taking just short of forever to get to her location.

She hissed with anger as another object, slightly larger than the earlier items, struck the back of her head with enough force to actually cause real pain. It felt like a golf ball sized rock.

Cassandra felt the back of her head and let out a howl of rage when her fingers revealed that a small amount of blood had been drawn. She directed her fury at the children, now huddled together on the log, looking quite terrified.

"What the hell are you doing?" she screamed at Cassidy, who simply shook her head at the woman's anger.

Jake was gripping the log tightly with both hands, looking at her with a combination of fright and, strangely enough, *sympathy.*

"Why do you have that look on your face, boy?" she barked out at him. Jake opened his mouth, but found that the words were stuck in his throat.

"Answer me!" Cassandra now sounded slightly hysterical. She was accustomed to feeling fully in control of a situation, and it did not set well with her right now, this feeling of vague uncertainty.

"I . . . I'm scared!" Jake managed, trembling all over now.

"Good!" Cassandra spat. "You should be!"

"I'm afraid of . . . what's going to happen . . . *to you!"* His voice was shaking as well. Cassandra glared at the small boy, and then burst into a high-pitched shriek of laughter.

"Don't you worry about me, sonny boy," she snorted. "You have plenty to worry about for yourself and your sister, there. You can worry about your mommy and her friend, too. You all are going to have a whole new life, if you can call it that, very soon!"

She watched with her lip curled as Cassidy wrapped her thin little arms around her brother to calm his fear.

"You!" she spoke harshly, gesturing to Cassidy. "Get over there by that angel statue!" She point to a monument standing about ten feet away. Both children stood, and she stopped them with a screech.

"Just her." She pointed at Cassidy. "You stay where you are, boy!"

Cassidy dragged her feet as she covered the short distance to the moss covered sculpture. She sat down at the cold base, and looked back miserably at her sibling. Jake began to cry, quietly.

"Dry it up, kid." Cassandra was unmoved by this display, merely becoming more annoyed. The little boy looked up at her; his face streaked with his tears, and spoke softly.

"Why are you doing this to us?" He shivered out the words pitifully.

"Because you all are unnatural freaks from some other world, or something. I don't know what you are, really, and I don't care. I just know that I am to hunt you and anyone like you, and bring you in to my bosses. I'll probably get a raise and a promotion!"

"So this . . . is for money?" Jake asked, in what sounded like disbelief.

"Money, glory, maybe a little of both. It's all good." She shrugged, then tossed her hair back and looked at her watch. Shawn Baker had five more minutes before she called him again, and ripped holes through his eardrums.

She decided to ignore the thing dancing around just out of her view, its shadow playing games with her imagination. She would not let some dumb animal creep her out.

As she looked up through the trees, she could not keep back the small gasp that escaped her lips at the sight of the giant orange ball of flames that seemed close enough to lick the trees and ignite them.

Was this normal, she wondered.

She knew there was such a thing as a harvest moon, but was there a harvest sun, or some equivalent?

She had never noticed it looking like this before. Then again, she wasn't exactly the outdoorsy type either, and not one to notice things like beautiful *or* unusual sunrises and sunsets, for sure.

The sound of a large vehicle slowing down on the main road diverted her attention from the natural phenomenon above her head.

*　　*　　*

As Shawn parked the truck in the small alcove of trees and high grass, he looked at Will and felt all but certain that he wasn't going to make it.

Will's eyes were half-closed, with one of them looking horribly wrong, slightly rolled back into his head. His color was dreadful, and his breathing rasping . . . irregular.

Somehow though, he still had managed to keep himself semi-upright in the seat, and Shawn was sure that Will's finger was still curled around the trigger of the pistol that he was also positive was in Will's pocket.

He had to shake his head in admiration. For an old guy, he was tough as nails; that was indisputable.

And he could still whip *ass!*

I can personally vouch for that, he thought, as he gingerly touched the puffy and sore area to the left side of his face, and then moved his hands down to his ribs that were also feeling the pain of this morning's abuse.

Yeah. That was going to leave a mark.

As he looked again at the slowly slumping form of his partner, Shawn felt another surge of conscience. He owed the man, and he had decided that he was going to get his kids back safely for him.

He also felt that it was entirely possible that Will would not live to see this feat accomplished, but it was the least he could do, since apparently he was going to be required by Will himself, to let the man die.

He knew that he could not call an ambulance or anything right now, given the current situation.

It really did suck.

"Will, buddy, listen to me."

Determination wrapped its horned claws tightly around Shawn Baker's throat, lifting him . . . shaking him now . . . urging the man to make things right.

"It's gonna be okay, understand? I am going to get your kids. I'll take them back to your mom's house, I guess. Then, if you want, your wife can pick them up from there, okay, partner?"

Will's eyes were working hard to focus, until he finally found Baker's, and he nodded. Speaking was nearly out of the question, but he tried.

"What would Machiavelli say?" he rasped.

Shawn was silent for a moment, and then he smiled valiantly. "Let's not tell him then, alright?

"You . . . you'll be okay, Will. After I deal with Lockhart, I'll get EMS out here." Shawn tried to sound matter of fact, but what he felt was dread.

"Hell, man. I'm probably going to have to let Cassandra have some of the good stuff, to get her to let go of all this! I am going to have to sacrifice myself to her. How will I go on?" he tried to joke, and Will's mouth twitched almost into a smile as he shook his head and made a grimace appropriate to the idea of anyone actually having to have sex with Lockhart.

Then he sighed.

"Tell Indie I'm sorry," he croaked. "That I love her and the kids. You're right, I'm an idiot . . . but they didn't deserve this."

How weak he sounded to himself. How could this be? He really *wasn't* going to survive. He knew it now. Of all the ways he thought he'd go. All the times he'd come so close . . . surviving just so he could die of a heart attack.

Well . . . *shit!*

Shawn suddenly reached out, ignoring Will's startled move back against the truck door, and put his hand on his partner's shoulder. He gingerly tugged his own beloved gun out of Will's waistband and spoke urgently.

"Will, I understand if you don't fully trust me right now, but you can, okay? I don't think you have a choice anyway, do you? I am gonna put this right. Just stay here and don't move, you got it?"

Will closed his eyes in response.

Shawn quietly pulled himself out of the truck, and screwed a custom-made silencer to the end of his weapon. He smoothly shot out the left front and back tires without so much as missing a step as he moved toward the graveyard, tucking the gun briskly back into his holster.

*   *   *

Cassandra leaped up, having seen that the sound had come from a large, four-wheel drive Ford pickup truck, with someone behind the wheel who looked exactly like Shawn Baker.

Finally! She all but shouted to herself.

She'd watched the driver pull over to her side of the road and move the truck forward until it became concealed from passers-by, for the most part. After an agonizing few moments, he had slowly exited the truck, and shut the door softly. Cassandra breathed a sigh of relief.

It *was* Baker.

She noted the absence of his always-present tailored jacket, and his dirty and disheveled appearance. He looked like he'd been in a fight, and she'd be willing to bet that she knew who the other contestant had been.

Well, he must have kicked Will's ass, she thought with pride. *Otherwise he wouldn't be here.*

Not that she was surprised. She had the utmost confidence in her hero, and wouldn't have given odds of any kind to Will. He was too much like somebody's dad, or something.

Not a fighter, she was sure.

With a stern look of warning to the forcibly separated children, she waved her hand in the air, and called out Shawn's name. He looked at her with an expression that conveyed nothing short of pure horror at the hiding place that Cassandra had chosen.

"Are you *kidding* me, woman?" Shawn shouted back to her. "I'm not coming in there!"

"Oh get over it, you big baby!" Cassandra grinned. She knew it. He was a superstitious namby-pamby, *although a very hot one,* she added to herself.

Grunting in disapproval, Shawn began to awkwardly step his way through the graveyard toward the woman and her captives, making quite sure that he stepped on no unmarked graves.

He was trying to hold his breath as well, although this, he obviously could not keep up for any length of time.

He stopped halfway and pleaded to his co-conspirator;

"Please . . . come on Cassandra, don't make me come all the way in there! It's . . . *dark!*"

"Don't worry, I'll protect you from the Boogeyman," she laughed, in much better spirits now that she was not alone with these creepy kids.

With a pained and martyred expression, Shawn sighed, and moved forward. God damn her . . . he was going to make her pay for this when it was all over, if it was the last thing he did.

He *REALLY* hated graveyards.

Shawn finally made it to the small party, and looked at the miserable faces of the children. He felt instantly ill at the misfortune that he had brought upon them. As he cleared his throat to speak, Cassandra called out to him.

"Hey, Shawn, look at this one!" She pointed down to a small and very old looking grave marker. Shawn had to squint and crouch down to see the writing on it, which was very faint. As it dawned on him what the letters he was reading spelled out, he recoiled angrily, falling on the seat of his pants in the damp earth.

He looked around, and was horrified to see that he was now sitting directly on a grave that had only the small headstone that lay flat, level with the ground.

With a shriek that would have done any thirteen-year-old girl proud, Shawn was back on his feet.

"*Fuck,* Lockhart, you're a real sick-o, you know that?" He was trembling with outrage and disgust, now also pissed off that she had made him blurt out the grand-daddy of all curse words in front of the kids.

Cassandra bent double with laughter at Shawn's antics. His reaction had been better than she could have dreamed.

"Oh, my God!" She gasped for breath. "That was the funniest damn thing I've ever seen!"

"Yeah, well I'm glad you're so easily entertained!" Baker retorted, angrily.

He then pulled himself up to his full height, closed his eyes and drew upon every ounce of training and experience that he could, in order to regain control of his traumatized mind. This was no time to allow himself to freak out over his own personal little phobias. He remembered his new mission, and put it into action, swallowing down the burning acid rising in his throat in anticipation of the words that he was about to speak.

"Ok, sweet thing, you've had your little joke." He forced out his most charming smile at Lockhart. "Now, we need to get the hell out of here, if you don't mind." Cassandra was instantly agreeable. Baker's small endearment hadn't escaped her notice, and she was only too happy to comply with his wishes.

"Where to now, Sugar?" Baker kept the smile in place with a Herculean effort, and wished the blond at the bottom of the ocean.

She *really* didn't need to return the favor with the pet names.

"Well," he began, trying to sound very much in charge. "We need to get back to town. There is going to be a slight change in plans. I've thought of a better way to get Will's wife and her guy to come to us." Cassandra's face changed imperceptivity.

"Go on." Her voice was now all business, no trace of the flintiness of only moments ago. Baker pulled in a deep breath.

"I want to take the kids to Will. He said he knows of a way to get Indie to come to him, and, no doubt, the guy will come with her. He wouldn't allow her to show up at Will's place alone, right?" Cassandra regarded Baker thoughtfully, with her arms crossed.

"What's going on, Baker? Why the change of plans? I thought Will didn't want his wife captured."

"Yeah, well, he's had a change of heart. He's decided that he's not really into staying married to a different species after all."

Cassandra looked around uneasily, over her shoulder before speaking again. That damned shadow.

"Um, Shawn . . . sweetie . . . when were you going to tell me about the kids?" She was looking at him unhappily now.

Baker's heart sank. She knew. Damn it all, she knew.

"I wasn't sure about the kids, Cassandra." Baker spoke honestly. "Sure about what, Shawn? Their status . . . or taking them in?"

"Both, kind of," he sighed. "Cassandra, I don't want to bring in the kids."

He held his breath again as he waited for her reaction. With Cassandra, you could never be sure what you were going to get. Lockhart looked pensive as she kept her arms tightly crossed, poking at the clumps of soil at her feet with the toe of her ruined shoe.

"But, Shawn," she protested. "These kids are the *most* important. I don't know for sure, because I don't work in your department, but I am willing to bet that they've never caught any so young before. And I think they're a set . . . *Equals* or whatever, which is kind of nasty, actually. I thought that *Equals* were, like, you know, boyfriend-girlfriend or something."

Baker was wracking his brains to come up with an explanation for Lockhart. He too, was baffled by the idea of the two kids being *Equals*. Obviously, they didn't know everything about these beings, but he had thought the same as Cassandra. He looked up at her to see her watching him very carefully.

He tried another tactic. His ace in the hole.

Shawn smiled fully at her again.

"Come on, Cassandra; let's do this Will's way. Then we'll be rid of these kids, and we will still get to bring in the others. We'll get plenty of credit, and reap the rewards." Baker stepped closer to Cassandra, and pulled her close to him.

"Besides," he whispered. "Just think of how we could occupy our time while we wait to hear from Will."

Cassandra's jaw dropped open. As many times as she had dreamed of hearing just these kinds of words from Shawn, the reality of the moment astounded her.

She allowed Shawn to pull her toward him, and caught the faint remnants of expensive cologne. Her breath caught as she felt his lips press softly against the sensitive area just below her ear.

Oh, he was good . . . just like in her dreams. She could even force herself to ignore the feeling of the children's eyes upon them.

The sound of something crashing through the underbrush yanked them back to their surroundings. "What the hell was that?" Shawn was already on edge.

To him, there was nothing worse than noise coming from unknown sources in a graveyard.

"It's just some animal," Cassandra told him breathlessly. "It's been hanging around here the whole time." She hadn't been quite ready to give up the moment, but Baker was now looking around, distressed. He wanted to see this "animal" with his own eyes. Just to make sure. But he saw nothing.

Uneasily, he turned back to Lockhart. She was still gazing up at him, dreamily. "We are going to take these kids back to Will's mom. Then we will . . ." Cassandra stopped him with a light smack to the chest.

"Silly boy! We are not giving these kids back, are you *crazy*? This is too good to give up. Don't get all wimpy on me now, Shawn. You can handle this!"

Baker was surprised to find that Cassandra was still resisting, after his offer. He had been so sure that she would go for it.

Actually, she *was* going for it just fine, yet still resisting. He was going to have to get tough.

"Listen to me, Cassandra. I am calling the shots, here. This is my plan, my deal, okay? Just do what I say and everything will work out fine." The woman stepped back and narrowed her eyes.

"Shawn Baker, obviously you don't have the guts to do what is necessary, but that's okay. I have enough for both of us. You can turn your back, if you'd like, and let me do the dirty work, but we *ARE* bringing in all four of them. Your plan has been modified!"

Crap. She *was* going to fight him.

He thought for a moment, glaring at the woman before abruptly shifting gears. He'd actually covered plan "B", as a backup . . . he just never thought for a moment that he would have to use it. Shooting out the truck tires had turned out to be the thing to do.

Shawn raised his hands in mock defeat. "Alright, you know what? Let's load up and get to a hotel, and we will talk about what to do from there . . . how does that sound?"

"Now you're talkin'." She smiled.

He made a great show of rounding up the kids and walking ahead of Cassandra before he let out a yell. "The truck has two flat tires!" he tried to put the right note of irritation in his voice.

It wasn't hard.

"So change it, big man!"

"There's only one spare, Lockhart!"

"Oh, yeah. Great. Well, what the hell are we gonna do *now*," she wailed. "I'm sick of this place, and sick of these kids and . . ."

"Alright, I hear you! Jeeze, relax girl!" Shawn was still working to keep her loyal to him.

"Let's go back here so we can sit, and I'll make some calls." He moved the kids quickly back to the thick woods, and let them sit together on the log again. He wanted to keep Cassandra away from the truck, obviously, and he needed to think.

And try to figure out what to do next.

With an angry sigh, Cassandra went to sit back on the crypt, jerking around a couple of times as the shadow in the corners of her eyes continued to torment her.

Shawn noticed as well, and moved well beyond the area where he had seen it last, shifting to stand near a large headstone that rose to the middle of his back.

He pulled out his phone and stood, thinking. Cassandra helped him think, by yelling at him.

"Baker, you've got to get us out of here and now, or all hell is going to break loose!" His response was lost as a blast of hot air whipped around his body, nearly burning his eyes. A heat storm, maybe?

Shawn thought the sun looked awfully bright and . . . um . . . *close*. Freaky.

CHAPTER 33

"The wolf also shall dwell with the lamb, and the leopard shall lie down with the kid; and the calf and the young lion and the fatling together; and a little child shall lead them."

Isaiah 11:6

The road was unusually deserted, especially considering the fact that it was a very sunny spring Saturday. They had passed only one other car on their hasty journey, not counting the police car, of course. Jackson had clearly seen the officer's intention of stopping them.

A warning, eh? Well, the man was nice enough, Jackson decided, and under normal circumstances, he would never have dreamed of interfering with the man's thoughts. He would have pulled over and taken the official warning gratefully.

Ah. Yes. He had not been the one to interfere!

He did not have that gift, did he? Jackson and Indie were meshing so seamlessly in thought, now, that it was becoming difficult at times to separate whose ideas were whose.

Jackson filed away his intention to tease Indie about her effect on men for a more appropriate time.

That poor officer didn't stand a chance, he thought, as he remembered the completely befuddled look on the man's face, just as he had been preparing to pull out behind them.

He glanced over at her now, and noticed her lips, pressed tightly together.

Consider it noted, came her distracted thought.

Jackson spoke aloud, now. "I thought you were going to let me have some private alone time with my evil thoughts," he commented as he scanned the sides of the road. They should be getting close now.

—

301

"Maybe I've decided that I had better keep an eye on you and your thoughts," she returned, anxiety riddling her features. He could feel her tension building, in spite of her earlier calm, and her pledge of confidence in fate and himself.

Jackson was anxious as well. He was very unclear about the outcome of this ordeal, but he already knew this; the same senses that had warned him that they were going to have to face their pursuers head on, now told him something else.

Something awful.

People were going to die today, in connection with this little adventure, and he had no idea who they were going to be. He was appalled by this revelation. He knew that Indie had felt this as well, accounting for her rising anxiety, and he had nothing with which to comfort her.

He couldn't even enjoy a moment of selfless bravery, and hope that he would be one of the doomed, to spare anyone else, because of the strange workings of having a permanent soul mate, whose fate was intertwined with your own.

The end of him would bring about the end of Indie as well. Unthinkable.

It did cross his mind, that perhaps this *was* it. That their destiny was that they were to meet, and do something very important, and then move on. He could not help but remember Ms. Conner's dying words. "*She is in possession of something so precious . . . .*"

Something that must be protected. He then thought of her last words.

"*At all cost.*"

Maybe they were not meant to have any length of time together in this life.

He and Indie. That could account for two souls that he knew would be moving on today. Although he knew moving on was not exactly the end, he wanted to enjoy the here and now with her; *the pleasures and joy of the flesh.*

At least for a little while.

"What will be, will be . . ." he thought with a sigh. He was ready to do whatever was necessary.

He glanced upward at the sun raging in the sky and shivered. He wanted to go to one of the observation centers to check on the status of the sun, but he could see from here that it was expanding with an excess of negative energy.

Usually it was too subtle for the average person to notice, especially without the benefit of viewing it from one of the focus areas, like Mystery Hill, or the better-known Stonehenge.

Today, however, no one could help but notice the change. It was frightening.

Indie spotted the back end of the PT Cruiser, its nose deep in the muddy ditch. Jackson abandoned his chaotic thoughts and guided the Mercedes to the opposite side of the road, pulling over an appropriate distance, and turned off the engine.

He pocketed the keys, and turned to face Indie, grasping both of her hands before speaking.

"I suppose it's pointless to ask that you remain here, and let me go see what I can find, right?"

"I knew you were a smart man," Indie replied. There was no way she was staying in the car.

Jax looked into her eyes and spoke silkily, in his singsong mesmerizing voice. "Don't you want to wait for me, and stay where I know you'll be safe?"

Indie's eyes misted for only a split second, before she tossed her head. "Oh, don't *even* try that with me . . . are you kidding?" she huffed, pushing against his chest.

He placed both hands around her face, and kissed her quickly before giving her a tight, miserable smile. "I figured it would work exactly like that, but you can't blame a guy for trying, can you, love?" They sat looking at each other for a full thirty seconds, before speaking in unison.

"Let's go!"

They left the car, and began silently working their way through the tall grass and huge rocks that were littering the area. As they moved around a particularly thick cluster of trees and rock, Indie sucked in her breath as she spied Will's truck, obviously purposefully concealed. She also noticed the two flat tires.

Jackson squeezed her hand and whispered fiercely. "Don't assume the worst, Indie. Let's check it out."

Indie nodded, but felt a knot of dread in her belly. She almost didn't want to look, but knew that not looking would not make what was frightening her go away.

As they began working their way toward the truck, trying to be very quiet as the dried weeds and grass crunched under their feet, Jackson saw movement deep within the cemetery housed within the clearing ahead.

He saw the blond woman, and read immediately from her heart and mind that this was the real threat. This person was cold. This person was heartless. This person had the features of *darkness*.

A true demonic soul.

Jackson's strong infallible heart skipped a beat, and a frost seemed to wrap around his entire body.

They were in trouble. He'd never had any problem confronting one of *them* before, but her close proximity to the children, and having his *Equal* so close to the foulness of evil, disturbed him greatly.

Killing them off here and there was part of his job, but it was never a direct confrontation. He always made sure to take them out before they even knew what was happening, because active confrontation was dangerous with these creatures.

The lost souls who had no idea what they were.

Just walking anger and hate.

Jackson turned to speak to Indie, but saw that all of her attention was focused on the truck. He also took note of the fact that there was no way to get to the truck without coming into clear view of the woman.

Instantly, he knew that he and Indie must separate.

Indie! He sent an urgent call to her mind. She turned with a start, to face him. *Listen, Indie, you can get to the truck if you use your gift. You will not be noticed. There is enough cover from the woods to allow me to make my way closer, to the back of the cemetery where they are, without being seen . . . what do you say?*

Indie hesitated, and then answered silently.

Yes, you go. I feel like I need to get to that truck right away.

"Be careful," they whispered aloud to each other, and Jackson veered to the left to circle around, feeling Indie shut down as he moved away from her. He didn't like the feeling of separation and isolation that this caused him, but he knew that it was the best option. He focused on getting through the crackling grass unseen.

Indie approached the truck cautiously, still moving with care. She wasn't physically invisible, just unlikely to be noticed, so she moved with deliberate stealth, to avoid any sudden movement that could possibly give her away. Her heart was pounding so loudly, she felt sure that anyone within a half-mile radius could hear it. All attempts at calming it had proven ineffective so far. Deep breaths, calming focus . . . nothing was helping.

She finally made it to the right side of the truck; the one facing away from the cemetery, the truck itself now offering shelter from any searching eyes.

Carefully now, she grasped the door handle, and opened it ever so slightly. She was unprepared as the weight of something large pushed back against her, causing the door to open all the way.

Indie covered her mouth to stop the scream that nearly escaped as she recognized first, that this was a person, and then in almost the same instant, the identity of that person. He had fallen half out of the truck, like a scene from a horror movie.

It was Will. Most of his body remained on the seat, but his head and shoulders now hung treacherously outside the truck.

It was obvious that he had been leaning heavily against the door. Shaking violently, Indie knelt near Will's head, and could just hear the faint sounds of breath, and a faltering heartbeat in the full throes of cardiac arrhythmia.

She didn't want to touch him. To look at him was telling enough.

Indie covered her face with both hands and burst into silent sobs that threatened to tear open her chest.

She looked at the face of the man she had married.

The father of her children.

He sucked in a desperate gasp as he began struggling to right himself, and Indie knew that she could not put it off. She had to get him back into the truck.

Swallowing her sobs, she wrapped her arms around Will and lifted him quite easily into the cab of the truck, straightening his body to make a more comfortable arrangement of his limbs. The tears pressed through her tightly shut eyes, and the heaving sobs began again.

The burning in her belly was so strong that it extended to her entire torso.

She pressed her face against his, holding him tightly. Will stirred, and tried to look around to find the source of the arms that held him. "The pain . . ." he whispered weakly.

Indie sat up instantly. She had the power to comfort, to soothe and to take away pain. She also had the power to help heal, but only that which *could* be healed. She could diagnose hopelessness through her touch. And Indie had almost never felt such hopelessness. However, she could bring him peace and ease his pain.

"Will," she whispered to him, fervently. "I'll make it go away," she promised. "All of the pain will leave you." As she spoke, she slid into position to cradle Will in her arms. She slipped her free hand under his shirt and pressed her palm to his skin, directly above his heart.

Will stiffened and pulled in another deep breath as the blood flow increased, allowing more oxygen to nourish him.

The damage to his heart, however, was catastrophic. This would bring comfort and nothing more.

The burning in Indie's gut was almost unbearable now, but she would endure it. Her warm tears fell, touching Will's face, and he finally focused on her.

"Indie?" His whisper was uncertain. "I'm here, Will," she answered in a trembling voice. She gently rubbed his chest, seeking to ease his breathing.

Will lifted his shaky right hand, just enough to stroke a tear from Indie's cheek, and spoke in a sad attempt at humor.

"That bad, huh?" he breathed out the words.

"Pretty bad," Indie admitted. She knew there was no point in lying to him. He wasn't stupid. Besides, she was the world's worst liar under the best of circumstances.

"The kids!" Will's face clenched in a different kind of pain, as he remembered his mission. It slammed back into focus as he struggled to sit up, but Indie held him firmly.

"No, Will, you mustn't move. Jackson is out there. He is going to rescue our kids." Indie hoped that she was not inadvertently telling a lie, now.

She held tight as Will continued fighting to sit up with surprising strength, the temporary fix helping him immensely. "Will! Don't move, unless you want to experience the phrase 'sudden death.'" Indie's voice wavered as she said this, but she had to keep him still.

Maybe he could at least hang on to see the outcome. If it was good, then he could die in peace . . . no chance of his becoming one of the lingering souls hanging around Earth, bemoaning their fate.

If the outcome was bad, however . . . .

No. She could not think about that possibility.

"Indie." He stopped struggling now, and was looking up at her with a heartbreaking expression on his face. "I . . . I'm sorry. For everything. I am a jerk. I never did right by you. I . . . ."

He broke off as a nasty cough took him by surprise. Indie cringed at the sound of fluid beginning to fill his lungs.

He began again.

"How could I not see? I look in your eyes, even now, and get lost, somehow. I know you were unhappy, and I never did a thing about it. I don't know how, but I never even noticed, until it was too late. Now, all of a sudden, for the past twenty-four hours, I can't think of anything *but* you and the kids. I don't get it." He rasped in a wet breath. "Can you forgive me?"

"Will," Indie kissed his forehead gently, hesitantly. "Don't torture yourself . . . it wasn't anything in you. It was me. I have . . . I mean, there's something in *me*, that makes people, well, kind of ignore me. It's sort of an odd defense mechanism. I didn't even know I was doing it before, but I understand it a little better now. I learned how to let down the wall yesterday, so maybe that's why you were so able to . . . to think about me."

Will was quiet as he contemplated this.

"So, my being the worst husband in the world wasn't *all* my fault?" He coughed again.

"Stop it, Will." Indie was trying not to be tearful, but it was difficult. "You were the best husband anyone could ask for." Will looked at her skeptically.

"Except for the snooze alarm thing . . . that was really annoying." She was trying desperately to take away his fear.

"Ah, that damned snooze alarm. Somehow I always knew I'd go to my grave hearing you complain about that." Will smiled drowsily at her. He was beginning to feel lightheaded and sleepy, as if he had received an injection of morphine.

"Whad'ju do to me?" he asked, thickly, as his eyes became heavier

. "Just relax, Will." Indie forced herself to assume a professional demeanor, but aware that the lack of oxygen was starting to take its toll on his body. Talking was not helping.

"You listen, I'll talk, okay?" She stroked his hair and felt his body relax in her arms. "You provided for me, for our family. You took care of me, and saved me from a horrible fate. If you and I had not married, I might have had a very different outcome. And the kids . . . they never would have been. I don't regret one second with you, Will. You're a good man, just as I knew you were when we met." She wiped impatiently at her tears that would not stop flowing.

"I'm sorry for what has happened, for leaving you. But I had no *choice*. I don't want you to ever think that you were . . . inadequate in any way. This is a phenomenon that goes with what we are.

"We're not aliens, Will, or anything exactly other worldly and definitely not evil, although the explanation would be tough for you to swallow. It's a little theological, to say the least." Will was struggling to keep his eyes open, and he started to speak. Indie pressed a finger to his lips.

"Shh, no. I'm just going to say it, okay? We are descended from . . . *angelic beings* that came into the flesh of man, to procreate and to perfect humankind. We are *like* humans; the *forbearers* of humans, just the way we were all meant to be, and will be, eventually. If the human experiment survives its own tendency to try to destroy itself."

There. It was out there, for him to do with what he would.

It crossed her mind that she was already breaking one of the biggest Society rules, but revealing herself to someone who already knew that she was, well, *different*, did not seem wrong somehow. Especially since he was—she gulped—dying.

Will's eyes were now closed. His breathing was more regular, and even, although the sound of fluid building was impossible to ignore. He smiled, and reached up once more to stroke her cheek.

"An angel," he murmured. "I *knew* it!"

*   *   *

Jackson made it through the tangle of woods to the back portion of the cemetery. He kept a tight eye on the blond she-devil, who was now pacing angrily.

He noticed a tall young man standing near a large headstone, and felt the jolt of recognition.

Well what do you know? He knew this man. They had crossed paths before, briefly.

Not in person, exactly, but the man had been stalking one of the law firms, a few years ago, attempting to follow the money trail that kept all Society Members afloat, and afforded legal protection, when needed. Jackson had been asked to monitor the man, and find out his habits.

After noting his penchant for expensive things, Jackson had decided that a visit from the IRS to ascertain *HIS* money trail, might keep him busy enough to stay off the backs of the Society's legal team.

An anonymous tip detailing Mr. Baker's spending habits and various other insinuations, had resulted in a lengthy and irritating investigation, that had almost cost Shawn his security clearance, and thus, his job. Fortunately, for Shawn Baker, the investigation had found nothing unlawful.

Just a tax error from years before, requiring the IRS to actually pay Shawn five hundred dollars.

This had not been enough to placate him for the trouble it caused, but it did interrupt his pursuit of the law firm's money source. Jackson had accomplished that mission.

He was now directly behind the headstone where Shawn was standing, and he knelt on the ground while he whispered a small prayer.

The woman held all the cards. She had the kids. He had nothing to bargain with. He was able to peek around the headstone and steal a look at her.

He shivered with revulsion at the sheer evil emanating from her every pore. It seemed impossible to believe that everyone couldn't see it.

Jackson was able to pull from her mind an infatuation for the man standing nearby. Not any kind of love, but a lust-driven obsession. Hmm. Maybe that could prove fortuitous.

He backed up a bit to shift his position, wanting to be able to see both the blond and the other Agent, at the same time. He waited patiently, until the moment the blond was busy speaking to the children, whom he could see only the very tops of their heads from this vantage point.

As luck would have it, Shawn Baker chose that very moment to back up closer to the headstone in response to something that had frightened him. Jackson made his move.

With a speed and strength that would seem inconceivable, Jackson stood up, lurched forward, locking his arm around Baker's torso, covering his mouth with his other hand, and snatched him off his feet. This brought Shawn over the headstone, and some twenty feet back into the woods.

They were now completely hidden by the brush.

Shawn Baker suffered a near cardiac arrest of his own, being lifted and dragged through a graveyard by unseen hands, as if in instant replay from one of his darkest nightmares. For a moment, he was grateful for the hand clamped tightly over his mouth, as it prevented him from screaming like a girl for the second time of the day.

As he was slammed down to the ground with terrific force, he grunted in pain, his ribs quite sore from his make-out session with the end of Will's boots. The impact now didn't help.

"This has turned into one bitch of a day!" he thought as he looked up at his assailant. Shawn's eyes bulged with disbelief, as he recognized immediately the man from the video Will had shown him.

"Aw, *hell!*" was all he could manage, in response to Jackson's finger to the lips indicating that he should not try yelling. He backed up this gesture with a broken-off stick which was short, sharp and about as thick as his thumb, pressed ominously against Shawn's throat.

Really?

Well. Wasn't this some shit? A gifted Federal agent such as himself. Held helpless.

At *stick-point.*

The humiliating spots in his day just continued to get better and better. Shawn stifled a sigh.

"Now, I know what you're thinking, Shawn Baker. But don't feel bad. Others have suffered far more than simple humiliation at my hands, and with much more crude instruments. I am bound to use only my hands and what I find in nature as my weaponry. Call it a handicap, if you will."

Shawn grappled furiously with the impulse to try to find an escape, only to be nudged with the point of the stick; the sharpness catching the skin of his throat.

"Mr. Baker," Jackson whispered. "It would truly be in your best interest if I had your cooperation in this matter, so if you don't mind, be very quiet, please!"

"Hey," Baker whispered ferociously. "Listen, I . . ."

"Yes, Mr. Baker," Jackson cut in. "I see the turmoil in your mind, and I'm happy that you don't want the children harmed. That is the *most* important concern, but I am afraid it's not quite enough. You see, I don't want Indie hurt or captured and unfortunately, this means that nothing can happen to me either. Our destinies are one, if you will pardon the hyperbole."

Jackson gestured toward Lockhart. "I do have to say; you certainly found a real *non-compos mentis* to be your helper. Most unsettling."

"What in the *hell* does that mean?" Shawn asked, rubbing his damaged ribcage.

"Insane. Not of sound mind, get it?" Jackson spoke while looking around the tombstone at the object of this description. Shawn said nothing. He had never been in such a position. He wasn't sure if he was an ally to this thing or not, even in his own mind.

He looked at the Society Member, who clearly had the strength of a bull and the speed of a cat, noting once more, that he looked like a teenager.

And spoke like an English professor.

How deceptive. He wanted to ask him his age, absurd as this would be right now.

"Forty." Jackson spoke while straining to see all movement in the clearing, glancing down only to check the other man's reaction. "That's crazy!" Shawn hissed, in hushed tones. The guy was almost twice his age. Jackson threw him a distracted nod.

"Not too shabby, for an old goat, eh?"

Shawn was speechless.

He thought about the children, now alone with Cassandra, and pictured, with a stab of guilt, the fear on their faces. At that moment Jackson turned, and seized him by the shoulders, staring at him in shock. He did not speak for a long moment, simply burning a look through Shawn with scorching eyes.

"No!" he whispered. "It can't be . . . it simply can't be possible . . . *can it?*"

"What can't?" Shawn was startled by the man's swift change of mood. Jackson stood and dragged Shawn along with him, to get closer to the cemetery.

"Hey, man, you don't have to drag me around. Can't you read my mind? I'm not going anywhere!" Jackson pulled him back down into the cover of grass. "I have to see them. I have to get closer. Are you *sure?*"

"What are you talking about? Am I sure about *what?* I don't know that I've been participating in this whole conversation!"

Jackson stared back at him before answering. "Forgive me, but I forget." He swallowed hard, and spoke slowly.

"You think Indie's children are Society Members, too? Both of them?"

"Well, yeah, I'm sure. Especially now. They are twins, so they must both be, right?, And maybe that's why they are a set, because of . . ."

"*NO!*" Jackson cut him off again. "It does *not* work like that. I mean, they would *both* have to seek their *Equals.* They would . . ." His voice faded away to an even softer whisper.

"They are brother and sister . . . they can't . . ." He stopped again as he began to comprehend.

"*Something so precious that it had to be protected at all cost!*"

Jackson's jaw actually dropped. He floundered for a moment, seeking strength, seeking a plan . . . seeking *anything* that would help him succeed in this mission that had just tripled in magnitude.

Oh, I must not fail! The responsibility was all but suffocating.

Baker was incredulous. "You didn't *know?* What is going *on* with all of you people? Why am I always the first to see it?"

"I've never seen the children," Jackson responded, a little desperately. "If I had, *I* would have known." He shook his head, and looked at Baker.

———

310

"Look, this is monumental. Those kids *must* be rescued unharmed. I cannot impress upon you the imperative nature of this fact. It simply must be! The impact of these children coming to harm at the hands of that . . . that *woman*, would be unthinkable.

"I'm not sure, but somehow I believe that this might be more than the Creator will tolerate. The negative energy would be immeasurable!"

Baker struggled to remove a sharp stick that was stabbing him painfully in the back, mirroring the one at his throat, and tried to comprehend what Jackson was telling him.

What did he mean, *"the Creator"* would not *"tolerate"* it? He knew that hurting the kids, or subjecting them to harm was wrong, but what was he saying about negative energy, and the impact?

Before he could voice these questions, Jackson suddenly tossed away the pseudo-knife, and scooped Shawn up onto his knees, lifting him with ease and gripped his arms with iron strength.

"They are the children of the *Seraphim*, Mr. Baker."

This meant nothing to Shawn, not having much of a background in religion. Jackson sighed in exasperation. He was about to seriously break some rules, but he had to explain, to make him understand. He drew a deep breath, and pulled Shawn very close.

"You've heard of angels, I presume?" Jackson continued without waiting for a response. "The Seraphim are the highest order, those closest to the Creator. In the realm of ancient history, the Creator sent a number of his angels to mingle with man, for a quick explanation. They were to breed with mortals, and perfect the race. However, the Creator sent one of his highest order, who spread his genetics to only a handful of females, in a pure and sexless union. The descendents of this one, the Seraphim, is the rarest, most pure and powerful of us all.

"But these are young and unschooled members. They cannot even *begin* to know of their powers. In addition, they *can* be *Equals*; brother and sister, because theirs is a loyal and innocent, pure partnership. The destruction or harming of beings so good and so pure is the foulest of evil, and will create enough negative energy to . . . to bring about . . . *great destruction!* And possibly irreparable damage to the planet!"

Now Shawn's face was slack with horror.

The simple fact was, that it was well within the realm of possibility for him to believe this. In his line of work, he had learned to accept the existence of all manner of impossibilities.

"Look at the sun, man!" Jackson shook him, pointing up at the furious ball of fire in the sky. "The negative energy creates this turmoil . . . draws it *closer*. Can you not see it?" Baker nodded mutely, staring up at the awful sight.

A shrill scream cut through the moment. Shawn recognized his name in the middle of the harsh sound. Cassandra had obviously noticed his absence.

"Shawn, where the hell are you?" she shrieked again.

"What do you want me to do?" he asked Jackson, who was now deep in thought. Jackson had thrown out a desperate call to Indie, only to receive no response. He remembered that she was now cloaked in her protective world, apparently preoccupied with something, or she might still have heard him. He would have to go to her.

"Indie must be told. It is her children whose lives are on the line. I need her input and now! Keep down and keep quiet. It will offer a distraction if the woman either feels you've abandoned her, or if you have just inexplicably disappeared. Just please stay here. I *can* trust you, right?"

"What do *you* think?" Shawn answered, staring up at the sky.

Jackson placed his hand on Shawn's chest, the heat shocking the other man, even through his shirt. "Be careful, brother, and . . . I am glad for what . . . Jackson's face was intense, serious, as he faltered; " . . . for what you will achieve here today."

Then he was gone. Shawn began gasping for breath. The urge to begin hyperventilating had been with him for the last five minutes. He could hold back no longer.

There was no time to ponder Jackson's words to him. The echo of Cassandra screeching his name was rebounding around the valley, growing more desperate or angry; he wasn't sure which, by the second.

He crept carefully up to a large boulder, and peered around. The children and Cassandra were in plain view. An obvious solution made itself known to him immediately.

Jackson, as a Society Member, might be required to use only weapons found in nature, but *he* was under no such obligation, was he? It was a clear shot. Simple. Shawn knew exactly what he needed to do.

He slowly moved to draw his weapon, and then froze. He looked down at the empty holster.

What. The. *Fuck?*

Where could it have gone? he wondered in a panic.

Christ. When he had shot out the tires, he had quickly shoved the weapon into his holster. He had not snapped it into place. That fact, coupled with the extra bulk of the silencer, had allowed the gun to fall out at some point. It could be lying anywhere on the leafy, debris-strewn ground.

He felt positively naked without it. Shawn clenched his fists and silently cursed his carelessness. What a colossal blunder.

"Son-of-a-bitch," he sighed, deflated. Sending some lead into Lockhart's fucked-up little head would have brought this whole nightmare to a swift and easy end.

"I guess all I *can* do now is sit here and wait." Looking up briefly at the solar light show hovering uncomfortably close above his head, Shawn positioned himself to better see into the clearing, and watched as Cassandra ran around in circles, calling his name.

Could this really be it, he wondered? What a bizarre kind of fame he could enjoy in whatever afterlife awaited him. He could brag to all of the other bastards in Hell that he, Shawn Baker, had put into place the situation that ended the world.

Yay, me.

Wouldn't they all be impressed? And how could this be, anyway? *Negative energy?* Of all the ways he'd ever guessed that Man would finally jerk the plug out of the wall on life here, this was so not on his radar screen. It was too . . . simple.

It seemed that someone had been very tolerant of all the crap taking place on Earth for a very long time, and now, He'd seen just about enough.

Not that Shawn could blame that Someone, but this was *NOT* going to happen because of him . . . *was it?*

Surely not.

Definitely. Not.

CHAPTER 34

Nick slowed his patrol car as he came upon the two-mile mark, according to his odometer. He was looking for a black, "new-fangled" car, in a ditch.

He didn't know which side it was on, or how far exactly in the ditch it was, so this slowed him down considerably.

As he crept along, he reached down to snap on the air conditioning. He hoped it worked, never having had to use it before. Not even on the hottest August day had he indulged, simply soaking up the heat to store it for the winter.

This was different. It seemed an ominous, oppressive kind of heat that might suddenly flare outward and singe the hair on your head.

Nick was relieved when the unit kicked on, and, after a few seconds of expelling stale, hot air, it began sending out nice icy streams of an artificially cooled breeze. He wrinkled his nose at the plastic-y, moldy smell that blew out with it.

"I guess I've gotta take the bad with the good," he sighed as he continued his search.

He made his way north approximately another mile before he saw something reflecting light on the right side of the road. The back end of the PT Cruiser was glaring with the reflection of the late morning sun, its front end so deeply into the ditch that the rear was nearly parallel to the ground. It might have been easily missed, were it not for the bright sun creating a beacon of sorts.

Thank God for small miracles.

Nick grimaced as he pulled up behind the car, and silently asked for another miracle; that no one was hurt or trapped inside. He picked up his radio handset.

"This is Captain Brocatto, I'm conducting a ten-sixty-h, on US two, over."

"Uh, sorry Captain . . . *what?*" came the sheepish reply.

Nick banged the handset on the dashboard. He would never get used to Vermont State Police's disregard for using or even wanting ten codes. The New York PD ten codes were welded to his brain, and he still used them every single time.

Jesus, you'd think they would pick up some of them just because of him; like inadvertently learning bits of a foreign language to which you were continuously exposed.

Not these people.

"I'm checking out a disabled vehicle, okay! Doin' a little research. And after that, I will be ten sixty-three. Can you guess what that one is?"

"Er . . . ah . . . lunch?" answered the crackling voice, hopefully.

"Hey, you *have* learned somethin' huh? I'm out!" He threw the handset down into the seat with a snort of disapproval.

He felt that the professionalism of his chosen field was beginning to dry up, and he didn't like it. Ten codes were a police tradition, and kept most nosey eavesdropping people in the dark as to exactly what was taking place.

If those people needed to know something, he would tell them! Your average Joe citizen did not need to hear that there was a domestic dispute at any certain address. Around here, they probably knew the people, and this was a shameful lack of privacy for individuals.

Bringing himself back to the now, he stepped down from his mental soapbox for the moment. Nick climbed out of the cruiser, and blinked at the brightness, allowing his eyes to adjust.

The ground was slippery and muddy as he began to descend in to the ditch. He could see that the airbag had not deployed, which surprised him. The impact had to have caused quite a jolt to the occupants, and he could see even from where he stood, that no one was opening either of the front doors. They would have had to exit the back.

Nick was relieved that so far, it appeared that the car was unoccupied, although he would have to get all the way down there to know for sure.

He concentrated on making his way to the bottom without falling on his ass. It was a little tricky as he tried to work toward the side of the car, having to leave the convenient path that the vehicle had carved for him. With a sudden slip, his footing gave away.

Nick caught himself as he was thrown against the passenger door of the car.

Yeah, this is what they pay us for! Nick thought, cranky now at the mud covering his boots, and the thought of the climb back up. He peered through the window.

It was empty.

Both relieved and annoyed by this, Nick was attempting to find a better way up when he heard a horrible shrieking.

It was a woman's voice, and she was calling out a name hysterically.

Did someone lose their kid? he wondered.

The sound made him remember a time years ago, when during the holiday season, a woman had run up and down forty-second street, screaming in a similar fashion. She had lost sight of her five year old son, and was understandably in a state of panic.

Luckily, it had a happy conclusion. The child was found in a small toyshop, lured by the brightly colored treasures.

Nick had never forgotten the sound of the woman's voice as she shouted so desperately, and the screaming he was hearing now sounded pretty urgent. He now struggled in earnest to gain a foothold in the slimy hole that he had just plunged down.

It was a heck of a lot easier getting down here, than it seemed to be getting back out. He wondered as he struggled, who could possibly be out here looking for a child. There was nothing around here but woods.

Campers, maybe?

One of the occupants of the car he was now trapped with?

Whatever it was, the cop in him was becoming very distressed with every second that ticked by that he was not helping this person.

At this point, what he was accomplishing mostly was covering himself head to toe with green-tinged mud, too slippery to allow him a foothold on either the ground, or to climb onto the car for leverage.

He looked at the radio on its shoulder clip and thought about calling for help, but then decided that he would exhaust every option in the universe first, before calling for help out of a mud hole.

Oh, he would never hear the end of that!

"Helloooo? Is someone down there?"

Nick looked up and could see nothing at first, due to the stream of sunlight clawing at his face. As he made a visor with his hand, he saw the silhouette of a person standing at the top of the ditch that had imprisoned him.

His eyes quickly adjusted, and Nick saw that an elderly man was looking down at him with obvious amusement. He had the look of the older Vermont woodsmen, and was holding a very long, thick stick, on which he leaned heavily at this moment.

"Hey . . . uh, yeah." Nick was embarrassed. He was still a city boy after all, he had to admit.

"I'm kinda stuck!"

"I see." came the man's mirthful reply. "Would you like a hand?"

"Um . . . ." Nick hesitated. The man looked to be at least in his sixty's, and was just under average height. Nick knew he was a big man, and even heavier than most people guessed, due to his high muscle mass. How could this man pull him up?

But the screams he had heard. He had to get out here, although, he noted that the screaming woman was now silent.

" . . . or perhaps you are enjoying yourself down there?" The man asked, kindly. There was nothing sarcastic or offensive about the older man's words or voice.

Just a sort of gentle teasing beneath his words.

"No! I mean, yes, I would like a hand, but do you think you can pull me up? I'm a pretty heavy guy, yeah?"

"Well, let us find out, shall we?" The old man stepped down on to the flat back end of the car, and extended the long stick that he carried toward Nick.

He did not move with the natural caution of the elderly; his step was firm and sure, Nick noticed. "Hold fast to the stick, son," he spoke with confidence.

Nick paused, and took a deep breath. He seized the end of the thick stick and gingerly pulled. The man did not waver, so Nick grasped the lifeline more firmly now, and hauled himself out of the hole, slipping and sliding along the way.

And then he was out!

Nick's feet were heavy with the sticky mud caked on his boots, and his uniform would probably never recover, but he was relieved to be free of his trap.

"Hey, thanks a lot, sir. I really appreciate the help. I would have hated to have to call for back up to get out of there!"

"Yes, well, it's fortunate that I happened along, then." He hesitated, and then asked, "Did you hear a woman's voice a moment ago?"

"Voice? She was screaming like a banshee!"

"Ah. So you did hear it." The old man sighed, as if this was not the answer he wished to hear, and then spoke again.

"Well then, it is obvious that you are meant to be involved, wouldn't you say?"

Nick didn't know exactly what to say to this odd statement. Meant to be involved? He shrugged it off.

Vermont old timers sometimes had a unique way of expressing themselves, he had found, although, the cop in him noted automatically that the man had no classic Vermont accent. He actually had no discernable accent whatsoever.

Weird.

"Yeah, I heard it while I was down in there, and I was planning to check it out. I don't hear it anymore, though."

"It seemed to come from across the street . . . in the cemetery." The old gentleman offered helpfully. Nick shuddered.

Screams from an old cemetery.

Great. Yeah, that was exactly where he wanted to go right now.

He looked back at the old man, who had inadvertently become his savior.

The man was dressed in grey pants made of a soft material, and a long-sleeved shirt of exactly the same color and cloth. Nick's keen senses took this in, thinking it strange, somehow. Clothing items didn't tend to fade so uniformly.

His walking boots were obviously very old, and had buttons on them, rather than laces. As he looked more closely at the man's face, he was startled for a moment at the man's brilliant blue eyes, which stood out fiercely against the steel gray hair and his neatly trimmed bead.

His face was open and friendly, and Nick somehow felt . . . *small* in his presence. It made no sense, as he physically towered over the man, who could have been no more than five feet seven inches tall. As he met the eyes of the older man once more, he took in his expression of calm amusement as he waited for Nick's response.

Nick coughed nervously, irritated with himself for having such a vivid imagination. He tossed aside his visual interrogation and began backing toward the road. But he'd also noted the absence of any traffic whatsoever during his ordeal, and felt the sense of unease that had touched him earlier, return with a hair raising creep.

"Thanks. I appreciate your help, mister," he called over his shoulder as he moved across the road toward the thick wooded area that encircled the clearing that was the old cemetery. The officer barked a sharp expletive as he suddenly found the old man walking next to him. He hadn't seen him cross the road at all.

Nick recovered, and spoke in the most official voice he could muster.

"Sir, you should just go on about whatever you were doing before, if you don't mind. I can take it from here."

"Oh I am doing just exactly what I was doing before." The gentleman smiled absently. "I was in on my way to this very resting place for the departed."

The older man studied Nick's skeptical expression. "Does this surprise you?"

Nick once again found himself with little to say. The man's arrangement of words was very strange to him, as were the things he was saying.

"I . . . guess not," he began uncertainly. He had no real reason to keep the man away.

"I just would have liked to check this area first, to make sure that everything's safe before y' head in there, y' know?"

"Yes, but *'Quis custodiet ipsos custodies?'*" laughed the old man, softly.

"What does that mean?"

"'Tis Latin, son. It means but 'who will guard the guards.' "It also means that we shall check it together, Officer Brocatto," the man's amused tone returned. "For surely, no harm can come to me as long as I am with you!"

Nick stared at the man, unable to decide if he should be annoyed or flattered. And then he shrugged. "Sure, then. Come on!" He gave the man the famous Brocatto grin. "I'll protect you!"

He stopped short. The old man had called him by name. Then he relaxed immediately. Of course, he had seen his nametag.

He really needed to get a grip.

As Nick crossed the road, he spotted the back of a car several yards ahead, the top of the trunk area reflecting the sunlight with a brownish metallic gleam.

It was a Mercedes.

He stopped again, as a thought tried desperately to make itself known to him. Something about this car.

He had seen it before, hadn't he? As he moved toward the vehicle, he experienced a vague clouding of his mind, which jolted his memory. Yes! He was going to stop this car earlier, for speeding. But, something had stopped him . . . or distracted him in some way. He wasn't sure now.

However, why was it parked here? This was not a cemetery that people visited, as a rule, which was why he had looked at the old man curiously when he claimed that this was his destination. It was old and out of the way, the only recent interments had been the remains of those with no family, the unclaimed deceased given free eternal napping privileges here by the state.

Something just wasn't right.

Nick moved with purpose now, as a small mystery began to unfold. The old man walked silently beside him. As he came around a dense area of trees and rock, he spied something that was truly disturbing to him.

There was no doubt about it. It was Will's truck. Complete with front-end damage from its hostile introduction into the side of a Nissan Sentra earlier in the day.

Focused on the truck, Nick stalked carefully now, eyes never leaving the vehicle. Was there someone inside? He thought he saw movement, but wasn't sure. As he crossed the open area towards the truck, he was just reaching to pull his weapon, when Nick heard the shrill voice of the woman he had been so worried about earlier.

"Hold it right there!" came the rough command.

He looked up to see her standing some twenty yards away, toward the back of the cemetery, expertly pointing a small silver handgun directly at him. Nick froze, his eyes darting worriedly to the old man just behind him.

"You need to get out of here!" Nick spoke out of the side of his mouth. Perhaps he had not yet been seen. The old man simply shook his head, calmly.

Nick briefly wondered if the old man was crazy. He seemed to have no sense of self-preservation.

"I'm talking to you, cop!" The unpleasantly nasal voice of the woman jarred him as she moved closer. "You have wandered, uninvited, into the middle of a federal investigation. I am advising you to leave."

"Now!" she barked, angrily.

Nick was defiant. "How do I know that? You got some ID?"

Who did this broad think she was, pulling a gun on him at the drop of a hat? What the hell did they teach these Feds, anyway?

Cassandra fished in her pocketbook, held across her chest by the long straps, the weapon never wavering. She drew out a leather case and flipped it open. Nick stepped forward to see.

"Easy!" she warned. "Take slow steps, and keep your hands where I can see them."

"What is your problem, lady? If you're a federal agent, why are you treating me like some kind of enemy combatant, for Christ's sake?"

"Because the case I am working is complicated, and it's not necessarily so easy to tell the good guys from the bad, alright?" This caused the woman to release a small snort of amusement for reasons Nick could not fathom.

"So then, what's going on?" he demanded. Cassandra swiveled just a fraction of a degree. "Who's your friend, here?" She gestured with the weapon toward the old man.

"He's a civilian. He was coming here to the cemetery to visit a grave, I guess. He just happened to walk in with me, okay? Let him go!" Cassandra's mouth hardened.

"Get over here, gramps!" She motioned with the gun for the man to step forward with Nick. She was furious. Where in the hell was Shawn? And why, of all people, did a *cop* have to show up. And toting along some old geezer, for good measure.

She ground her teeth.

"*What* is going on?" Nick repeated, angry as well at being held at gunpoint, and at the careless endangerment of an innocent bystander. He was so going to file a complaint about this lady, as soon as he got back to the station.

Cassandra was thoughtful for a moment before she spoke.

"This is your lucky day, officer. I am going to ask you to turn around and trot on outta here, and you can just carry on with your little safety patrol. This little meeting never happened, alright?"

At the same time the woman spoke these words, Nick looked past her, and saw two very young children sitting huddled together on a log, obviously terrified.

Cassandra followed his gaze, and shouted at him. "Get out of here now!" Nick glared at her.

Walk away and leave this nut with those little kids? That was a big negative.

"You hold on a second . . . What are you doing with those kids? They don't seem real happy to be here, lady!" He took another step forward.

Without preamble, Cassandra fired her weapon, hitting Nick in the left shoulder. Nick gasped in shock, and dropped to one knee.

"Jesus Christ," he yelped in pain. "Are you crazy?" He looked around for the old man. Nick's main concern now was to find a way for him to escape.

The man was looking back at Cassandra with no shock evident in his expression.

Just a very odd mixture of disappointment and displeasure. The woman was eyeing Nick coldly, now.

"Okay, have it your way . . . *officer!*" She sneered the word.

"Just what the hell kind of agent are you supposed to be?" Nick was cradling his left arm, nursing the shoulder that was now bleeding profusely.

"A very successful one," was her response. "Get up! You help him," she ordered the older man.

Nick tried to wave away the old man's assistance, but he found himself gripped firmly under the uninjured arm and lifted to his feet, almost with no effort at all on his part.

Nick looked him in the eye, and then looked away. This man was too strong. It wasn't . . . right, somehow.

He had no time to explore this fact, as he was ordered to walk forward with the stranger at his side. Cassandra unsnapped Nick's holster, and removed his weapon.

"You got anything else on you?" she asked with a jab to Nick's shoulder with the end of her pistol. He winced with pain, but did not make a sound.

Oh *hell* no. No way was she gonna make him voice his pain. He shook his head, teeth gritted. This was Vermont. He didn't exactly feel the need to pack an arsenal of heat to go on routine traffic patrol.

"Okay, Hero, now you can come join our little party! And how nice of you to bring a friend along, too. He will be so grateful that you did, when this is all over!" Nick stared at the woman. He was feeling quite sure that he had never met such a bitch in his entire career. And that was saying something. She seemed to take an obscene amount of pleasure in what she was doing.

He began walking in the direction that she'd indicated, unenthusiastically. Something told him that unless he came up with something really clever, this was not going to end well for any of them. *Those poor kids.* He could see the misery in their faces as he approached. Another cold thought hit him now. *Where was Will?*

*　　*　　*

Shawn watched, sickened, as he observed his simple plan spinning wildly out of control, highjacked by the crazy woman in the clearing. They were supposed to just pick up the kids, go to a quiet location, then contact the other two Members, and let them exchange themselves for the kids.

Simple.

The idea of bringing them all in had been there, yes, but even so, they would have merely snatched them all up when the grown ones came to make the exchange.

Again, easy.

Involving that woman had proven to be a very grave mistake, but he had no idea that she was this far gone. He knew that he didn't like her, and that she was ruthless, but now, it was clear that Cassandra was quite violence—oriented. What did that guy call her, "*non-compos mentis*"? Hell, yeah she was.

Pulling back, Shawn leaned heavily against the large granite headstone that was currently giving him cover, and banged his head, none too gently, against it. He shut his eyes and tried to decide how much more wrong this little fiasco could go.

"You crazy, crazy bitch! Shooting the cop, well that's just great, Lockhart . . . brilliant!" He was ill with disbelief.

It was one thing to shoot up people when you had no choice, or if it is imperative to the mission, but she just . . . *did it*. He was beginning to feel that Cassandra must have already decided to leave no witnesses, and so she wasn't concerned with any repercussions for her wildly careless actions now. In addition, some poor old guy, coming to visit his grandma or whomever he knew that was buried in this creepy old place. He certainly did not deserve to die for this, but it was pretty clear that this was her plan.

From his vantage point, he could just see the Society Member guy, what was he calling himself . . . Jackson? He hadn't made it to the truck when the cop showed up. Jackson was backed up against a large tree, and Baker could easily see his expression. It looked identical to the one Shawn wore, which conveyed near madness from his despair.

Shawn thought furiously, and decided that he needed to do . . . *something*.

He couldn't just sit here and watch any longer, or he was going to start punching the granite in front of him, just to vent some frustration, and draw a little blood.

Maybe he should just step out from behind his cover of stone, and simply stroll out into the clearing. He didn't know what he would say to Cassandra about his sudden disappearance, or reappearance for that matter.

Maybe I could just yell, 'Surprise'! he though desperately. Tell her he had decided that an impromptu game of Hide and Seek was in order? He didn't know.

As he firmed up the decision to walk into the clearing, a movement to his right caught his attention. Jackson had pointed straight at him, and was shaking his head vehemently.

Oh yeah? Shawn thought, caustically. *Well, what are YOU doing, powerful creature that you're supposed to be? I'll tell you what . . . NOTHING!*

He saw the look of frustration on the Society being's face, as he again gestured, almost frantically, for Shawn to stay put.

With a sigh, Shawn decided to listen to him. *Maybe he knows something I don't*, he decided. Who knew? Maybe he could see the future, and knew that it would be counter-productive for him to rejoin the group in the clearing.

But it was maddening. The kids were less than maybe five feet away from where he had stealthily moved. If he had Jackson's speed and strength, he probably could have reached out, snatched them up, and run away though the woods.

But Shawn had no gifts to use in order to save the children, did he? Therefore, he remained on his unwilling standby status for now, and waited.

*   *   *

Cassandra forced Nick and the old man to join the children on the log. The older gentleman moved gracefully through the brush, and sat next to Jake. Nick took the opposite side next to Cassidy, and perched himself precariously on the edge, pushing back the brush that extended over the log, scratching against his side and back.

Cassandra eyed them all with disdain.

"Well well well, what a motley crew we have here, huh? Bet you're glad you decided to choose this day to make a visit to the graveyard, aren't you, Grandpa?" The man did not respond, simply continuing to regard her with distaste. Her lips twitched into a snarl. She did not like being ignored.

Nick spoke hastily, to try to distract her. "Why can't you let these kids, go? They can't be part of your 'investigation', can they? I mean, someone is going to have heard that gunshot lady, and probably call the cops. Don't you want to stop all this now, before something really bad happens?"

"Why don't you, shut your mouth, copper," she returned, hostilely. "Haven't you learned what happens when people stick their noses where they don't belong?"

Nick was disgusted. Copper? What the Hell? Had this woman actually called him 'copper'? What, was she channeling Al Capone, now?

But she looked worried, and began looking around, trying once more to find Shawn. She wanted to scream her frustration. The shadow that had been tormenting her had been still for the last several minutes, but now, she not only saw the darting of something dark and slinking shoot around the perimeter of her vision, but she could hear the sound of it trampling the grass and weeds.

It had to be a raccoon, right? She knew that raccoons couldn't move that fast, but could come up with nothing else. She jumped at the same time Nick did, as the officer reacted to something thrashing around very close to his back.

He leaped to his feet, alarmed, which was the final addition needed to snap Cassandra's nerves. She began shrieking at Nick, and pointing her weapon at each person, alternately, as if playing a deadly game of the children's classic 'one potato-two potato'.

"There are too . . . God . . . damn . . . many . . . people here!" she screamed, and finally, apparently deciding who the first to go had to be, she leveled her gun at Nick's chest.

From directly behind Agent Lockhart, came a horrific sound of snarling rage, and the crashing of under brush and branches breaking, causing Cassandra to spin around in a panic. Her mouth and eyes were open wide in shock as a large dark object hurled itself down on top of her.

CHAPTER 35

The sound of the gunshot made Indie's stomach lurched dangerously. Her head had been bowed, watching Will's face when the shot rang out. She had observed through the side mirror of the truck, the approach of the police officer and an elderly man who looked familiar to her, somehow.

She could swear the man had made eye contact with her through the mirror, although he apparently gave no indication to the officer that he had seen anyone in the truck.

The officer had been focused intently on the vehicle in which she hid, holed up with her dying husband. Indie had been paralyzed with fear as the officer had come dangerously close to discovering them; Will in her arms, the life slowly ebbing from him by the minute.

He was completely unresponsive now.

Indie shuddered with grief, but her attention was focused outside, on the issue of her children and the woman holding them, now at gunpoint, as well as two additional hostages.

She had been afraid that she could not escape notice when the officer had attracted the attention of the evil woman. It seemed every eye was turned in her direction.

It would have comforted Indie to know that her defense mechanism was such, that the more threatened she felt, the more efficient her gift became, cloaking her even more effectively. Her defense was practically impenetrable now.

She watched through the driver's side window with horror, realizing that the crazed woman had shot the police officer without a moment's hesitation.

Indie noted with relief that his wound was not life threatening, as long as the bleeding did not get out of hand. Even from this distance, she could sense the strength of the wounded officer, and that his body was already in the process of frantically attempting to mend the injury. She was still shaken by the woman's utter willingness to pull the trigger with so little provocation.

And this woman had her children.

She pulled Will's old sleeping bag from where it was stashed behind the driver's seat, unrolled it and wrapped it tightly around Will, to offer him the continued feeling of arms around him.

She rolled his jacket and slipped it under his head, then pulled her hands through his short, sandy hair. "I have to go, Will," she whispered. "You should be comfortable, okay? The kids . . . I have to go try . . ." Her voice failed her.

No one should die alone.

But had no choice. She said a small prayer, and then whispered against his rough, bristly hair.

"Goodbye, Will. I'll always love you." Resolutely swallowing her tears, she opened the door and slid out of the truck.

Indie made her way around the back of the vehicle and took a deep breath, preparing to cross the clear area that would leave her in the open, and possibly attract the attention of the mad woman. She spotted Jackson about thirty feet away, hidden in a dense cluster of trees, and he returned her stare, eyes on fire.

Moving silently toward him, she kept her eyes locked in place on his. She resisted the overwhelming urge to look over to where the woman was now screaming again. Some deep, long-suppressed instinct told her that this was key in maintaining her "invisibility", shielding her movement from the others.

When Indie had stealthily covered all but the last four feet, Jackson, seemingly unable to help himself, shot forward and dragged her to him, pulling her into his arms. He crushed her silently to his chest before releasing and turning her to face the activity in the clearing.

Jackson was having a refresher course in the lesson that sometimes the most difficult part of any tactical maneuver was observing and biding your time.

It was nearly impossible to stand and watch, taking no action.

He'd tried a little experiment, on the unlikely chance that he could influence the motion of objects with his mind. No descendents of the Archangel blood lines had this gift as far as he knew, but hell, it was worth a shot.

Focusing all of his concentration on a small boulder directly behind the deadly blond, Jackson attempted to make it rise.

It was as pointless as he'd figured it would be. Apparently he was doomed to remain the "hands on" kind of guy he already suspected he was.

Which kind of sucked. That rare type of gift would have been most appreciated right about now. He tugged Indie back tightly against his chest as they took in Cassandra's murderous tantrum.

Out of the corner of his eye, Jackson spotted the elusive projected image of the Fallen, dressed in his favorite incarnation of *Sobek*, sporting the reptilian head of a crocodile.

It was the most fleeting of images, sifting through and around the trees, but it sent a quake through his belly all the same.

He felt the instinctive rise of bloodlust snake its way up his spine, as his genetics went to work, planning for the kill. But killing or harming a projection was, he knew, impossible. There is nothing to touch, and the actual body could be anywhere.

So Jackson suffered this, as he glared at the image with disgust

Naturally, an act of such evil and negativity as the potential harm of the children of the Seraphim would attract the sniffing and hissing presence of *Evil Incarnate*, if only in his dreams. The Fallen was forced to travel with only his mind when he was the Speaking Man, if he wanted to cover a lot of ground, and in his dreams he could take any form.

He'd shown a long time preference for his character of *Sobek*, having enjoyed the feeling of being worshipped for that brief moment in Egyptian history.

As quickly as he appeared, he vanished in a shimmer of thin air. However, Jackson felt his continued presence all around, and had to shake off his need to fight.

He turned his attention back to the screeching blond.

The woman was in a perfect pitch of hysteria now, and waving her weapon ominously at the group. Indie and Jax watched as she singled out the police officer to withstand the worst of her rage.

"No!" Indie's cry was heartfelt, but nearly soundless, as the woman raised her gun and took aim. She and Jax drew back as one at the sight that met them next.

The woman spun crazily around in panic, and was knocked to the ground as an animal, black and caked with mud, launched itself at her with a furious growl.

Max's front paws hit Cassandra squarely in the shoulders as he simultaneously sank his sharp teeth into the side of her face.

Lockhart shrieked in pain and rage as she struggled with the animal, which, having knocked the woman to the ground was now biting and tearing at every part of her within reach.

Nick, as soon as he recovered from his shock, leaped backwards, grabbing both children and gathering them close to his side. He looked up at the old man, who also rose, but was watching the attack with fascination, as if it were a scene from the National Geographic channel. Nick was hesitant.

He wanted to scoop up the kids and bolt but, incredibly, the psycho blond had not dropped her weapon, and was waving it wildly now as she fought the angry animal with vicious kicks and unceasing curses. He did not dare try to run with the kids.

Not yet. He was afraid that she either would intentionally or inadvertently blow holes in them as they fled.

With a final and brutal kick to the dog's ribs, Cassandra separated herself from the raging animal, and climbed to her feet, shaking with outrage. Max rolled several feet to the front of Cassandra, whimpering in pain. He rose to his feet also, to face her, still ready to fight.

As Cassandra lifted her silver Berretta, and took aim, Cassidy tore herself from Nick's grasp and put herself between the woman and her pet. She knelt at Max's side, speaking softly to the animal.

"Out of the way, Princess," Cassandra ordered. "That dog is dead, one way or the other!"

Trembling from head to toe, Cassidy stood her ground defiantly.

"Get back over here, kid!" Nick was beside himself. He had no doubt that this woman would shoot a child, no problem.

"I would listen to the officer, if I were you, little girl. I have had enough of this whole thing, and I'm ready to call it a day. Now move!" Cassandra stood, bleeding and disheveled from the attack, yet cold and calm, ready to kill.

"Kid, please!" Nick begged. "I know you don't want the dog hurt, but come on . . . it's not worth your life!"

"He was ready to give his life for us, and I will do the same for him," the little girl stated firmly, although her voice trembled as her body quaked.

"Hey, no problem, freak." Cassandra spoke now as a shower of debris rained down upon her, the protests from the creatures of the forest becoming deafening once more. "Just know that you're not saving anything. I'll shoot you, and then I'll shoot the dog. What a hero you'll be!"

The woman's evil sarcasm was making Nick feel like a trip to Lourdes was in order, assuming he came out of this twisted little adventure alive.

"You're causing all of this, aren't you?" she continued, as several larger stones began bouncing across the brick pathway toward her.

"I knew it was you all along. You caused everything to go wrong, and now, I am done. I shoulda just done away with the both of you at Grandma's house like I wanted, but that's what I get for being nice, huh?"

She ignored the rocks and pinecones hurled in her direction, focused only on her need for revenge upon this creature, and the tiny little girl trying to shield it with her body. The creature that was the source of all of her angst of the day, in Cassandra's small mind.

She raised her weapon once more.

Indie nearly gagged when she read the horrible woman's intentions, and leaped forward to race into the clearing. She was shocked as Jax grasped her by the back of her shirt, and jerked her backwards, catching her as she fell. He wrapped both of his arms around her, unyielding.

As she struggled, he stroked her hair and breathed his words into her ear. "Indie, no. Trust me. I have seen. You have to let him earn his redemption. It is almost our time, and we will go to the clearing . . . very soon."

She stared back at him in disbelief first, then as she studied his face, and opened her mind, allowing his knowledge to flow into her, she swallowed down her instincts, and stopped fighting him, tearfully resigned.

"I've *seen* it, Indie!" Jax repeated hoarsely. His eyes were wide; clear and piercing. "It's all because of . . . *Will!* Something in him; he is the *gateway*."

He shook his head. "I can't make it clear now, but I didn't know I could see . . . I mean I couldn't, until moments ago." He turned her to face the clearing once more, standing behind her and holding tightly around her shoulders and waist, and they watched.

As Cassandra's finger tightened around the trigger, Nick let out an anguished cry . . . ."*NO!*" His shout joined with another, emitted simultaneously.

"*Cassandra, no!*" The shouts were cut through by the sharp crack of the pistol firing.

The moment Cassandra squeezed the trigger, she heard and saw Shawn as he leaped in front of her, tackling the little girl, his arms forming a protective barrier between her and the harsh fall to the ground.

Cassandra's mouth fell open in shock as she saw the spurt of blood shoot from the dime-sized hole in Shawn's back, just to the left of his right shoulder blade. She knew that the hole from the exit wound in the front would be considerably larger.

"*Oh, God. Cassandra, WHAT DID YOU DO?*" Shawn choked out the words, struggling on the ground as his hands sought automatically to clutch at the fist-sized hole in his chest.

Cassandra stood frozen, staring at the writhing figure of the only man she had ever given more than a passing thought.

Nick leaped forward once more and dragged the now sobbing child from Shawn's arms, pulling her into his. Over her head, he could not tear his eyes from the awful sight of the man attempting desperately to stem the rapid flow of blood from the wound.

"Oh, *no!* Oh, you psycho . . . *why* . . . how could you do it?" His voice was wracked with fear and disbelief.

Shawn looked directly at Cassandra and screamed; "*Don't let me die here!* Not in this place, for God's sake, *please!*" Cassandra jumped at the sound, but still made no move.

She noted in a disconnected way, that the dog had fled and was nowhere to be seen.

The sounds coming from Shawn were sickening, as the blood rapidly and painfully rushed into his lungs.

Cassandra's sudden scream startled them all.

"You idiot! Why did you do it, Shawn, *damn you! Why*?" She backed away from him, still shrieking. "You stupid, stupid idiot! You've ruined *everything!*" All Cassandra could focus on, was the fact that her little fantasies that had sustained her for the past year would never be realized.

She was infuriated to have this taken away from her. These people had robbed her of her dream. The sight of a man and a woman approaching together, striding right up to the clearing drew her attention.

The woman stopped to embrace both children, and then moved to kneel at Shawn's side. The man stationed himself beside the elderly man and the children.

As Cassandra watched, speechless, the woman pulled Shawn's torn shirt away, and placed her hands on his face, and then his chest. Shawn's screams stopped abruptly, like a tap shut off by the faucet and his body began to relax.

Jake stood close by the old man, his fists clenched tightly. He looked up at him questioningly, and the old man smiled sadly, and shook his head.

"No, son. We do not, as a rule, interfere with the fate and destiny set forth by nature, unless, of course, as directed by our Creator. It is one of Society's most important rules." Jake looked back at the man who had saved his sister, and by proxy, himself.

The gentleman spoke again, softly. "Shawn Baker has achieved *Tabula Rasa*, meaning, a 'blank slate' or a state of innocence. His actions here have saved him. His future in the hereafter did not look promising before this day."

Jake sighed, and nodded, his face filled with sorrow.

Indie spoke soothingly into Shawn's ear, offering words of comfort and gratitude as he exhaled noisily. Although his respirations were increasing, his face and body were becoming more and more calm after Indie's touch.

"I can't see anything, you know." He spoke in a conversational tone, his voice thick and bubbly with blood.

His eyes were open very wide, curiously blank.

"Is that . . . *normal* . . . ?" Shawn's hand shot spastically outward, and he grasped the air. "Ah . . . man. Yeah . . . *is* she okay? The little girl . . . Will's kid?" The congestion was strangling him.

Indie touched his face. "You saved her," she whispered.

"Oh!" Shawn shuddered. "Do you hear it? *Can you?* Sounds like . . . they're *singing!*"

His chest convulsed once and did not rise again.

He was still, and the clearing was heavy with an unnatural silence.

Nick had watched people die before, but this was especially hard for him somehow. Maybe because he'd had a little history with him earlier in the day. Knowing that there were children here to witness this made it worse.

He was dimly aware of the bizarre conversation taking place between the old man and the boy.

Did they know each other? He had only been half listening, his eyes riveted on Shawn.

A movement at his side caught his attention.

Nick stared with utter amazement at the vision standing next to him, semi-concealed in the underbrush, and rubbed his eyes. He *must* have wished himself a vision, because a hallucination was surely what stood before him now.

No, it was still here.

The dog that had attacked the woman, and saved his life only moments ago, stood next to Nick in the thicket. But this was not the cause of Nick's disbelief. It was what the dog was holding that had the officer stunned.

In his mouth, Max carefully held a heavy burden.

It was a gun. Not just any old gun, either. It was a Walther PPK 7.65mm, obviously conjured out of thin air by a guardian angel, Nick decided.

"*How* . . . ?" Captain Brocatto shook his head.

Never in a billion years would he be able to convince someone of this story.

Max whined, softly. Urgently.

Watching the blond woman very carefully, Nick slowly bent to his side, reaching down toward the weapon that the animal held in his teeth.

The moment Shawn's breathing ceased; within a single second, Cassandra came back to life.

"Get away from him," she whispered coldly to Indie. Indie touched Shawn's face once more in thanks, and rose to stand before agent Lockhart. All reason had left Cassandra now, and she narrowed her eyes, first at the woman standing in front of her, then all of them.

They were all going to pay for her loss; the object of her obsession. No one was walking out of here, except for Cassandra herself. She would come up with a story later, when she dragged the bodies of the alien beings . . . these *Society Members*, in to the lab.

The other two could just rot here. They were already in a cemetery. Perfect. No one came here, and the animals would take care of the remains.

Jackson moved forward to stand next to Indie. "You don't need to do this, you know." He spoke to her smoothly, carefully. "You could end this the right way. Shawn died to save that child. You would take her life now, to spite his sacrifice?" Lockhart wavered.

The man's voice was compelling. It seemed to pull her thoughts away from her anger. For a moment she drifted, soothed by his thoughts.

She snapped back, suspicious. That thing was using some kind of mind interference on her, she was sure.

Goddamn aliens.

This one was dangerous. Incredibly handsome, she could not help but notice, but he couldn't be kept around for one minute; not if he could get into her head like that.

Yes, he would be the first to go.

"Shut up. You're dead." Her tone was flat. She looked around once more at the small group this had inexplicably become. "You're all *dead!*" She repeated, her voice rising to a scream.

She pointed her gun at Jackson, and the sound of the gunshot echoed around the valley.

Indie screamed.

Cassandra stood with her arm still outstretched holding her weapon, eyes wide. She lifted her hand and touched her chest, her white blouse becoming saturated with rapidly spreading crimson. She held her blood-covered hand in front of her face, and then looked past Indie and Jackson at the police officer, now crouched in position, aiming a familiar weapon in her direction, the silencer that had been on the end of it was cast aside, for better deadly accuracy.

She began to scream again and gripped her gun tightly. Another gunshot exploded through the clearing and Cassandra went down as the second bullet hit its mark.

The woods were filled with her shrieks of agony as she flopped on the wet ground.

Indie rushed forward and placed her hands on the woman, and Cassandra hissed as Indie's hot hands connected with her cold one. "Don't touch me!" she screeched.

Indie, although repelled by the iciness of the woman's skin, held fast, and Cassandra's thrashing halted.

"Why?" Cassandra demanded harshly. "Why would you move to ease my pain?"

"Because even unadulterated evil should be the recipient of a simple act of mercy."

"You and your kind . . . you're nothing but unnatural freaks! Freaks and cowards, living in hiding!" Lockhart snarled.

"Yes," Indie spoke gently. "You're right that I fear for you, and what's waiting for you. It's horrible, because I know nothing can save you now."

"You sound just like your wimpy son!" spat Lockhart, unmoved.

"Don't mistake compassion and love for weakness." Indie replied steadily. "Don't you realize the strength one needs to maintain self control, to not become simply a knee-jerk reaction of anger and revenge? No, our reactions take a measure of strength that you can never understand!"

Cassandra jerked her hand away from Indie, and gasped as the pain returned with a vengeance. She clawed desperately at the air, and began a horrible wailing as her body convulsed.

Her screams were suddenly joined by a screeching, howling sound that made Indie cover her ears in alarm.

The sound rose, deafening as Lockhart's shrieks mingled with the new grating sound. It seemed to surround them in an eerie stereo-like hissing movement, and seemed loud enough to be heard throughout the entire state.

With a silent shout of fear, Jackson rocketed forward and lifted Indie, still kneeling by Cassandra, and carried her back away from the woman.

The hissing and wailing grew louder, and Nick pulled Cassidy more closely to him.

He looked at the old man, who had stepped toward him now, summoning Indie and Jackson to move back closer to the small group. The old man moved to stand the closest to the convulsing woman, and whispered . . .

"*Vade retro Satana . . .*"

The officer had already concluded that this was not just some ordinary citizen off the streets, and instinctively moved closer to him as well. He also had a fleeting memory of the Latin inflicted upon him as a child in school.

The man had clearly spoken the words "get behind me, Satan." He had never thought to hear those words spoken in quite such a literal sense.

Nick's strict Catholic upbringing was surging to the forefront of his brain as he thought of devils, demons, possession and every other nightmare-inducing teachings from the schools of his youth.

This was worse. Much worse.

He watched in wonder as his hand made a decision without his involvement, lifting and performing the sign of the cross.

Twice.

"What is it?" screamed Cassandra, as blood began pouring from her mouth. "What's happening?"

"They are the *Shadow People*." The old man spoke quietly, yet somehow his voice was perfectly clear, audible even above the chilling din. "Your ancestors have come to claim you, Cassandra Lockhart . . . mercy be upon you!"

As the man spoke, hideous dark figures began swirling through the cemetery, rushing through the trees toward them They moved with a serpentine undulation, never touching the ground.

The shapes were *more* than opaque black . . . it was as if light had no ability to shine even near them; holes in the fabric of this astral plane. They varied in lengths; some less than two feet long, while others approached eight feet in length.

Hideous humanoid shapes without features.

Like wisps of jet-black smoke, they wove in and out through the headstones, finally concentrating on the area where Cassandra lay shrieking. The small group watched, mesmerized as the Shadows took turns diving underneath Lockhart, nudging her body upwards slightly, and then dropping her.

Crying out in terror, she batted uselessly at the figures, unable to make contact with anything solid, although they were able to force the movement of her body.

As one particularly long figure came from underneath her, it floated toward the others, and circled in what looked like curiosity around the body of Shawn Baker.

"You dare!"

The old man spoke angrily, raising his right hand and the thick stick with it. The figure was instantly propelled backwards with terrific force, howling in rage as it went.

Jackson turned Indie toward him, and held her tightly to spare her the disturbing images. Normally these types of entities would receive the wrath of the Archangel blood, dispatched with Jackson's skill . . . but he held his place now, allowing the demonic beasts to torment Lockhart as he shielded his *Equal* from the awful sight.

Nick was doing the same with Cassidy, and wishing desperately that he could look away. The old man held Jake with his left arm, allowing the boy to bury his face in his side.

The ground where Cassandra lay, tormented, began to change. Shimmering, it became dark and soft. It was taking on the appearance of a puddle of oil, or maybe tar.

Cassandra began to sink; pulled by the wispy Shadow People downwards in a show reminiscent of a boa constrictor leisurely swallowing a very large meal.

The earth seemed to yawn, and the woman's head and shoulders began to sink into the soft, sticky-looking mass underneath her.

Her gurgling screeches became muffled as the top half of her body disappeared.

The Shadow figures moved more quickly now, as if in a feeding frenzy of sorts, wailing and shrieking, mingled with an awful sound similar to long fingernails raked across aluminum siding. Cassandra's feet began to tilt at an odd angle as her body began to sink fully, only her shoes visible.

These quickly slipped under now as well, and one by one, the Shadows plunged into the earth where Cassandra had vanished, their screams and howls' becoming fainter until finally, all was silent.

The ground where she had disappeared was no longer shimmering black. The grass had returned, although there was a circular area in that particular location, that seemed to have a scorched appearance.

The silence was almost tangible, hanging heavily in the air after the unbelievable sounds that had just been raging through the air.

Nick was the first to move, clearing his throat to speak, or at least give it a try. He couldn't comprehend why law enforcement officers had not converged upon the clearing, for surely people had heard the gunshots and the screams as well as the other ungodly sounds that had ripped through the air.

No one had reported this?

"I, uh . . . think it would be great if someone wanted to explain to me what just happened here," he began uncertainly. All heads turned in Nick's direction, although no one was ready to speak yet.

The old man finally answered.

"Officer Brocatto, I think we should take a walk, and I will enlighten you to the best of your ability to comprehend." The older gentleman placed his hand on Nick's shoulder as he spoke.

Indie awoke from her stunned horror with a jolt, and reached with a sob to gather her children to her. Cassidy left Nick's side and threw herself into her mother's arms.

Indie hugged her tightly, and then looked over her head to find her son. She looked all around, in between the lanky limbs of Nick, and behind the softly draped garments of the old man. It became very clear in the span of less than ten seconds.

The indisputable fact was, Jake was gone.

CHAPTER 36

Being dead was not so bad, Will decided.

It didn't hurt. He wasn't hot.

Or cold.

Like the baby bear's bed, it felt just right. He wasn't one hundred percent sure that he was all the way dead yet, but he knew that he had a good running start.

The only thing that tugged on him in a most irritating fashion, was a nagging feeling that he had left something undone. Something very important, although he could not imagine right now, what that very important thing could be.

Will was seeing what appeared to be a bright white empty screen. He remembered terrible pain, and a sense of impatience at how long it was taking him to actually die, while he was alone in the truck. Something had happened to pull away the support he was leaning on, and then . . . he remembered Indie.

Comfort and love.

Who would have believed that he would be given the opportunity to apologize? Apologize and say goodbye.

There was a distinct feeling, for a moment, where Will felt better, somehow; as if, when he pulled in his breath, oxygen actually followed. But it was a brief sensation.

He could not move or speak now, and felt nothing of his body. It was like he'd become just a brain, endlessly pondering life outside the jar in which it was housed.

His mind journeyed back to the day he'd met his wife.

Strange. He had never reminisced before about such things.

Then, the first time he'd held his newborn babies.

So alert, even at birth. Will remembered all of the nurses commenting on this. They were reaching and grasping for fingers, able to track faces, eyes wide and knowing.

Short flashes of his career popped through his mind, as if in a slideshow set at an impossible speed.

Then, he had been lifted and carried in what he had determined must be the arms of an angel. Strong arms, but ever so gentle, supporting him as they made their way up.

Thank God, it was up!

He felt sure of this, although he had no point of reference. What were those vague cracking sounds, though? They did not seem to belong. Neither did the other sounds.

Voices screaming, but as if in a vacuum. Muffled and faint.

Shouldn't he be concerned? He wasn't sure that he would be able to force his mind to react with any kind of fear or stress. Everything was just so calming. Even the screams became soothing.

As Will continued to float upwards, he felt the angel remove her arms. He wondered idly if he would fall, but was not afraid. She would surely not let him drop.

He wasn't surprised when he continued on his upward swing.

He could even feel a breeze gently stroking his face, but noticed that he could not feel any movement, like hair stirring.

So odd.

"Don't worry, Will . . . she's okay!" A familiar voice danced past him, as he was slowly rising.

He could not image who this could be, but the voice sounded jubilant. It was also, most definitely male. He didn't understand it just now, but somehow, the words that wisped past Will, filled him with the most incredible sense of relief.

The annoying, nagging feeling of unfinished business appeared to have joined that voice as it had flowed past, taking away the last of the strings that Will suddenly realized were binding him here.

He felt a surge of power as his ascent became much faster now, steady and swift. As Will reached the pinnacle of his journey, he was met with a brilliant feeling of light, calm and joy. He found that he had arms now, although he could feel no other body part. Those arms now rose of their own accord, like a toddler asking to be lifted by his father.

"Daddy!"

For a moment, Will though he had spoken aloud.

"Daddy, stop! We need you!"

These words did not come from him.

Will was confused. He wanted to keep moving forward, but this voice was causing him pain, and slowing his progress. He didn't want to feel the pain anymore.

Determinedly, Will pressed ahead, feeling very close to his goal. Just a little further.

"Daddy, NO!" The voice commanded him back. There was no alternative offered.

He felt himself yanked backwards roughly; a disorienting drag through mist and light, only on some sort of crazy inside-out trip through time and space.

Will didn't like this.

He was beginning to feel a pinpoint of heat; a burning sensation dead center in his chest. No. Not the pain.

Not again. He didn't think he could take it.

Will struggled to free himself from whatever had caught hold of him and was pulling him the wrong way, but it was no use. He felt himself falling now, as if from a great height. When he reached the bottom, it was not going to be pretty.

Will could feel limbs beginning to re-form, and he flailed clumsily now as he gained speed. The pain in his chest intensified, burning, searing and suffocating.

Finally, with what should have been a tooth-shattering jolt, Will found himself in a reclining position, wrapped tightly in a familiar thick fabric.

The pain was insufferable.

And then it was gone. A little child was crying. It sounded very close.

What's wrong? Will wondered, sleepily. He still wasn't breathing.

"Daddy, I thought you weren't coming back!" The voice was sobbing. Will's eyes snapped open, and he focused on the face in front of him. Jake's tiny hands were clutched together, resting on Will's chest as if caught in the middle of his bedtime prayers. His eyes were red and damp.

A blast of air was forced deep into Will's lungs by an unseen entity, causing him to sit abruptly and violently upright. He grabbed the little boy, and pulled him into a feverish embrace that might have cracked the bones of a less sturdy child.

A sob broke loose from his throat, and he let it. He felt that he would never be able to cry long enough, or hard enough to release the overwhelming emotions that he had suffered in these few short days.

After several minutes of self-indulgent bawling, he pushed Jake back and ran his hands around the boy's face before asking breathlessly, his voice still unsteady.

"Your sister?" Jake nodded his head, conveying that she too was okay. Will sagged with relief, tears leaking once more.

"How about your mother? Is she . . . ?"

"She's okay too, Daddy."

"And . . . the man," Will swallowed hard. "Jackson? He's okay as well?"

"If Mommy's okay, then you know he is okay." Jake spoke with confidence.

Will winced at the words, but then sighed in resignation. True enough, he supposed. "So," he grabbed his son tightly again. "Everyone is okay, then? It's all over?"

"Yes, Daddy . . . except . . . ." Jake spoke doubtfully.

"What is it?"

"I . . . I think I might be in trouble . . . ." Jake's voice trailed to a whisper.

"I did something that I wasn't s'posed to do." His lip quivered, but then he spoke with defiance, and a hint of temper that Will had never before witnessed in his child. Not in either of them.

"But I don't care! I don't care what they do to me. I would do it again and again, if I had to!" His little voice trembled with emotion.

"Son, nothing bad is going to happen to you, I'm sure." Will was confused. "What are you afraid of?" Jake looked distant for a moment, and then looked at his father, and gave him a shy smile.

"Nothing, Daddy. But can you walk?"

Walk? Will stretched his arms, and then alternately each leg. He suddenly felt ready to take on a twelve-mile road march.

With a fully loaded rucksack at that. He also felt, unbelievable as it seemed, ravenously hungry.

"Yeah, son," Will laughed at the boy. "I think I can walk! Let's get out of this truck. I need to see your sister and your mom!" He threw back the sleeping bag that held him, struggling to kick himself free, and then shoved open the door.

The air smelled wonderful; fresh and clean, with a lovely breeze suddenly picking up and cooling him.

The heat seemed to have lessened to a more normal level. It was good to be alive. Why did he not feel this every day, he wondered.

He lifted his son into his arms, turned and walked toward the clearing, pausing as he noted the people present.

Nick, Indie and Jackson, Cassidy, and a stranger. An older man he did not know. Every one of these people were staring at him with a variety of different expressions of their faces.

Relief. Disbelief.

Cautious goodwill, and finally, on the face of his daughter, joy, as she shouted his name. The older man wore an expression of affection, tolerant amusement and resignation. Will suddenly found himself suffering from something resembling stage fright, uncomfortable to find himself the center of attention.

He looked at Jake, and took a deep breath. "Alright, son?"

"Yes, Daddy," Jake smiled. "I think it is!" And so they made their way through the weeds and brush to join the waiting crowd.

CHAPTER 37

The gift, tho' it's given
The war is not won
The call you hear next
Like a shot from a gun
Will lead you to triumph
A path full of glory
You must answer the call
To seek the end of your story

Katherine Whitley

After mere seconds of stunned silence, Indie slowly raised her head until she met the eyes of Jax. Then back again to Will. Could she see ghosts? Was that another one of the "gifts" that seemed to be surfacing slowly as the day wore on?

She had better not be seeing ghosts, because if so, that ghost was holding her son and that would mean things that she had no intention of accepting.

But no. Their heartbeats were solid and strong.

Both of them.

How was this possible? Will had been dead enough to go ahead and call off the code, had he been in an ER. That was no mistake. Yet, there he stood!

"Indie . . ." Jackson was hesitant, unsure himself why her husband was standing at the edge of the clearing right now, decidedly alive and kicking. He had clearly seen her thoughts on his condition, but as the thought dawned upon him . . . he sucked in his breath.

He understood now. It was the boy.

A boy who obviously possessed one hell of a gift.

"Your children. Cassidy and Jake . . . they are part of the Society," he began. "But not just any Members. They are even more . . . special."

The older man stepped toward Indie, as Jackson gently took her hand.

"What my good Brother is trying to tell you, is that you have born a perfect pair of Society Members, *Equals* together, and they are the Children of the Seraphim . . . or to be more specific, myself." He bowed to Indie as he said this.

"I am the *Paterfamilias*. *I* am the Seraphim sent to this earth eons before to, metaphorically speaking, toss a handful of seeds to the wind just to see what grows. These children are among the very few results of that little adventure."

The man looked over at Will and Jake, smiling tenderly, but with the faintest trace of exasperation.

"Jake has the gift to summon one back from the threshold of death, if he reaches them before contact is made with the light."

Indie, without taking her eyes off Will and Jake, took in the man's words, and heard Jax's unspoken acknowledgement.

"Cassidy has also demonstrated her gifts today here as well . . . creating a bubble of sorts, containing the sounds and events into a vacuum, preventing innocents from accidentally becoming involved." The Elder continued. "She communes with the beasts of the Earth, and they obey . . . objects move by her will. Yes, I will be very interested to watch her progress as she becomes properly schooled. In addition, the gift of invisibility is strong around these children, as well as yourself. Most impressive!"

Indie was awestricken by these revelations from the Elder. Her children. So small.

So innocent . . . . . So powerful.

She could hear nothing from the mind of the older man, only his words, although she understood that if this man was a Seraph . . . an *Elder*, of course, he would be powerful enough to shut her out.

But really? Her children?

"My son . . ." the Elder began. "And here I must interrupt myself, for I do not wish to diminish your role in bringing them into existence. Yours as well as William's." He touched Jackson's arm as he said this, as if to soften the blow that these words carried to him.

"But Jake *is* my son, and," the Elder sighed with the same expression of tolerant and affectionate bemusement that he wore earlier, "as such, has chosen to exercise his number one privilege. We talk about many things that are some of the most important rules set forth by the Creator for Society, but the rule that tops the list, and trumps all others, is the right of free will."

He smiled widely.

"The Creator gives each and every living thing, both human and otherwise, a brain, and the right to use it as they see best. The consequence of our choices becomes the continuously changing landscape of our futures, with each future touching many others.

"Jake has made his choice, and so it shall stand. We shall find out the implications of his choice to alter the course of nature in due time, I expect. But for now, I imagine you should go to him . . . our daughter has already taken that liberty!"

The Elder nodded in the direction of Cassidy, her blond head bobbing as she flew toward the clearing's edge.

Jackson turned Indie to face him, and pulled her face up to his. She saw a touch of pain in his beautiful eyes; the eyes that saved her life, and she wanted to weep.

But he shook his head.

"Go see Will. It's right that you care for him." He smiled and looked past her at Will, who was now busy fending off the energetic attacks of affection from both of his children.

"Remember your promise to me, Indie." Indie felt hypnotized by his voice. Just how could anyone resist his spoken word? "Besides, it looks like he might need help! I think the children are quite happy to see him."

Indie leaned forward and pressed a kiss to his lips.

"I know that you realize you have nothing to fear, right?"

Jackson shoved his hands in his pockets and looked at the ground first, then back to her face.

"*Right?*" She gave him a little shake.

He squeezed his eyes shut for a nanosecond, then smiled again, and nodded his head a little. "Yes, of course. I'm fine with it . . . go!" Indie turned and ran towards Will, who had just managed to peel the happy children off his chest as she reached him.

He stunned Indie by grabbing her, encircling his arms around her and sweeping her into a backwards dip, before planting an old Hollywood-style kiss on her mouth.

She gasped and began to struggle, but found herself laughing.

Will had certainly never done anything like that before, and especially with this level of enthusiasm. Keeping his face down to look at Indie, Will grinned impishly. "Is he watching?"

"Of course he is!" Indie scolded. "What are you trying to do to him?" She felt Jax's fists clench in his pockets, but without looking, knew that his face was outwardly calm.

"I just thought I would give him a little jolt. It's not so much, really, considering what he's taking from me." The smile faded from Will's face, and his eyes were serious now. "It's so unfair really, that I had to actually lose you in order to find you."

He looked at her now with eyes that sought to commit her face to memory. "I guess you had me at goodbye," he joked pathetically.

He brought a finger to Indie's lips so he could finish without interruption. "I just want to say thank you for everything you've ever done for me . . . and—" his voice cracked a little, "—and to say goodbye to you with something I should have been doing for you every day. I guess this was my last chance.

"Besides," he lifted his head and looked back at Jackson, who was staring levelly back at him. "It just felt damn good!"

Indie extracted herself from his arms, and took his hand. "I told you that it was never your fault. We are focusing on the here and now." She pulled him around to look at her fully.

Her lips began to tremble.

"Oh my God Will, I knew you were gone. I was watching you *die*. It was unbearable. But Jake brought you back. Our children . . . both of them are . . . what I am, only . . . ."

"I know, Indie. Baker told me." He shook his head exasperated. "Although how I didn't know about them, or *you*, still blows my mind. I must be blind. Or stupid. Both, maybe. I don't know, but . . . ."

Will stopped. Indie was looking at him with the "*I've got some bad news*" expression etched across her striking features.

He looked all around, and it began to dawn on him that there was no Cassandra . . . and no Baker. He vaguely remembered the sharp snaps of sound he had heard at some point earlier. His memory was unclear.

Gunshots?

"Where . . . what happened? Is he . . . are they tied up somewhere, or . . . ?"

"They aren't tied up, Will." Indie whispered with a tug on Will's hand. "Come on. I need the others around me when I tell you what took place here."

After a long look at Indie, a sickness began to spread through Will's belly. Something was pulling at his memory, like a dream awakening.

Words.

Wispy, floating words moved around him, and then away.

"Don't worry, Will!" The tone had been triumphant. Joyful, even. And very familiar.

Baker?

Will's brain hurt as he strained to hear the memory again. Where had he heard this? Very recently he was positive, and it had seemed to make him, well, almost happy in his memory. Now, the words filled him with dread.

"He's dead, isn't he? Baker is dead." Will's voice was flat and hollow. The scant contents of his belly rolled, and began to climb it's way up to his neck.

Unfathomable as it was, the death of the man that he was so ready to kill if he had too, was sickening him.

Baker had been turned, Will was sure of it. He had felt the goodness surge from him at some point, although he wasn't clear where this had taken place, exactly.

Indie pulled him along toward the others. Numbly he followed, the children at his side.

Jackson and the Elder observed the approach of the four in outward silence. Inwardly, Jackson was fighting to kill the disgust with himself, which was rising fast along with another emotion that he could not understand.

Not an emotion, really.

Yeah, this was more of a desire.

The irrational desire to rip Indie away from Will, and maybe just bounce Will's head around on the ground. Just a little.

Nothing that would hurt him. Not too badly, anyway.

He heard a low chuckle behind him, and realized with horror that the Elder had, of course, heard his shameful inner dialog.

No, Elder . . . I truly do not wish the man ill will. I don't know what is wrong with my thoughts. A strong hand grasped Jackson's shoulder, and spun him around to face away from the approaching family.

"So, are you a fighter or what, my Brother? Do you chastise yourself for feeling the discomfort of another male kissing your *Equal*? A male who loves her as well? They share a bond and a history that will not go away. You must allow yourself to understand that these emotions are quite . . . rational."

The old man spoke so kindly, so sensibly, that it brought a lump to Jackson's throat. It hit him hard that he was not only in the presence of an Elder, but also in the presence of *THE* Elder . . . the chosen one above all, and that this Elder was speaking directly to him.

Giving him his words of wisdom that in the past, with the exception of the Commitment, he had heard only in his head at the Sacred places.

Perhaps he should listen, he thought with an ironic laugh to himself.

"It is only my humble opinion, but . . . perhaps you should!" spoke the Elder, eyes twinkling. "Allow yourself to be a man, and feel what a man will feel. You were right before. You are no angel! However, the angelic genetics that flow through you are not of the pious nature, but that of the Archangels . . . the warriors.

"One of the failings of Society teachings has been the tendency to educate toward a response appropriate to the Virtues, with their kindness and endless patience, but this, I know, is asking a lot. Therefore, you struggle with your fighting nature, and feel unworthy when . . . shall we say, *less than gentle* feelings surface." The Elder's hand dropped and he held his stick with both hands.

"Don't deny your feelings, Brother. There is no shame in them, for it is not weakness. However, know this; it is your response to those feelings that makes you a true man. Self-control and confidence are what keep you worthy.

"Make no mistake, she is yours, and she wants only you in the way that a woman will want a man. She continues to have love for the father of her children as she should, do you agree?" Jackson's body relaxed at the Elder's words, and he nodded gravely.

"I agree, my Elder."

"I will add here one more thought for you to ponder. You work so hard to keep your warrior tendencies from your *Equal*, pointless as you know it to be . . . but *why*? Can you not fathom the idea that as her *Equal*, you are her perfect match?" He narrowed his eyes briefly at Jackson.

"You. Not the version of yourself you try to project to her . . . what you *think* she would like to see. This woman of yours finds a little danger in her men, er, how shall I put this . . . *exciting!*"

Jackson smiled and had to look away.

The Elder was actually blushing! "Just something for you to think about, my Brother."

Shaking his head now, the Elder pulled himself back, and sighed. "I brought myself here today simply to observe. I had no intention of stepping in, or altering whatever course events took, but I knew I had to witness this unfold."

"You helped the officer get here, didn't you?" Jackson spoke with barely suppressed humor. "That's why you were with him!"

The old man's eyes sparkled. "I was simply out for a walk, and found a man stuck in a ditch! Would you have me leave him there?"

He then turned his shimmering blue eyes back toward Nick, who, at this point had decided that he was either stuck in the middle of a very strange dream, or he had slipped through a very large crack in reality.

After he'd shot Cassandra, and all of the stuff that he was going to try really hard to forget he ever saw was over, Nick had come forward and covered Shawn's body with his muddy jacket and sat down close by. Max lay, panting heavily at his side.

He didn't know why, but he felt that Shawn should not be alone, even if he knew that the man inside the shell was long gone. Besides, he wanted to stay back and try to observe the rest of the happenings taking place, and maybe, just maybe, he would figure out what was what on his own.

So far, all he had done was grow more confused.

So, okay. The old man? He was *not* a human being.

Nick had already registered this in his mind, crazy as it might sound to anyone else. He also knew that when the man had put his hand on his shoulder, assuring Nick that he would tell him all that he would be able to comprehend, Nick had winced, and braced himself for the pain.

The old man had grasped the shoulder that was the recipient of a lot of unwanted attention from the wrong end of Lockhart's gun. Not only did the expected pain never materialize, but also, the wound was gone. No sign of any injury remained.

None. Zip. *Nada!*

Yeah, yeah. It was impossible, he knew. But whatever.

It was a fact. Christ, even the hole in his uniform shirt was gone.

He might have thought he was going insane, except that Nick had the stubborn confidence born of his upbringing.

Nick Brocatto saw what he saw, end of story. If anyone thought he was crazy that was their damned problem.

He'd remained huddled in his own private vacuum while the happy family scene had taken place. When Will had appeared at the edge of the cemetery, Nick was relieved beyond measure; however, it seemed that the rest of the group had been a little more than relieved. They had been flabbergasted. As if somehow, he should not have shown up. Like, ever again.

They were, thank God, obviously *glad* to see him alive, or else he might have suspected a little foul play, shocked as they had appeared. In between the surreal feelings, Nick also felt a gut levitating sense of relief, now that the crazy blond was taking a dirt nap.

Nick had only drawn his weapon to kill once before in all his years of duty, and it had taken him a while to get over it.

But popping that one had felt all kinds of right. He was over it already. Probably nearly over it as he'd drawn his weapon to fire.

Sick bitch.

As for what had happened to her afterwards? Well, *that* he would never get over. Not if he lived to be a thousand. *That* was the kind of stuff that nightmares were built around. Maybe the kind of stuff Stephen King dreams about for inspiration.

Nick started shaking, as whatever autoimmune-anesthesia he was under began to wear off, and shock seeped in to take its place. He watched the old man greet Will, and then look back at him, gesturing for him to come toward the two of them.

Nick rose slowly, advancing on his friend and the stranger. The stranger who had just happened along, showing up at just the right time, and in just the right place.

Right.

"Um, hey Will. You all right, guy?" Will shocked the officer by pulling him into a bear hug.

"Nick, man, I don't know how this would have turned out without you. I owe you forever." Nick looked at the rest of the faces surrounding them, and cleared his throat self-consciously.

Will released him and stepped back, his copper-brown eyes fixing on Nick's obsidian ones. "I don't know how I know this, but you saved my family. I can never repay you. Not even with a semi-tractor trailer load of 'snobby' beer!" His face froze when he looked down and saw what Nick held.

Nick followed Will's eyes down the length of his own arm, and was startled to see that he still had a death grip on the weapon that he had used to talk business with Lockhart.

The weapon that was brought to him as if wished from a star.

"How . . ." Will's voice was strangled. "How did you get that gun?" Nick was a little unnerved by Will's tone.

"Um, well, this is gonna sound crazy" He looked around, thinking of the recent events and reconsidered. "Or maybe it won't. A dog brought it to me. That dog over there." He pointed at Max, who lifted and cocked his head at the sudden scrutiny of the gathering.

A terrible noise came from Will's chest as his eyes drifted from Max, to the sight of Nick's huge jacket nearly completely covering an inert form on the ground. He looked back at Indie, and she nodded, her eyes suddenly sparkling with unshed tears.

"He saved Cassidy, Will. He sacrificed himself; put himself between the gun of that horrible woman and our daughter."

Will sounded as if he were choking. "Give me . . . I mean, can I have that weapon, please, Nick?" Nick immediately handed the gun to Will, realizing at once that there must be some significance to it that he didn't understand. Just add this to the pile of other mysteries of this day.

The pile that was rapidly becoming quite deep.

"Officer . . . our walk?" The old man had spoken, and Nick, grateful for an out, as well as the chance for explanation, leaped forward as if he had been tasered, and set out on an easy stroll with the man beside him.

Will moved forward toward the lifeless form on the ground as Indie turned into Jax's arms. Jackson gathered her in one embrace, and the children he pulled in with his other arm, gently steering them close. He turned the whole group back and led them toward Will's truck, sensing the other man's need for privacy.

Once more, Jackson caught the slithering sight of evil incarnate moving through the cemetery, a furious scowl in place on his reptilian face.

You lose. Yet again, oh Fallen One. Today, you walk away with nothing more than what you already possessed. Go back to your stolen body and bring yourself to me, whenever you're ready for another go 'round, my perpetual adversary! He fired the thoughts toward the scaly-headed beast, who disappeared with a snap of his shiny teeth, and an angry snarl.

Hesitating, Will gingerly lowered himself to the ground beside the covered body. He could handle dead bodies. He had done so many times before, hadn't he?

So why was he shivering so hard?

Why was he sitting there with his hand hovering above the jacket, afraid to touch it? He took a deep breath and dragged the jacket off Shawn's body.

The pool of blood drying around him was evidence of the fatal gunshot wound that drew Will's stare. Along with the gaping hole in Shawn's chest. Will's eyes hardened.

This was an exit wound. The man had been shot in the back.

Oh that bitch! He hoped she died hard . . . suffering.

Pain shot behind Will's eyes as this uncharacteristic feeling blew through him.

No. Her suffering would fix nothing, would it? He dragged the top half of Baker's body into an upright position, and held on to him.

"You can trust me, right now . . . I'm gonna put this right, okay?" The words drifted back to him foggily. Baker's voice . . . in the truck.

"You did it, alright, bro'. You put everything . . . right. We defeated the enemy." Damn, was he going to start wailing again? What the hell was happening to him? He looked down at Shawn's face once more, and a word melted through his consciousness.

Absolution.

That word had probably never crossed his lips, but now it was in his head, as though whispered by a chorus of beautiful voices.

Absolution.

Redemption.

Shawn Baker had achieved it. Of this, Will was sure. He forced himself to his feet, lifting Baker easily into his arms, and carried him toward his truck. It was time to get out of this place.

CHAPTER 38

Out, out brief candle!
Life's but a walking shadow, a poor player
That struts and frets his hour upon the stage,
And then is heard no more; it is a tale
Told by an idiot, full of sound and fury,
Signifying nothing.

William Shakespeare
From Macbeth act five, scene 5

As the giant room separated by double occupancy office cubicles began to fill up, tensions began to ease.

The echo of emptiness was shattered by the sound of heavy boots and high-heeled dress shoes marking their way through the building, each pair seeking the hidden comfort of their own little office cubby-holes. People were talking, and wired-up nervous laughter was heard in short spurts, bringing the place back to life.

The aroma of food wafted through the building.

Someone's take out, Will thought, absently. Thai, from the damp-dog smell of fish sauce permeating the air.

Life goes on.

Someone dies, and then someone has lunch. It is the strange cycle of humankind, he supposed.

He had neither seen nor heard one single thing from Indie or his kids since the . . . *incident*, but he was oddly unable to freak out about this. It was as if his body instinctively knew that they were fine, and he would see them all in due time.

Will brought his mind back to today.

—

It had been one crowded funeral; the old Lutheran church on Main Street was overflowing with the entire staff of the Homeland Security branch, and a truly impressive number of weeping females. Quite the fleet of conquests for the very short time Baker had been in town. Shawn would have been pleased by the turnout.

Will moved through the office with his trademark stealth, fidgeting impatiently with the sling and shoulder stabilizing gear he sported as he took a seat at his desk. He grunted only slightly this time, the pain lessoning.

The tape around his ribs constricting his breaths was really starting to get on his nerves, though. Maybe he would take them off AMA tonight. His doctor said that he was healing with supernatural speed, which had made Will bark with laughter at his last check up. The magnificent black eye that he had been sporting for the last week was finally beginning to fade as well.

He could not stop his eyes from traveling over to the desk on the opposite wall, now empty and sterile. It had been stripped and packed up by Shawn's mother who came alone, her tiny frame shrunk down even further from the weight of her grief.

Her only child, gone.

It had caught Will's attention, for some unknown reason, that her last name was different from Shawn's . . . Tilman, or something like that. She must have remarried. Where was Shawn's father, he wondered. Didn't matter, did it?

His eyes dropped to the wastepaper basket next to Shawn's former desk.

There had to be fifty or more half-chewed packs of Tums, Pepcid and Zantac that Mrs. Tilman had tossed. The woman had politely declined all offers of help in clearing out Shawn's apartment, stating tearfully that she needed some alone time with her son's possessions.

Will had winced as he'd run through a list of potential possessions that he thought Shawn might have had around the house that would cause any mother a small case of the horrors.

Like the Costco-sized boxes of condoms he liked to stockpile.

Or the enormous collection of Kama-Sutra type books that he bragged about collecting, which was why Will had decided that a little breaking and entering had been in order the night before. He'd made his way easily through Shawn's security system, and removed as many mother-unfriendly items as he could find, which were now charcoal in Will's fireplace.

Will caught himself smiling as he thought of his partner and his minor league bad-boy ways. The kid enjoyed life to the fullest, there was no doubt about that. He was going to miss the wise-ass, that's for sure.

The wise-ass that just happened to save his little girl.

Shawn's debt to him was far more than repaid.

He thought about the fact that all actions and choices are so interconnected. A sort of chain reaction of events set in motion by one small act. He saved Shawn's life. Had he not, then Shawn would not have existed to save Cassidy.

But then, there also would have been no Shawn Baker to call, and the event might never have happened in the first place. The circle he mentally traced made his temples pound.

Will covered his eyes with his right hand, as it was the one still on a mobile shoulder joint, and tried to find some sort of definitive answer.

Maybe . . . maybe it was possible that all of this *needed* to happen, so that Shawn could earn his way to a better outcome in the afterworld. He could only imagine how tarnished the guy's potential halo had been prior to this little caper.

"Hey Will!" The cautious voice of Ben Blackstone interrupted his musings. "Oh, hey there Ben. What can I do for you?" Will answered, rubbing his eyes.

"Ah, no, I don't need anything. I was just seeing how you're holding up. I mean, it's tough, I know . . . losing a partner. Or a friend." Ben looked at Will quizzically.

Will leveled his gaze to hit Ben's.

He was good people. *Quiet and studious, kind of heart and deed.* Will choked on a laugh. Since when did he use phrases like that, even in thought? He was turning into such a sap.

"Yeah." He spoke quickly now, to catch up to a proper span of time between question and answer. "It is hard, Blackstone. I'm still kind of trying to press it into my skull to make it stick, you know?" Ben draped his arms over the cubicle's wall.

"I know. I still can't believe it myself. Who knew Lockhart would turn out to be some crazy, homicidal maniac, huh? I mean, we all knew she was kind of a loose cannon, but hell, killing Baker in some kind of jealous rage?" He shook his head. "I never saw that coming."

Will closed his eyes for a moment, reciting the "official" story in his head once more. He was a pro at this stuff.

There would be no contradictory statements coming from him.

"Yeah, I couldn't believe it myself. She must have overheard me and Baker making plans to head over to the bike show on Saturday, and decided that was her window of opportunity to get Shawn."

"What exactly did happen, Taylor? I never did get the full story. There's lots of rumors, but . . . ." Ben was leaning over the partition, looking a little hopeful. He didn't like second hand information.

"I kind of wouldn't mind hearing what really happened, unless of course . . ." Ben flushed, clearly embarrassed. "I mean, uh . . . I can understand if you don't want to re-live it, Will."

Now was the time.

Will knew that this was the opportunity to set in stone the official report filed by the first officer on the scene. Captain Nick Brocatto. Will's mind backtracked to the aftermath of that horrible day.

*   *   *

Nick had returned from his walk with the man they were calling the "Elder"—alone—and with a slightly foggy look about him. Will had just laid Baker's body carefully in the back of his truck, and stepped around to the road.

He watched, more than a little confused, as Nick had walked directly past him to his patrol car, and made an urgent call on his radio asking for back up.

There was just enough time for Will to note with a start that first, he was all alone, and secondly, Shawn's Nissan was now just yards ahead of him, wrapped violently around the front grill of his truck.

It was exactly as it was before when he had plowed into the guy's car miles down the road.

Except that it was here.

Then things moved quickly as a tornado of time, space and a lot of dust lifted him off his feet, and threw him around roughly, but strangely, without anything touching him. At least, he didn't feel anything had touched him. At first.

When the dust cleared, Will found himself face down, with a mouthful of mud and feeling freakishly disoriented.

The pain was sure as shit a surprise, searing through his left shoulder violently as he attempted to push himself off the ground. He reached up automatically to seize the offending body part, and felt liquid warmth. Without looking, he knew he was bleeding.

A lot. Pulling his hand toward his face, he confirmed this interesting fact.

He could also feel a tight pressure under his left eye, and his ribs? Well, they felt as though his chest had caught on fire, and someone had kindly put out the blaze for him.

With a fucking *bat!*

Will struggled to put at least a few of his extremities under him, managing to rise up almost on all fours.

Ow. The ribs. Oh, man!

The sound of gunshots startled him and Will felt himself hit the dirt face first once more.

What in the hell was happening? And what in the hell had happened to *him*, although at the moment, he was much more concerned about the answer to the first question.

Not 'what in the Hell,'" Brother! The gentle voice sifted through his head clearly; a shimmering laugh. However, before Will could react, or do anything more than work toward closing his mouth, someone flipped him over on his back, oh so gently.

"Will! Will, 'bro, can you hear me? You're gonna be fine, right? EMS is on its way!" Nick's voice was carefully controlled to hide what Will could tell was a hard case of the panics, although what in the H—(he retracted the oath quickly)—*world* . . . he was talking about was a total blank to Will.

"What . . . ? What's happened?" Will's voice sounded strange. Hoarse and torn.

"You've been shot, man. Been in a car accident and shot!" Nick's voice was also raw, but oddly triumphant.

Car accident? Shot? Well, that could explain why he felt like someone had beaten him with a bag of quarters. Will shook his head hard. Holy crap, when had all this happened to him?

He had obviously missed out on one very big adventure involving himself, and someone's pistol party. But how?

"S'okay, Will, just the left shoulder. But I got the bitch. She took off in the woods somehow, but I'm sure she won't get far. We'll pick her up. We'll just follow the blood trail!"

It was beginning to become clear to Will that the events of the morning had just been violently rearranged, and for reasons that were obvious. What, was Nick going to go back to the station and fill out a report on what he had actually seen? No way was the Society going to allow that, he was sure. He didn't know the extent of their powers, but, hey, sure . . . so they maybe could totally screw with the order of time and events.

Why not?

At this point, there was almost nothing that Will couldn't believe in. The story. Well, the story had to be made . . . *possible*, right?

At least in the realm of the human world.

He almost laughed aloud, because it suddenly reminded him of how his department worked. Take care of the problem, clean up the mess, and fabricate a suitable reality. The irony of his Homeland Security unit and, uh . . . . Will choked for a moment. Anything, well . . . *Holy*, was absolutely incongruous, but there you had it.

He was suddenly quite at home, familiar with the tactic, and decided that it was his job to simply go along with whatever Nick told him. He knew Nick wasn't lying or covering up anything. The man was incapable of a lie, no matter how pressing the excuse.

Nick's brain had obviously been implanted with a scenario, and Will had found himself dropped into the final act, without a script. No problem. He could follow as well as he could lead.

Soft laughter rippled through his head once more, feeling like a cold wash of rain.

I knew you were worthy, my Brother!

Who WAS that?

Oh well. William Taylor decided that he would worry about the who's and the why's later. Right now, he had a job to do.

Feigning a little extra weakness and confusion, Will looked up at Nick's face, which was dark with anger and concern. Will reached up and touched a mighty fine fist-sized knot on the side of his head, and grit his teeth.

"What happened?" Will asked again, aware that he was repeating himself. "You don't remember?" Nick sat him up carefully.

"Well, I guess that's not surprising, considering the whack you must have taken to the head!" Nick's anger flared again. "Did you know that woman? She seemed to know you and that other guy pretty well." Nick suddenly turned his eyes away from Will's; a look of sickness on his face.

"Your partner, right? That was the guy, Shawn Baker. He *was* your partner?"

"Uh, yeah. Shawn Baker is my partner . . ." Will held his breath. Even knowing what was coming next did not soften the slam to the gut that he felt when Nick spoke the words.

"He, ah . . . was shot too, Will. He . . . he didn't make it. The guy is DOA."

The grief swept into him, as if he was hearing for the first time, which was very helpful to the part he was playing, he supposed. Didn't make it any better, though.

"Jesus, Nick. Tell me what happened. All of it."

"Well, man, maybe when you are feeling better, you can fill in some blanks for me, but near as I can tell, it was a woman scorned kinda thing, yeah?

"I guess this chick had a thing for your partner, and . . ."

Will cut him off. "Lockhart." He hissed the name between his teeth.

"Cassandra Lockhart. Yeah. I mean, yes she did have a . . . *thing* for Baker. She was a Fed, too."

"I'm not surprised." Nick nodded his head. Sirens were approaching now, and fast. "She seemed to handle the play-dirty cards like a pro. Looks like she ditched her car on purpose, probably knew you two were headed this way somehow, and I guess you saw her first, and stopped."

"Yeah."

A story was materializing in Will's head, flowing like a breeze through his skull. "I'm starting to remember stuff, Nick." Will spoke weakly, working his role well.

"Me and Shawn had been talking about going to this bike show in Burlington. We were taking separate cars because Baker wanted to hit some sports bar afterwards.

"Lockhart flagged me down. Said she wrecked her car, and then she jumped me. I wasn't expecting it, so she kind of got the upper hand . . ."

"Well, why in the hell should you have expected a fellow agent to attack you, man?" Nick was furious. Disloyalty was incomprehensible to him.

Nick, in spite of his gentle heart, had a zero-tolerance policy regarding bullshit, and betraying your family, country or friends and partners was a definite sharp turn off the freeway of the acceptable. In fact, those particular offences had their own special parking garage in his heart.

"Baker was behind me in his car," Will continued, his eyes squeezed shut so that he could better read the script in his brain. "Lockhart was trying to make me drive . . . I think, and then she caught me in the head with something, I'm not sure. Anyhow, next thing I knew, she was driving, and she rammed Baker's car with my truck." Nick hissed in his breath in anger.

"I got thrown around pretty good, I guess." Will tried to move his body to ease his breathing as he said this. "Baker crawled out of the car, and Lockhart just started screaming at him, about how she wasn't going to take his 'humiliating' her any more. She made Baker pull me over next to him, and when I tried to talk some sense into her, that's when she shot me."

"Yeah, and that's when I pulled up." Nick spoke bitterly. "I *saw* the broad cap you, man." His eyes were burning black toward the spot where this scene had supposedly taken place.

"I got out and told her to freeze, and she starts firing away like a deranged monster, and clips my gun right outa my hand like a God damned sniper!" "She had me walk forward, and I swear to you Will, I just knew somehow that this chick was gonna finish me. *I knew it!*"

"It was like a dream. She lifted that weapon of hers, and pulled the damn trigger, cold as can be, and . . . ." Nick swallowed down something, as if his sickness was trying to spill right out of him.

"Your partner. Jesus Christ, Will, the guy yells out, and jumped in front of her, right when she fired. He . . . he saved my life. And I didn't even know the man!" Nick could not hide the choked up sound working its way out of his throat now.

It was clear that Nick did not think himself worthy of another's sacrifice. Not by a long shot.

Yeah, well you're wrong! thought Will, fiercely.

"Um, yeah, so anyhow," Nick coughed and cleared his throat before continuing. "The woman clearly hadn't really planned on hurting this guy . . . uh, I mean Baker, and she pretty much flipped out when she saw what she did. That's when I noticed that when Baker crawled out of his car, his gun fell out of it's holster, I guess. I saw it there, on the ground and just grabbed it and fired!"

Nick shook his head once more. "And she took off into the woods."

Two squad cars and an ambulance pulled to the roadside behind the two men, and skidded to a stop, the drivers all kinds of jacked up, anticipating action of some kind. They were disappointed.

There was definitely nothing to see now.

Will had the wherewithal to note that Indie, Jackson and the kids had simply vanished into thin air, as far as he knew. Yet . . . Will knew they were all okay, somehow.

The old man . . . whoever or whatever he was, he was not here either, at least not in the physical sense that was for sure. Will allowed himself to be scooped up by the EMS team, and raced to the hospital. During the quick ride, while IV's were started, and bloody bullet wounds were cleaned and pressure dressed, Will had laid quietly, listening to the most amazing voice; wispy and soft, playing through his head.

I am truly sorry for the pain you must bear, but there must always be balance. You have absorbed the injuries inflicted on young Shawn Baker, as well as the very fine Captain Broccato. They did happen, so they had to be accounted for to appease our Creator's penchant for continuity.

You did not suffer Shawn's fatal wound, obviously, because he has born that himself. Captain Broccato has had his memories of events altered, somewhat.

The voice sounded a little remorseful.

But yours, as you are well aware, have been left intact.

"Why?" Will breathed softy, as the medications began to take effect.

Your destiny has been found, William Taylor, and you must fulfill it. No need to go looking, for it will find you, and it will find you many times over. You are the Redeemer, and they will come through you. You are the gateway . . . your pain affects others profoundly. You will need your knowledge that you carry forth to succeed.

"They will come . . . through . . . *me?*" Will was leaving consciousness behind rapidly, and his thoughts were crumbling like ash.

"Redeemer." He mumbled on his way out.

Will was taken to the hospital, where he was cleaned up, patched up and taped up, and then forced to be an overnight guest for observation purposes. The bullet was extracted from his shoulder and sent to forensics.

Arguing had gotten him exactly nowhere, and finally Nick, who had decided to play guardian pit-bull for the night, told him that if he didn't want a lungful of teeth for supper, he needed to shut the hell up.

Will shut up, breaking his forced vow of silence only once more, to again refuse to allow the hospital to try to contact his wife or his mother.

Nick spent the entire evening there, alternating between Will's bedside, and gazing wistfully at a tiny, pony-tailed nurse sitting behind the glass doors in the ER. In between bouts of pain-medicated slumber, and wakeful stressing,

Will had a moment of overwhelming gratitude for the man who'd saved them all, and didn't even know it.

He wanted him to find the happiness he deserved, and wished he was a genie, able to grant Nick his biggest wish.

Somebody needs to do it, if I can't, he'd thought drowsily, as he began to slip away once more. The unaccustomed drugs in his system worked amazingly well. He was soon out again . . . .

Will snapped it back together, realizing that he'd finished his tale, and was now dwelling in his own memories.

Ben had listened, wide-eyed to the official story, his fingers unconsciously digging into the fabric of the cubicle walls.

"God, Will." He sounded horrified; "we almost lost you too, man. I didn't know about Baker saving the cop, though."

Holy shit! How had Will allowed that to happen? Baker died a hero, and everyone had damn well better know about it.

"That's right, Ben," Will looked at him gravely. "Shawn Baker died to save another. He knew that he was the reason for Lockhart's breakdown, and he didn't want Nick to die for it."

Ben stood for a long moment, unsure what kind of reply would be appropriate for such an act of selflessness, finally deciding that he couldn't come up with one. He made a noise in the back of his throat before speaking again.

"They haven't found Lockhart yet either, have they?"

"No, the APB still stands." Will could see that Ben had had enough. Actually, he wasn't looking very well. Ben was an office guy . . . good with the paper, but not into the whole *Die Hard* scene.

"I'll see you later, Will. And, uh, thanks for telling me the story. I really am sorry, man." As Will gave Ben a salute of dismissal, his suit jacket fell open slightly, revealing the soft glow of expensive leather, running in a one-inch wide strip of well-polished mahogany across his chest.

The holster and shoulder strap fit Will like a glove, as did the handgrip of the Walther PPK 7.65mm that rode proudly in it.

Ben nodded his head toward the exposed leather and weapon. "Baker's mom let you keep that, huh?"

Will didn't answer, and simply stared steadily back at Ben Blackstone.

Understanding flowed to the surface of Ben's eyes, and he inclined his head once more and left, as Will re-buttoned his jacket.

He'd asked no one's permission to keep the weapon.

Enough said.

Will's supervisor popped his head around the corner, and spoke in his usual diplomatic style. "Taylor, get in my office!"

Will deliberately took a little more time than was necessary to get around the corner to the man's space, even stopping to pour himself a cup of coffee, just to show Mr. Hard-ass how well his approach to management worked.

He calmly added creamer to his coffee, and stirred with methodical thoroughness, enjoying the burn of the man's glare from the corner of his eye.

Mark Levinson liked Will just fine; however, everyone who worked under him enjoyed the crap treatment. The man was confident in his belief that the way to run a tight operation was to be sure everyone hated you. Meant you were doing your job.

"Glad you could make it, Taylor!" The sarcasm was heavy in his supervisor's voice.

"Glad I could, too, Levinson. What do you need?" Will strolled into the slightly larger cubicle space allotted the anointed members of management, and realized that they had company.

A woman with sharply angled, chin-length red hair, who Will guessed to be in her early forties, was perched lightly against Mr. Hard-ass's desk, arms folded and all business.

"William Taylor?" She offered her hand. "I'm M." she inclined her head briskly. "M Townsend."

Will snorted hot coffee through his nose, choking and splattering the cream covered walls of Hard-ass's cubicle with small flecks of brown.

"Jesus," muttered Levinson, reaching for a handful of Kleenex.

"Are you okay?" she asked dryly, withdrawing her hand rapidly, to avoid the coffee shower.

"Uh . . . yeah." Will coughed a few more times before regaining control. *M? Oh my God.* Wherever Baker was, he hoped he was hearing this.

"No . . . I, uh, I'm sorry. The name just caught me off guard. M? *Really?*"

"Yes, Mr. Taylor. Is there a problem?"

"Oh, no . . . just, you know, the James Bond thing. You must get that all the time, huh?" Although M's tone remained crisp, Will thought he could detect a little warmth sneaking its way through.

"My name is Meredith, Mr. Taylor, and I feel that the name is a little cumbersome. Since the available nicknames for Meredith are limited to Mare, which, nothing against horses, but I don't want to be called one, and Merri, which merry I am most definitely NOT, all we have left over I suppose is Death, and death is not a title I am comfortable with. Therefore, that left me with "M". Is this okay with you, Mr. Taylor?"

"Absolutely . . . *M!*" Will smiled and extended his hand, wondering who this person was.

"You put in for a transfer, Taylor, to Texas." Hard-ass was speaking again.

"That's right."

"M is . . ."

"I can speak for myself, thank you Mr. Levinson. I am head of the Security division in Corpus Christi, and I flew down to interview you in person, although I must say, your resume is quite inspiring. Can we go back to your office and talk?"

Hard-ass was irritated by the woman's dismissal, Will could tell. Hell, he *liked* this lady.

"After you!" Will made a sweeping gesture with his good arm, indicating his office around the corner, and gave a nod of *"see you later, jerk,"* to Hard-ass.

Mr. Hard-ass.

Will did not want to be disrespectful, after all. As Will was exiting the office, Hard-ass called out to him once more.

"Oh, and Taylor, when she gets done with you, get back in here so I can introduce you to your new partner."

"What new partner?" Will demanded, stopping dead in his tracks. "I'm getting transferred out of here. Why would you assign someone to me when I'm leaving?"

"'Cause this guy requested you, specifically, and the top boys think a lot of him, apparently. He goes where you go."

"But . . ." "No 'buts,' Taylor. This came from Washington."

Will started moving again, straining his brain mightily to try to guess who in the hell would request to be his partner in such an imperative manner.

Someone with pull in Washington, huh?

Just as Will rounded the corner to enter his office, a cool voice called out to him from the front lobby.

"Hello, Will."

Will dropped his coffee, dumbstruck. No. Not possible.

No freakin' way!

"Mr. Taylor, are you coming this way anytime soon?" came the brisk voice of M from Will's office.

"Yes ma'am," Will called over his shoulder as he stepped toward the lobby. "Be right there."

Will took a very deep breath, blew it out slowly, and decided he had just learned something the hard way; whenever you think you've hit rock bottom, there is always an asshole standing by to throw you a jackhammer and a shovel.

He extended his hand shakily. "Hello, Jackson!"

CHAPTER 39

Will maintained eye contact with Jackson as he backed his way toward his office cubicle.

He had no explanation as to how he managed to have a sane and rational conversation with M, but he must have done so, because she offered Will the position in Texas on the spot. As if in a surreal fog, Will smiled and accepted the job, thanking her and even seeing her out to the lobby.

He even managed to go back into Hard-ass's office to be formally "introduced" to Jackson.

A week gone by and not a word from anyone about his family, and then *HE* just shows up like this?

Part of him wanted to collapse with relief, even though he truly had felt sure that his family was safe, there was no substitute for seeing and hearing for yourself.

But part of him was beginning to feel a little belligerent.

First, Will basically had to hand over his wife and kids like taxes to the government, and now he was going to have to work with this guy, too? This was beyond unfair.

It might even fall into the "not doable" category of possibilities.

Will finally made his escape to the men's room. He backed up against the far wall, and slid to the floor, checking under the stall doors for feet, just to make sure that he was alone when he started screaming.

Or puking. He wasn't sure which he wanted as a first course yet.

"Are you alright, Will?" Christ, the man had come from nowhere. Will hadn't even heard the door open. Without asking or waiting for permission, Jackson reached down and unceremoniously pulled Will to his feet.

As Will was pondering whether he wanted to option his right to punch the guy in the face for this violation, Jackson spoke first, his voice even and controlled. "I really hope you don't try it."

Mind reading bastard.

Hmm. Will thought he could detect a slight contradictory emotion from the man. He almost laughed.

Hell yeah, the guy was hoping he *would* give it a go . . . maybe just a little. Jackson sighed. "Not really, Will."

He crossed his arms and leaned against the wall.

"Believe me, I have some very . . . mixed feelings about this placement myself, but I go where I'm told, and do what I must. It is the blessing of my genetics, I suppose."

Will thought that the way Jackson spoke the word "blessing," sounded like the man meant something more along the lines of "curse." Jackson shrugged.

"It is a burden I bear with pride."

"*Sure* you do." Will assumed a stance similar to Jackson's, arms awkwardly folded, accommodating the shoulder gear, with a dead steady look back into his eyes before firing off his wrath at the idea of this cozy little arrangement.

"Just what the hell makes you think you're qualified to do what I do? I mean, what training did you get in your fancy law school, what, was it Harvard?"

"Oxford." Jackson replied calmly.

Of course. Even better.

"Whatever. What training did you receive at *Oxford*, qualifies you to be a federal agent for the United States Department of Homeland Security, and our classified unit especially? And furthermore . . ."

Will hit on something that should have been a major complication. "How long do you expect to be able to mingle in a nest of people trained to spot you and your kind, huh?"

"Yes, well that would have put an end to things rather quickly, but you see, I have been allowed to share in Indie's gift, by the grace of the Elders. You know, the one that allowed *you* to remain ignorant of her status for quite some time."

Will's jaw muscles were clenching ominously as Jackson continued. "As for my credentials, perhaps I've had more education than you are aware of, Will. Education, training and maybe even some relevant experience."

"Care to elaborate?" Will asked through his teeth.

"Not particularly, if you don't mind."

"Suppose I do mind?" Will was now psyched and primed for action. He decided he could overlook his vow to get along with this guy for Indie's sake, just for today.

"Look Will, can we not do this . . . please?"

"What's the matter, can't handle a little macho bullshit posturing?"

"I can handle whatever I need to handle," was Jackson's maddeningly passive response.

"Well, that makes one of us, Jackson. When I decided to try really hard not to harbor any hatred toward you, that did not mean that I was up for us becoming best buddies. I put in for that transfer to Texas mostly because I didn't want to hang around and watch you and my wife making lovey-sick eyes at each other, you get me?"

Jackson's eyes seemed to tighten briefly with an emotion that Will had recently had the pleasure of brushing up against.

Jealousy.

He leaned toward Will ever so slightly, arms crossed. "Then you'd better learn not to look." He spoke in a cold whisper, his eyes suddenly nearly black . . . and murderous.

Will was surprised.

"Oops. Better be careful Jackson; your show is slipping!"

Well well, what do you know. The pious priest does have a streak of man in him after all, Will thought.

With a slam and a grunt, Will discovered that his healing rib bones had somehow become one with the men's room floor. He found himself staring at the filthy tile as he strained to keep his head up.

Jackson's knee was planted painfully in his back.

Shit fire, but the man was inhumanly fast. Imagine that.

"I would respectfully ask that you do not think of me as anything less than a man." Jackson's voice was soft, calm and lethal, his cultured accent somehow making the statement even more menacing.

Will had to admit it, at least to himself. He was impressed. So, okay, maybe the guy could handle himself in a fight after all.

"Point taken," Will gasped. "But I do have one thing to say . . . ."

Jackson's knee provided a little more pressure to the area between Will's shoulder blades. "And that would be . . . ?"

Jackson's voice was still perfectly calm and controlled. "If you let my face touch the floor of this damned place, so help me God, I will find a way to kill you!"

Instantly the pressure disappeared, and Will found himself lifted and set on his feet for the second time of the day. He dusted off as best he could, gagging at the thought of all of the germs he had just been up close and personal with, and looked over at Jackson.

His posture was unchanged, just as if he had never moved from his position against the wall. Will couldn't be sure, but he thought he could detect a glint of amusement in Jackson's slightly hooded eyes.

So obviously, Jackson was worthy of a little respect in the fisticuffs department, no doubt about that. But still, Will had a need for a little "back at ya" action.

Thinking quickly, Will focused his mind.

David Ortiz . . . Josh Beckett . . . Hunter Jones . . . Nick Green . . .

He took a shifty step toward Jackson, who now wore a slightly confused expression.

Will caught Jackson completely off guard with a right hook to the side of his face, delivered with respectable force, nearly taking the man off his feet.

Jackson recovered instantly, and stared back at Will in disbelief.

"Unfair. That was a sucker punch!"

"That's probably going to be the only way I'll ever get one in on you, so yeah!"

"Aw, you *jerk!* I think you knocked loose a tooth!"

Jackson rubbed his jaw and began to smile. "So that's why you took a sudden interest in providing roll call duty for the Red Sox. Brilliant distraction!" There was clearly a tone of grudging admiration in his voice now.

As both men stood quietly petting their respective sore spots, an uneasy truce announced itself, silently. Jackson extended his hand toward Will.

"Shall we start over? Think of it this way, Will . . . you will be able to stay close to the kids, and Indie will not have to worry about you. Nor will you have to worry about her. I will take care of her forever, do not doubt that. She is the gravity in my world."

Will hesitated for only a moment before accepting Jackson's outstretched hand, and smiled a sad little smile.

"I know that. God help me survive it, but, yeah . . . I know it."

As they exited the men's room, Will slapped Jackson on the shoulder, none to gently, and spoke gruffly. "I guess maybe you won't be so bad to have around . . . for back-up. We'll need to loosen up your vocabulary, though. Too fancy for me!"

"Right. I'll get to work on that right away." Jackson replied sarcastically. He glanced over at Will's profile.

"Texas, is it? Another move. Indie will be thrilled."

Will stopped and faced Jackson with a genuine smile this time. "And just think, my man. This time *you* get to be the one to break the happy news.

A small tip from me to you; bring home flowers and chocolate!"

CHAPTER 40

Indie sat cross-legged on the floor of Will's living room, surrounded by boxes and small crates, along with several rolls of bubble wrap. She wrinkled her nose at the mounds of anonymous objects, mingled with the potentially obsolete items she had yet to go through.

"How did we get so much stuff?" she wondered, beginning to feel slightly overwhelmed.

Jackson bounded into the living room with an annoying amount of energy. "Come on, love, you promised Will it would all be finished today! Looks like you need another week or so!" He seemed to dance, rather than dodge around the shoe Indie threw at him, and he dropped down beside her with a heart-stopping smile.

Indie's breath caught, and she tried to stay focused.

But, God, he was such an adorable little pest.

"What's wrong, my precious, too much for you?"

"Either make yourself useful, or sit over there, be quiet and look pretty!" Indie growled, thoroughly in a state of huff.

"Oh, but I can sit right here beside you and be all annoying and still look pretty!"

Jax was working her, but good, Indie decided. She had shot him down on his offer to have a moving company come in and pack up the place, telling him that she absolutely had to handle this herself.

Will had been all on board with the moving company plan, especially if Jackson was springing. But Indie would not hear of it. She was an old pro at this, she reminded Will. After all, the family had moved how many dozens of times? Indie pretty much considered *herself* to be a professional moving company at this point, but it seemed that a couple of things had happened in the last two and a half years; she had forgotten how much she actually hated it, *and* they had collected more belongings.

Especially Will and his freaky packrat self. What was she thinking? "Ready to wave the white flag yet, beautiful?" Jax tried to hide the mirth behind his words, as he rolled Indie onto her back and pinned her to the carpet, which was now littered with the horrible static-y crumbs left by the countless bags of packing peanuts.

Unbeknownst to Indie, Jackson had been watching in fascination as the little white balls had been rolling toward her, and even zipping through the air to attach to nearly every part of her body, and much of the back of her hair, magnetically attracted by the snapping electric charges she generated by crawling around on the carpet.

He was having quite a lot of fun today, or at least he was now, having finished sulking after Indie would not even let him help her. So now, he'd decided that tormenting her for her bad decision making skills on the subject of packing and moving could help ease his suffering.

"I will never wave the flag, do you hear . . . *NEVER!*"

Indie put as much force into the vow as she could, while Jax ignored her, covering her with silky, shiver-inducing kisses.

"Oh, but just think, Indie . . . the kids are at their Grandmother's. We could get the moving people here in a half an hour. I hired them for the day anyway, so that they could be ready to roll if you changed your mind!"

"*OH!* Are you crazy?" Indie fumed. "Do you *know* how much a moving company costs?"

"As a matter of fact I do, since I paid them this morning at the same time I paid them to pack up my . . . I mean *our* house." Jackson gave her his most disarming smile; the one he knew she could never resist. He allowed the front of his hair to flop down over his eyes, and tilted his head to look up at her through the tangle of chocolate colored silk and closed his eyes halfway.

Ah. He had her. He knew it.

Jax could feel her struggling with her natural tilt toward stubborn defiance, and another need he could feel beginning to build in her.

One that he had been fighting all day.

"Come on, Indie," he whispered against her ear, his voice a little off kilter from the ache of needing to be alone with her.

In their house, not Will's.

With a little moan of defeat that exited her lips simultaneously with Jackson's laugh of triumph, Indie grabbed a small dusting cloth that was lying nearby and waved it feebly in the air.

"Will this do?" she asked, a little breathless from the attention Jax was giving her neck and shoulders with his lips.

"Quite nicely," was his muffled response.

Indie had allowed the television to remain switched on, in a fruitless attempt to distract Jax from harassing her. It suddenly blared the tinny, generic orchestra music that someone long ago had decided was the logical intro to every single newscast shown on the planet.

The female anchor wore a heavily sprayed hairstyle, and a suitably furrowed brow to compliment her look of contrived interest, as she continued the weeks-long story about the dangerously high amount of solar activity that had occurred recently.

It had died down to within normal limits now, but the parade of "experts" that were being shuttled through the studios to offer their opinions on the causes, and the dire consequences of drinking bottled water and driving pretty much any vehicle other than a skateboard, was painful to watch.

The anchorwoman nodded her head in the most serious manner, eyes vacant and utterly bored. "Yes, we need to see this as the sign of things to come," stated expert number eight thousand and seven, a gaunt gentleman, who needed a shave and a good meal, was droning, turning directly into the camera and boldly suggested that people cut down on their toilet paper usage.

This caused Indie to burst into laughter as Jax helped her to her feet. Who knew? To save the planet, all we need to do is start wiping with leaves . . . or maybe pinecones.

Jackson gripped Indie by the waist and pulled her into a spine-bending embrace, cutting off Indie's laughter with a kiss that conveyed a message.

A very urgent one.

As Indie responded with equal enthusiasm, wrapping her arms around his neck and pulling him, impossibly, even closer, he broke contact with her mouth just long enough to growl in her ear.

"We've got to get out of here. Now!"

With a small leap, Indie wrapped her legs around Jax's waist, and her held on to her tightly as he all but ran through the house to the front door.

Jackson couldn't understand what had become of his self-control lately. Something was dreadfully wrong with his restraint now. He was randy as a seventeen year old whenever he was around her.

Basically, all it took was a full-length glance at Indie, and parts of his anatomy sprang to life with a completely unmanageable urgency. It was embarrassing, actually, but then it wasn't like he had forty years of celibacy to make up for or anything, right?

What made it even more difficult, was the fact that she was always on board for any naked time; as long as they were in an appropriate place.

Unfortunately, Jackson's body had no such mandates, hence the cause of his usual state of discomfort lately. The feelings were something utterly alien to Jackson prior to his connection with Indie.

He was having to re-school himself on control nearly constantly, it seemed.

"Hold tight, now," he whispered, eyes glinting with excitement as he jogged down the deck stairs, doing his best not to bounce her around too badly.

She wasn't complaining.

They reached the Mercedes, and Jackson stowed Indie into the passenger seat, buckling her up, and pulled a Starsky and Hutch-worthy scramble across the hood of the vehicle, and was in the driver's seat. He started the car and looked over, noticing Indie was panting, her hand pressed to her heart.

Alarmed, he reached out to her. "Are you okay?" He was instantly on edge . . . and then instantly back in the game. He could feel her thoughts.

She wanted him just as desperately. But Indie thoughtfully answered his question. "No, but I will be!"

The look in her eyes nearly drove him to take her right here in the car. Right here in this driveway.

Will's driveway.

Oh no. That was so not happening. The thought cooled him enough to decide that they could make it back to their house . . . if he drove very, *very* fast.

He threw the car into reverse and screamed down the driveway, hit the street and nailed first gear. They made it to the stop sign before Indie shrieked. "Wait!"

Jackson skidded to an abrupt stop, and grabbed her hands. "*What?* What is it . . . ?" His eyes were wide with concern.

"Stop right now . . . and call that moving company! Tell them we will be back here at five o'clock, and that we need them to be finished by then!" After staring at Indie for a full minute, Jackson simply began cracking up.

The car shook with his laughter as he grabbed her and pulled her to him.

Still laughing, and still gripping her in one arm, Jackson pulled out his cell phone and dialed.

"Okay, my leader!" He shook his head. "All business, aren't you, love?"

"You'd better believe it, baby!"

*　　*　　*

"*Say* it, Indie . . . *please.* Say it out loud!" Jackson's voice was hoarse with need. "I need to *hear* it from you."

Jackson looked down at Indie before burying his face into her sweet smelling hair, and then once more rolling his forehead into the soft space between her eyes, right at the bridge of her nose. They were drenched in sweat, their bodies connected fiercely.

Jackson was trying not to be a savage, but he found himself in the throes of some very male need to possess and to claim. It wasn't helping his mission of restraint that Indie was matching his urgency move for move.

He was hovering near the edge, but he simply needed one more thing. The sound of her voice in his ear, whispering the words that he knew she was feeling, but needed so desperately to hear.

Jackson used both hands to push back her damp hair, stroking the sides of her face with his thumbs, and made direct eye contact. "Please . . . *tell me!*" He was shivering with anticipation.

And so who is the needy one now, Indie silently chided him, enjoying his desperate need for her to the max.

Deciding that he'd suffered enough, Indie drew up her knees, pulling him even deeper into her, and clenched her fists full of Jackson's hair. She whispered in ragged breaths.

"I need you, Jax! I love you and I'll need you *always!*"

Oh yeah! That was it.

Jackson topped the mountain and began the slide toward home plate, his groans of love and satisfaction coming from deep within his chest, breaking through the kisses as he staked his claim. The sounds drove Indie to the top of her own precipitance, where she felt her body rise, and then fall as she arched her back into a swan dive, riding the rippling current back down to Earth.

Indie had never in her life felt so wanted.

So *needed*. And so treasured.

She could feel in Jackson unequivocally, that she was his top priority, his deepest need. The words he spoke to her on that fateful day, when she invited him into her house, came back to her . . . ."*I'm afraid I am a slave to your wishes.*" It felt like a promise kept, because she knew without a doubt, that there was nothing he would ever deny her. Never would she feel forgotten, neglected or unimportant again for the rest of her life. She felt an absurd urge to cry, but only tears of joy. Soft gentle kisses, full of love, pulled her from her thoughts.

"You are right on all counts, Indie. You will want for absolutely nothing from this moment on. Anything you wish for, I will lay it at your feet!" He kissed her once more, as if to make sure she understood.

" *. . . but you'll never see the end of the road, while you're traveling with me . . . .*" Jax quoted with a laugh.

"*Crowded House?* You are *such* a corndog!" Indie whispered, but clearly pleased and a little dizzy with love.

"It's a great line, and also just a statement of fact." Jackson pushed up on his elbows to look her squarely in her eyes. "It is my vow, to you!" Then he smiled.

"It's four-thirty, my love . . . care for a quick shower? I know you want to be somewhere at five!"

CHAPTER 41

Will glanced at his watch as he worked his way down I-89. It was four forty-five. Indie had sworn to him that the house packing would be done by this evening, but judging by the amount left to do this morning, and knowing her tendency to shun all help, he seriously doubted it.

He had watched with conflicted amusement as Jackson had tried to persuade her by any and all means at his disposal, to allow him to hire movers for the job, but to no avail.

Jackson had been all kinds of put out, but he could have told him to save his breath.

When Indie set her mind on something, just step out of the way. She would never be swayed. Oh well, maybe by this evening when she realized the amount of work left to do, she would break down.

Will's eyes blinked.

From nowhere, an overwhelming exhaustion sledge hammered him with such force, he wasn't even sure that he would make it to a rest area.

Gasping, and taking huge gulps of air from the window he hastily let down, Will struggled to hold his eyes open as he finally spotted the small blue sign pointing toward exactly where he needed to be.

What is happening to me? he wondered, as he pulled into the circular curve off the highway. Could a person suddenly develop a severe case of narcolepsy? He had never been hit with fatigue like this, just out of the blue.

Will just managed to throw the truck in park, and snatch up the small lever next to the seat and slam backwards.

He was out before the seat came to a stop; unconscious and instantly in the middle of a dream.

He felt himself lifted . . . pulled upwards as he wondered without any real concern, if it was going to hurt when he smacked into the roof of his truck. In his dream, he closed his eyes and braced himself for the impact, which never came.

When Will opened his eyes again, he was facing downward, watching the road and all of the traffic move further and further away.

He felt a current of air roll him lazily onto his back, and he felt the distinct sensation of being held so gently, so tenderly in the palm of someone's hand, like a premature infant in an Anne Geddes print.

So utterly at peace.

Safe and calm, as he was rocked gently from side to side.

A voice that was the distillation of love and kindness wrapped itself around him, cradling him even more tightly in its embrace.

Redeemer, it whispered softly.

The gifts you receive will keep your footing sure, your stance on equal terms with your worthy partner and adversary. You will never betray one another, and you will fight for the same cause, as you grapple with your own relationship.

You will love as brothers love, and fight as brothers will fight, but always united as one." The voice circled Will like a hand caressing his face.

You will awaken with a small token of my gratitude for the salvation of my creations; the gifts aforementioned will soon make themselves known. Use them well. The sound of the wind rose.

Sleep now, my Redeemer . . . .

The voice dwindled until only the sound of the wind remained, soft and soothing on Will's skin.

It seemed to Will that he remained suspended in the palm of the unseen hand for hours, comforted and cleansed, before feeling a gradual downward float drift him back toward his truck. He closed his eyes once more as the roof of the truck approached, but this time, he knew he would not feel an impact.

He was laid gently back in the seat of the truck with all of the care of a mother for her child. Will's eyes opened and he looked around, his mind hazy.

The time on his watch read five-fifteen.

There was a small piece of paper on his dashboard, obviously from a memo pad. It was covered with words, written by a very firm hand.

"You had better be out taking a walk, buddy. You call me as soon as you get back to your truck, so that I can swing by your house and kick your ass!"

"P.S. I hope you're okay."

It was signed, "Nick."

*　　*　　*

Nick was headed back to the station to wrap up the humdrum stack of paperwork required simply so that he could go home.

He was already off duty, and listening to music in his patrol car when he experienced a sickening feeling of deja vous.

He spotted Will's truck parked in the rest area. It was one without facilities, so there wasn't much else around, just a few picnic tables and benches. Frowning, Nick pulled in through the exit side and came to a stop beside Will's truck.

As he feared, it was empty. *What the hell . . . ?*

Nick parked the patrol car, and quickly looked inside the truck to make sure Will wasn't curled up in the floorboards or anything. He noticed then, that the truck was unlocked.

Nick ripped the door open and tried to ascertain whether there were signs of any foul play.

No, no signs of a struggle. No blood (thank God) and everything else seemed to be in order.

Will's cell phone was resting in the passenger seat.

Maybe he had to take a leak. Nick looked around.

The area was heavily wooded, but had hiking trails everywhere. He waited for about ten minutes, and then uneasily decided that maybe Will had simply wanted to take a walk. Have some alone time.

God knows, the guy needed it. He most definitely had enjoyed a very difficult couple of weeks.

Nick looked at his watch and fumed. He knew he had to report in, but was uncertain what to do.

If Will was simply taking a walk, the last thing he needed was to think that he had to worry about Nick freaking out about him all the time now. The man would not want a cop with nanny-syndrome hanging around, would he?

Heaving a giant sigh worthy of a man of Nick's stature, be pulled out his little notebook, and his best ticket-writing pen, and tried not to rip the paper as he wrote. He snatched it out of the little spiral binder, and slapped in onto the dashboard of Will's truck.

Indulging himself with one more moment of hesitation, Nick reluctantly climbed back into the cruiser, and with a last look around, pulled back onto the highway.

*   *   *

Will sat in the cab of his truck just long enough to convince himself that he was still alive, truly awake, and relatively sane.

This took just under half an hour.

He held his hands up in front of his face, turning them first front to back, and then he opened and closed them several times. Next he checked the legs. Yep, both were working.

His mind seemed okay, as he ran through a few sets of multiplication tables, and some states and their capitals for good measure.

He finally deemed himself fully awake and one hundred percent sure that what had just happened to him was not a dream. Something had really happened.

Something amazing and unreal.

Nick had apparently driven by and seen Will's truck parked here with—Will shuddered—no one inside; hence the note.

Redeemer. The word seemed to hiss through the interior of the truck. It had the effect of jogging several memories at once.

They will come through you.

"Me?" Will whispered. It sounded a little scary, but suddenly, in a blinding flash of understanding, Will got it.

Everything clicked nicely in his head with a satisfying snap. He still wasn't sure just exactly what he was supposed to *do*, but he figured this would make itself known to him in due time.

He just hoped he didn't disappoint anyone.

With hands now steady, Will reached forward, started his truck and rejoined the traffic on the highway. He put his cell phone's blue tooth capabilities to good use, and dialed Nick's number.

Nick answered on the first ring.

"Will, you sorry sonofabitch, I am going to kill you."

Will smiled. One thing about Nick . . . you never had to wonder where you stood with the guy.

"I love you too, 'bro! Hey, what are you doing tonight?"

"Besides kicking your ass? Nothin' much."

"Then why don't you swing by the house? This is my last night I'll be hanging out there, and we should have a beer or two. Indie is supposed to be wrapping up the packing, but I'll believe that when I see it. It's a mess. But I want to hang with you before I take off."

"Yeah I'll come, as long as you don't try to make me help load a truck or anything. But, uh . . . ."

"What? What's the problem?" Will demanded. There was a moment of embarrassed silence, and then Nick spoke in a rush. "Can I bring someone with?"

"Like who? One of your sisters?"

"No, jackass. A, um . . . yeah . . . a girl. Her name's Rebecca."

Oh. My. God.

Nick had a date? Will had to shake the sound of disbelief from his throat.

"Well, hell yes, bring her! Who is she?"

"She's a triage nurse at the hospital. I saw her the night we brought you in to the ER. I somehow got up the nerve to talk to her. She's pretty quiet, though.

I think she's shy, which gets me every time. Anyhow, one of her girlfriends dropped a dime on her; told me she thought I was . . . uh . . . ."

Nick stopped talking.

"She thought you were what? Tall? Gay? Into S and M?"

Nick exercised his right to remain silent. Will drew in a deep breath, and burst out laughing.

"Aw Nick . . . she thought you were *CUTE* didn't she? *Oh, man!*"

"Yeah well, maybe I ain't so bad, huh? Anyway, she may say no."

"You haven't asked her, yet?"

"Naw, still workin' up the courage."

"Alright, Nick. I'm hanging up this phone so you can call her now. And I'll see you both at my place, right?" Will could swear he could hear Nick blushing through the phone. "Yeah, okay. Wish me luck."

"Luck! Later, man."

Will hung up, and realized he had a big dopey grin on his face. Nick on a date. What a concept. Will had almost decided the guy had taken a vow of celibacy or something. He just never seemed interested.

His gut told him that Nick had been on the receiving end of a suitcase full of heartache, but he didn't know any details. He was really happy for the man, and hoped the lady was worthy.

Slowly, the smile faded as he thought of his own situation.

He tried to imagine himself with another woman, but all images of any female he dreamed up, had long, dark hair like satin, and shimmering pool-water blue eyes.

Oh well. It wasn't like finding someone was any kind of priority in his life right now.

As it stood, Will couldn't care less if he never touched another woman again, but he knew that this was not going to be the case always. He was too much of the husband variety. He liked being a family man.

Will drove in thoughtful silence until he turned on his street and realized that his driveway was blocked by a huge tractor-trailer, with the name Allied Bonded Transportation professionally fused onto the length of the beast. Will saw that his mother's car was pulled up next to the truck, and on the other side was Jackson's Mercedes.

Oh yay, the gang's all here.

Even though Will was happy to see that Indie had relented and allowed the use of the moving company, the very fact that it was here was just another swift kick in the balls, as far as he was concerned. Obviously, Jackson *did* have the power of persuasion over Indie. One that *he'd* never had.

And just what tactic Jackson had used to get her to see things his way, was something that Will did not care to think about.

Will parked his truck out on the road, and made his way up the drive, hands shoved deep in his pockets. He took a seat on the hood of his mother's Subaru Forester, and looked up at the house, his mind churning.

How can you feel so conflicted about someone, he wondered.

It should be cut and dried. Will should hate Jackson, and in a world full of perfect balance, Jackson should hate Will right back.

Simple. A nice, easy, well-defined relationship, right?

But no.

Will knew Jackson to be honorable and honest. Decent and kind. He was also extremely intelligent and could apparently be a righteous ass-kicker, when the situation warrants the need. All fine qualities in a man, in Will's humble opinion.

In fact, if Will didn't have to suffer with the knowledge that Jackson was probably getting busy with Indie at every available opportunity, they would probably have been the best of buds. Instead, whenever he thought of the two of them engaged in that kind of recreational activity, Will became sorely tempted to offer the guy a nice new belly button piercing, free of charge.

Compliments of his new friend, Walther.

He decided that he could be friendly with Jackson only as long as he kept his head from detailing what was happening behind closed doors with those two.

Will looked back up at the house that had become the last home that would be shared by himself and Indie, as a family. All of the curtains had been removed, and he had a clear view through the picture window into the living room. The lights inside were bright, and Will knew that no one could see him sitting out here in the grayness of dusk.

He watched, arms folded lightly across his still sensitive ribs, as his mother flushed and giggled like a teenager at something Jackson said to her. Marie had described Jackson as "charming", when she had first been introduced to him.

Charming!

The woman is a traitor, Will thought with a snort.

If anyone should have been able to hate Jackson in the proper way, she had been his ringer.

So much for that. The guy seemed to have an intoxicating effect on the ladies.

His kids loved him too, and ran to him, squealing with joy whenever they saw him. That was a good thing though, wasn't it? Will wanted them happy, and was glad that Jackson clearly loved them too.

He sucked in his breath as Indie moved into his line of vision, trying to help the movers, naturally. But everywhere Indie was, Jackson was there also; brushing back her hair, running his hand lightly down her back, touching her.

His hands seemed nearly constantly at the ready, in case she stumbled or needed someone to steady her. He let her lift nothing, and threw a protective aura around her by his very presence.

There was something almost animalistic in his stance; like he would tear apart anyone or anything that threatened her.

With his teeth!

The look on Jackson's face whenever he looked at Indie was that of an almost sickening devotion, and it was mirrored perfectly in the eyes of Indie.

Will swallowed hard.

Damn it, but she deserved that. All that and more.

But I could do that for her! Screamed his heart.

Too bad you never did, his brain reminded him harshly.

He couldn't stop dwelling on it. Why couldn't she just cocoon-up again now, and make him forget about her?

Will had to concede, that it probably wouldn't help anyway. Her loss was such a commanding presence now, that he was always at attention.

And it sucked. It really did.

A voice startled him out of his pity party. It was Indie's voice . . . *but how?* She was upstairs.

He could see her now, speaking to Jackson. "What's keeping Will, I wonder?" He heard her voice, plain as day.

Will watched the scene, more carefully now. Jackson's voice hit his ears. *You're worried about him?*

It sounded different.

When he heard Indie's voice, it was strong, and had the hard edges of vibration . . . like a tuning fork. When he heard Jackson's reply, it had sounded all fluid and smooth.

As if the vibration had been removed. Indie spoke again. "Should we call him?"

Jackson was now speaking. "Sure, give him a call. I'm sure he wouldn't mind hearing your voice!"

I'm sure he wouldn't mind at all . . . .

Will realized with mouth-dropping acuity what was happening.

He heard the first part of Jackson's statement, with its rougher vibratory sound . . . and then heard the added ending in the smooth and silky timbre.

And Jackson's mouth had stopped moving when he heard it!

Holy hell! He was hearing Jackson's thoughts! Will strained to hear anything from some of the others.

Nothing.

Finally, he noticed he could hear them if they were speaking aloud to Jackson. He was guessing that he was hearing them through Jackson's thoughts.

And it was *very* clear that it was only Jackson's thoughts he heard.

Will was immediately able to tell what was spoken out loud, and what was internal dialog from Jackson. The vibrations were the sounds breaking through the air. Words in his mind made no such motion in the atmosphere. They were like silk.

Ha! *The gift.*

Will now had a good idea what gift he had received. He could read Jackson's mind. But why?

There will be no secrets between brothers! The answer glided through his ears, curling around his brain.

Oh, this was going to be good.

Equal footing. Jackson could read his thoughts; now Will could read his. Will had an inspiration.

JACKSON!

He sent the silent shout. He watched in satisfaction as Jackson jumped, and looked around, a little confused.

Out here, pal!

Will watched as Jackson slowly turned his head toward the picture window, and heard clear as daybreak:

Oh, not possible! There is no damned way!

Will couldn't stop the laugh bubbling up from his belly at the look on Jackson's face.

Bingo!

And he'd made Jackson bust loose with the "D" word! Will felt like he'd scored the winning touchdown at the Super bowl. He just had one more thing to say.

Honey, I'm home!

With another gut busting laugh, Will raced up the stairs.

CHAPTER 42

Nick's girl was cute, Will decided, as he took another hard pull on a Magic Hat brew. She stuck close to Nick's side as he fawned over her in the most embarrassing way.

So what, Will thought, as he perched himself on the threshold of the fireplace since all of the furniture was gone. Nobody had ever accused Nick of being a smooth-talking player, and anyhow, the girl, what was her name . . . *Rebecca?* Yeah, Rebecca seemed to be eating it up; pleased with all of Nick's clumsy attentions.

She wore her fine, light brown hair in a ponytail, and little or no make-up obscured her heart-shaped face.

She was a tiny thing, incongruous next to the giant of a man standing beside her. Her head just past Nick's waist, but they looked cute together.

Cute? Ugh. Sap.

The evening had turned into quite the little party after the movers pulled out.

Will had realized with a jolt, that Nick would not remember meeting Jackson, Indie or his kids. It was really weird, introducing him to everyone, knowing all that they had actually been through together. Hell, they might have all been daisy root inspectors by now, if Nick had not planted some lead accessories into the center of Lockhart's chest.

He didn't need to look at Jackson to know that the man was staring at him again. But then, Jackson had barely been able to stop since Will had walked in the door, flaunting his shiny new gift from either the Elders, or the Creator himself, he didn't know which.

Eyes straight ahead, watching Cassidy show off her mad cart-wheeling skills through the now empty house, Will raised his beer bottle in a salute in Jackson's direction. He felt the man's internal scowl, and smiled.

Cool!

—

He could hear the guy sigh, even in his mind. To all outward purposes, Jackson had been the flawless gentleman.

Funny and oh so charming, as Marie would say.

But on the inside, the man was struggling. He couldn't believe that the Elders had given Will this gift.

Will wanted to tell him to go to Hell; that what Jackson had gained was a lot more valuable, as far as he was concerned.

He saw Jackson's head whip around, and Will widened his grin. Oh, well. He guessed he just did.

Boy this was handy.

"So, Mom, I guess we should be looking for you in Texas in a month or so, huh?" The woman followed them everywhere. "Just think; this time you can actually stay with me!"

Will waited for her screams of excitement at the news. Wasn't that her dream come true, after all? To have her boy all to herself again? It took a moment to dawn on him.

No screams.

His mother was fussing with Jake's shirt collar, and smoothing non-existent wrinkles out of his clothes.

"Mom? Did you hear me?"

"Marie, you're blushing!" Indie's voice was shocked at first, and then a knowing smile spread across her face.

"What's the deal, Mom? So you're not planning a move after a discreet waiting period?" Marie released a squirming Jake, and turned to face her son.

"I don't know, William. I might just stay here. These moves are getting hard for me, and at my age, I think it's time I settled into one place."

"Yeah, well you should've been doing that years ago, Mom, but that never stopped you. What's so great about this place? I mean I . . . ."

Will stopped.

Second hand info, stepping up to the plate. Indie and Jackson's brains had just exchanged the news, and so now, Will felt it seep into his mind, like warm caramel sauce.

His mother had a boyfriend. Marie was beet red.

"I . . . I've been . . . *talking* to a very nice man recently, that's all!" *That's all?*

The information that Jackson now gleaned from Will's mother was a little more specific, and now, by proxy, it was in Will's head too. Marie and this "nice man" were doing a little more than talking.

Oh Christ! God no!

He had to get that image out of his brain, like, *now*. How sick was that? Maybe if he set his head on fire . . .

Indie broke the awkward silence.

"That's wonderful, Marie. Do you think it's serious?"

Oh, it had better be, Will thought. *If the guy was going to be allowed to do all that . . . .*

So not going there again.

Marie was now only faintly pink. If she only knew.

"I think it might be, but we'll see. At any rate, I'm not planning on moving to Texas, Will. Sorry to disappoint you!"

Everyone laughed and the grossness of the moment was absorbed. Will tried to remember that at least Nick and his date couldn't see it. That made it only unbearably sickening, is all.

He slinked into the kitchen to grab another beer. Will raised a questioning chin up toward Nick, and the man nodded, then looked at Rebecca. She shook her head, so Will grabbed two.

Jackson could get his own.

Oh, right. The guy didn't drink alcohol. So he could pop himself another juice box, then.

Indie and Marie cornered Rebecca, and Will watched with sympathy as the women went to work learning everything about her. Indie was genuinely curious, as they both worked in the same field. Marie, as Will knew very well, was just plain nosy. But it came in handy for social gatherings.

As Will handed a cold bottle to Nick, he gestured toward the French doors and the men filed out onto the deck. It was very dark now, and the temperature was perfect.

Will could hear Jackson and the kids playing hide and seek in the large backyard.

What a cheater. Jackson could read their little minds, so what a challenge *that* game must be.

Oh. He remembered that the kids could read his as well. Hmm. Maybe it was pretty interesting at that.

"So . . ." Straight talking Nick got right to the point. "This is pretty weird. You know that, right? You and Indie and the whole boyfriend thing?"

"Yep. You're right. Pretty weird," Will agreed.

Nick waited.

"So you got nothin' t' say about it, then?"

Will hesitated. Damn. What *could* he say?

"It's beyond complicated, Nick. Let's just say that nobody cheated, and nobody's at fault."

Except me, Will added silently, swallowing bile.

"Bullshit. How is that even possible?" Nick was unimpressed.

"It isn't, in the world as you know it. But trust me when I tell you, that it had to end up this way, and that Indie is all the better for it."

"Hmph!" Nick snorted into his beer. He looked over at Will.

"You know, I wanna hate this dude, right? But somehow . . . I just . . . *can't*." He took a hard hit of his beer. "And I've been watchin' him. It's like he looks at Indie with this . . . physical touch. It's crazy. His eyes are all about her."

"You . . . are . . . right, Nick. That's *exactly* right." Well, wasn't he becoming quite the yes-man this evening?

"And now . . ." Nick looked around and consciously lowered his voice. "And now," he spoke in a stage whisper, "you're gonna have him as a partner? And you're all up and movin' to cow-town together? That borders on kinky, 'bro!"

Will heaved a sigh.

God, he wanted more than anything to blurt out the whole story to this man. He thought that if anyone would understand, it would be Nick. He might think Will was a raving lunatic, but he would understand.

"Look, Nick . . . ."

The police officer held up his hand, and then clapped him on his injured shoulder, gently. "No worries, Will. I know something's up. I even know that you really wanna tell me about it, but ya can't. I don't know why, but if ya can't . . . well then ya *can't*, s'all. Right?"

Will ate the lump in his throat.

"Thanks, man," he choked. Nick *was* the man, and he wanted him to know that. He looked up at him. Nick wasn't looking back at him, but across the yard, staring off into the distance.

"Hey, Nick,"

"Yeah, bud?"

"One of these days, I am going to find a way to tell you everything, because you deserve that. You're a damn good friend, and to tell you the truth, Nick, there aren't that many like you out there. I wish . . . I wish . . . aw shit, never mind!"

"God, Fed, you sound like a *girl!*" Nick was casual, but Will thought he could hear a strange thickness in the man's voice.

Out of the corner of his eye, Will caught him dragging his thumb under each eye. Under all the tough guy action, Nick was such a softie. *Just don't piss him off*, Will thought with a little smile.

The game of hide and seek ended, and Will and Nick made their way back inside.

Jackson had joined the woman standing around the kitchen island, and they were all staring at him, and hanging on his every word with disgusting star-struck faces.

Will and Nick looked at each other. Nick made a show of taking his pointer finger and doing the gag-me thing down his throat, and Will cracked up.

—

"What's so funny?" asked little Rebecca, floating instantly to Nick's side. "Your date," Will replied, sneaking a peek at Jackson, who was leaning in way too close to Indie, whispering in her ear. Will's laughter dissolved.

Abruptly, he decided he'd had way more than enough.

"Well folks, we're closing up the bar, I guess. We've got a long day ahead of us, right Indie?"

Yeah. He'd *definitely* had enough for the evening.

"Hmm, what Will? I didn't hear you." Indie answered in a distracted way. Oh, but Will heard what Jackson was saying in her ear, though. Heard it just fine, thank you.

Whatever.

"I said we all have a long day tomorrow, right?"

"Oh, right! We do. Cassidy and Jake!" She called out to the children, who appeared at once.

"Time to go. Remember, tomorrow you meet your new teacher, Lorena."

"We remember, Mommy," the twins sang in unison.

The Society had arranged for the home schooling of the twins, and Lorena St. John was set to arrive in the morning; a live-in nanny-slash-teacher.

Indie had dug in her heels at the idea of boarding school for the twins, and Jackson had not even attempted to change her mind about that one. Besides, he wasn't so hot on the idea either. They could be taught just fine right under the same roof as the rest of the family.

Much easier for him to watch over them that way.

No need to speak of anyone crossing the ocean for their education for many years . . . not until college.

Nick and Rebecca said their goodnights, and "nice-to-meet-ya's," and pulled out first. Marie and Jackson gathered the kids together and loaded up the car. The kids and Will were spending the next couple of nights at Marie's house, and then the caravan to Texas would begin.

Will stood next to Indie, and caught himself leaning slightly toward her, letting his arm touch hers; the heat from her body warming him.

She allowed this, and spoke softly. "I know this is a freaky situation, Will, but I am glad for it. And furthermore, it's going to all work out, I know it!"

"You think so?"

Will couldn't help himself. He reached up to brush her face lightly with his fingertips, hating the concern he saw for him in her eyes.

Hating that he loved it.

Indie closed her hand around his. "Yeah, I do. There is a reason for all of this; we already know it, don't we? It's like a movie being played out, and we are the characters. I don't know . . . it's weird, but it's okay. And we're safe with him, you know."

"Yeah. I know."

Will patted his shirt pocket, and caught himself.

Whoa, how wrong was this? He'd been feeling for a pack of cigarettes.

Will had quit smoking over fifteen years ago. What had he been thinking? He had been thinking he needed a smoke, was what!

Ah . . . . Nothing like nearly dying from a fatal heart attack to bring about the urge to light up.

"William Taylor, don't you even *think* about it!" Indie was appalled.

"Never mind what I'm thinking . . . or doing, for that matter. I'm a bachelor now. I can eat Cheerios for supper, and have bacon and beer for breakfast, right? And smoke like a chimney if I want!"

Indie narrowed her eyes at him.

Well, maybe he would do all that stuff on the sneak. She could probably kick his ass.

"And *don't* you forget it!"

Hell, she was serious!

Will laughed out loud, and wrapped his arm around Indie.

"Come on; let's get out of this place. Can't you hear your man out there, throwing a thrombo, 'cause I've got my hands on you?"

They walked to the front door together, and looked back at the same time.

Both wore slightly wistful expressions. Will looked down at Indie once more, his eyes sad and serious. He kissed the top of her head, and pulled her through the door.

Then he shut off the light, and closed the door behind them.

Epilogue

Knights of Redemption

Chapter 1

The state of Texas had three temperature settings, William Taylor decided as he baked like a spiral sliced ham in the driver's seat of a decrepit nineteen seventies Dodge Dart.

Hot, hotter and "Holy shit, it's hot."

Will figured that they were on the high setting of def-con three right about now as sweat hosed down his clothing; his form-fitting Levi's now welded to his thighs from the moisture. He was feeling like a definite shoe-in for any nearby wet tee-shirt contests.

It sucked.

Isn't it lucky, he thought to himself, *that the United States Army's infantry division takes great pride in making sure that all of their soldiers get lots of practice in the fine art of being absolutely miserable?*

Having proudly served nine years in that club before taking his current government position, Will was a pro. This is not to say that he *liked* it. He just could stand it much longer than your average citizen could ever possibly contemplate tolerating.

But he was beginning to reach his limit.

He fired up yet another cigarette, inhaling and then releasing a blast of Marlboro flavored smoke, finishing with a perfectly formed ring. He used his forefinger to clip the smoke ring neatly in half, ridiculously thinking of the old teenage-smokers' rule: *"Don't let it die a virgin!"*

He chortled at his self-acknowledged act of immaturity.

What could he say? He was bored.

Will caught his partner, Jackson's, mental cough, though his head never lifted from the Corpus Christi Caller-Times, the newspaper that he was making a point of devouring column by column. He seemed determined to read every single word contained in the local paper.

This inspired Will to pull another deep drag on the butt, and accidentally blow a mushroom cloud of the stuff out of the corner of his mouth toward the unfortunate Jackson, whose hands, he noted, clenched slightly on the edges of his paper.

This gave Will a satisfying case of the warm cozies.

"The Elder's aren't exactly thrilled about your relapse," Jackson spoke lazily, defying his irritation. He kept his eyes determinedly focused on page B-nine.

"Sure they are," Will replied distractedly. "They're all about free will up there." "Well then, I'm not so sure I'm into it anymore," Jackson complained. "I really hate cigarette smoke!"

"Hmmm, how can I put this the right way? *Tough shit!*" Will's eyes were scanning the parking lot that had been their gracious host for past two hours.

Jackson snapped the newspaper, eyes still on the pages.

"For God's sake Will, must you *always* behave like such a wanker?"

Will grinned at Jackson now; his brown eyes crinkling appealingly at the corners.

"For the most part." He paused to pull another drag from the almost finished cigarette. "I have to say, I'm impressed. Your vocabulary is coming along quite nicely. Especially your discovery of some of the more colorful adjectives."

"Well, I have only you to thank for that, brother."

Still smiling, Will pinched the remnants of flaming coal from the end of his cigarette, extinguishing it fully before slipping the butt into his pocket. Some military training never died. "Now I'm going to take that as a compliment paid, Jackson!"

He slugged back his Aquafina bottle and drank greedily, before shaking another Marlboro from the pack. Will had just resumed smoking again after fifteen years of cigarette-celibacy.

Will had started at the tender age of fifteen, but by the time he hit twenty, decided it wasn't conducive to the hard training lifestyle that the Army provided. At least not for him, so he'd quit.

But Will did nothing in a half-assed manner, and that included bad habits. If he was going to smoke again, then he was going to be a chain smoker, *damn it!*

It was a tragic show of weakness, in his opinion, and he hated himself for it. But in light of recent events, Will saw it as a better option than taking up self-mutilation as a hobby. He told himself that it was just a temporary crutch, to see him through the process of acceptance.

Jackson rearranged the newspaper, crinkling it noisily in that special way that only he could, knowing that it really got under Will's skin.

It was now his turn to release a contented sigh after feeling the grinding of Will's teeth from across the front seat.

Will made an impatient noise as he reached out to click the dial of the antiquated A/C in a desperate attempt to create a little air movement in the stifling car.

Thank God, they both were Metro enough to be into cologne and effective deodorant, or else the car would have been unbearably rank.

"I seriously doubt that the thing has repaired itself since the last twenty times you've tried it," Jackson noted dryly.

Will draped his arms through the open spaces in the steering wheel of the classic seventies-era bad-guy mobile in which the two of them were imprisoned—undercover and overheated.

He rested his forehead on the center emblem of the wheel and stifled a groan.

"Where the Hell is this guy, Jackson?" Jackson shrugged. "Probably sleeping. I can only see darkness around him, and I can hear the sound of an air conditioner running."

That really burned Will.

Here they were, waiting to meet this guy who claimed his friend was acting strangely after being supposedly abducted by one of the rumored "flying witches", melting their asses off in the hot sun, while their boy napped in cool comfort.

Working undercover as researchers doing a documentary on these increasingly reported mysterious dark figures was a lame idea in Will's opinion, but it was not his call.

In his new role of investigator, he had been looking forward to calling his own shots. Unfortunately, his new boss, M, had turned out to be something of a micro manager, and this was all of her brilliance in action.

The criteria for documentary filmmaking seemed to be simply ownership of an outdated video camera, a crap car, and another person dumb enough to work with you.

As far as crap cars went, this one, assigned by Supply, was a shining example of the idea that most documentary makers must be notoriously short of the green.

He estimated the value of this mobile-oven to be around fifty American dollars.

That meant that the supply team probably paid two thousand.

Yep. Nothing too good for the MIB.

"I'm sure he's not coming."

"Will turned his saturated blond head, still resting on the steering wheel and looked at Jackson.

"You don't say? And yet, here we still sit!"

"M's orders are to give the man a few more hours . . . he may just be nervous, considering what he does for a living." Jackson closed his eyes for an instant. "Although now I have just seen clearly that he won't be coming. I got a flash of us leaving at three o'clock and you're practicing your gift of colorful language, because he didn't show."

"Too bad we can't share that useful bit of info with M. It sure would save time." He paused to grab a towel from the back seat and mop his face. "And misery."

"Unfortunately, that's not a situation we can change. I was afraid that getting a bunch of drug-runners to meet up with us was going to be . . . *challenging* at best. Even if they are terrified of getting attacked by flying witches!"

Over the last year, increasing reports and even plenty of video footage had been collected about these strange, dark figures moving through the sky. They seemed to have somewhat of a humanoid shape, and hooded cloaks that came to a point in the back, which spurred the name "witches."

The whispers of these creatures had spilled over from the campfires of low-level drug traffickers, giving away to full blown panic as many of the men, poor and superstitious illegals, began reporting attacks and abductions by the beings.

It had grabbed the attention of Homeland Security finally, when a Mexican police officer was attacked near the border, the man in an undeniable state of shock, but a very reliable witness.

Now, it was the matter of getting people to come forward about the attacks and alleged abductions that was proving difficult, to say the least, as the people who had the most experiences happened to be people who were doing their work under cover of night; criminals, drug dealers and transporters.

These people were certainly not talking to any Feds . . . and they didn't seem overly keen on confiding in researchers either.

Jackson abruptly slapped the newspaper down onto his lap, and unceremoniously ripped off his tee shirt. He snatched up another towel from the bag at his feet and rubbed his dripping hair.

It was the closest thing to a show of irritation Will had seen from him yet.

He liked seeing Jackson blow his cool. The guy was too controlled.

Funny.

People always said the exact same thing about him.

Jackson was even more so.

Unnaturally and irritatingly controlled.

"A little uncomfortable are we, 'bro?"

"Not at all. I just felt a need to intimidate you with my rock hard abs."

Will guffawed.

"Hey, I'll match you six pack for six pack, punk!"

He spoke while gripping his smoke between his front teeth, momentarily forgetting that Jackson was almost six years his senior.

It was all too easy to forget this. Jackson looked as if he couldn't legally buy a beer, when in truth, the man was knocking on the door of forty-one.

This, however, was one of many secrets about Jackson that Will kept. According to his paperwork, Jackson was a mere twenty-five, working hard on twenty-six. Even getting people to believe *that* was asking a lot, but it wasn't unfathomable, as was his true age.

At thirty-five, Will was as rock solid as ever, his body looking exactly as it had fourteen years ago, during his hardest military years, but his face looked at least his age, maybe older.

Will had the tough and ruggedly handsome air of George Clooney, in the movie "Three Kings", or perhaps Daniel Craig's 007 appeal.

He contrasted sharply with his partner's inhumanly youthful perfection. No matter what he wore, no matter what the situation, Jackson looked like an AWOL Calvin Klein model, with his longish mop of dark chocolate hair, and deep teal eyes, framed with jet-black lashes.

Even M, their crisp no-nonsense boss, who had initially ordered Jackson to chop his unruly locks, had fallen under Jackson's spell. Now, not only did she allow his non-regulation hair, but she wore that sick, sappy look on her face that Will was beginning to associate with all females, whenever the guy was around.

Will was becoming quite used to playing second string in Jackson's band, where woman were concerned.

First, with his now ex-wife, Indie, and now with every female they ran into. Every single working day of his damned life, he had to observe it.

Women might notice Will and smile . . . then they would notice Jackson and gawk. And *that* . . . was all she wrote.

They never looked in Will's direction again.

When you topped off the rock-star looks with the man's mesmerizing voice, and Brit-lite accent, then threw in his old world gentleman-like manners and cat-like grace . . . well, there you had it. A potent cocktail of female-ensnaring assets, all wrapped tightly around Jackson's firmly muscled frame.

Of course, Jackson never gave any of them even a cursory glance. And why should he? He had *THE* woman.

The only woman in the world, as far as they both were concerned. Because she used to be Will's.

Will was still learning to deal; first with the fact that his wife of ten years had turned out to be part of a genetically superior race of beings descended from angelic bloodlines. The *Society Members* that his co-workers were always on the hunt for, the purpose being dissection and study, under the guise of an implied threat.

He had since learned the true objective of the Society, as explained by Jackson himself, and knew that the idea of a threat from these people couldn't be further from the truth.

Boring, is what they were, from an investigative standpoint, Will had complained to Jackson after the revelation.

Oh, they were interesting if you looked at it from a historical point of view, and the things that their ancestors had brought to the world, but as far as mystical beings from other worlds went, eh, it wasn't too exciting.

Sure they were resistant to disease and illness, had telekinetic powers, and some other crazy abilities that he wasn't even sure about their extent, which was kind of cool, but not jaw dropping for the most part.

"So your purpose here is to basically improve the human race, and promote positive energy, like, getting all the countries together to sing cum-bye-ya, and that sort of crap?" Will had asked incredulously. "Yeah, good luck with that!"

Jackson had also explained that he also kept certain undesirable "beings" that often appeared on this earth, at bay, annihilating them with a ferocity that would terrify any mortal who had to watch. They also kept an eye out for the latest incarnation of the *Fallen One*; AKA Satan, among the other names he chose for himself.

Society Members were sort of the time-keepers of the world, monitoring the sun and the aging effect on it from negative energy that would eventually end this little experiment called mankind.

This had chilled Will just a little. He hoped that the *"Creator"* as the Society called God, wasn't ready to throw in the towel just yet.

After all, he had season tickets to all of the Red Sox games.

He, himself had been on a task force assigned to the capture and study of these, Society Members, meanwhile, unknowingly living with them under his very own roof.

He never saw the "markers" as they called them; the perfectly geometrically aligned features, as well as other small signs, noticeable only to the trained eye, because one of Indie's gifts was an ability to force the eye to skim over her, rendering others unable to really focus on her clearly unless she commanded attention. This was something she did unconsciously; some deep-seated survival instinct.

Oh, and there was also the little catch that they are born with a predetermined mate. After contact is made between the two Members, they are rendered hopelessly devoted to one another for life.

A very long life, as long as nothing ends it prematurely, which accounted for their insanely youthful appearance.

Jackson just happened to be the Society Member who had appeared in their lives to claim his mate, Indie.

The fact that Indie was already married to Will, and unaware of her own status, had been a sticky situation, but ultimately Will had realized that Indie was faultless, as well as helpless to fight the inborn draw to her rightful mate.

It had nearly killed her as well, to hurt Will, but things were getting better.

One of the quirks of these pre-destined mates was that they shared the same date of birth, and consequently after the Commitment to each other, the same date of death.

They were called *Equals* for a reason; their destinies were truly entwined.

It was for this reason alone, Will told himself, that he knew he would protect Jackson with all of the weapons and skill at his disposal, because who he was really protecting, was Indie.

He chose to ignore the idea that he might be protective over Jackson because he actually found himself kind of liking the guy, against his will.

Just a little.

Will preferred to believe that he simply suffered his company because he had no choice, and liked to prove it to himself often by deliberating goading and harassing Jackson at nearly every available opportunity.

This abuse Jackson bore with remarkably calm acceptance, only returning the gestures occasionally and in a very mild fashion.

He understood where Will was coming from, and tried to indulge his need to vent his still-simmering angst.

The next shocker for Will had been the revelation that he and Indie's children were not only another set of Members, but a rare and powerful type, descended straight down from the angel of the highest rank.

They were in possession of nearly unspeakable powers, including Indie's "invisibility" gift, and now had a specially assigned trainer and teacher living with them now, to educate the children and teach them how to use and contain their power.

Will had no idea exactly *what* they were capable of, but he already knew that his son, Jake, had the power to remove Death's hand from one's shoulder.

Jake had saved Will, who had died, for all intents and purposes, dragging him back from the very threshold of death, much to the chagrin of the Elder who had sired the original Society Members from which they had descended.

It was a big rule, that one did not tamper with destiny or fate, but a bigger rule was the function of free will, which Jake had exercised when saving his father.

Whether there would be horrible ramifications later, remained to be seen, although it seemed that Will's destiny had been such that his rescue from Death's claws was part of the plan.

Will had been visited in a dream; one that he was sure was actually real, but he had to call it a dream to maintain his sanity. In this dream, he was informed that he was the *"Redeemer,"* and that *"they will come through"* him.

He still wasn't sure what it meant, but hey, now he knew he had a purpose in life. He just had to figure what being *The Redeemer* actually entailed.

It was a strange title. Sounded like a super-hero. He'd wondered if maybe he should purchase a cape, just to be safe.

The final sledgehammer to Will's ego had been the forced assignment of Jackson as his new partner, after the death of Shawn Baker, his partner of the previous two years.

Shawn's death in itself was a sore subject with Will. Because Shawn had died saving the life of Will's daughter, Cassidy.

The situation was complicated, with Shawn starring as the villain in the beginning, and winding up the hero at the finish, his position in an afterlife of peace firmly sealed.

At any rate, Jackson, who Will knew only to be an Oxford-educated attorney, was now his partner, simply because the Elder Society Members had determined that Will had a higher purpose to serve, and that he needed Jackson to assist in fulfilling his destiny.

They had used some sort of Divine influence, Will supposed, in getting the open position of partner for Will, filled by Jackson.

As it turned out, Jackson obviously was hiding a carton full of kick-ass and some serious training somewhere in his past, so the placement at least wasn't totally ridiculous, as he had originally feared.

Go figure.

The man was also steadfastly avoiding any conscious thought about the origins of professional ass-kicking resume' for reasons unknown and Will wasn't going to ask him again.

He knew it was only a matter of time before Jackson Allen slipped up and gave it a cursory thought. Some memory would show itself, and he would think about it, and then Will would know.

Because the only part of the whole sorry deal that didn't suck, was the gift given to Will by the Elders, just before the move to Texas—the ability to read Jackson's thoughts.

This leveled the playing field a bit, as Jackson had, among many other unusual powers, the ability to read the minds of those around him.

Indie was able to shut him out at times, if she felt threatened and retreated in fear into her invisibility mode. But aside from that scenario, they were an open book to one another.

So far, Will was enjoying the hell out of the gift he was given.

He especially loved the knowledge that his receiving this gift had caused Jackson distress.

It was an odd coupling, to say the least—neither man hating the other, in fact, sharing a reluctant respect for one another. However, Indie remained the epicenter of unrest.

For Jackson, it was the fact that Will had her first, and gave her the children that he never could—Society Members having no ability to procreate.

At least, not with each other.

Not that Jackson resented the children. He did not, and loved them just a loyally as he did Indie.

It was just the bond that having children together creates between two souls that had him all itchy and scratchy.

The possessive and territorial nature of Jackson's genetics were constantly rattled by Will and Indie's continued closeness; something that the cultured and rational side of Jackson totally understood.

Really. *He did.*

But, his Archangel genes snarled whenever he thought of Will's body wrapped around Indie's, performing the act that had resulted in children.

The visual of it nearly killed him at times, flaring to the surface whenever Will and Indie had physical contact of any kind.

Jackson also had the burden of being tormented by the guilt he felt over these feelings, having been raised to believe that such feelings were wrong, and to be in total control of his emotions at all times.

This he fought, even after reassurance from the Elder that he should embrace, as well as control his warrior bloodlines, and feel no shame.

He was trying.

Honestly he was.

There was also the promise that Jackson had made to Indie, that he would never allow harm to come to Will, to his best ability. This promise was made to reassure Indie that Jackson understood her love for the man who was the father of her children.

After all, it wasn't as if they had had a huge blow up fight, decided that they hated each other and gotten a nasty and dirty divorce. It was much more complicated than that.

Will's struggle was simple and painfully obvious. He was still in love with Indie, and saw no future where changing *that* fact was going to be an option.

Will loved her, and Jackson had her.

The end.

He should be going quietly into the 'good night', he knew, but so far, that wasn't happening. It was a sharp and bitter pill to swallow, and so it ended up going down in very small, hard pieces, with a lot of liquid to wash each bit down—and many long breaks between bites, until it could be finally finished in the end.

He figured he was almost halfway there.

Maybe.

Shaking his head, Will abruptly had enough waiting.

"To hell with M, Jackson. If we pull out now, do you see us suffering any repercussions?"

"No. But . . . ."

Jackson's honorable nature was, as usual, trying to cause problems.

"Then we're out of here. This is ridiculous, hanging out here when you *know* it's a waste of time, right?" Jackson hesitated, then agreed. "Sure Will, whatever. You're the team leader anyway."

"That's right. I'm making a career decision here. Besides, I am starving to death. Are you into Tex-Mex? There's a place up the road I like . . . good salsa and I'm sure that you'll find the gazpacho to your liking," he threw in a little sarcastically, knowing that Jackson ate only healthy things.

No burritos for him, poor bastard.

"Sounds good. I could use a bite." Jackson stretched, ignoring Will's jab.

"But I'd like to share this little mystery that's unfolding here in town, actually. It's at least a *real* unknown to me. There have been a string of murders in the last several months," he gestured to the paper in his lap. "And last night, there was another."

"Why, do you think they're connected?" Will asked, fanning himself with the sports section.

"Well, I'll say this; all of those murdered were registered sex offenders, and all of them died pretty violent deaths in quiet allies or secluded areas after dark."

"What a shame. Those poor, poor pervs. All males then?"

Will was abruptly disinterested, actually. If someone was in the business of whacking perverts and predators, who was he to interfere in the free market?

Jackson was mildly exasperated.

"Will, random murder is not okay. Even if the people are monsters, the Creator will judge them, and prior to that, a jury of their peers. If they are found guilty and sentenced to death, *then* that is their fate"

"Spoken like a real attorney, dude." Will tried, unsuccessfully, to stare Jackson down.

"Listen, if my heart isn't broken by the murders of a bunch of the lowest bastards on the planet, my apologies. But really, I just don't care."

Jackson laughed.

"My heart isn't broken either, Will. I just think tracking down a serial killer sounds a lot more fun and intellectually stimulating to me than pretending to hunt for the answers to questions I already know, that's all. I think I'm going to follow up on this."

"Help yourself, bro'," Will replied as he fired up a smoke, inhaling deeply. "All I can think about right now is La Fiesta and an ice cold Dos Equis amber!"

Will looked at Jackson as he started the car.

So, you know about these flying witch things then, don't you?"

After a long delay, Jackson answered.

"Yeah. I do."

"So what are they? I mean, really. I know we can't use any of your knowledge for work purposes, but I'm curious."

Will felt a break from the heat at the chilling look in Jackson's eyes as he answered.

"Will, my brother, some things you're better off just . . . *not* knowing. Trust me."

Will stared back at the man, finally turning to face the road again.

"Right. Maybe I don't want to know after all."

Look for Knights Of Redemption on Amazon.com!

LaVergne, TN USA
15 February 2010
173175LV00002B/3/P